MERLIN OF THE MAGNOLIAS

A NOVEL

MERLIN

OF THE

MAGNOLIAS

GARDNER LANDRY

GREENLEAF
BOOK GROUP PRESS

Published by Greenleaf Book Group Press
Austin, Texas
www.gbgpress.com

Distributed by Greenleaf Book Group

For ordering information or special discounts for bulk purchases, please contact Greenleaf Book Group at PO Box 91869, Austin, TX 78709, 512.891.6100.

Design and composition by Greenleaf Book Group
Cover design by Greenleaf Book Group
Cover Illustration by Jeremy Wells

Publisher's Cataloging-in-Publication data is available.

Print ISBN: 978-1-62634-755-7

eBook ISBN: 978-1-62634-756-4

Part of the Tree Neutral® program, which offsets the number of trees consumed in the production and printing of this book by taking proactive steps, such as planting trees in direct proportion to the number of trees used: www.treeneutral.com

TreeNeutral

Printed in the United States of America on acid-free paper

20 21 22 23 24 25   10 9 8 7 6 5 4 3 2 1

First Edition

But God hath chosen the foolish things of the world to confound the wise; and God hath chosen the weak things of the world to confound the things which are mighty;

And base things of the world, and things which are despised, hath God chosen, yea, and things which are not, to bring to nought things that are.

1 Corinthians 1:27-28

· *Spring*

· One

It was the kind of bright, halcyon morning that would have augured for a chamber of commerce day for Bayou Boughs had Bayou Boughs been an incorporated city. Instead, it was a raft of privileged serenity buoyed upon the surrounding maelstrom of Houston, Texas. From the vantage of his observatory, all seemed placid despite the negative energy rotation he believed had gripped his city for decades.

Merlin rose and, inspired by the light dancing on the freshly bloomed neighborhood azaleas, began to play his glass armonica with greater vigor and concentration than usual. A winsome melody issued from the instrument suited to elegiac dirges and eerie phrasings. Up-tempo notes flowed freely from the spinning discs in the multipartite glass assemblage, as if Merlin's fingertips were channeling the very essence of spring. Even the cacophonic whir of blowers, mowers, and edgers was at bay, allowing his notes to float over the neighborhood without competition from the drone of internal combustion lawn tamers.

The glass armonica, Merlin believed, was an instrument ideally suited to his outlook and personal magnetic calibration, its ethereal tones bespeaking so much more than the mere notes it produced. He sensed it intimated depths and dimensionalities few could fully comprehend and appreciate. Benjamin Franklin must have envisioned a player such as Merlin himself interpreting time-honored arrangements generations after he invented this most original and beguiling of American instruments, he mused. He believed also that he was providing a service for the neighborhood and any of its outdoor workers who happened to be within earshot of his expert musicianship. His inspiration soared as he inhaled the morning air. *Sumer*, Merlin thought, is indeed *icumen in*.

Merlin believed the very existence of his observatory must have been predetermined in conjunction with what he reckoned as his life's mission—its springing into form as seemingly inevitable as the burden he would bear for the city of his birth, rearing, and adult residence. Far different from the hackneyed residential addenda of so many quotidian garage apartments in the neighborhood, this structure was thoroughly sui generis. The observatory was round—utterly cornerless. It was of substantial height, rising at least a story above the rooflines of even the tallest surrounding houses. The northwestern to southeastern exposure of its top floor was a semicircle of windows and on the north-facing side there was a modest balcony for sitting, reading, morning coffee, nighttime telescoping, and the taking of readings from various instruments installed on the outside of the structure at the little balcony's side—temperature, barometric pressure, humidity, et cetera. The building had been the retreat of the former owner of the property, on the nether reaches of which it stood in defiant iconoclasm.

The owner, Merlin's late and beloved grandfather, had provided in his will for a trust to be created for the benefit of the observatory's current occupant. Merlin's grandfather, as family friends and relations understood it, had created this arrangement with the understanding, considered by all familiar with the case to be both insightful and thoughtful, that the subject beneficiary, although having proven himself quite capable academically, lacked certain connective capabilities that made interpersonal exchanges practiced daily and without reflection by the majority of people moving through the world a belabored endeavor, taxing him in the way a corporate tax exam might tax an English major. Human interaction for Merlin was, at the least, difficult and, at the most, utterly bewildering. This did not mean, however, that he did not desire it. He truly longed for real friendships, and the few people in his life who were able to connect with him he treasured as much as life itself.

Then there was his weight. Not just his weight, but his size, also. Perhaps it was better to speak of it in more or less scientific terms as his mass, the presence of Merlin's personage often described by those who beheld him for the first time as so massive that they would have sworn they had encountered some sort of urban Sasquatch had they not been apprised of his Christian name and provenance. His height? Some six and a half feet or better. But that was not really the biggest visual impact. Merlin's width was astounding. And it was not just because he was overweight, which he unquestionably was. No, the astounding thing was the huge frame on which all the excess weight hung. Ursine comparisons abounded from his earliest post-pubescent days, as in addition to his mass, a gene marking hirsuteness expressed itself with relentless and reckless abandon. After many seasons of meticulous shaving, he became weary of the whole enterprise and let his beard and hair grow, with the occasional trim and cut the only interventions keeping the whole unruly affair moderately in check. Strangely though, as large and even coarse seeming as his physical presence was, Merlin's facial features were rather fine. This dynamic created an arresting juxtaposition. Big thick hairy body, round thick hairy coconut head with bushy beard, but glimmering through the follicular forest was the unexpected sunlight of his face, anchored by sharp, gunmetal blue eyes that the world usually observed behind the thick circular lenses that brought his days and nights into focus. The nose—more aquiline than the rest of his physical person would have suggested. The effect of this compounded strangeness was so disjunctive as to be arresting for the first-time beholder. One saw a big stupid body and expected a big stupid face to center it; instead the face intimated significant, if idiosyncratic, synaptic activity between those two jumbo ears out of which more errant hair protruded.

Concern for personal orderliness was not in the ascendant on this bright antipodal morning, and justly so, as its sunlight-through-dew-drop perfection seemed to cause the armonica to wail more plaintively and at ever higher volume. A few hundred yards away the ethereal strains of Merlin's inspired playing wended their way to the desiccated ears of a twosome of leathery old golfers, who on hearing them regarded each other with momentary befuddlement as they ambled up one of the back nine fairways before acknowledging simultaneously what the sound was, and, more tellingly, its source and the identity of its generator, for although Merlin was not easily knowable, he was far from unknown. He was one of those neighborhood characters whose vagaries seemed to be tolerated not so much with contempt as with benign bemusement. He was a type who, if a stranger were to see him ambling down the street, would elicit an immediate reaction, but as it is with all local oddballs in their own neighborhoods everywhere, the display of his eccentricities became a commonplace part of neighborhood life.

His impromptu playing morphed into the *Ode to Joy* from Beethoven's Ninth Symphony, and the effect was so pleasant that even the usually complaining neighbors desisted and allowed the armonica's notes to fall unprotested on their ears. Could the feeling he sensed this morning bode well for a world wider than his own visual purview? Could it extend to the far-flung boundaries of Houston itself? Might it intimate the long-awaited energy shift that would finally bring an air of the positive and hopeful to this place that, although the birthplace of many profitable business concerns, was an energy sink for much of the melancholy and malaise the not-too-distant Gulf of Mexico seemed to deposit into the area? The regular heavy inundations, sometimes in the form of tropical systems, reminded him of this dynamic—Hurricane Harvey only the most recent of such phenomena as it parked itself over the area and deposited a year's worth of rain in just a few days. *Hmm*, he thought. *I must consult the instruments and tables.*

Finishing the final notes of the iconic classical piece, Merlin shifted his focus from the lyrical to the analytical. First he recorded readings on his instruments outside—barometric pressure: relatively high for this time of year; humidity: tolerably moderate. Light breeze out of the north-northwest and an air temperature in the middle sixties. Additionally, the azaleas were popping, adorning the neighborhood with the floral equivalent of its Sunday best. Although he realized the temporality of this display, Merlin somehow had a sense that all of these factors were combining to telegraph to him that change of a positive nature might be afoot, and that he might have a central role in effecting it. Was a window opening? Might it fall to him to defenestrate himself through it in sacrificial service to his fellow Houstonians?

That idea prompted a review of his printed and electronic tables of the phases of the moon, the angle of the sun, the earth's present course through the solar system, and the alignment of various celestial bodies. Additionally, he considered the old lines of navigation the Druids had understood millennia ago; he had extrapolated them from the other side of the world all the way to the Upper Texas Gulf Coast. He sensed that the geomagnetic ley lines influencing the area were beginning to light up, too. Everything pointed toward change. Merlin was unequivocally being communicated with, and it was time for him to pay attention to the subtle and maybe not so subtle messages being sent his way.

One of his tried and true methods for achieving this active listening beyond his observatory was to ambulate while wearing a device of his own creation—a metal crown of sorts with protruding but retractable antennae, internal magnets, rather complex electronics, ear buds, and a volume control that allowed him, he believed, to pick up subtle signals regarding his environs. Merlin's walks while wearing it were among the eccentricities to which the neighbors had become practically oblivious. He had incorporated the device into season-appropriate headwear, so he could stay in sartorial step with the seasons even as the apparatus helped him tune in to faint messages in his own changing world.

Today, he chose a retrofitted Ecuadorian fedora, a style that for generations has gone under the misnomer of a "Panama" hat. Not having donned it so far this spring, he felt a frisson of pleasure as he appraised its classic lines and the discretion with which his contraption had been incorporated into its circumference where a wide, black satin ribbon would normally have encircled it above the brim. Merlin had even gone so far as using navy blue and crimson felt-tip pens to draw a faux hatband on the exterior electronics to further conceal his head-borne device. He removed it from a hat rack, wiped clean the small solar power cell blanketing the little valley of its top crease, and prepared for his constitutional to breakfast.

As the morning fairly cried out for it, Merlin chose an off-white linen suit, but left his shirt tie-less, as he knew a few footsteps, even on this pleasant morning, would be all it would take to incite his eager sudoriferous system to frenzied activity, causing him to resemble a living fountain over which glistening rivulets of unctuous liquid seethed incessantly. As to footwear, Merlin required furnishings more practical than style-forward. Owing to his substantial mass, he wore almost exclusively a little-known brand of heavily cushioned, wide-soled urban hiking boots. With a nod to what he considered the most basic of sartorial requirements, he owned several pair, each dyed a distinct hue, per his instructions to the shoe hospital, to complement his daily ensemble, in accordance with the season and meteorological conditions. He dusted off a pair that had been unused since the previous summer and appraised them with winsome fancy. The lacing up of the white boots was a rite of the season's arrival and meant that he was publicly averring that spring had unquestionably sprung.

He emerged from the base of his tower, opened the driveway gate, and stepped onto the neighborhood sidewalk. He adjusted the earpieces dangling from the hat's sweatband into the cilia-dense jungles of his outer auditory canals, listened for a moment, and slid the frequency locator bar on the left side of the hat forward and backward very delicately until he zeroed in on what he believed to be a legitimate signal. He adjusted the volume, and then, crucially, adjusted his angle of ambulation.

He believed the frequencies his listening device picked up should determine his approach to the world—his literal approach, that is. Today, hearing a compelling whir through his left ear bud, he adjusted his person to an angle of approximately 33 degrees, his left side turning forward on the sidewalk. He adjusted the volume knob on the right side of the hat and began tentatively, then resolutely, to proceed on the sun-dappled sidewalk. The visual impression was like watching a wide-body jumbo jet angle against heavy crosswinds on final approach for landing, a maneuver known as crabbing.

The linen-besuited, white-booted barge of a man moving down the sidewalk was something to see, but the addition of the broad-brimmed straw fedora out of which protruded small antennae in four directions constituted another level of the unusual. The sight, augmented with Merlin's curious sidelong gait and frequent adjustment of knobs and rheostats alongside the hat's brim, would have been enough to induce in a hypothetical new-kid-on-the-block observer momentary catatonia, if not mild terror. Add an upward cock of the head inclined to the left and a visage that bespoke rapt listening, and one was presented with the most iconoclastic of Bayou Boughs' many eccentric denizens.

Lawn maintenance equipment was now audible from seemingly every direction, but leaf-blower- and grass-edger-wielding specialists desisted from their eardrum-assaulting vocations and stood aside so Merlin could pass undisturbed—intimating, perhaps, a degree of Catholic respect for a mystery beheld. Merlin turned left onto Bayou Boughs Boulevard. He passed a couple of hulking mansions and approached the gate house of the club at the end of the block. The majority of the traffic through the gates was vehicular. The pedestrians transiting the gate house were members on the way to a workout in the gym, lap swimming in the pool, a tennis game, or launching a few balls off the practice tee at the driving range—all of them in casual athletic clothing.

There was one member, however, whose walking ensemble was far from pedestrian, at least in his mind. Merlin angled past the guard with a gracious wave and nod. Regardless of his state of preoccupation, he made it a priority never to forget his manners. Looking like a cross between Charlie Chan and Bigfoot, Merlin sidled toward the members' entrance as a golf cart–steering new employee stared long enough to barely avoid a collision with a brand-new steel-blue Aston Martin entering the club. Oblivious to this near miss, as he was to many of the peripheral things in his world, Merlin kept a laser-sharp focus on his mission.

When he pulled open the heavy oak door to the locker room, a gnat of a natty man brushed past him. They both acknowledged each other wordlessly—Merlin with the bemusement of an elephant encountering a mouse and the little gadabout with a kind of momentary horror followed by unmasked disdain. The smaller man, Tite Dûche, scuttled off toward the members' entrance with impatient dispatch, the little tassels on his ballet slipper–thin cordovan loafers flicking this way and that, oscillating with the frequency and vigor of similar accouterments adorning the busts of the most enthusiastic of nineteen seventies–era Bourbon Street burlesque performers. Meanwhile, he had to adjust the cashmere peach pastel pullover sweater he had draped around his shoulders as it had fallen sideways during the little pas de deux with the club's largest and most geomagnetically attuned member.

Tite was everything Merlin was not: small, social (like a bee), and the clubbiest of clubby dressers. Merlin puzzled over Tite's preoccupation with the pettiest of social concerns and displays of the showiest of seasonal wardrobe extravagances. The annual professional tennis tournament, which was just a few weeks away, was the most extreme example of the latter. Tite had a big role in the event and took his status as annual license to wear the same garish neon green and pink plaid madras blazer as he strutted with inimitable officiousness around center court and other tournament venues. Merlin was thankful a few weeks remained before the international sports media would descend and the event would clog his beloved neighborhood's streets. He quickly regained his composure and, remembering to fold in the antennae protruding from his high-tech hatband, entered the great modern-day mead hall of the men's locker room at Bayou Boughs Country Club.

The locker room at the club was no mere utilitarian antechamber to the world of athletic striving. It was an oversized, over-the-top, yet broken-in-baseball-glove-comfortable man cave with staff, a bar, and food service from the club's downstairs kitchen. The room itself was a great soaring rectangular space with high dormer windows along the sides of its vaulted upper reaches. The center of the space featured square tables and wide leather chairs on rollers. At the end of the room, functioning like an altar, was a three-sided bar. Behind the bar was a high brick wall featuring an intricately carved wooden sculpture of the club's crest, lighted such that it seemed to glow, an effect all the more evocative during low-light outdoor conditions.

Merlin had never mastered the art of small talk, so as he lumbered past tables with members he wasn't sure whether he knew, he held his laser-like focus on an oversized barstool at the right corner of the bar counter next to the wall. Drying a glass and looking in the general direction of the locker room entrance with his usual mix of diffidence, deference, and a dose of genuine compassion for the locker room's latest arrival was Shep Pasteur, a Cajun from the prairie and bayou country of Southwest Louisiana and longtime club employee who had known three generations of

Merlin's family. It was with fond memories of Merlin's grandfather and a sense of Merlin's strange and sad-seeming life trajectory that Shep nodded after catching Merlin's locked-in forward gaze as he approached his usual spot at the corner—a place that, were this indeed an ecclesial altar, would have been reserved perhaps for a junior acolyte but certainly no one of even slightly higher rank. When he recognized who was awaiting his arrival, Merlin's anxiety eased a bit, and he focused his rare brand of intensity on the stalwart icon of a Bayou Boughs employee who Merlin could never remember not having known.

"Ah, bonjour, Merlin!" (Shep pronounced "Merlin" the French way: "Mer-lanh," in hopes this bit of levity might soften the serious fixedness of the young man's tunnel-vision gaze.) Shep, like many of his colleagues, had developed a precise radar for discerning club members' moods, and this morning, in addition to seeing Merlin's sartorial paean to the season, he noticed an unmistakable spring in the step of the massive linen-clad presence lumbering his way. An image of the Stay Puft Marshmallow Man's giant inflated cinematic likeness in the Manhattan parade in *Ghostbusters* flashed through his mind as he pulled out the large chair at the corner.

Additionally, Shep continued to call him by his first name, a practice that was rare among club employees when a member's son or daughter became a voting member of Bayou Boughs Country Club. Many people relished this aspect of their transformed status on attaining membership, but Shep recognized that for Merlin, such a suddenly formal if not stilted mode of address would be bewildering, and perhaps fray the tenuous strings that seemed barely to hold Merlin to the ground over which he moved so tentatively. Merlin returned the greeting with an unusually upbeat reply.

"Shep! The seasons are shifting—in the heavens and in the earth!"

"Like they say, looks like spring, she has sprung."

"Even though it springs quite early here, yet it springs indeed."

"That's right, Magic Man. Now how you gon' celebrate it?"

Magic Man was the nickname Shep bestowed on Merlin when he was a toddler. Shep hoped that Merlin might mention his attraction to a representative of the fairer sex, equally unusual though she might have been to be attracted to this great enigmatic walker of the neighborhood. He was not surprised to be disappointed.

"With a hearty breakfast commensurate with the vibrations of this auspicious day, of course!"

Shep emitted a barely audible sigh and asked, "The usual?"

"Yes, please! And could I have one of the large mugs of coffee?"

"Does the pope wear a funny hat?"

Merlin thought for a moment and then smiled and said, "Well yes, yes he does!"

Shep shook his head and chuckled as he sent a quick sidelong glance Merlin's way before signaling a younger employee across the room to put in Merlin's breakfast order. As the bartender placed a giant mug of piping-hot black coffee to the right side of Merlin's place setting, Merlin opened the paper to his favorite section, the weather, and looked at the map of the U.S. with its cold, warm, and stationary fronts depicted along with the isobar lines denoting barometric pressure. He checked the list for the temperature ranges and precipitation reports from cities around the country and throughout the world. He tried to jibe this printed meteorological snapshot with the complex matrix of his own calculations. Despite his good mood, he wasn't getting too far with this exercise, so he turned to the headlines on the front page.

One caught his eye and polarized his mood from jubilant to concerned. "Oil and Natural Gas Prices Plummet—Industry Analysts Say Bottom Not in Yet." He began to read the article. "Oversupply in the hydrocarbon industry continues to mount at an increasing rate. Many experts are predicting more shocks with no firm bottoming of oil and natural gas prices until late next year at the earliest. The first wave of layoffs in the energy sector is already impacting the local economy and many pundits are predicting successive waves of industry belt-tightening as fuel supplies increase and profits plummet."

Transfixing existential concern clouded Merlin's sunny mood, as the lion's share of his discretionary personal income arose from oil and gas royalty payments. The income from the corpus of his trust took care of his phone, utilities, insurance, and club dues, but most of his other expenditures were predicated on the whims of the oil and gas market. He supplemented his income by tutoring neighborhood children at their families' homes and had become a reliable resource for parents wishing to bolster their kids' chances at being accepted into the better colleges and universities around the country, but royalty income was the mother's milk that funded what he called his research, the importance of which was so great to him he considered it his life's work and calling.

Mercifully, just when the article's ramifications began to set in, his breakfast arrived, and what a breaking of the fast it was. Bisecting the main plate was a girthsome ham-and-cheese omelet covered in a generous ladleful of hollandaise sauce. On the left side of this centerpiece were hash browns with caramelized onions, while on its right side, the omelet hosted sharp cheddar cheese grits topped with diced fire-roasted jalapeño peppers and a pinch of roasted serrano peppers—the diabolically fiery *chiles toreados* that had been known to send many a locker room breakfaster running for the facilities if too liberally applied and consumed. A small satellite plate to the upper right of the place setting contained a side order of bacon and a side of venison sausage. A co-satellite to its immediate left featured a couple of slices of buttered wheat toast. The moon of the omelet-anchored sun was a medium-size plate bearing a short stack of pancakes with thick daubs of butter melting in its inner layers. The topmost pancake featured a whipped cream flourish in the shape of a gyre, evoking ideas of swirling eddies, hurricanes, or even distant galaxies. (They had done this for him since he was an eager youngster breakfasting with his grandfather and talking endlessly about his fascinations with natural phenomena and the cosmos.) At the central point of the gyre, a lone maraschino cherry topped the white peak. A gravy boat of molasses syrup orbited the pancake moon, an unctuous complement to the a.m. extravaganza.

Scooting the bar stool a couple of inches closer to the counter, he turned to another section and folded the newspaper to frame something reliable and nonthreatening—the crossword puzzle. He gingerly placed his draftsman's pencil on the paper and moved it aside. Unwrapping his silverware from its napkin-swaddled security, Merlin took manual authority over knife and fork and laid siege to the feast. Thermals of gastronomic pleasure bore him into progressively higher realms of enjoyment as he proceeded through the meal, the largest breakfast served at Bayou Boughs Country Club that morning—or on any morning, for that matter. The staff even had a nickname for it: the Magic Mountain. This clever moniker served as a streamlining shorthand for the kitchen. When a Magic Mountain order came in, the cooks knew exactly what to do. One time someone even snapped a picture of it before it left the kitchen. A breakfast this mind-bogglingly prodigious was worthy of memorializing with a photograph, the harried photographer must have reasoned. It also served as corroboration when disbelieving conversation partners were recounted tales of this feast in bodegas and cantinas on the other side of town.

Just as Merlin was annihilating the remaining few holdout morsels clinging to his little constellation of breakfast plates, his mobile phone buzzed in his trouser pocket. He fumbled for it as the ingestion of the meal seemed to be challenging his fine motor skills more formidably than such a food-hoovering session usually did, and finally retrieved it. Looking at the phone's screen, he registered that the number was coming from the offices of Southeast Texas Bank and all of the musculature throughout the length and breadth of his mass tightened simultaneously. His formerly calm stomach wrenched painfully around its copious contents. He knew this could mean only one thing: his trust officer was calling.

Merlin accepted the call and in a muted tone answered with a sheepish hello.

"Merlin, this is Curtis Bumpers in the trust department down at Southeast Texas Bank."

"Hello, Mr. Bumpers."

"We've covered this before; you can call me Curtis."

"Matters financial are of necessity grave by nature; I prefer to address you with the formality my forbears impressed upon me as appropriate for such interactions, thereby honoring the gravity of the subject, my memory of my bygone blood kin, and of your chosen professional métier in life."

Curtis Bumpers paused for a perplexed moment, caught himself while beginning to sigh, and continued. "I wanted to see if we could *visit* in my office as soon as is convenient for you."

Merlin was gripped and twisted from within. His valves of Houston, first described by anatomist John Houston in the 1830s, taunted him and threatened to give way like a breaching dam during a deluge. He pulled himself together to finish the conversation.

"When would you like to see me?"

"How about this afternoon?"

"That's fine."

"Four o'clock at my office at the Phal-Tex Energy Tower?"

"Yes. Very good. I will be there." Merlin ended the call with a quivering thumb and stared into the middle distance.

"What you say, Magic Man?" Shep was trying to get Merlin to snap out of the mental eddy he could see was spinning him.

"My trust officer." Merlin's speech was monotone.

"What he said to you, *cher*?"

"He said he wants to visit with me."

Now it was Shep's turn to register surprise. On hearing the word "visit," the aperture of his eyes grew a little and his spine straightened. He knew what "visit" meant in Houston, and it tripped his usually fluid banter. The pause in the conversation was just long enough for an eavesdropping member at the bar to chime in. Peter Pastime held forth: "Ha! That's one of my favorites! When they say 'confer' or 'talk,' never fear, but when 'visit' gets trotted out, look out! Something's about to go down that might not be too pleasant for the party summoned to 'visit.' This is one of my favorite hometown euphemisms! When I recounted it to my chums in Ivy at Princeton, it never failed to elicit uncontrollable guffaws!"

Shep remained silent; he couldn't disagree with Pastime, and even if he did he was not permitted to contend with him per club policy. It was true. Many times he had overheard a captain of industry saying he would like to visit with someone on the other end of a telephone conversation, and the next thing you knew, the two were locked in a fight pitting the visit requester's company against the requestee's company. After that, it was their lawyers who were "visiting" and then the litigation was all over the business section of the newspaper.

Shep, still off balance from this interjection, remained silent, but Peter Pastime continued. "We Pastimes get quite a chuckle over this local argot. It's just so unabashedly passive-aggressive. My great-grandfather said no one asks for a visit unless he's got a sledgehammer literal or figurative behind his back and in his firm grip. Ha! A visit with a banker! Ha! That is rich indeed!"

With that pronouncement, Peter Pastime went back to his *Wall Street Journal*, opening it theatrically and looking condescendingly down his nose at an article.

Shep took a breath and attempted to mollify the rictus that held Merlin in mute astonishment. "Hey, Magic Man, it might not be so bad. You can go down there and see what that banker has to say, but just don't let it get to you." Merlin's attention returned to Shep, and he relaxed slightly as he focused on the wry Cajun. "Okay," Merlin said just above a whisper, and then, feeling his breakfast do a karate move inside his vast gut, "I'd better go now."

Shep nodded, and Merlin rose to his feet, aiming for the door.

He was so close to completing his project to extend ancient Celtic navigational lines to the environs of Greater Houston, from which he could extrapolate a massive amount of crucial new data. He felt certain that with this information and a little more astronomical charting, he would have a pretty good shot at determining what was governing the negative energy gyre he believed held his beleaguered but beloved home city in its suffocating thrall. He might even be able to formulate a plan to reverse it, ushering in a new golden age of well-being in the ever-burgeoning metropolis (mirrored by his own ever-burgeoning waistline) about which he cared with a depth of concern he could neither fully plumb nor comprehend.

On his walk homeward, Merlin did not extend the antennae of his listening device. He left the ear buds dangling forlornly by each ear and didn't touch the gadget's on switch. Lost in thought and with his gaze fixed on the sidewalk pavement in front of him, he shambled toward his observatory, weighed down with his mountainous breakfast and the burden of a potentially destructive storm gathering on his near financial horizon. When his observatory was in sight, Merlin's valves of Houston began to give way. He trotted to the entrance, bounded up the stairway, and made it through the bathroom door in the nick of time.

· Two

Lindley Acheson sat low to the ground on a wheeled gardening cart scooting along in measured increments as she regarded a bed containing some of her prize roses, a few of many varieties that had won her significant notoriety among area gardeners. News of her accomplishments had even carried beyond the city into other parts of the South. The members of Bayou Boughs Garden Club thought of her as a gardening prodigy, a Mozart of the flower-bed, as she had exhibited an undeniable knack for growing things from her girlhood. Others thought of her as a kind of horticultural Amazon savant, for, inasmuch as the roses and orchids and irises she grew were delicate, through the inscrutable caprices of the gene lottery, she most definitely was not.

This is not to say she was not good-looking—even beautiful—with luxuriant dark hair framing green eyes and skin without blemish. It's just that there was quite a lot of her to behold. Earlier in her life, doting female relatives tried to comfort her by assuring her she was just big-boned and that there was a long and well-known history of women with this physical trait being seen as quite attractive. By the time of her early adulthood, however, she had become fully cognizant that the era of Rubens had faded into a tiny speck on the receding horizon of history's rearview mirror, and that her look, as the fashion police called it, was not remotely in vogue. In fact, she had come to believe that it really never was and that, well-meaning though their counsel was, those relatives' statements from bygone years were just attempts to mollify a girl who knew that, year in and year out, she would always be the biggest one in her grade school classes. And although some of her friends matured into their adult height on the early side before the boys caught up and often surpassed them a couple of years later, by the time Lindley reached high school, she remained the most physically imposing young lady among her peers. Her personality, however, was far from imposing or aggressive, the way so many Texas women, even those from more established families, can be. It was almost like her outsized physical being caused her innate gentleness to be amplified. This aspect of her personality, along with her prodigious talent in the field of cultivating flora, made her a beloved, if not quite pitied, minor neighborhood luminary.

A less sweet side, perhaps, was that as she grew older she actively channeled all her heartbreak and frustration into her impressive array of flowering plants. This morning she was paying attention to some particularly vicious thorns on the thick stem of a dazzling hybrid red tea rose in full bloom. She exhaled fully while reflecting on the thorns in what she considered her very confounding life. Just as she was about to sink a notch farther on the sadness scale, she heard it, and, unlike the superannuated golf curmudgeons, after listening for another moment to make sure of the sound's nature and general area of origin, her face softened, and with eyes brightening, she looked up with a wistful smile. She knew that those ethereal strains could emanate only from the lone glass armonica in Bayou Boughs, and that its player could be none other than someone she had known all her years, Merlin McNaughton.

———

On leaving the club after a late afternoon board meeting, Tite Dûche's step had quickened considerably from its usual fast pace.

Additionally, there was a kind of pucker to his mouth that, taken in view with his sharp little snout of a nose, made him seem all the more rodent-like. Not knowing this little man, one might have thought he had some serious business to attend to, was off to an important doctor's appointment, or needed to see a school principal about a miscreant child. On all of these counts, such an observer would have been wrong, as this was Tite Dûche's way of expressing excitement.

The business before the board this afternoon involved electing a new slate of officers for the coming fiscal year, and through years of machinations and shameless flattery of key decision makers, Tite's grand design had come to fruition. The new president of Bayou Boughs Country Club was none other than N. Teitel Dûche V, aka "Tite" Dûche.

A laundry list of items his new position would empower him to address extended its sharp little elbows into the cramped sides of his mind's alley-narrow breadth. He had to get going on this. It was his time. Finally. Tite skittered across the parking lot toward his yellow Porsche Cabriolet, his mind racing with a frenzy mimicking the high-pitched whine his little topless German roadster produced while redlining through the gears and spiriting him from one tony engagement to the next.

———

Merlin sat across from the desk and empty chair of Junior Trust Officer Curtis Bumpers in the banker's office sixty-six stories above the pavement in the Phal-Tex Energy Tower in downtown Houston, a place radically transformed from the malarial bayou-laced coastal prairie upon which the Allen brothers staked their claim and promoted to unsuspecting, credulous settlers back East in the 1830s. How their minds would have boggled had they been able to foresee their risky venture's spawn. Or maybe not. From its very inception Houston had been a city of opportunistic dreamers unashamed to believe that they could bring big business ideas to fruition in this new, freewheeling place.

Merlin McNaughton was not such a soul. Although he came from a line of adept businesspeople, perhaps through the untimely death of his parents and his grandfather's sphinx-like taciturnity, the chain of transmission of business-mindedness was broken. Also, and more importantly, Merlin was always more interested in ideas and concepts than in the feet-on-the-ground, hands-in-the-dirt world of doing business. It helped that he had always been provided for—not lavishly, but certainly adequately. As he waited for his trust officer to return with his file, he resigned himself to the reality that a heavy weight was about to be lowered, if not dropped insouciantly, onto a world that seemed to hang tenuously from its own private celestial firmament—namely his.

His eyes roved around the office. There were a few files stacked neatly here and there, the perfunctory photos of wife and children and a fishing tournament trophy, among other unremarkable mementos. From the walls hung what Junior Trust Officer Bumpers would doubtless have referred to as art, but what was really nothing more than an atavistic expression of basic ancient rites and impulses, albeit rendered with a more evolved hand. There were paintings of men wading in shallow saltwater and casting toward a schooling group of tailing redfish on an idealized Texas Gulf Coast morning. There were men in orange vests poised behind English pointers lifting their shotguns to bring down a couple of unlucky birds in an explosive covey rise of bobwhite quail against a backdrop of classic South Texas brush country, replete with cacti and mesquite trees. There was another idealized depiction of men shooting ducks from a reed and salt grass blind on a remote bay, one duck falling hard and another wounded and sidewinding toward the light surface chop as muzzle flash blows from the barrels of the second shooter's twelve gauge and a trusty Labrador retriever tenses to dive into the saltwater and swim toward the bobbing inanimate creatures.

All of Junior Trust Officer Bumpers' paintings were by the same artist—the painter whose work was on the walls of hundreds of bankers, lawyers, and energy professionals around the city—H. Gervey. A print, or if one were fortunate enough to have one, a painting by Mr. Gervey was a kind of religious totem signifying membership in a brotherhood or wannabe warrior class of subduers of nature and the out-of-doors. In the same way the painters of the famous Lascaux cave drawings in France functioned as artist-priests, Mr. H. Gervey officiated for this contemporary demographic and psychographic group. H. Gervey's paintings, although sometimes bordering on what the intelligentsia might deem a kind of Thomas Kincaid–esque shlockiness, were not without merit. It was just that the proliferation of them in the offices of so many former FIE-nance majors from various state universities around the region had rendered them the kind of predictable, unimaginative totems that they had become.

Although reflections on anthropology and aesthetics were not populating Merlin's thoughts, a quick glance around at the H. Gerveys brought to mind vivid memories of Merlin's youthful hunting and fishing trips with his grandfather, the legendary and quirky Arthur McNaughton. Renowned for his intuition for finding and developing productive oil and gas plays, McNaughton was as publicly taciturn as he was successful. In the company of a small group of family members and trusted friends, McNaughton did, however, drop his Mandarin opacity and reveal a genuine warmth and thoughtful, even whimsical persona. He was something of a polymath, especially in his era among his oilman peers, having studied philosophy along with geophysics in his college days. He had special compassion for his grandson who demonstrated a kind of serious inwardness from a very early age.

After his son's and Merlin's mother's death, Arthur McNaughton assumed responsibility for raising the young man. Arthur committed for his remaining years to making a concerted effort to connect with Merlin, and, as best he could, to connect Merlin with the world. One of his favorite ways to engage Merlin with the outside world was through hunting and fishing expeditions. McNaughton was a great club man and a member of the most prestigious private clubs in the region, including hunting and fishing retreats. One of Merlin's favorite spots was a place on one of the bays on the central coastal bend. And Arthur McNaughton took note that duck season animated his grandson thoroughly. In very short order, Merlin demonstrated just as much interest in fishing the shallow bay waters of the sportsman's club a few hours south of town. He wade-fished for hours with singular focus, and much to his grandfather's delight, developed quite a knack for it. That extreme focus was noted over time by club members and guests, and the club's guides, with a nod to The Who's rock opera *Tommy*, began to refer to him among themselves as the pinball wizard, underscoring his rapt attention on the activity and his uncanny ability to catch lunker trout and redfish, along with the occasionally gigged flounder the size of a large pizza pan.

Merlin was fascinated with the effect of the weather and the tides on his endeavors, and Arthur encouraged this line of inquiry. He settled on a particular memory of his grandfather and himself on a calm October dawn casting to a school of redfish tailing at the entrance of a salt grass–lined slough, methodically catching their limits before the sun was no more than a few degrees above the eastern horizon. His reverie broke like a dry rotten bough in a hurricane-force gale as Junior Trust Officer Bumpers entered the office.

Bumpers took his seat and glanced at the papers in his grasp and his computer screen at measured intervals. He then looked at Merlin with clinical professionalism and said, "According to the terms of the trust created for your benefit, distributions cannot be forthcoming at their heretofore previous rate without impinging on the corpus of the capital. And from what I understand from the level of income generated by your on-again, off-again tutoring of neighborhood students, even if you double it, it will not make up for the shortfall for what you have become accustomed to receiving from your trust on a monthly basis as long as oil and natural gas prices remain depressed." Bumpers looked across his desk at Merlin in stony silence.

"Very well," Merlin said, "so what you are suggesting is that—"

A peevish wince torqued Bumpers' pasty unremarkable face: "Full-time employment would solve the shortfall."

Now it was Merlin who was silent. He had known this was coming; nevertheless, like the arrival of the news of the expected death of a long-ill loved one or the demitasse signaling the end of a particularly satisfying holiday feast, the shock registered on a visceral level and his integument reacted with predictable violence. He felt his intestines twist into a kind of Gordian knot as his eyes widened and his right shoulder dropped in sympathy with his churning bowels. His valves of Houston threatened, then desisted. On seeing Merlin's discomfort, Bumpers held him in a cold, unblinking stare. He harbored deep-seated contempt for the beneficiaries upon whom his own livelihood depended, and especially for one as alien to the norms of corporate America as Merlin. The rare occasions when he was able to drop the hammer on a beneficiary he relished with the anticipation of a well-provided-for toddler awakening on Christmas morning.

"Very well," said Merlin with Roman stoicism and stood to tower above Bumpers' desk. Taking in Merlin's sheer upright volume quelled Bumpers' seething disdain for a few seconds. Merlin was generally not very adept at reading people's moods by their facial expressions and body language; however, he noticed as he rose to leave that Bumpers' unbroken icy glare did not meet his eyes. As he walked to the door Merlin imagined the concentrated twin negative energy vortices of Junior Trust Officer Bumpers' eyes burning through the posterior of his spring-weight ensemble. He grabbed the steely doorknob and turned to say goodbye, but Bumpers was already back to work, tapping on his computer keyboard. Merlin was not able to influence the capricious global oil and gas market, but he was determined not to let Bumpers' glare do permanent damage to his own internal energy balance.

———

There was another player holding the thick-gauged puppet cables of Merlin's financial fate; he was the erstwhile occupant of the house beyond which Merlin's observatory stood like a middle finger to the neighborhood. He landed in Houston on few occasions, his compulsively peripatetic mode a near runaway train of unsettledness teetering alongside the steep gorge of permanent dilettantism. Although he was only twelve years Merlin's senior, he was his uncle and Merlin's grandfather's youngest and sole surviving child. Merlin knew that Mickey McNaughton called himself a consultant, but about what and for whom he consulted remained veiled to him.

Mickey was named as the sole trustee for the Merlin Mistlethorpe McNaughton Trust created in the will of Arthur McNaughton. Mickey, in turn, had appointed the Southeast Texas Bancorp Trust Department as co-trustee to handle the day-to-day aspects of the management of Merlin's humble trust fund. His style of trusteeship was arm's length, to say the least, and he had never balked at, much less reviewed with the barest modicum of fiduciary acuity, any of the quarterly reports Junior Trust Officer Bumpers had provided him. Mickey McNaughton often demonstrated the attention span of a hummingbird and was known in Houston as a kind of Bertie Wooster of Bayou Boughs. Educated at some of the Ivy League's finest institutions and at a New Hampshire prep school before that, he was one of those Houstonians who didn't have a Southern or Texan accent, and, owing to his academic pedigree and coming of age at school among New England's elite, his clipped speech was peppered generously with "So . . ." at the beginning of his sentences and

"Right?" at their conclusions. In short, Mickey McNaughton was a type who born and bred Houstonians looked upon with dubious eyes, if not outright distrust. To many of them, with his Southern credentials so severely compromised, he seemed like a spy in enemy territory—a double agent.

After Merlin's meeting with Bumpers, Mickey was nowhere near the vicinity of Bayou Boughs or Greater Houston. As Merlin trudged to the bus stop for the Allen Parkway to Kirby Express, he contemplated trying to contact his globe-trotting uncle by telephone, but experience had taught him that attempts to implore Mickey for something regarding his trust almost always fell on deaf ears. Merlin could imagine his cant answers to his questions regarding the account.

"So . . . the terms of the trust are such that none of the corpus may be spent except in the case of extraordinary circumstances, right?" "So . . . Southeast Texas Bancshares Trust Department is one of the most respected such departments in the U.S., right?"

"So . . . I'm in Dubai doing org consulting, right? So . . . dealing with the minutia of the vagaries in the oil and gas market is really not in my wheelhouse, right?"

"So, you have a master's from Rice. You can probably get a job somewhere doing something, right?"

It had become clear to Merlin, through many previous interactions with Mickey, that his not-too-senior uncle had no interest in the grand personal projects Merlin deemed such important priorities. Every time he started to talk with Mickey about things like reversing the negative energy gyre of Houston, Mickey's spine would stiffen, his eyes would glaze over, and he would say something like "So . . . I've got a squash game in fifteen minutes, right?"

No. This time Merlin was determined to draw on all the internal resoluteness he could muster and face his financial headwinds head-on. He would neither contact Mickey nor allow himself to be humiliated by further interaction with Junior Trust Officer Bumpers. He was prepared to take the proverbial deep breath into his cavernous lipid-swaddled lungs and inject himself into the vast intertwined commercial vascular system of the cacophonous city that thrummed and clanged so close to his sacrosanct refuge of a home in the heart of tranquil Bayou Boughs.

· *Three*

Merlin fell into a deep funk in the ensuing days, confounded by his newly constrained situation and utterly flummoxed by the dubious prospect of prospecting for work. He had hardly touched his glass armonica or head-encircling listening device. Instead, his hands, or more accurately put, hand, found other occupation as an old nemesis returned to thwart him.

In the foggy zone between sleep and wakefulness, images of Celtic warrior queens and ancient goddesses crowded his imagination. Some were Wagnerian Brünnhilde types, replete with horned helmets and body-length spears. Some were on horseback, swords drawn and sporting armored war bustiers out of which tumbled fierce fulsome breasts ready to do battle in their own right. From mythic Britomartis to indomitable Queen Boudicca of the Iceni forward to red-, white-, and blue-clad Wonder Woman, the images came in increasingly rapid succession, intensity, and Technicolor vibrancy.

Simultaneously, a spear of a fleshly nature was rising in Merlin's nether regions. And then, most disturbingly, Merlin became conscious of his left hand abetting this development. As the images scrolled in his mind in even more rapid-fire succession, his sinister hand kept pace, and before he was fully aware of the intensity of this hijacking of his more noble self at the hands of base desire, double life-size images of Xena, Warrior Princess, blew up in his mind as his manhood followed suit and erupted in

Vesuvian proportions, leaving an aftermath requiring immediate attention in the laundry room on the observatory's ground floor.

Merlin's anguish was now even more profound than it had been over the previous days, and he was sure that a self-diagnosed condition was once again thwarting him. Merlin was right-handed at all times . . . except when it came to the above-described activity. Because of this idiosyncrasy he was thoroughly convinced that he suffered from alien hand syndrome.

Alien hand syndrome is a very rare condition in which the sufferer loses motor control of a hand such that it wanders and acts as if it has a mind of its own with no volitional agency whatsoever on the part of the person to whom the hand appertains. Video documentation of this neurological disorder is both stunning and rather disturbing—not unlike Merlin himself. Merlin realized that it was time for qualified medical professionals to address his predicament, confirm his self-diagnosis, and present reasonable options for a path forward that would bring his errant left hand once again under his dominion and put an end to its early morning southbound travels.

Fortunately, on this morning's agenda was a trip to the doctor's office for a regular check-up. Merlin would plead his case with McLean (Mac) Swearingen, M.D., a longtime family friend and fellow member of Bayou Boughs Country Club. A couple of hours had elapsed, and by now, Merlin was as put together a version of himself as he could be—in stark contrast to his frowsy daybreak mess. Today he chose linen trousers in a neutral beige, complemented beneath, of course, by his special urban hiking boots in their own matching hue of beige. For a shirt, he chose a simple blue oxford cloth buttondown. Merlin selected this humble outfit to give respect to the august institution in the Texas Medical Center whose threshold he was about to traverse. Dr. Swearingen's offices were in the Witlock Tower, a contemporary wonder of opulence and efficiency in the heart of the largest concentration of hospitals on the planet. Surely, if

Dr. Swearingen couldn't help him, someone in his vast network of colleagues in this city within the city of healthcare providers could get to the bottom of this confounding situation and tame his errant alien hand.

While considering his vexing condition during the Alles ride to the medical center, Merlin thought of old reruns of *The Addams Family* he had watched as a child and a character in the series that was a single, very expressive hand called Thing. He was beginning to think of his left hand as such a disembodied adversary in his life. Could this be what the old orators and writers were alluding to when they spoke of a red-handed mutiny? The moniker would seem appropriate as he had noticed the blood-flushed surface of his palm after its defiant morning romps in his crotch. What a boon that he happened to be on his way to plotting its imminent defeat.

After exiting the Alles car and entering the bazillion-dollar opulence of the Witlock Tower, whose soaring public spaces on the elevated lobby floor rivaled and indeed surpassed those of some of the most palatial of contemporary hotel lobbies, Merlin took the elevator to Dr. Swearingen's office. After responding when a nurse called him by his first name to an examination room with the indulgent upward-lilting sing-songiness of a pediatrician's or veterinarian's assistant, he found himself seated on an examination table awaiting the doctor's entrance.

Merlin went to Dr. Swearingen because he was one of Arthur McNaughton's best younger friends. But with the passing of time, the good doctor was now no spring chicken himself. Initially, he agreed to see Merlin as a patient as an homage to his friendship with taciturn old Arthur. As time elapsed, however, he had developed a genuine avuncular affection for the young man. He had noticed people flee from Merlin on sight when happening onto his path at church or at the club, and after registering it too many times for him to count, he resolved that, however outlandish the young man's appearance or topic of conversation, he would never disrespect him publicly and would make his best effort to silence anyone he heard doing so.

This morning's interchange with Merlin tried his resolve to the uttermost as his patient, with great passion and seriousness, explained that he believed he suffered from alien hand syndrome. When the doctor asked for examples, Merlin finally confessed, with much reticence and embarrassment, the singular activity that had established this belief in his oversize coconut of a head. At this point, the good doctor looked at his smart phone, acted as if he had just received an emergency message, and excused himself from the room to release a barely controlled snicker before gathering himself and retuning with his serious clinician's face in place. He asked Merlin to perform some simple motor tasks involving touching his nose with his right and then left index fingers. Then, with utmost gravity, he looked at something on a computer monitor and returned his attention to Merlin before pronouncing his diagnosis.

"I think I can say unequivocally that you do not suffer from alien hand syndrome."

Merlin's face dropped, and his eyes and brows took on a look of mild hopelessness. "I don't?"

"No, Merlin. I think we may be dealing with something else that will require a little more reflection on my part before I can get a grip on . . . uh, that is, a full assessment to you."

"Oh," Merlin offered, "I understand." His chin dropped toward his chest.

Doctor Swearingen's posture changed somewhat, and he attempted to take Merlin's attention elsewhere. "I have a completely out-of-the-blue question for you."

"Okay," Merlin replied with guile-free sheepishness.

"Have you ever thought about looking for a special lady friend? You know, like a girlfriend?"

Merlin sat up straight on the examination table. It was with lingering surprise and building insecurity that he said, "The world of potentially amatory forays with members of the opposite sex has never been a field in which I have shown great aptitude."

"Well, you know, I hear there are dating sites on the internet that put all kinds of people together—even folks who may not necessarily have seen eye to eye with anyone prior to registering with one of the services."

Merlin's back stiffened more, and he froze with terror. His eyes filled with the fear and bewilderment of a cornered animal.

"I'm not entirely certain of the motives of the owners of these sites. I have heard that in some cases they may be dubious."

The good doctor looked a bit surprised. "Really? What kind of motives?"

"My understanding is that some of these sites are owned by foreign companies interested in controlling the population through a kind of subtle eugenics experiment carried out through their matchmaking software."

Now it was the doctor who demonstrated wide-eyed bewilderment as he came face to face with a bona fide conspiracy theory proffered by the immensely odd and oddly immense young man who was probably one of its truest believers.

"I declare. I've never heard such a thing, Merlin." The doctor's nervous discomfort betrayed itself by his sudden default to a Texas folksiness peppered with mild oaths.

"Yes, some of my research has revealed that dark players may be pulling the strings of these seemingly harmless so-called dating sites. Some theorists say that is part of their strategy."

"Well, I'll be dipped!" The doctor seemed ready to shed his lab coat and stethoscope for a pair of overalls and a banjo.

"Yes, this is part of the reason for the quandary in which I find myself. Most of the women I honor are heroines of yore with grand missions and independent minds—very different from the sheeple traversing these questionable dating sites. I seem to have been born out of time, as it were, as my tastes and thought trajectories are so out of step with the mores of today."

That's not all that's out of step with you, son, thought the doctor.

"Perhaps I would have been better suited to the era of arranged marriages between scions and heiresses of palatinates and city states or shires and kingdoms. Surely the wisdom of kings, queens, and their sage loyal retainers of bygone centuries far outstripped that of the owners of these dubious so-called dating sites whose questionable motives may be inching daily now toward being uncovered and reproved by the authorities. No, Doctor Mac. I greatly appreciate the concern, but, alas, I find myself beached on the ebb and shoal of an era with a gait of which I seem consigned to be ever out of step."

Beached is right, thought the doctor as he stared at his patient whose proportions called forth images of the fluked baleen masters of the high seas, and "out of step" he once again registered as the understatement of the year, coming as it did from this marcher to a drummer of seemingly unknowable origin.

A lingering few seconds passed as bewilderment blanched Doctor Swearingen's wizened visage. Then, recognizing the uncomfortable unbroken silence, Dr. Mac Swearingen went back into Southern avuncular family-friend mode as he and Merlin exchanged pleasantries while departing the examination room, Merlin heading for the front desk and exit door, and the doctor in the opposite direction toward the safe harbor of his office to gather himself before resuming his duties on one of the higher floors of the gleaming state-of-the-art medical tower whose glass and steel exterior shone like a freshly unwrapped scalpel in the flat midday glare of the relentless subtropical sunlight.

· *Four*

On the Alles drive homeward, Merlin stared through the rear window of the nondescript Japanese sedan across the back seat of which he reclined in an angular sprawl to conform to its tight confines. As he gazed skyward, his thoughts ranged, discipline-free, across a host of barely interrelated subjects: From which direction were the clouds coming? Was it the southeast? Or the east? What was average full takeoff weight of the gargantuan Emirates A380 that would leave this evening on its daily marathon flight from Houston to Dubai? What was the average rate of rotation of a long-distance spiral pass thrown by a starting NFL quarterback? Would the local professional football franchise be looking down the barrels of doom for yet another excruciating season? Would the offensive line at St. James' stand a chance of holding together against its rivals' defenses nearly as well as it did when he was its anchor at right tackle during his high school days?

Although he was foremost a man of ideas, Merlin's cerebral nature had never snuffed out his interest in the world of athletics. Noting Merlin's dimensions early in his middle school years, the football coaches at St. James' encouraged him to try out for the team. Speed and quickness were not the obvious appeal. It was the sheer mass their little college prep line lacked that had them salivating over the potential wall the elephantine young man could present on the gridiron. The same coaches were pleasantly surprised to learn that, in addition to his size, he possessed an almost preternatural strength to match, of which he seemed barely aware.

When the coaches began to stress the role of the lineman as a protector of the quarterback, Merlin's interest was piqued. Additionally, they spoke of opening up running lanes for the other offensive backs, which also appealed, but it was this idea of defending and protecting that really seemed to excite the young recruit. Not wanting to risk losing this coup for their line, the savvy coaching staff spoke of "protecting the ball carrier's forward progress" and "defending and protecting the running lane" versus "opening up a hole," et cetera. Merlin took the bait and became a standout lineman, bringing his singular focus to the football field and intimidating defenses with his astounding dimensions and tonnage.

As the car turned northward from the tree-lined calm of the boulevard alongside Rice University to the retail jungle of Kirby Drive on the southern reaches of which the professional football stadium was situated, Merlin lamented the fate of the Houston Texans. Tales of the heart breaking Oilers' choke during the play-off game against the Buffalo Bills tormented him along with stories of excruciating defeats at the hands of the Pittsburgh Steelers. The Oilers were champions before the AFC and NFC were united, but since the dawn of the era of Super Bowls, no victories had accrued for the Bayou City's pigskin pros. Would the Texans ever rise to the occasion, if the occasion presented itself? Surely, this city of wild-eyed redneck football fans on the very buckle of the football belt should expect a victory, but the waiting continued. It must be the malaise brought on by the negative vortical energy and unfortunate rotation of the city's psycho-spiritual gyre, he deduced. The nineties bore witness to two Houston Rockets NBA championships and, more recently, in a post–Hurricane Harvey thumbing of the nose at the gyre of the malaise, the 2017 Astros brought a first World Series victory home to Houston, but a Super Bowl victory, much less appearance, remained elusive.

A Texan Super Bowl victory would be the acid test that would prove a definitive energy reversal had occurred.

On his arrival home, Merlin entered the front door of the main house and sorted through the mail, leaving everything addressed to Mickey McNaughton on a front hall table and taking everything pertaining to him back to his refuge. As he approached his observatory, he noticed what looked like a raw egg and encrusted broken shell smashed against the lower part of the tower. Perhaps a nest had fallen from a tree. As he washed the mess away with a garden hose and brush, he noted the runic phrases he had painted near the entryway of his abode were in much need of a touch-up. Ruminating on their significance did not lift his spirits, so he entered the door and trudged up the staircase to his residence with his stack of mail. Downcast, he opened his door and looked across the room to his bookshelf.

The first book to catch his eye he always left leaning perpendicularly against other books behind it, so he could see its cover facing the room. It was his favorite from childhood and brought back memories of his beloved nanny who spent much more time with him than did his parents in his formative years. The book was *The Story of Ferdinand* by Munro Leaf, and its timeworn cover featured a colorful drawing of the big bull dreamily sniffing a beautiful red rose under the shade of an ancient tree in some fantastical rural Spanish locale, distant in both time and place. His pause on seeing this favorite story brought a melancholic smile to Merlin's otherwise droopy visage. "Ferdinand the Bull," he mused. Why did he like that story so much? He couldn't really come up with a good answer but thought that his preference for it came from its exotic Iberian setting.

A monthly newsletter from Bayou Boughs Country Club dropped from the stack of mail he was still clutching. He picked it up from the floor and put it on top of the other pieces while enjoying more pleasant childhood memories of reading about Ferdinand. That moment fled with jackrabbit dispatch as he looked down at the club newsletter on top of the mail stack and in frozen disbelief saw Tite Dûche's photograph on the front page of the monthly bulletin and his name and signature beneath the president's letter. Merlin dropped the remaining mail on a side table and went to his window wall to read the letter.

What an honor to realize a lifelong goal of being elected President of Bayou Boughs Country Club! I am grateful for the confidence shown in me on the part of the Board of Directors of Your Club.

Merlin hesitated before continuing, noting Tite Dûche's penchant for capitalizing the initial letters of random nouns and other parts of speech. As noun capitalization is compulsory in German, was this evidence of Dûche's Teutonic roots showing?

Providing the Premier Club Experience is the goal of Your Board and my foremost responsibility as Your President. Part of that charge is to make certain that all Club Members follow all Club Rules to ensure a calm and respectable Club Environment. I will publish a comprehensive list of Club Rules in the next issue of the *Bough Branch,* but for now, I would like to bring to your attention a new rule that Your Board believes requires immediate attention and enforcement.

We all know that hats are not allowed inside any part of Club Property. Of course, out-of-doors, hats are appropriate, and we particularly encourage members' wearing Bayou Boughs' branded hats, visors, caps, and sportswear, but even out-of-doors, it has come to Your President's attention that certain types of headgear are completely inappropriate and therefore, from now forward, have been banned by Your Board.

Certain Members seem to have deemed it necessary to

wear unusual headgear improvised with various antennae and electronics. It would be improper of Your President to name names, but the offenders are hereby served with notice that Your Board and Club Staff have been alerted and Know Who They Are. Specifically, effective immediately, no headwear of any kind may be worn that contains improvised electronics, dials, levers, or antennae—protruding, retractable, or otherwise within the confines of Club Property or Airspace—both Indoor and Outdoor. Offenders will be dealt with harshly, swiftly, and appropriately.

It is Your President's goal to make Bayou Boughs a comfortable, welcoming place for all Members and Their Families. Compliance with the new headwear rule is one more way to achieve this stated goal. Thank you for your continued support.

Sincerely,
N. Teitel Dûche V
(and with a handwritten signature)
"Tite"

Merlin noted that in the handwritten reproduction of Dûche's signature, the dot of the *i* in "Tite" was drawn with great care to make it look like a golf ball, while the *i* was tweaked ever so slightly to represent a tee. Stunned, Merlin collapsed into a large easy chair. In his place of refuge since his earliest memories, he would now be under attack. "It's open season on Merlin McNaughton," he lamented. How would he survive this onslaught? The full authority of the board was behind it, and Tite's animus toward him had now found a way to throw a wrench capable of lodging itself squarely in the gears of Merlin's spinning world.

Were more bans and constraints on his horizon? Merlin stared out the window toward the golf course and the top of a tree line behind a perfectly groomed, impossibly green fairway. Above it, a hawk wheeled in a tight predatory circle, its vision fixed intently on its next meal, most likely an unsuspecting bunny rabbit, Merlin mused, grazing at the course's edge where it abutted the relatively savage wilds of Buffalo Bayou.

· *Five*

Merlin shambled down the street in a neutral tone outfit, a plain beige baseball cap corralling the unruly mop of hair on a downcast head. He stumbled over a protruding section of sidewalk as neighborhood lawn specialists enacted their rite of stepping aside and silencing their leaf blowers and edgers as the gargantuan gringo traversed a strip of their outdoor workplaces. Merlin had never thought about it, but none of them had ever made fun of him as he passed. Always minding his manners, he tried to give each a slight smile and a nod as he walked by, and perhaps it was this modicum of noncondescending respect that the yard men sensed and returned in kind as appreciation of the simple gesture.

When the Dûche family walked through Bayou Boughs, if any of this type of personnel were working near street or sidewalk, they actively ignored them as they strutted with jutting chins, frowning pursed lips and wrinkled noses that had become a kind of behavioral trademark of the family. All the Dûches seemed hell-bent on letting the world know that they were in charge and said world just needed to get out of the way.

Merlin's only fleeting thought, however, as he passed the workers was conjecture as to whether they had all graduated from specialized vo-techs or trade schools in Mexico or Central America. He imagined a ceremony that included the graduates walking across a stage at the far end of which the dean of horticultural management slipped the harness of each graduate's very own gas-powered leaf blower or weed whacker over neck and shoulder in sash-like fashion, announcing to the world the individual's readiness to depart to the land where leaves needed to be blown and weeds whacked incessantly.

Merlin was still distracted by ideas of the pedagogy of botanical management when the door of the locker room surprised him by opening just as he reached for the knob. This shock sent Merlin reeling backward, teetering and waving arms to steady himself. Tite Dûche, clad in one of his signature spring outfits, looked Merlin over with unmasked contempt. As Merlin caught his balance, Tite's trademark pinched-face look returned, and he marched toward the exit. Merlin had doffed his ball cap on entering the clubhouse, so Dûche couldn't cite him for a wardrobe misdemeanor. Nevertheless, he sensed no goodwill emanating his direction from the fastidious little flea of a man. What sort of geomagnetic imbalance had caused him to reach for the door just as the misbegotten incoming club president pushed his way through it? Were the wheels of his world beginning to spin away from each other into their own chaotic and unrelated orbits?

Merlin entered the cavernous man cave with ball cap in hand and eyes wide as he approached his corner spot where Shep Pasteur, like a kind of animate and bemused drugstore Indian, awaited his arrival. And it was definitely the approach of an air-displacing presence, as in his depressed state, Merlin had put on more weight. Shep thought for a second that he should have a couple of those orange plastic-coned flashlights like the tarmac crew use at the airport when guiding jumbo jets to their gates. He released that notion like gafftop catfish and took the human wide-body's hat as he pulled out a high bar chair and offered Merlin his usual spot at the counter.

Perhaps the chair had sustained some previous hairline fracture because on arranging himself into it and placing the small, if one could still really call it that, of his back into the place where the chair's seat met its back support, the unfortunate piece of furniture let out a cracking sound and gave way, first assuming the form of an angular, elongated trapezoid, then flattening onto the floor with Merlin sprawling atop the wooden and leather ruin. Shep went into lightning-quick action, asking another employee to bring in the shoeshine guy's chair—a large, high office chair that belonged to Chappy, the resident bootblack. Shep then summoned a clean-up crew by phone, all the while checking on his charge's well-being.

"I . . . I'm . . . so sorry, Shep! I—"

"Hey now!" Shep interrupted. "Don't you worry a minute about it. I saw a little crack running down that ole chair yesterday afternoon an' thought to myself, it's time for a replacement."

Shep and Chappy helped Merlin to his feet and then into the big black rolling chair that was, fortunately, the same height as the other barstools. Merlin sat in stunned, embarrassed silence as some of the few members who were there at that hour stared in the direction of the mayhem—the superannuated members glaring like mute, miffed snapping turtles, while a trio of younger members snickered under a large-screen television at the far side of the room. Merlin regained his spot at the bar, but he hunched over it with hands clasped atop a bowed head and elbows planted on the countertop, trying to fade into the woodwork.

Shep continued, "No now don't you worry there at all Magic Man! You got nothin' to be ashamed of! That chair was fixin' to go an' it was just a matter of who was gonna sit in it next. I seen it happen before! You just got the unlucky draw!"

Forlorn, Merlin looked at Shep as the wise Cajun spoke and repeated his final words. "Unlucky draw?"

"Dat's right. Sometimes, that's just how the cards fa—, uh, get dealt to you. True for everybody, not just you or me, Magic Man."

Merlin's facial muscles began to relax slightly, and his stiff posture began to ease into its usual slump.

Shep looked across the locker room toward another attendant and mouthed the words "Magic Mountain" while pointing at Merlin out of the broken man's field of vision as he continued to console his rotund charge.

"Shep?"

"What you say, Magic Man?"

"Shep, I gotta find work. More than just working with the St. James' kids on their homework."

"I thought your granddaddy left you well fixed!"

"Pretty well, but there have been some twists and turns lately, and I need something more than part-time. I think I can do it. I could do school pretty well. Maybe I can do a real job, too?"

"You can do more than you think you can right now, but you gotta believe that's true before you try."

"Believe it's true?"

"Yeah, it's just like going fishin'. Don't nobody go fishin' thinking they're gonna get skunked! An' even if they don't catch even one, they gotta keep believin' for the next time!"

Merlin gave Shep a blank face, but Shep was determined to continue until he saw a spark of the slightest kindling of hope where there was only ashen firelessness. Merlin thought of some of the more productive fishing trips from his youth, and his mind wheels began to move. Shep detected this slight change and kept Merlin interested at the other end of the line as the wily Cajun continued to reel in the lure. The spark of another idea animated Shep. "Hey now, do you know Mr. Mondeaux?"

This question caught Merlin off guard and caused him to recoil a bit. "You mean the billionaire T. Rex Mondeaux?"

"That's him!"

"He probably wouldn't remember me, but I know that he and my grandfather were friends."

Shep hesitated as he thought no one after having encountered the hulking obtuse egghead of Bayou Boughs would have an easy time forgetting him and kept angling to raise Merlin's spirits.

"He was in here just yesterday afternoon at the cocktail hour."

"Oh . . . okay?"

"Yeah, and you know I don't make it a habit to listen in too much on conversation between members, but I heard Mr. Mondeaux playing his violin about how much trouble one of his company's been having with what he said was 'its main advertising vehicle.'"

"Is that like an investment vehicle?"

"No, no! Mr. Mondeaux's company owns Fandango Utilities."

"You mean the company with the blimp?"

"Exactly! In this case the advertising vehicle is really a vehicle!"

Merlin brightened. "An airship!"

"Dat's right! It's the Fandango Utilities Blimp!"

"One time it flew right over my observatory!"

"Dat's the one!"

"I wonder what they need."

"I don't know, but if it's anything that don't require a pilot's license, I'm onna be your recommender for the job."

"How can you find out?"

"That's not your worry, Magic Man. You let Shep do his magic an' then you can do yours."

Merlin's Magic Mountain arrived, and he dove into it with renewed gusto. Between bites, he picked up a golf scorecard pencil and notepad and began to doodle images of blimps from various points of view. To Shep, Merlin's sudden excitement seemed so palpable the whipped cream gyre topping his pancakes might begin to rotate, but Merlin quashed this notion as he attacked the carbohydrate-rich discs with the ardor of a grizzly devouring its first kill after awakening from hibernation.

Shep began to wonder how he might broach the subject and suggest the unconventional candidate to the eccentric mogul Rex Mondeaux. Regardless of how tough a businessman Mondeaux was reputed to be, he knew that Mr. Rex liked him. It would all be a matter of reading the captain of industry's mood and timing his query and pitch with finesse. Mood radar and timing were skills at which Shep was beyond expert.

He resolved to risk crossing the usual club employee boundaries. He had known Merlin's grandfather. And he knew Merlin. And he deduced that since Arthur McNaughton's passing, there wasn't a soul in this world to look out for this well-meaning but clueless young man. At this moment, however, Shep relished his success in turning Merlin into a hopeful mass of blimp-dreaming, breakfast-gobbling anticipation.

· Six

With his acutely tuned human radar, beat-perfect timing, and rarely erring intuition, Shep Pasteur took full advantage of the opportunity to ask a post-business-deal-sealing, post-golfing, post-second-cocktail-quaffing Rex Mondeaux, chief executive officer of Mondoco, Incorporated, of which Fandango Utilities was a subsidiary, to take a chance on Merlin, who, Shep assured Mondeaux, might be just the right fit for the gap in Fandango's pesky blimp operations. After a quizzical moment of reflection, Mr. Mondeaux—never one to mince words or overthink a deal—said okay. Shep considered this one of the major victories in his storied history of clubhouse diplomacy. Now, it was imperative that Merlin not let him down.

———

Merlin was duly impressed when the Alles driver was flagged into the blimp base after giving his passenger's name. The large white hangar loomed before them with a diminutive office attached to its side like the entryway to an elongated oversized igloo. The entry sign read "Fandango Utilities Blimp/Airship Resource (FUBAR)—Home of the *Airmadillo*." Reading this official-sounding name and looking at the looming hangar as the car approached the office induced reverential awe in Merlin. He mustered all the presence of mind he could to steel himself for the interview.

In a few minutes, Merlin was sitting in a rolling office chair across the desk from Lyudmila Sukhova, sales and marketing director for Fandango Utilities. Above and behind Ms. Sukhova, the entire wall was covered in what Merlin considered a very bold and striking graphic of the *Airmadillo* in all its garish orange, blue, and silver glory, its nose pointed bravely toward the heavens. In bold type framing the airship on the background of a cloud-specked blue firmament toward which it soldiered were the words "Fandango Utilities" and "A Dang Good Idea!"

The auburn-haired Ms. Sukhova eyed the unconventional job applicant with a raised eyebrow reminiscent of Natasha of Boris and Natasha fame from the *Bullwinkle* cartoon show. The lowering of the eyebrow was accompanied by fixing Merlin with a piercing, unsmiling gaze. "Bleemp eez problem," Ms. Sukhova intoned flatly. She even sounded like Natasha as far as Merlin could remember from the reruns. He would have liked to hear her say, "Moose and squirrel must die." But that thought vanished as the no-nonsense marketing director continued.

"Well. Not exactly. Bleemp eez fine. In good functioning order. Management of bleemp eez real problem."

Merlin nodded silently.

"A lot of turnover here at office. No consistency. This is bad for corporate image; bad for client relations."

Merlin nodded again as the svelte Slavic executive scrutinized the single hard-copy page of his resumé.

"Nontraditional resumé, but at this point we will try anything. Also, very strong suggestion from upper management that you be hired."

"I have good skills at organizing data," Merlin offered with a quavering voice.

The eyebrow went up again as Sukhova glanced quickly at the hulking, disheveled blob across the table.

"Bleemp Operations needs two things as soon as possible: We must have program to organize scheduling of passengers and program to remind mechanic when to service vehicle and what service to perform. We need better communications with parts suppliers and manufacturer, so bleemp stays operational as many days as possible."

Merlin listened and responded tentatively, "I have written a lot of software programs."

"What kind of programs?" Sukhova said with an unveiled tone of challenge.

"Many kinds. I like solving problems," Merlin responded flatly.

Lyudmila Sukhova's eyebrow remained raised in its unconvinced arch as she froze Merlin in her gaze for a moment and looked again at the resumé. To Merlin's surprise, she relaxed into the chair, turned, and sailed the lone sheet nonchalantly toward the bare surface of an empty credenza behind her beneath the blimp graphic.

"Here eez description of benefits and salary."

She sailed another sheet vaguely in Merlin's direction, and he reached awkwardly to catch it as it slid off the desk.

"You start Monday?" Merlin glanced at the data on the official-looking glossy printed page and nodded in compliance.

"Okay," exhaled Sukhova as she pushed back from the desk. "Time to meet staff."

· *Seven*

Tite Dûche left the club through a service entrance after conferring with an employee at its doorway. In a couple of minutes, he was ripping his yowling little roadster through its gears as he careened down Kirby Drive and onto Allen Parkway. Vitalized by what he considered to be a productive board meeting, Tite crinkled his rat nose in the breeze as he made each gear whine at high RPMs before jerking the stick into the next one. Now he was on his way. Now he, he believed with the certainty of a new proselyte, could remake the club to suit his fancy. Board resistance was a nonissue as his cronies would back him on all his proposals.

Neither charity cocktail reception nor gala-planning party were on Tite's itinerary today. He pointed his cheeky two-seater northward from the Allen Parkway entrance ramp onto I-45 and quickly exited toward a neighborhood where the rich-man's car would stand out like a zoot suit at an Amish funeral. What business could a Bayou Boughs stalwart have on the near North Side? It was a land where the signs were written mostly in a language on which he did not have the loosest of grasps, although, on entering the barrio, it surrounded him like water surrounds a fish.

Despite his bafflement and subsequent glee on getting the job at the Fandango Utilities Blimp/Airship Resource base and meeting some of the staff members, Merlin's sense of isolation increased over the ensuing days and so did his appetite. Driven by a hunger nothing short of global in its span and proportions, he hit all of his local go-to spots, covering a broad spectrum of ethnic and regional cuisines.

He led off with a culinary flight of whimsy to old Indochina, alighting at a favorite haunt in Houston's Midtown, where he was known in Vietnamese to the restaurant staff as the Water Buffalo. Merlin was, as usual, single-mindedly unaware of past instances of waiters' snickering as he lumbered down the sidewalk to the restaurant entry and angled himself to slip through the glass doorway to the basic but comfortably appointed restaurant. The staff shot each other looks of instant alarm, then turned on their perfunctory greeting smiles to welcome him. Having had too many experiences with his rupturing support slats undergirding booths alongside the far wall of the restaurant, an employee ran to retrieve a large, wide rolling chair as another motioned him toward a four-top table. On Merlin's arrival tableside, the big sturdy chair rolled into place to allow him to slide into it with comfort and confidence.

He did not seat himself before producing a black portfolio he had clutched under his left arm. He opened it and removed its sole contents—a translucent smock of the sort that a child's art class might distribute. It started at the neck with a rigid collar of metal entwined in some kind of bright red fabric and descended into the vast tarp-like amorphousness of the gargantuan smock. This version was modified to have some basic sleeves, sort of like a poncho, allowing both greater freedom of movement and more protection from flying morsels and liquids.

Unfazed, the waiter was a bodhisattva of patience.

"Usual starters?" he inquired.

"Yes! Of course!" returned Merlin with the exuberant security of the recently gainfully employed, his smock flapping in a show of unrestrained glee. And the onslaught began: First with soft spring rolls and spicy sweet peanut sauce, followed by fried summer rolls with fresh mint, cilantro, bean sprouts, and sliced jalapeño peppers all swaddled in crisp, fresh leaves of romaine lettuce ready for the dipping into the sticky-sweet, unctuous fish sauce ubiquitous in Vietnam and in Vietnamese cultural outposts around the world.

Merlin rolled through the summer rolls with great relish, his eyes rolling back in his head as he chomped down on the cold of the lettuce and vegetables before hitting the hot fried density and intensity of the roll itself, the coral-colored fish sauce dribbling down his chin and coursing through the thick tendrils of his beard with his smock and plate serving as catch basins for the overflowing condiment. As Merlin finished his last bite, the waiter once again appeared.

"Pho?"

"Absolutely!"

This is when the smock's efficacy rose to a particularly high level. As much as Merlin loved the iconic Vietnamese soup, he had learned over and over that he could not make it through even a small bowl without depositing a significant part of its contents on the frontispiece of his shirt, with a fair residuum making its way onto his lap. Time and again Merlin had stained himself to the point of great embarrassment, even for a soul as unselfconscious as he.

Determining never to leave a Vietnamese restaurant again looking like Jackson Pollack had painted his torso with seasoned broth and sauced, fried, and sautéed tidbits, Merlin initiated a search for a suitable barrier between himself and the objects of his gustatory pleasure. After careful consideration, he decided that the art smock was an ideal choice. It covered the threatened corporeal areas thoroughly while allowing for unencumbered freedom of movement to reach for platters, condiments, and other items as he orchestrated each bite of his mealtime symphonies.

After a server refilled his teacup, while yet another brought a fresh pot of tea, the piping hot tureen of pho tai with all its attendant trimmings and condiments arrived. A big plate of the same vegetables that accompanied the summer rolls also appeared, with a few additions, including tiny leaved rao ôm, which Merlin thought particularly beguiling, as no Western cuisine of which he was aware used an herb with a similar flavor. Merlin used all of the vegetables and healthy glops of each of the sweet and spicy condiments, creating a dark brew—the thinly sliced pieces of beef and wilting vegetables swimming in a hot turbid broth reminiscent of flotsam, jetsam, discarded household items, and perhaps even body parts bobbing in the chocolate milk–colored, post-hurricane churned waters of Galveston Bay. Remnants of pho descended in glistening tear-like rivulets down the creases of the smock as Merlin finished his soup and awaited the main event.

With his lunchtime preamble complete, Merlin was ready to dive into the heart of his feast. First there was a crisp salad of shredded cabbage, bell peppers, and herbs topped with torn strips of roasted and flash-fried duck and covered with a thin, vinegary pepper sauce that piqued his desire for the forthcoming dishes— and forthcome, they did. There were salt-and-pepper-fried whole prawns he devoured with such gusto he barely removed their shells before pawing them toward his insatiable maw. There were flat pieces of pork surrounding central oval bones he dispatched with equal speed but with enough dexterity and dental precision to eat to the very edges of the bones. Merlin the bone edger moved to a dish of beef short ribs in a savory sauce with whole roasted garlic cloves that alit piping hot from the kitchen. With a judicious nod to his health, he ordered a dish of baby bok choy and tofu fried with aromatic herbs, leeks, and lemongrass. He liked the name baby bok choy and wondered if there was ever a midget wrestler in the days of yore from perhaps colonial Hong Kong who was called Baby Bok Choy. He considered the yin and yang of bok choy—how when cooked it remained firm and crisp at its core while becoming supple at its leafy edges. He was certain that, with a stage name like Baby Bok Choy, such a wrestler would have had an automatic leg up on his opponents and a thoroughly successful career.

Finally, there was a whole fried red snapper topped with a dark brown sauce featuring shallots, scallions, sliced fresh ginger, and fresh-quartered kaffir limes. Merlin processed the top side of the fish, removing the flesh from its skeleton and flipping the entire filet deftly onto a bed of rice he had prepared for its bull's-eye landing on his plate. A few moments later, he flipped the plattered fish with the aplomb of a seasoned teppanyaki chef and fileted its other side as fresh pillows of rice awaited its imminent flop onto his plate with the attendant spectacle of drops of sauce spattering upward onto the already food-pummeled smock. For dessert, he decided to be judicious and opt for a simple, yet cloyingly sweet, Vietnamese sua da coffee with condensed milk as thick as the Gulf Coast air into which he would soon wobble after his noonday culinary romp.

Merlin's other stops during the ensuing days included South Asian buffets of Sri Lankan, Pakistani, and northern and southern Indian provenance, a Japanese *robatayaki* restaurant, several Central American *pupuserias* in the Bellaire area, a Persian place, and an enormous Lebanese lunch buffet line, the contents of which were so vast and varied that even Merlin could not imagine sampling everything on offer at one sitting. One of his more astounding performances came at one of those all-you-can-eat Brazilian churrascarias where the staff continues to bring freshly fire-roasted meats to diners until they turn their green dining cards over to the red side to signify that the onslaught of animal protein has vanquished them. Merlin's level of consumption at this place was so prodigious that, after his departure, management convened to reconsider the all-you-can-eat policy and the restaurant's price structure.

In addition to the world of global cuisine, Merlin descended on reliable haunts featuring regional favorites. As it was crawfish season, he hit all the spots—the true Cajun places and, his favorite, the hybrid Vietnamese/Cajun crawfish restaurants in the Southeast Asian enclave on the west side of town past the beltway. He devoured pound after pound of the cayenne-and-Vietnamese-spiced critters that after their sacrifice in the spiced boiling pot were strained from their final swim, and in the style unique to the Vietnamese preparation, were dusted in spices and doused in massive amounts of butter in a big aluminum bowl for serving. He also felt obligated to get the full experience and avoid insulting the staff by consuming the boiled potatoes, corn on the cob, onions, garlic, and Andouille sausage accompanying each of his orders. Strategically, Merlin scheduled these feasts late in the afternoon, as these restaurants filled up at night and westbound evening traffic was horrendous.

No tour of Houston would be complete without a deep dive into the world of Tex-Mex, so Merlin went to his top spots until he was *relleno* with every Mesoamerican chile imaginable. He even departed from the culinary borderlands and found himself in a Yucatan restaurant for a little *cochinita pibil*. Later he landed at another interior Mexican place with rich mole sauces from Puebla and Oaxaca. Burgers, fried chicken, straight-ahead Gulf Coast fish and seafood, and a whole kaleidoscope of barbequed favorites were also on Merlin's list, as he had a sense that when his new career began, he would be limited to rare visits to his cherished spots. At the end of this binge, his already fulsomely cut wardrobe fit him like so many form-fitting surgical gloves. Even from the depths of leaden self-unawareness Merlin heard the whisper of a cosmic suggestion that he consider dialing back his intake. Although his ballooned girth limited his mobility more than ever, he was satisfied that he had not missed out on the vast variety and quality of culinary comestibles his steaming mishmash of a city offered. This satisfaction afforded him the opportunity to focus on the task at hand—his new role at the Fandango Utilities blimp base.

· *Eight*

Merlin's arrival at the Fandango blimp base proved to be nothing less than a revelation. First he responded in A-student fashion to Lyudmila Sukhova's directive to organize passenger and maintenance scheduling and parts requisition for the blimp. Although customer rides were a secondary aspect of the blimp's promotional purposes, recent miscommunications had upset the balance of harmonious corporate/client relations as his predecessor had been far from fastidious in matching blimp passengers to acceptable and available flight times. The ensuing grumblings of the crestfallen clients made their way all the way back to Rex Mondeaux, who on getting a look at the individual in charge of the scheduling and knowing the amatory proclivities of the chief blimp pilot, immediately deduced that her service was most likely entirely focused on the pilot and not the clients. A little more research on the part of his cold-blooded Russian marketing manager confirmed Mondeaux's suspicions. He congratulated himself (as he often did) that he had hired the polar opposite to do the attractive young woman's previous job. He was particularly satisfied knowing this would thoroughly frustrate the chief pilot, Captain Dirk Kajerka, whose prospects for similar pay and hours beyond the blimp base dwindled with each passing season.

In very short order, Merlin put his formidable left-brain abilities to work creating software to manage the administrative problems his predecessor had ignored. He wrote a program to show available passenger flight times for a solid year in advance. Another program sent e-mails advising future blimp riders of their flight dates and times while simultaneously entering their information in his main scheduling database for in-house purposes. He spoke with the chief of blimp maintenance and learned that there was no regular communication regarding blimp upkeep and management at Fandango. In fact, the maintenance chief was using guidelines in an outdated printed manual from the blimp manufacturer. Merlin wrote a program that allowed the engineer to click and mark an electronic checklist at regular intervals and automatically communicate that information to management at Fandango and to the blimp manufacturer. With this program in place, Fandango was able to keep the blimp flying more of the year, as parts requisition became a much quicker and easier process.

Notwithstanding his frustration at his sassy little sidekick's departure, Captain Kajerka overcame his initial revulsion at the sight of the new administrative coordinator and actually started to interact with him in a vaguely civil manner. He could not deny that Merlin's tech skills had made everyone's life at FUBAR considerably less stress-prone and that the incoming good reports to management from happy blimp passengers lowered the collective staff blood pressure by several digits. Nevertheless, his sky-high libido squirmed within him as he longed for an assistant like the comely but less than competent one so recently departed from the service of FUBAR.

After the passage of several weeks, and with the new system whirring like a well-oiled machine, an inkling of an idea rose on the foggy horizon of Dirk Kajerka's imagination. With all the new goodwill flowing from corporate in the direction of FUBAR, he reasoned, it might be acceptable to ask for at least a part-time hospitality employee to greet arriving blimp passengers, check them in, and accompany them to the lighter-than-air vehicle before takeoff. Likewise, she (and he saw the new employee as none other than a she, and a certain kind of she at that) could usher blimp riders on their way after landing, providing them with certificates memorializing their flight and thanks for participating in the FUBAR/*Airmadillo* story. He reasoned that he could sell this proposal to his bosses on a couple of counts. One: as competent as the new admin at FUBAR was, he was the opposite of what you would want a client to see on arrival at the base. Far from instilling a sense of security and confidence in passengers, one look at Merlin, he would argue, might strike serious doubt, if not fear, in the about-to-ascend passengers. Anyone would agree that, regardless of his competency, Merlin was an unsettling presence to encounter.

Two: if the prospective air hostess were only a part-time employee, she would not be a significant financial burden to Fandango Utilities. Surely it would be worthwhile for Fandango to make the newly tightened ship of blimp operations thoroughly professional by presenting a pleasant greeter and facilitator to VIP clients. He knew he would have to first overcome the cold raised eyebrow of the Russian marketing director, but if he could win her advocacy for the idea, she might be able to sway Rex Mondeux to agree to the plan, even though the departure of the less-than-professional recent admin/greeter was still relatively fresh in the renowned mogul's memory. Mondeaux didn't micromanage his other companies, but the *Airmadillo* was different; it was a pet project into which he invested personal pride. Maybe, just maybe, Dirk Kajerka reasoned, if all the stars lined up, he could once again have a comely sidekick at the base. Conceiving this whole scenario was as much strategic thinking as Kajerka had done in years, but his motivation, base though it may have been, was equally strong and now grounded in determination. The blimp would have a stewardess (he cleaved to the antiquated sexist term) and an accompanying wardrobe of professional but ever so slightly sexy blimp stewardess outfits suitable for every season. But could he sell it? He didn't want to get ahead of himself. He decided that although Merlin was a low man on the totem pole, it might be judicious to win him over to his plan. After all, keeping the big fella happy and generating good work product could do nothing but redound to an overall positive atmosphere at FUBAR. Making Merlin feel a part of the decision to hire a part-time blimp attendant would also, Dirk reasoned, make him feel like a part of a team, regardless of how much Merlin seemed like a lone jumbo planet in his own obscure solar system.

One morning when the blimp was undergoing a scheduled maintenance thanks to Merlin's new software, Merlin was getting hot water for his hibiscus tea in FUBAR's commissary. The captain ambled in to fill his coffee cup just a moment later and realized that this was his chance to reel Merlin into his scheme. Merlin's spine straightened a bit in deference to aeronautical authority as he noted the pilot entering the commissary and angling toward the coffee machine.

"Kind of a quiet morning here at the old FUBAR, huh?"

Merlin steadied himself to prepare to respond to the unexpected query from the base's on-site alpha authority figure. Captain Kajerka had never asked such a seemingly innocuous question of him. Was it a test? Merlin pondered this for a long moment before responding in what he considered the most professional of manners.

"Yes, the zephyrs of the incoming norther appear to have arrived ahead of the meteorological sages' prognostications."

"Wow! Zephyrs! I used to know an entertainer named Zephyr," enthused the mustachioed captain.

Merlin tried to mirror the pilot's conversational tone with his response: "It sounds rather like the name of a thoroughbred racehorse, perhaps."

"Oh, she was a thoroughbred alright—from head to tail."

Merlin faltered, wide-eyed and silent.

The captain recognized Merlin's unease and changed the

subject. "Well, everybody, myself included, is talking about what a great addition you have been to the team here at the base."

Although they seemed to be already at full aperture, Merlin's eyes widened a bit more. "Th . . . thank you," he stuttered.

"You've taken care of a lot of stuff that got overlooked around here, but I am kind of thinking we need a little something else to round out the FUBAR experience."

Merlin cocked his head like a befuddled golden retriever.

"Yeah, what with me flying, and you and the mechanics handling the scheduling and technical stuff, not to mention the ground crew, don't you think we may be swimming in a little too much testosterone around here?"

"Oh! Perhaps?" Merlin ventured.

"I knew you'd feel the same way," the pilot cajoled his easy-to-hit mark with more shameless flattery. "Yeah, so what I'm thinking is we put an ask in for a part-time air hostess, a young lady who could really convey the Fandango vibe. She would welcome clients, get them settled in the blimp, and maybe even provide a little tour guide banter in the airship if she has a flair for performing."

Having grown up in a largely male household, Merlin knew how dull a single-gender milieu could make the atmosphere. "Yes!" he offered with sudden enthusiasm. "I can visualize such an addition to the staff."

"I mean, you know, this would be only a part-time position, but it could be a real enhancement to the whole show." Dirk Kajerka lingered on the words "position" and "enhancement" and noted that Merlin accepted his statement without the slightest suspicion of double entendre. *Great*, Kajerka mused to himself, *this guy could be the perfect accomplice*. "Okay, then," he said, "I will run this up the flagpole with Lyudmila and see if she thinks it might fly."

"Oh, okay," replied Merlin with the amiable bemusement of those born in the manger of naiveté. He was relieved to have

managed a verbal parley with the swaggering captain of the vehicle for which the base existed, but reflecting on the interchange in
his office, he felt newly at ease—like a real team member, someone the pilot would chat with while getting coffee on a slow day.
Little did he suspect his suddenly solicitous superior imagined
a flight attendant whose primary attendee would be he of the
bouncing epaulets, Captain Dirk Kajerka, himself.

· Nine

Lindley Acheson decided to walk to her meeting at the Garden Club this Saturday morning. If Indian summer signified warm weather that persisted into fall in New England, then there needed to be, she reasoned, a term for coolish spring weather that lingered into the relentlessly encroaching heat and humidity of an approaching Houston summer. She was enjoying her walk in this nameless cool, when she heard the familiar strains of the armonica careening through the neighborhood. Her route would take her past Merlin's observatory, so she made a game of trying to determine what he was playing as she approached.

The lively tune was Merlin's arrangement of "La Primavera" from Vivaldi's *Four Seasons*. As she got closer to the tower, she realized that Merlin was doing a kind of glass armonica karaoke this morning. A recording of the classic Baroque-era piece blared on his sound system and the armonica was accompanying it. Lindley thought this a rather ingenious solution, as the Vivaldi piece's rapid-fire violin solos and punchy passages were not ideally suited to the mechanics of Merlin's instrument. The armonica, however, did add a certain resonance to the recorded piece that, she had to admit, enhanced it considerably.

When she was within a few hundred feet of Merlin's tower, the music stopped, and by the time she neared the McNaughton address, Merlin was emerging from the garden gate onto the sidewalk, a clipboard clamping a jumble of penciled papers. He seemed to be in a hurry as he started his walk to breakfast, so Lindley quickened her pace to catch up with him, calling ahead to him before he set out in earnest.

"Merlin!" Lindley called with sufficient vigor to be heard above the tuned-up lawnmowers of Bayou Boughs. He stopped, looked up, turned slightly, then continued to walk. Lindley called again, and he turned around completely and saw her. She was wearing a Mexican-style sundress and pulling a little cart with her gardening implements: some topsoil, a few flower bulbs, and other related items.

"Hello, Lindley!"

"I liked what you were playing this morning."

"Yes, well, thank you. It's something new, a kind of collaboration between armonica and a masterful recorded rendition."

"I could tell. It was nice!"

"I was concerned that I might be cheating in my musicianship, but I decided the armonica might complement rather than simply imitate the recording."

"It was very complementary. I really have never heard anything like it."

At this, Merlin's face lightened, and he stood up a little from his slump.

"Really? Perhaps I have stumbled onto something!" Merlin offered as he stepped backward and tripped slightly on an uneven section of sidewalk, causing his clipboard nearly to escape his grasp.

"I think you should play more pieces like this when you get the inspiration."

"Thank you. I think I will!"

Lindley's phone rang, and she apologized for having to take the call. Merlin waved and headed for the club. After the call, Lindley looked up toward Merlin's backyard abode. She noticed that there was a strange kind of writing painted on its walls near the doorway. She also saw a clipboard like the one Merlin was carrying hanging on a nail on the outer wall next to the tower's balcony, its papers flapping in the mild spring breeze.

———

As Merlin entered the locker room and rounded the corner of the opening foyer, something spun him with a jolt, sending his formerly clipped assortment of notes snowing onto the floor around him. He looked down and saw a designer golf outfit–wearing Tite Dûche grimacing back at him, fire in his beady close-set eyes. Merlin couldn't tell whether he ran into Tite or Tite ran into him this time, but never one to err in the direction of the unmannerly, he began to apologize. Tite met this offer with a stony stare and marched off like a toy hussar for his tee time. Merlin scooped up his notes and shuffled toward his usual spot at the bar. Shep Pasteur was staring at his shoes as Merlin angled to dock himself at his corner spot.

———

Mickey McNaughton poured himself a bracing gin and tonic and stood at his hotel room window looking out onto the Persian Gulf, or the Sea of Arabia, as the Emiratis call it. The weather was turning warmer, heralding the incoming heat missile barrage that made summers in Houston seem temperate by comparison. His patience was once again wearing thin—not only with the weather but also with his Dubai-based clients.

Normally, he could go into a meeting, spew a bunch of Ivy League/East Coast platitudes, and leave his audience dumbfounded but rarely enlightened. Clearing things up always took a back seat to stirring them up, Mickey's theory being that, as long as he was the stirrer and continued to be sought out for counsel, this mode of operation was good for business—not necessarily for his clients' affairs, but most certainly for his own.

But this job was different. Mickey's time-honed techniques did not faze the consultees, who continued to ask probing, substantive questions.

Their foray into the dialectical didn't suit him. After all, Mickey was trained to act as a consultant and believed his role was not to actually solve problems but to point them out with as much moxie and theatrical spark as he could summon. The problem-solving bit was the work of a turnaround CEO, and Mickey could serve as a gating mechanism, a recommender of such an expert at most, but never one to step into his shoes. All the arrows now pointed in the same direction; it was time to fly. He freshened his cocktail and began to rehearse his exit speech in his mind. "So, I do diagnostics of organizational inefficiencies. I'm not a turnaround specialist, per se, right?"

———

After sinking a two-foot putt, Tite Dûche strode to his golf cart and took the scorecard from the little clip at the center of the cart's steering wheel. "This is how clipboards were meant to be used," Tite mused with the unwavering sanctimony that had come to distinguish the Dûche brand. Etching his score for the hole into the confines of the little box on the card with the short, eraser-less pencil, Tite simultaneously etched a plan for the forthcoming club newsletter in his mind. This one was obvious: a lay-down, hand as the card-playing members would say. It was time to tighten the bolts at Bayou Boughs Country Club, and Tite Dûche was ready to assume the role of wrench-wielder-in-chief.

· *Ten*

Despite Lyudmila Sukhova's initial skepticism, Captain Dirk Kajerka's flight attendant gambit was successful. This win was in no way attributable to any silver-tongued powers of persuasion on the part of the pilot. Instead, while they were talking, Ms. Sukhova had an idea. A younger relative of hers had recently moved to Houston and needed work. She realized this role might be well suited to her cousin, a former finalist in the annual Sturgeon Queen pageant in a small town on the northern shores of the Caspian Sea not far from Astrakhan.

Additionally, Ms. Sukhova was sure that with her solid Russian backbone, her cousin would have no problem rebuffing the pilot's inevitable advances. Pitching the idea to Svetlana Slahtskaya was really no pitch at all as the new arrival to the inland concrete-covered prairies of the Upper Texas Gulf Coast had no prospects other than that of a retail position at a national chain store in a mall on the city's outskirts. The possibility of getting to fly in a blimp excited her. In her trademark terse and humorless fashion, Sukhova ended their conversation, "Okay, you will be at blimp base Monday morning at eight. Wear heels and skirt—not too short."

Svetlana's arrival at FUBAR created a frisson of excitement. The mechanics and ground crew did their best to catch a glimpse of the striking young Slav, like long-incarcerated inmates craning their collective necks to see a barely visible woman passing in a vehicle outside a prison's perimeter. Regardless of the novelty of her arrival at FUBAR, Svetlana's presence lent an immediate and palpable sense of lightness to the air at the base. Yes, she was attractive, with straight blond hair and crystalline blue eyes that bespoke Siberian ice floes, but it was the surprising unvarnished warmth of her personality that lightened the atmosphere around the facility. It seemed that a new and optimal equilibrium had been reached—just like when Dirk Kajerka held the blimp in a static hover on an almost windless day.

Merlin found Svetlana thoroughly fascinating, having never been in such close proximity to a woman of such physical appeal and charming personality. On meeting her, he had a hard time mustering a verbal greeting. After a long, wide-eyed pause, the stunned giant finally stuck out his paw and uttered a nervous "Nice to meet you," as Svetlana returned the gesture by lightly clasping a portion of Merlin's hand with the most delicate and poised female hand Merlin had ever remembered touching him in his adult years. Although he looked at it for a moment too long while they exchanged greetings, Svetlana did not seem at all disturbed when they regained eye contact to complete the introduction.

Merlin was unaware of the grumblings of the mechanics about his getting to work in the office next to the newly arrived client relations specialist, and after recovering from the initial shock of his close encounter with what seemed to his eyes Svetlana's blinding beauty and effervescent charm, he began to work efficiently with her to create an ideal experience for blimp passengers from near and far. After getting comfortable with her new environs, Svetlana added some of her own cultural touches to the sterile FUBAR office atmosphere. She brought an authentic Russian samovar to work and initiated a welcome ritual that included a cup of tea and sweet stuffed blini she served to each blimp passenger around a conference table as Captain Kajerka debriefed the blimp riders on a few aspects of lighter-than-air aerodynamics and the flight's route.

Of anyone at the base, the finer points of Miss Slahtskaya's appeal were least lost on that swaggering swain of dirigible dirigisme, Captain Dirk Kajerka. Realizing that he would need to be circumspect in his strategy and tactics with Svetlana, given her relationship to marketing director Sukhova, Dirk hung fire, restraining himself as best he could from amatory efforts to close the deal with the new arrival. And so, for the first time in the frequently stormy history of FUBAR, in relatively short order, operations achieved a previously unreached high level of excellence. Word of this positive new state of affairs at FUBAR made its way back to the corporate overlord himself, Mr. T. Rex Mondeaux III. Mondeaux met the news with a tentative sigh, as by now, he had come to view the blimp as an endless source of tedious headache-fostering personnel problems, although it had become a critical aspect of the company's public identity. At least for the time being, the blimp, it seemed, could remain off the radar screen of organizational issues that merited attention.

Over the ensuing weeks, Merlin experienced something he had never known—being a part of a well-functioning team in the workforce. He was a part of the football team in high school, but there he always felt like an outsider—uncomfortable to join in the locker room banter with its egotistical talk of status and girls and physical prowess on and off the gridiron. Merlin felt he was looked upon as a necessary, but strange and maybe even repulsive part of the St. James' offense. Not so in his new station in life. It was as if for the first time his world was opening up, and the constraint of his financial challenges had actually served to bring him to this surprisingly satisfying place.

It was in this environment of a smoothly humming FUBAR that Dirk Kajerka could contain himself no longer. He had to make his move, or at least get the prop spinning so a move was makeable. Once again, the pilot addressed Merlin in another seemingly chance encounter in the coffee room at the blimp base. Merlin was almost done filling his teacup with hot water when

Captain Kajerka sidled into the room and angled toward the coffee maker next to where Merlin was standing. The pilot was holding his favorite coffee mug, an oversized all-black corporate promo piece featuring white Playboy bunny ears. Merlin looked at the pilot and quickly focused on the mug, allowing Kajerka the perfect entrée to start a conversation.

"I got this back when Playboy decided they wanted to start an airline—you know, to ferry whales to Las Vegas and to parties at the mansion in L.A. It was pretty short lived, but let me tell you, it was a boatload of fun while it lasted."

"Oh, yes, I'm certain it must have been," stuttered Merlin.

He was once again terrified at the captain's casual reference to what must have entailed some thoroughly illicit, if not illegal, mischief. Seeing this, Kajerka changed his tack and sent the conversation in the direction he had rehearsed.

"So you know, with things going so well here at the base, I'm thinking this might be a good time for you and Svetlana to learn a little more about airship operations. That is, if you're interested."

On hearing this, Merlin's guarded mood did a 180, and his eyes remained wide—not in fear, but with a sense of fascination.

"Operations?" Merlin replied tentatively.

"Yeah, as you know, a big part of blimp life is flying around the city on advertising missions, whether it's to sporting events or festivals, or just around town on a nice day where people can see the *Airmadillo*, and after sunset check out the messages on the big screens on both sides of the ship as they light up the night."

"Yes, I know there are a lot of advertising missions."

"You got that right."

"And at night the blimp puts on an awe-inspiring aerial show with its state-of-the-art screens. I have researched them and learned that Fandango Utilities spared no expense in purchasing the very finest technology."

"And you got that one right, too. Mr. Mondeaux figures that if you're gonna have a blimp, you might as well get the most out of it."

"Yes, I understand. Very logical."

"So that's kind of where I'm going with this idea. Kind of making the most of the ship for some key employees while I make the promotional runs without guests of the company."

Merlin was now doing his golden retriever cocked head quizzical look, which gave Dirk Kajerka all the permission he needed to continue.

"Yeah, so what I'm thinkin' is that there's no reason you and Svetlana shouldn't spend more time in the blimp. You know, when your schedules permit."

"You mean flying . . . in the blimp . . . around Houston?!"

Merlin couldn't believe his ears. Here was a chance to observe his woebegone hometown's vortical energy from the sky and from various angles at different times of day. How could a more perfect opportunity arrive to help his great project along its way? His silence was of the enraptured variety, as his head inclined upward while he envisioned himself aloft above the city.

"So, what do you say? Are you in?"

Merlin snapped out of his reverie.

"In?"

"Yeah, what do you think about my idea?"

Merlin's thoughts returned to earth, and he uttered with uncharacteristic force and resolve, "I'm in!"

"Good!" The corners of Kajerka's mouth curled fiendishly toward the outer perimeters of his pilot's mustache as he could not contain his glee that his plan was underway.

With his unwitting accomplice in the bag, Dirk turned his attention to the svelte Slavic ingénue. He was surprised that she seemed even more enthusiastic and naïve regarding the prospect of comprising part of his flight team than Merlin. "This is like slicing a hot knife through butter," Kajerka mused.

· *Eleven*

Merlin was on another high after his first night flight on the blimp. Although he wasn't able to discern any traces of the city's spinning energy vortex, he was thrilled to see Houston at night from the relatively low altitude of the blimp. The city lights dazzled him as the *Airmadillo* flew above some of the most populous parts of town toward the Oz-like majesty of downtown. It wasn't a huge world city like New York, Shanghai, Paris, or Mexico City, but it was what Merlin knew, and he took it all in while listening to Captain Kajerka's running commentary with mute, wide-eyed amazement.

————

Back in Bayou Boughs he neared the hatch-style door into his observatory cradling a full stack of mail in one arm. He pushed open the door and stepped up into the room, flipping on a light switch. Once again, the club newsletter slid out of his grasp and fell onto the floor before he could place the mail on the table. He still hadn't become accustomed to seeing Tite Dûche's photo on its cover next to the president's letter, but he picked it up and started to read anyway:

As you know, it continues to be the Greatest Honor of My Life to serve as President of Your Club. Getting married was important and kids being born was great, but this is Truly Special. In a continuing effort to provide you with the Premium Private Club Experience, Your Board and I are addressing problems and advocating for a change in Club Bylaws as Counsel advises. Counsel assures me that we can address most of the issues under our current Bylaw, Rule, and Regulation structure.

Of Immediate Concern is an issue that affects many of us: Reading.

Specifically, I am referring to the Types of Materials that are appropriate for Club Members to be seen reading while on Club Premises. It has come to Your President's attention that Certain Members have deemed it suitable to bring onto Club Property looseleaf papers precariously secured to common clipboards you might encounter on a Construction Site. Besides being materials unbecoming of Club Members (we should have Other People carrying clip boards for us, shouldn't we?) this type of activity poses a Safety Threat to other members should an Accident Occur and the Papers Go Flying—scattering like so many Illegal Aliens during an INS raid. Such papers could land on a noncarpeted surface, making it slick and an Automatic Falling Hazard. Additionally, they could fly up into the faces of Club Members and cause their sight to be dangerously occluded. All of this said, I think you will agree with me that Clip Boards are not acceptable to be in Members' Possession while on club property. Your Board will take action to Sternly Discipline any member found in violation of this rule.

This discussion caused the Board to consider the more General Topic of appropriate Reading Materials for Club Members while on Club Property. Besides the ban on reading from any electronic device anywhere on Club Property, the types of reading material appropriate for Club Members to be seen with needs to be addressed. For men, the business or sports sections of the newspaper are appropriate in the Locker Room or on loungers by the Pool. For the ladies, fashion and decorating magazines are highly appropriate in the Ladies' Locker Room or Poolside. More serious news magazines are a gray area and will be addressed in future newsletters on a publication-by-publication basis.

Novels are another difficult area—some are appropriate, but in this Day and Age many are not. Your Board has determined that Staff are not equipped to make this determination, so in the interest of consistency and a peaceful and merry Club Environment, we are henceforward banning the Reading of Books on Club Property. Books can be good—especially when they are the kind you read in school to get a degree that will Generate Capital—but many can cause unrest.

With this concern in mind, I have instructed Staff to confiscate all books that they find left on Club Property. Once every quarter, to encourage a festive atmosphere, we will have a small bonfire for 'smores near the lake in front of the 18th green. Any books found during the preceding quarter will be shredded, doused with lighter fluid, and set alight beneath Specially Dried and Split Logs—providing the kindling and flame of heart-warming authenticity only a Real Fire can impart, and making s'mores cooking such a memorable part of Family Life. Your Board and I thank you for your compliance in these new regulations and extend to you and your family a warm invitation to attend our quarterly inappropriate reading materials burning/s'mores roast as Your Busy Schedules permit.

Yours in solidarity,
Tite

P.S. A longtime friend was complimenting me on my newsletter writing and humorously offered, "Remember, a message from the Head of the Club is better than a Club to the Head!" I know you will all take my urgings to heart as we strive to make the Club a Better Place for All Members.

Merlin held the newsletter in disbelief and felt the blood drain to both of his supersize feet. He wondered what would be next. Maybe this was evidence that the energy vortex of Houston was indeed spinning more tightly and rapidly than in times past. He wanted to consult his instruments, tables, programs, and website references, but sleepiness overtook him like a freight train, and he barely had time to get undressed before it took him to a land where no institutional overlords dictated what he could wear or read or constrain how he conducted his person through his days and weeks in the spinning energy vortex that whirled over his hometown.

———

In another part of the neighborhood, Mac Swearingen, M.D., was reading the same newly arrived missive. As he finished, he let out a sigh of untempered anguish along with several shakes of his freckled head. "What in the sam hill is the world coming to?" he thought. Resigned that the *ancien régime* had been thoroughly vanquished, he reminisced about the days when the club had a comfortable, family-oriented atmosphere—always nice, but a family place with genuine connections of friendship and kinship. Now it seemed the old guard was being systematically overthrown by an invasive species of nouveau riche peacocks and generously compensated corporate robots.

He thought back to his own youth at the club—the smell of cigar smoke at the first-hole tee box, the worn leather chairs in the grill, and the families together with kids and grandkids running around like the place was a giant family room, which it basically was. It had become progressively quiet, and he wasn't sure, but he thought he discerned fear or at least uncertainty in the eyes of some of the longstanding employees the last couple of times he had been there. He pursed his lips and shook his head again.

Although he had served on the BBCC board in the past, Mac had never been one to get involved in politics of any kind, especially club politics. That was one of the reasons he pursued a medical career in the first place—even though, as he learned quickly, organizational politics are a big part of the healthcare profession. Still he avoided these situations when possible, but this clamping down on so many rules and now banning and burning books was sailing even normally even-keel Mac Swearingen, M.D., toward the edge of his world. *What in the blue blazes is coming next?* he wondered.

That night, Mac dreamed about blue blazes of unquenchable flame consuming stacks of his favorite novels from his younger days. Then volumes from his medical library began to fall into the fire. He woke up with a start and registered a cold sweat on his brow. It was a long time before he was able to return to sleep.

· Twelve

As spring nose-dived toward the torrid, torpor-inducing months of the Houston summer, two aspects of Merlin's world bifurcated and diverged. On one hand, he was facing more constraints from Tite Dûche and his board cronies at the club; on the other, his professional life seemed to be in a dizzying ascent. While he fine-tuned his skills in blimp passenger appointment management and notification, the blimp manufacturer was so impressed with Merlin's software program streamlining blimp maintenance and repair that they sent someone down from corporate to have a closer look. After this visit, which prompted Merlin to wear one of his best season-appropriate outfits, the blimp manufacturer let it be known they wanted to license the program for all of their customers.

News of this unexpected business coup quickly made its way to the vast hardwood desk of T. Rex Mondeaux III, who met it with the unrestrained delight that he never failed to experience when happening on unexpected good fortune. This was like finding the golden egg at the annual club Easter egg hunt when he was a kid. (Little Rexie had several early 1960s golden eggs to his credit.) Mondeaux was smiling and shaking his head in a state of surprise approaching disbelief, and after the news bearer, Ms. Sukhova, left his office, he thought of old Arthur McNaughton and how happy he would have been to know that his grandson had created something of value that stood on its own in the business world.

Usually one to take as much as he could when a pecuniary opportunity presented itself, Mondeaux decided to consult with Merlin regarding how Mondoco and Merlin could share in the profits from his high-tech creation. His memory of his friendship with Arthur, who was an advisor in his early days of business, spurred Rex to make this decision. Mondeaux himself made a trip to the blimp base to talk with Merlin about the arrangement, explaining that even though the employment contract Merlin signed provided that any invention during his employment would belong to Mondoco, he was personally overriding it and instructing Mondoco's lawyers to create a special agreement so that Mondoco and Merlin could share in future profits from the sales and licensing of the program. Mondeaux did not expect the software to generate massive amounts of money or provide anything approaching a sinecure for Merlin, but whatever it did generate, Merlin would have the knowledge that he would always get a significant percentage of it.

Although this development was as pleasantly surprising for Merlin as it was for his corporate overlord, and gave him a sense of previously unrealized self-worth, what really fired Merlin's excitement and imagination continued to be the ride-alongs in the blimp with Captain Kajerka and Svetlana. One day on one of their daytime flights, Kajerka threw out a surprise of his own.

"Anyone wanna give this blimp-flying thing a try?"

Svetlana immediately piped up. "Me? Fly bleemp? Da! Yes! I want to try!" And in a flash, Kajerka had exited the pilot's seat in midflight and motioned Svetlana to take his place. The svelte young Slav slid into the worn black leather of the seat with the nimble ease of a Soviet-era gymnast mounting a pommel horse at the Olympic games. Although the seat was far too commodious for Svetlana, Dirk Kajerka wasted no time in moving levers to scoot her nearer to the airship controls and instruments, relishing this first chance to move so close to her under the auspices of providing her with an optimally comfortable first-time-at-the-blimp-controls experience.

With a spine frozen upright like an ice-encased birch in a protracted Siberian winter, Svetlana stared with single-minded focus, taking in the privileged pilot's view through the cockpit windshield of the *Airmadillo* as it traversed the dense humid airspace a couple of thousand feet above the concrete-encrusted yet fetid coastal plain of Greater Houston. She glanced quickly at each of the controls and instruments as Dirk pointed them out.

"Here on the left, this is the throttle. It makes the engine go faster or slower. The big wheel at your right hand is called the elevator wheel. It controls the up and down direction of the ship."

(Dirk liked to call the blimp "the ship" from time to time to make himself feel more substantial, if not important. "Captain of an airship" sounded a lot more formidable than "blimp pilot," he reckoned.)

Pointing at a row of switches just above the windshield, Dirk continued: "These right up here are your envelope pressure controls. You can add more helium into the ballonet, which is the big balloon inside this thing, or you can release it into the atmosphere. With these, you can actually maintain the trim and shape of the ship, and of course, they really come in handy when you need to do a fast descent for landing if the wind picks up."

Svetlana's gaze locked onto the switches and gauges, but Kajerka broke her reverie as he continued his monologue and looked toward the floor in front of the pilot's seat.

"Now these pedals down here at your feet . . ."

Dirk saw that Svetlana's feet were barely reaching the pedals. "Hold on," he cautioned.

Dirk took this opportunity to once again adjust Svetlana's seat, enjoying every second of it, as he moved her forward so she could rest her feet on the pedals. He resumed his former posture and tried to continue in a professional manner, although he had begun perspiring at the collar.

"These here are your rudder pedals. They control the left and right direction of the blimp. Push on the left one and it goes left. Push on the right one and it goes right."

He sensed a tingling feeling where the perspiration was soaking the back of his neck on registering the contrast of Svetlana's delicate high-heeled feet resting on the big black rubber rudder pedals of the blimp.

Dirk encouraged her, "Okay, toots, take us somewhere!" With that Svetlana took a good look at the landscape below the blimp and pushed firmly on the left rudder pedal. With the strange slow delayed reaction to instrument promptings that is a hallmark of lighter-than-air flying, the blimp slowly, then more resolutely, began to turn. Svetlana turned the elevator wheel backward and in a few seconds the blimp began to rise. "I want to get better look," she said. As she surveyed the formless suburban landscape, her eyes looked eastward toward the Post Oak–Galleria area. "Da. There is Galleria." She looked at the compass on the instrument panel. "Heading is east northeast. 61 degrees." She located the GPS on the instrument panel and entered the address of the Galleria mall complex, a number she had committed to memory not long after her arrival in Houston. A red line to the address appeared on the navigation screen, and she followed it with the same focused single-mindedness that she demonstrated on occupying the pilot's seat moments earlier.

As they approached the upscale mall complex, Svetlana turned the wheel downward and the blimp began to descend. "How low can bleemp go?" She asked Captain Kajerka with icy efficiency, not releasing her fixated gaze toward the Galleria. Mildly alarmed by her focused resolve, Dirk responded, "We need to keep her above a thousand feet." Svetlana gave a slight, silent nod and watch the altimeter as it approached one thousand feet, turning the elevator wheel upward to level the dirigible just a few feet above the low-altitude flight restriction for lighter-than-air vehicles over Houston's airspace.

"I will circle," Svetlana declared flatly.

She gazed down on the high temple of Houston upscale retailing as she circled it, an act reminiscent of the way pilgrims to

Mecca circle the great stone monolith of the Kaaba during the culmination of their Hajj to the holy city. As Svetlana venerated the shopping mecca from above, images of countless storefronts crowded themselves into her imagination: Fendi, Prada, Gucci, Tiffany, Burberry, Moncler, Vilebrequin, Brunello Cucinelli, Hermès, and Cartier. Dirk continued to find her intense concentration a little disconcerting, but Merlin reveled in the sight of someone other than Captain Kajerka flying the airship.

"I want to come back at night and program sign to say 'I love Fendi! I love Moschino!'" Svetlana enthused.

"Uh, we can't just do that," ventured the captain. "Advertisers pay good money to share sky space with Fandango when we run their ads on the outdoor screen."

"Not even for one minute?"

"I don't think so," Kajerka said.

For the first time since taking the pilot's seat, Svetlana's posture slumped a little, and she took her eyes off the Galleria. "Hey, what do you say we give Merlin a chance at helm?" Kajerka asked.

Svetlana craned her neck around to see the largest blimp rider in the history of the *Airmadillo* and queried with subarctic chill, "Him?"

"Yeah, maybe you could relax here in the back and take in the sights while he has a go."

The young Russian transplant shrugged her shoulders and said, "Why not?" She seemed to let go of her disappointment in not being allowed to program adulatory messages regarding overpriced European fashion brands as she rose and angled her way toward the passenger seats.

After a sidelong appraisal of the newest blimp-flyer's figure as she moved past him, Dirk changed his conversational tone to suit the next student pilot. He looked Merlin in the eye with avuncular benevolence and said, "Okay, big fella, you ready to fly?" Merlin met this direct question with one of his all-time most stunned, deer-in-the-headlights looks. He was mute as his eyes locked in terror with the captain's. The great circles of Merlin's wide-open eyes were now at full aperture, the big round metal frames of his eyeglasses providing perfectly symmetrical little rings for the bright Saturns of his ocular orbits.

Dirk asked again, "Well?"

This time Merlin knew he had to respond. He steeled himself, and with an uncharacteristic confidence, continued to look Dirk Kajerka in the eye while out of his vast chest cavity boomed a resounding "Yes!" With that utterance, it was like a force from somewhere beyond himself gave Merlin a kind of supernatural ability to move toward the pilot's seat.

Dirk exhaled and said, "Great, right this way." He barely had time to step aside as Merlin began to squeeze past him toward the lone cockpit seat. Realizing that the seat remained in position for Svetlana, Dirk exclaimed, "Wait!" Merlin froze, and Dirk leapt to slide the seat backward on its tracks; he then cranked a seat-side lever backward to lower the seat several inches toward the floor. Merlin had done everything he could to arrest his forward momentum when the captain interrupted his progress, but it seemed there was a latent propulsive force that he had contained, but not tamed, as at the moment Dirk Kajerka finished the seat adjustment and moved away from the chair, Merlin swept past him and landed his mass in the seat like a jumper from a burning building falling backward into the safety of a cartoon-esque fireman's net.

Merlin was wedged sideways into the seat at an acute angle. On registering that the seat still was not adjusted adequately for Merlin, Dirk went into action again.

"Hold on, big fella."

Kajerka let the seat all the way back and with Merlin's weight, it hit the back of its tracks with a loud metal on metal clank. He then cranked Merlin's seat down as close as possible to the cockpit floor. Even with this extreme adjustment the seat seemed to barely accommodate its occupant, but barely would have to do. Svetlana had looked almost childlike in the pilot's seat, and Merlin was the polar opposite, rolls of his mass tumbling out of the seat's confines in every direction with his clothing barely preventing a dam break of hairy, sweat-covered flesh. Merlin didn't notice any inconvenience as he gathered his composure and, again, drawing on a well of confidence whose source he could not identify, he turned to face forward.

A wave of intense recognition washed over him. He beheld the controls and flight data instruments and sensed this was a view he was destined to see and that this pilot's seat was somehow *his* seat and *his* place. He surveyed each instrument and control, nodding a little as he took it all in.

Kajerka queried, "So you want me to go through this with you?"

"No, no," Merlin replied looking at the dials and levers. "I think I understood it when you explained it to Miss Svetlana."

"Why you call me *miss*?" Svetlana yelled from the passenger seat.

Not wanting to explain the years of training in manners that still happened in parts of the American South, Merlin replied, "Sorry." He then retrained his attention on the *Airmadillo*, which had veered from its tight circle over the Galleria.

As he rested his meaty right hand gingerly on the elevator wheel and his enormous hiking boot–clad feet on the rudder pedals, he felt strangely at home. Merlin, who had never gotten a driver's license and found the prospect of driving a car in a crowded city with so much ground-level sensory input beyond daunting, felt serene and in control at the helm of the blimp. He got his bearings and looked out on the city, and with the authority of a seasoned lighter-than-air pilot, pressed hard on the right rudder pedal while turning the elevator wheel backward to gain a little altitude. When Bayou Boughs came into view a couple of miles away, he straightened the blimp's course and programmed his home address into the airship's GPS. With an even greater intensity of focus than the seat's previous occupant, he was primed to see his observatory and its environs from the inexplicable comfort of his newfound airborne digs.

· *Thirteen*

The arrangement Captain Dirk Kajerka had created continued with the unlikely blimp trio. Over the following couple of weeks or so Dirk took off, Svetlana flew, Merlin flew, and Dirk landed the blimp back at FUBAR. Dirk did his best during the critical time while Merlin was flying to ingratiate himself to the striking young Slav. He figured that about two weeks of chitchat with Svetlana while Merlin was at the controls would be required before he could make his move.

During the airborne banter with Svetlana, he eyed the little curtain attached to a bar at the top of the blimp passenger compartment. From the blimp's delivery several years earlier, the curtain had never been unsnapped and drawn closed to separate the pilot's seat from the passenger compartment. He glanced at the little snap while he was talking with Svetlana the way a frisky teenager would consider the clasp on the back of his new girlfriend's bra during their first make-out session. When would he have the opportunity to unsnap it, draw the curtain closed, and begin a new chapter in his checkered libidinous history? The left and right edges of his mustache twitched a little when he thought about it, so animated was he by the prospect. The object of his desire was not as immediately easy to woo as he had hoped, raising a dubious eyebrow here and there during their initial conversations and demonstrating a Russian shell that seemed as hard as the wintertime surface of a Ural Mountain lake, but, eventually, she thawed as the *Airmadillo* plied the Houston skies with the largest blimp pilot in the entire history of blimp pilots at its controls. Dirk was ready to pounce.

The night was muggy and nearly windless, portending the greater unpleasantness of the oncoming Houston summer. The trio rose aloft, and when Dirk had leveled off the blimp at a suitable cruising altitude, he stood and motioned Svetlana to the pilot's seat. She sat and adjusted the seat with the authority and confidence of a seasoned MiG pilot. Before takeoff, when none of the ground crew was looking, Dirk secreted aboard a small ice-filled cooler containing a bottle of good Russian vodka and a tin of caviar from the Caspian Sea. He had also stashed glasses, mixers, and toast points. (Someone at the liquor store had told him the fancy way to serve caviar was on toast points, of which he had never heard. He was quick to find a specialty bakery that prepared them to order and made his first pur-chase of fresh toast points that afternoon.) As before, Svetlana was drawn to the lights of Uptown Houston like a Burberry plaid-patterned moth to a Tiffany lamp. Her level of excitement and animation was just as great as it had been on the first night flight, and her upbeat mood continued as the captain suggested that she let Merlin fly for a while.

She sat near Dirk in the passenger compartment, smiled slightly, and said, "Such a nice night." That was all he needed to segue into his pitch. "I brought along something to make it even nicer," he offered with a fiendish half smile and mustache twitch. He lifted the small cooler up to seat level, opened it, and showed Svetlana the elixir within. Her eyes brightened considerably, and she exclaimed, "It's my favorite!" Not wasting a nanosecond, Kajerka produced and opened an indigo velvet–lined box con-taining two crystal highball glasses. On seeing these, Svetlana exclaimed, "Baccarat! My favorite fine crystal brand!" The Kajerkan smile cracked a little more broadly.

"Would you like a mixer?"

"Meexer? No! We drink the Russian way!" Svetlana took the vodka bottle and one of the glasses and poured a couple of fingers. She almost ceremoniously handed the glass to the wily pilot. When he accepted it from her, she poured a glass for herself, making sure to dispense just a little less than she had poured for Dirk. She looked him in the eye, her smile leaving for a moment, and raised her glass to toast him, and he complied, surprised by what he perceived as some kind of exotic drinking ritual. They maintained eye contact as they took the first sip, after which Svetlana nodded approvingly. "Da, is just like Russian version of brand."

Not wanting the energy level to drop, Dirk offered, "There's more." He showed her the little tin of caviar, and she exclaimed even more exuberantly, "*Ikrá*! From Caspian Sea! And Petrossian! It's the best export marque!"

Dirk handed the tin to Svetlana and brought out the toast points. Svetlana echoed the drinking ritual by spreading the roe from the other side of the world onto a tiny bread triangle and handing it to the captain. She did the same for herself, and they savored the delicacy together. Her eyes became a bit dreamy as she said, "I miss this."

Now it was Dirk who toasted Svetlana and motioned that they should down the remaining contents of their glasses. This was the first of several glasses and caviar-spackled toast points, and the conversation began to flow as freely as the vodka. When Svetlana was mildly intoxicated, she exclaimed, "How I would imagine life in Texas to be like this?!" This was Dirk's cue. The mustache made successful contact with the Cupid's Bow and then the remainder of the fetching young Russian's lips. With his left hand cupping the small of Svetlana's back, he reached his right hand for the dividing curtain snap and popped it open with fluid aplomb. Svetlana took quick notice but was already under the Czech-Texan's spell as Kajerka pulled the curtain across the breadth of the passenger compartment. Merlin turned his head for a moment on hearing the curtain drawn but quickly refocused on piloting the *Airmadillo* through the thick night air.

———

Just before leaving Dubai, Mickey McNaughton remembered he had a special board meeting to attend in Nice for a global society dedicated to raising awareness of environmental threats to the world's oceans. Although he was on the board, he wasn't exactly sure what the organization accomplished. With his Ivy League pedigree, he was an asset to the board nonetheless. At every meeting he stood and made a very confident, erudite comment and always asked the speaker a question that wowed the attendees, but learning what he termed the granular aspects of the society was below his radar screen, as he would say. One thing he did know was that there was always excellent food and drink in plentiful supply at the meetings, and if history proved any guide, there was usually a lone female marine biologist whose connubial situation was at least in flux. All this and the French Riviera in springtime made the stop for the meeting in Nice a complete no-brainer for him. After a day of pontificating, a night of excess, and a couple of days of R&R *à la rivière*, Mickey decided to head to Amsterdam for a few days before his flight back to Houston. He had always liked the city, and it had been a place of many pleasant surprises for him over the years. This itinerary extension found him traversing the bustling streets of the Dutch capital one cool, overcast day.

His half-day hike took him through many of the city's storied districts, including some of the more infamous quarters. As he strolled along the far side of the Geldersekade canal near the part of the Red Light District some now referred to as the Leather District, Mickey spotted a slight, intense-looking man emerge from the Umber Tulip Hotel. The man was wearing what seemed to be a rather tight-fitting black leather jumpsuit, kind of a onesie for an adult customer. His feet were shod with shiny black patent leather ankle-high boots. When Mickey got a good look at this individual's face, he was astounded. The outfit was out of character, but the face was 100 percent Dûche—Tite Dûche, to be exact. On recognizing this little fish out of his home waters, Mickey immediately yelled in his direction across the wide canal even though he was not sure whether the jump-suited flaneur was quite within earshot.

"Hey Tite! Tite Dûche!"

When he heard the shoutout, the character in the leather onesie froze and looked around. Mickey piped up once again, "Hey, Tite! It's me! Mickey! Mickey McNaughton!" The terrified leather-clad tourist went into action. He put on a dark-colored knit cap and a pair of wraparound reflective sunglasses. He also wrapped a Dutch orange scarf around his neck, covering his face from the nose downward. He then took off and ducked down a side street. At the same moment, a bus obscured Mickey's view. When it had passed, Tite Dûche had vanished.

Mickey thought about confirming the identity of the leather jumpsuit wearer by leaving a message for Tite Dûche at the front desk of the infamous hotel, but he wasn't sure about darkening its doorway. Mickey had friends all over the world, and if some-one saw him emerging from the Umber Tulip, they might get the wrong idea. Nevertheless, this nonencounter was strange enough to cause Mickey to stop and consider it on the sidewalk. As he looked at the scene and wondered what in the world the presi-dent of Bayou Boughs Country Club was doing there dressed the way he was, he thought, *So that was weird, right?* He walked past a bar featuring artisanal genever, turned back, and pushed open a narrow door to a dark shotgun barrel of a barroom.

· *Fourteen*

Merlin had just gone medieval on a family-size platter of enchiladas verdes, using knife and fork to draw and quarter them like so many prone, side-by-side condemned prisoners before dispatching them to their doom past the eager chomping gates of his maxilla and mandible. They were drenched in the classic green tomatillo sauce flecked with bits of cotija cheese and topped with a drizzle of squeeze bottle–dispensed sour cream. With most enchiladas verdes preparations, the chef squeezes on the sour cream in a zigzag pattern, but the kitchen staff at the club applied it in the signature galactic/hurricane whirl that made its first appearance atop the pancakes in his Magic Mountain breakfast extravaganza. Years before this late spring day, someone in the kitchen aware of the dish's destination had decided to carry the theme beyond the early morning breaking of the fast.

For the kitchen staff, seeing the whirl atop a dish automatically signaled two things: 1) this was an astoundingly large portion in a city known for the size of its servings, and 2) the recipient was none other than the Magic Man himself. Merlin had not considered that this gesture could have amounted to personal branding in the making—an inkling of the authenticity so many aspiring young professionals of Merlin's age groped for in the foggy obscurity of indeterminate personal identity. He simply received the flourish as a homemade-style touch with a specific diner in mind. Others might have recognized the uniqueness of this gesture and story and perhaps started a clothing line featuring a galactic/hurricane whirl insignia, but not Merlin, who never considered the gyres so unusual as to be noteworthy.

As he finished the remnants of the enchiladas verdes, Merlin looked up from the platter and turned to Shep, who had returned to his post at the far-right corner of the locker room bar a few feet away.

"You doin' alright Magic Man?" Shep offered with a dubious frown.

Merlin's eyes widened as he looked at Shep, and then he said in a loud whisper as Shep approached, "Shep, I've been flying the blimp!"

"You mean the whole way?"

"Not for takeoff and landing, but during the advertising route. Even at night a few times."

"And where's the pilot?"

"He's in the passenger area. Supervising."

"He supervising on his own, or does he have some help?"

"Miss Slahtskaya is new to the city, and Captain Kajerka says it is helpful for her if he points out areas of town as we traverse the urban, suburban, and exurban landscapes."

"Sounds like you got a lotta free rein while he's 'splainin' her the sights."

"Well, it does seem that the captain's confidence in me is increasing. He let me fly the whole advertising route last night."

"Sounds like the captain's got his hands full."

"What? No! His hands are free to point out buildings and neighborhoods to Miss Slahtskaya while I fly!"

"Oh," said Shep credulously, "I see."

"Yes, the captain seems more and more at ease with me at the controls and when we exit the ship both he and Miss Slahtskaya even giggle at times. They seem to be quite content."

"I reckon they are, Magic Man, I reckon they are."

"Maybe I can salute you from the blimp over your house someday soon!"

"Now, that would be something the neighborhood wouldn't be expecting."

"I will call you and let you know when the *Airmadillo* is on its way to your area."

"Okay, my friend. Just be careful up there."

"I am, Shep. I am very focused in the ship."

Merlin looked at the big clock above the bar and realized it was time for him to return to his observatory to check readings on his instruments and comprehensive computer programs. Had there been a change in the energy field since he had begun to assist on the blimp's night missions? He rose abruptly and looked again toward the patient and loyal Cajun.

"Okay, Shep. I gotta go. There's a lot going on back at the observatory."

"Okay, Magic Man, take on off. Now you're a pilot, you gotta be places."

"Not a pilot, but I am flying!"

They waved goodbye. When Merlin was out of earshot, Shep said quietly, "You always been flyin', Magic Man. You always been flyin'."

———

Merlin finished his homeward walk on the same upbeat note and didn't stumble over a single protruding concrete dagger of contorted sidewalk—unstable gumbo soil and unruly oak roots the dual culprits for this unfortunate Houston phenomenon. Somehow, Houston's no zoning policy seemed to have created an atmosphere that affected even the order of public sidewalks. Or was it the other way around? His mood began to shift as he entered the front gate of the compound and noticed some haphazard yellow streaks on his observatory. He wondered if there could be some kind of strange neotropical migratory songbird traversing Bayou Boughs whose calling card was defecating in large yellow blobs. As he got closer and the stains came into clear view, he saw bits of egg-shell mixed with the yellow and sticky translucent accompanying goo. When he looked down, eggshells were scattered at the observatory's base. In his exuberance to get to his enchilada brunch at the club, Merlin had not looked back at his home after shutting the door and beginning his single-minded march. It was probably for the best, as his temporary ignorance had afforded him a pleasant noontide of feasting and talking with Shep in comfortable surroundings. He now realized that his refuge had been willfully attacked. Who would want to mar such an iconic and visually compelling Bayou Boughs structure? Merlin had never imagined this kind of malice would intersect with his life, much less deface the castle, keep, home, and refuge of his cherished observatory.

He backed away from the observatory toward the front gate of the property to take in the full view of the defacement. As he neared the gate, he heard someone call to him.

"Merlin! Hey, Merlin! What's going on?"

He turned to see Lindley Acheson, who was once again on foot to the garden club with her wheeled basket of supplies in tow.

"Lindley! I didn't know you were there!"

"That's okay, you wouldn't have seen me with your back to the street."

"That's because of what someone did to the observatory while I was gone."

"Looks like it must have happened last night. The eggs are pretty stuck on there."

"I guess you're right. I'm not accustomed to observing the observatory before I leave."

"This is a drag, Merlin. Why would anyone want to do this to your place?"

"I don't really know. I don't."

"Well, I think I remember how to get that out."

"Really?"

"Yeah, we had a bird's nest smash into a wall last year in a high wind. The eggs weren't as big, but they behaved the same way."

"Oh, okay."

"You need equal parts warm water and white vinegar in a spray bottle, and as crusted on as they look, you may need to scrub a bit on top of that."

"What about the spots up high?"

"I have a portable power washer you can use. You can put vinegar in the reservoir and maybe scrub with a long-handled brush."

"Oh! That's great, Lindley. Thank you!"

"Sure. No big deal. I'll bring them by in a little while."

"Thank you. Defacement of the observatory is something I have never contemplated and now that it has happened, I think I have a strange feeling."

"Well, get it cleaned up and maybe the feeling will go, too."

"Okay. Maybe. I will try."

Lindley started walking and stopped after a few steps to look back at Merlin, who had gone back to staring at the vandalism. She felt a strong wave of sadness pass through her for an instant and quickly turned to resume her walk as if to flee from it.

Head down, Merlin proceeded back to the observatory, and on entering the cocoon of a top floor nest he called home, he was once again taken aback as he saw a flashing message on his computer monitor. He had coordinated his array of programs into a kind of large orchestrated meta-program that could synthesize, and perhaps even symphonize, all of the information into a unitary, integrated data feed—both graphical and narrative. He had considered calling it Argus Panoptes after the many-eyed god from Greek antiquity, but on learning Argus was killed by Hermes, he opted for his original choice, dubbing it the Agglomerator. The flashing message on the monitor read: "Event Horizon—Deep Summer." He clicked on it and saw, amidst the cross hatches of ley lines and Druidic navigational arcs, a pulsing gyre that seemed to be tightening and brightening east of Houston near the Louisiana border.

Now he was even more frozen in his tracks than he had been a few minutes earlier when he realized the stains on his observatory were not exotic neo-tropical bird droppings but ordinary eggs from the grocery store. This time, however, his feeling was markedly different. It was one of awe, wonder, and amazement. It had worked. All these years of deep data dives and arrangement of inputs into an intelligible whole seemed to have yielded something which he had hoped for longer than he could remember: a reliable prediction. But what was it predicting? Merlin knew that it had to center on the negative energy gyre holding his home city in its relentless thrall, but what exactly was this event horizon intimating?

· *Fifteen*

Merlin veered and wheeled the *Airmadillo* down through the airspace just above the twinkling towers of the Texas Medical Center. He removed the marketing department's thumb drive from the computer that controlled the giant high-definition video screen on the blimp's outer skin and placed it in his shirt pocket. From his right trouser pocket, he produced a thumb drive of his own, as generic in appearance as the one he had just removed but containing files bearing slogans and graphics prompted by his interpretation of the Agglomerator's increasingly alarming messages.

He recognized that this nonapproved switching of drives was a transgressive act, and he had engaged in a mental wrestling match for days before this pivotal moment. He had finally arrived at the decision that the greater good of preparing citizens of his home city for a major energy vortex event justified his surreptitious temporary hijacking of Fandango Utilities' airborne advertising and that of the clients who paid for their own products or services to appear on the giant screen in the sky. His strategy was to alternate the Fandango messaging with his own, thereby diminishing his chances of getting found out by Ms. Sukhova and the higher-ups of the company. He felt certain his days were numbered as a Fandango employee, but what he had not considered was that, since his messages had to do with the concept of energy, to the vast majority of casual observers, their language would not seem terribly out of the ordinary for a video screen on a blimp owned by a utility company. As Captain Kajerka continued pointing out the sights to Ms. Slahtskaya with great vigor behind the closed curtains separating the pilot's seat from the passenger compartment, Merlin's night flight now became a mission, and his concentration intensified accordingly.

Mac Swearingen was working late because his wife was traveling in Europe with a group of women. He glanced through his Witlock Tower office window in the Texas Medical Center at the flickering lights in the skyscrapers of downtown Houston up Main Street northeast of the giant hospital complex. Out of the corner of his eye, he registered something unusual in the night sky, something bright and big and arriving. He rose from his desk and went to the window. As he began to take in the view the intimation of light became a pronounced presence in the skies above the towers. The Fandango Utilities Blimp—aka The *Airmadillo*—was crossing just above his vantage point, and its giant color video screen lit up the night. The effect was so arresting that even steady Mac Swearingen was inspired to utter aloud one of his trademark oaths. "Well, I'll be dipped," he said and surprised himself with the genuine wonder with which he said the words.

The blimp came into full view above him, and he read some of the text that scrolled along with the images. There was something about lowering power bills with Fandango's Summer Chillaxation Program. He didn't know what chillaxation meant and mused that it sounded like a medical condition. He then read a sentence that seemed even more puzzling: "People of Greater Houston! Prepare for a pivotal deep summer event horizon!" Dr. Swearingen once again let out an audible response: "What in the sam hill?" He let go of his befuddlement as quickly as he had after reading the message about chillaxation, figuring this cryptic-seeming phrase was something that all the young people must understand. As the blimp careened onward through the night, Dr. Swearingen gave a single, incredulous shake of his sun-burnished bald head and returned to his desk.

After following the navigational computer's GPS routing through the medical center, Merlin turned the blimp toward downtown, crossing airspace above an area that had become known as Midtown, with its concentration of condominia, mid-rise office buildings, and a variety of restaurants and bars. This part of town had a younger demographic and more pedestrian traffic than most other areas. The back of Merlin's neck tingled as he imagined scores of young professionals looking to the sky to see the sobering Agglomerator-prompted messages foretelling an imminent event that would affect each of them viscerally and mentally—at least as long as they called Houston home. He thought he spotted a group of hipsters in front of the Continental Club pointing at the *Airmadillo*. Could the exuberant gesture by this group of young people mean that they understood what his outdoor sky-borne messages intimated? Merlin hoped so with all his being.

As the towers of downtown loomed, Merlin heard a high-pitched squeak from the passenger compartment. He turned to look toward the curtain and saw something sharp jab forward at its center. He then heard the sound of something hitting the floor of the compartment. He looked down and saw a woman's stiletto heel pump slide out from beneath the curtain. He speculated that Captain Kajerka and Miss Slahtskaya must be craning their necks to see some distant landmark, maybe the illuminated San Jacinto Monument near the bay.

———

Jetlagged, but focused on the day's business, Tite Dûche perched in a chair too large for him behind his baroquely filigreed desk carved from an endangered species of tropical hardwood at the corporate headquarters of Dûche Ovens. The family business had grown since the time of its founding by Tite's grandfather, N. Teitel Dûche III, as with a burgeoning global population and desirable cemetery plots becoming increasingly difficult to procure, cremation had become a more reasonable option for many bereaved families. And Dûche Ovens enjoyed a near monopoly on the design, manufacturing, and distribution of high-end cremation furnaces and their attendant chambers. Although Tite's interests now ranged from real estate to oil and gas to a line of golf apparel, Dûche Ovens remained the cornerstone of his commercial livelihood and viability.

With what he believed to be his heightened aesthetic sensibilities, Tite had recently spearheaded the rolling out of a line of sleek, high-tech, high-efficiency chambers. Unaware no one in the undertaking business cared what a cremation furnace looked like or whether it had automatic features to make its operation as hands-free as possible, Tite was still gloating over the debut of the Super Dûcherator 5000. He had made a special point to hire particularly good-looking and well-spoken models to showcase the new product at the big annual funeral directors trade show. Tite looked across his office at an easel holding a photo of himself with hired models showcasing what he called "the 5000" at the convention in Florida. He approved of the sanguine smile he sported standing between the poised young women who towered over him in their high heels.

His mobile phone rang, and he answered it with "Hello, junior partner." He listened and a half smirk scratched itself onto his face as he said, "Good. Good work." He listened for a few seconds longer and closed the call with a curt directive: "Do it again." The half-smirk widened as he thumbed the red button to end the call.

· Sixteen

A thick haze met Merlin's view as he fumbled with his big fingers to get the sandman out of his eyes after a particularly satisfying sleep. Still in bed, he put on his fingerprint-smudged, round-lensed glasses to get a better look at the close enveloping nothingness surrounding the top floor of the observatory in the form of an unseasonably dense fog. Fog, Merlin felt, was a fitting symbol of the energy he often sensed in his hometown. Its density and weight bespoke the nearby yawning Gulf of Mexico. Merlin thought of the coastal bay system as straws the gulf used to suck the energy out of Houston. Even though he knew the vast gulf and the littoral waters of the bays teemed with life, and even though he greatly relished his saltwater fishing experiences, his conviction that the big gulf's energy gyre was largely responsible for draining energy from the Greater Houston area remained. Houston's vaunted status as the energy capital of the world made the whole experience worse, like some kind of cosmic joke told by a capricious and relentlessly cruel water deity. But fog, he conjectured, could also be considered benevolent, like an enveloping and comforting cloud blanket.

Satisfied with his reflection on fog, Merlin bounded toward the bathroom. After finishing there, he went into the observatory's galley. He selected a small silver bowl he had carefully polished and dried the day before and filled it with highly alkaline mineral water. He believed the pH value of the water he used to wet his fingers to play the glass armonica was important; the more alkaline the water, the better it wet the glass surfaces to produce an optimally mellifluous sound.

He placed the bowl next to the instrument near a far window of the observatory and flipped a switch to get the glass discs of the armonica moving. He looked skyward in contemplation, then with a resolute nod, touched his fingertips to the spinning wheels and began to play Albinoni's Adagio in G Minor. After eliciting a few bars of the soul-woundingly poignant classic, he heard his mobile phone buzz with a text message. It was from marketing director Sukhova. "Because of fog, no work at blimp base this a.m. Come in after lunchtime." "Roger," responded Merlin with what he deemed appropriate aeronautical aplomb. Relishing the prospects of his free half-day, he returned to his armonica with increased vigor and focus, interpreting the Baroque dirge with more emotion than, he was sure, it had ever been played on this instrument so suitable for the production of mournful tones. He was so taken with his playing that he decided to crack open a window to allow the notes to escape through the thick neighborhood air.

As he unlatched one of the observatory's casement windows, he thought he smelled something strange. He looked outside the window onto the tower's walls and saw it. The building's surface was plastered with eggs, and although he couldn't take it all in from his vantage point, it seemed the volume of egg splatter was considerably greater than it was the first time the observatory endured such a shameful defacement.

Merlin stood still and silent as he registered this most egregious affront to his abode, and by extension, to himself. He seemed to actually feel his heart sink, and reaching down inside for a thread of resolve, he decided that, before starting the clean-up process, he would play the adagio in its entirety.

He returned to the silently spinning glass of the armonica, and with even more interpretive motivation, wet his fingertips and played the time-honored piece to its conclusion. His performance became an act of defiance against the continued thwarting of his tower-home's dignity at the hands of shameless nighttime hoodlums. For an instant, Merlin saw himself standing head and shoulders above the pettiness of his home's assailants as he deftly touched the spinning glass to play the final heart-wrenching notes.

He still had the power washer Lindley had lent him. He also had plenty of white vinegar left over to blend the cleaning concoction. As he looked at the observatory from ground level outside, he counted some three dozen eggs smashed against the observatory's street-facing side.

On finishing the job, Merlin had worked up a considerable appetite, and given that it was early midmorning, he decided a proper brunch was in order.

He showered and dressed to greet the slowly unfogging day, choosing an off-white and celadon green ensemble to complement the season. The fog of his uncertainty concerning breakfast had also lifted, and he directed himself resolutely down the steps of the observatory and out the door toward the sidewalk, where he awaited the Alles car to spirit him to Tellicherry, a favorite neighborhood spot serving an inspired nouvelle version of Indian cuisine. It was a short ride to the place with high glass windows framed by rectangular steel interstices, one set of which functioned as the restaurant's front door. Merlin liked that the big heavy door seemed size-appropriate for him, and there was something about its transparent aspect that appealed to him too, although he couldn't really say what it was.

He reasoned that, since the restaurant didn't have a separate brunch menu and because brunch was a combination of breakfast and lunch, it was only fitting that he should choose from both menus. This time of morning he could stage his orders, getting his breakfast first and asking the staff to put in the order for his lunch items at eleven when the midday menu items became available. Merlin led off with a railway omelet stuffed with aromatic greens, paneer, and spicy ground lamb keema. He rose from his spot on a banquette along one of Tellicherry's walls to retrieve house-made ketchup from a shelf in front of the kitchen to add even more complexity and dimensionality to the savory keema in his omelet. When he turned to return to his table, he heard "Hey, Merlin." Lindley Acheson was getting water from the same shelf.

"What's going on?" Lindley inquired of the ketchup-toting giant.

"I got egged again. I mean, the observatory was egged last night."

"Again?!"

"Yes. It was particularly disturbing because when I became aware of it, I was having a very productive musical session on the armonica."

"I bet it was disturbing! And it happened again? That's terrible!"

"Yes. It seemed like three times as many eggs this time."

"That's bizarre, Merlin."

"I used your power washer and the vinegar mixture and cleaned as much of it as I could this morning."

"I'm not attempting to foretell the future, but why don't you just keep the power washer for a while. I don't need it right now."

"Okay, thank you, Lindley."

"You know, now that this has happened twice, you might want to consider installing one of those security cameras with night vision."

Merlin was taken aback for a moment and uttered a surprised "Oh! I guess you're right! Maybe I should."

"I would," Lindley offered. She looked at Merlin for a silent moment and then said, "Take care of yourself, Merlin."

Merlin looked almost forlorn and offered a quiet "Thank you, Lindley."

Lindley returned to her breakfast meeting and Merlin headed toward his place on the banquette by the window. His breakfast had arrived, and before attacking it with knife and fork, he delicately held the little squeeze bottle of spicy ketchup between his right thumb and first two fingers and squirted his signature design atop the center of the stuffed omelet. The orange-red galactic whorl was set off nicely against the yellow of the egg mixture and its enfolded greens. Thinking the whorl seemed isolated and alone, he decided to flank it with two lesser whorls on either side, creating a more balanced visual mise-en-scène. Merlin didn't consider that the three whorls might reflect a situation in his airborne life, but he did pause and regard the addition to the top of his omelet with approbation. He even took a picture of it with his mobile phone. After his unsettling early morning, it was as if the railway omelet had redeemed the universe of eggs. Then his hunger sprang like a bear trap, and he devoured the plate's contents with workmanlike vigor. He found a copy of the *New York Times* and began to work the crossword puzzle, but after only a few of the squares were full, the first of his lunch items arrived.

He led off with a South Indian dosa, a rice, lentil, and ragi crepe filled with chili-laced shrimp, peanuts, and bell pepper. There was a small metal bowl of turmeric soup, too, and Merlin picked it up in one of his big paws and downed its contents in two or three gulps. (He had heard turmeric had healing powers, so he made a special point to prioritize the soup.)

Just as he finished the dosa, a plate containing naan, jasmine rice, and a dish of Goa pork curry with caramelized onions and a host of aromatic warm spices arrived. His fork remained in the air from his final bite of the dosa and landed without pause in the middle of the curry dish. Sides of tamarind chutney and eggplant with walnut raita also arrived to Merlin's chomping and nodding approval.

On finishing this main event of the lunch phase of his brunch, Merlin decided that, since he had been judicious in not ordering any samosas or pakoras before lunch, he would allow himself the indulgence of a dessert. He returned to the ordering counter and asked for pistachio kulfi ice cream, a mango lassi, and a couple of flat triangles of chocolate besan mithai, a pumpkin and sesame seed–topped chickpea fudge with a density reminiscent of the early morning fog, and so flavorful it sent his taste buds into meal-concluding orbits of bliss. The wide-eyed register attendant nodded and uttered a kind of amazed and dubious "okay" before ringing up the order. Merlin decided eating the Indian pistachio ice cream first was the strategic thing to do, as the lassi could be placed in a go-cup if necessary, and, as it was already in liquid form, it would not melt. Additionally, the besan mithai triangles were portable in a small paper bag, should he exercise enough control to save one for the afternoon. He ate the kulfi, savoring each bite of the delicately flavored cold dessert, and then, looking at the time, realized he needed to go. He called for the Alles driver on his mobile phone and asked a lithe young tattooed woman behind the counter to transfer his mango lassi to a plastic cup and the besan mithai to a container to take with him.

Satiated, Merlin gathered his things, rose, and headed for the door. Still astonished at his intake, the dining room staff watched him leave. Even the cooks behind the high counter separating the kitchen from the seating area stood on crates, silent and wide-eyed, to witness the man who had eaten enough for three people as he waddled toward the exit.

· *Seventeen*

The next morning, Merlin sat at his desk in his small window-less office at the blimp base. Several lines of thunderstorms were moving through the area, and blimp flights were canceled until the base's weather service gave the all clear. Merlin was normally quite fastidious in sticking to his work during business hours, but Lindley's strong suggestion that he install a camera on the exterior of the observatory had stayed with him, and he was now scouring the internet for a suitable device.

He decided on a model reputed to have excellent night vision capabilities, short between-shot intervals, and very high reso-lution (for zooming in on specific areas when reviewing video). Although the camera he chose was rather pricey, he justified the expenditure as a service to the justifiable cause of self-defense. Also, if any more eggs marred the observatory's surface, this souped-up security camera might give him a fighting chance at unmasking the perpetrators. He thought the whole thing over once more then entered his credit card information and clicked purchase. Resolution was firming up somewhere in the neigh-borhood of his spine, and as he saw the "Thank you for your purchase" message, he sat up straight as if receiving electronic orders from a military superior.

He chose the quick delivery option, and within a couple of days, he found himself unboxing and inspecting the surveillance camera. It was tiny, so he could hide it in a strategic place on or near the observatory. He picked a spot and installed it with screws specially made to hold in stucco exteriors like that of the observatory. He had enjoyed the trip to Southland Hardware to purchase necessary odds and ends for the installation. The funky old store was a neighborhood holdout against the big-box retail onslaught that had swept the nation. Its employees were quirky, yet mannerly, like Merlin himself.

With the passage of a mere three or four days, it happened again, and Merlin's stealthy new night-vision camera performed as advertised. Deep sleeper that he was, Merlin was unable to catch the offenders in flagrante delicto. He reviewed the act in high-definition clarity on one of his large monitors, and he was astounded at the brazenness of the egg-hurlers. The number of ovate projectiles had at least doubled or maybe tripled over the volume of the previous attack—so much so the offenders had lined up cartons just inside their SUV's rear tailgate. They even backed the vehicle into the McNaughton driveway to launch eggs with slingshots fashioned from medical tubing. His amazement unabated, Merlin watched the whole thing several times from start to finish before he settled down to focus on specific aspects of the video.

Although their faces were somewhat obscured by ball caps, the egg flingers seemed to be young. Additionally, their all-terrain vehicle—with a jacked-up suspension and knobby mud tires—was the kind favored by the privileged young bucks of Bayou Boughs. Although this egging had wounded his sense of self-sovereignty worse than the previous two combined, Merlin counted it a distinct fortuity that the young rogues had been so shameless as to back their vehicle up the driveway in the direction of the camera's lens. The camera captured the vehicle's license plate letters and numbers twice: before the tailgate's lowering and after the delinquents closed it for their getaway.

Although Merlin was not the most self-aware of thirty-somethings in greater Houston, he recognized that many people gave him a kind of bemused look when he spoke to them; being taken seriously by authority figures—from the neighborhood patrol all the way up to the local constabulary and Houston police—might pose a challenge, even with his video evidence. He thought and thought about the best course of action, and he finally reasoned that, regardless of his past rebuffs, Mickey McNaughton was the individual to whom the evidence should be sent first. Merlin risked being ignored by his globetrotting young uncle, but he believed Mickey had a basic sense of fairness. He knew a phone call would not be the best option because Mickey had a way of hitting him with a barrage of words instead of listening—always deflecting whatever it was about which Merlin was inquiring. He chose to e-mail his uncle.

Dear Mickey,

I trust life is treating you well, wherever on this largely blue orb you may find yourself these days. I'm not writing to bore you with local happenings or to implore you to communicate with Trust Officer Bumpers on my behalf. My missive is of a completely different timbre and nature, concerning a series of property assaults that affect both of our residences. Several days ago, I returned home on a pleasant Saturday morning after a particularly satisfying Tex-Mex-influenced brunch at the club. On arrival at the side gate leading to the observatory, I noticed strange yellow streaks on its street-facing exterior. I tried to think of any local blooming flora that might jettison biota of such a hue and consistency and came up empty-handed. As I approached my residence, I noted that next to the yellow spots there were dried clear translucent daubs into many of which were encrusted tiny white shards that I quickly determined were the shrapnel of exploded eggshells. Confused and alarmed at this realization, I was grateful that a friend happened by on the sidewalk who had the equipment and proper non-home-exterior-harming liquid solution recipe for removal of this unsightly, tenacious, and odoriferous effrontery to a dwelling place whose grounds, structures, and improvements have been sacrosanct for many years—at least for me.

The real problem is that this was not an isolated act of vandalism—not a one-hit wonder, if you will. It happened three times previously, with each successive assault featuring an increased number of ova defacing my place of repose, musing, and creative ideation. After the second occurrence, a friend suggested that I install some sort of monitoring device in hopes of identifying the offenders, should they get up to their nefarious nighttime shenanigans yet again. Purchasing equipment to identify criminals is not the kind of thing that occupies my imagination, but desperate times call for measures of commensurate desperation. With earnings from my newfound career in the world of lighter-than-air locomotion, I purchased, installed, and connected a discreet night-vision camera facing the direction of the unknown egg hurlers, aka the street. The upshot of all this effort was that the fourth assault did not go unrecorded. That is why you see links to short videos I have attached below this communiqué. Most importantly, the camera captured the license plate of the vehicle the perpetrators used to transport themselves and their ovate ammunition. I thought you should at least know about this as an unsightly attack on the observatory affects the value of the property in its entirety.

Thank you for taking time to read this. I wish you travels sans travails and continued professional preeminence.

Yours in domiciliary vigilance,
Merlin

He inhaled and exhaled deeply, then clicked Send.

· *Eighteen*

Days passed and Merlin did not hear from Mickey. He had steeled himself and tried to keep a stiff upper lip. And then late one weekday evening, like a lightning bolt from a capricious minor deity, a response from Mickey arrived. He rubbed his eyes in disbelief when he saw the message in his inbox. The subject line read: "Sorry about delayed response."

Hey Merlin:

Sorry I'm slow to respond—got a new project in Amsterdam.

So, this egging by night business is the real thing, right? Quite disturbing and warranting action. Frankly, viewing the videos from the most recent incident caused a major rise in my blood. As soon as we can synch up on schedules with the Houston-to-Holland time difference, I'm going to call a friend in the Harris County DA's office so we can get a fix on the bad guys. This kind of renegade, continual vandalism, as they say in the merry old country across the North Sea from me, is just "not cricket." And beyond not being good form, in point of fact, it is criminal, right? Very sorry about the distress all this has caused you. I am on the case.

Best,
Mickey

Although Mickey's writing style never conveyed the warmest of filial sentiment, his e-mail was a prompt and sympathetic reply to Merlin's plea, and that was enough to cause a wave of comfort to wash over the distraught eggee. Additionally, Mickey's willingness to enlist the help of a prosecutor friend in the district attorney's office gave Merlin the sense that the tide could actually be turning in his favor as the justice system might soon power up its big fine-grinding wheels on his behalf. This thought was enough to elicit a deep exhalation and simultaneous upswelling of weariness. He shambled toward his bed and lay down thinking of what he once heard a country preacher call the sleep of the justified. "That must be one of the more satisfying forms of sleep there is," he mumbled, before his eyelids closed and he began to snore.

———

It was a red-letter day at the blimp base, as a cross-country run was on the agenda. The flight plan was to take the *Airmadillo* over downtown and then straight toward the coast in the direction of Galveston Island. The winds were very light throughout the area, even along the coast, where they had been known to play havoc with the blimp. Calm also prevailed at the base, where the whole team had settled into a smoothly operating routine, notwithstanding Dirk Kajerka's pushing of the envelope with his clandestine amatory exploits with Svetlana. The grounds and mechanical crew took note that marketing director Sukhova had not inspected the facility with her raised eyebrow in quite some time, and those who had been at FUBAR long enough knew her extended absences were a sign of workplace tranquility and a harbinger of stress-free days until the arrival of the next fiasco they had learned would surely manifest itself at this most idiosyncratic of workplaces.

Merlin was ahead on all of his office tasks and was grateful to get the nod to go on the trip. At midmorning the trio of lighter-than-airgonauts cruised above Buffalo Bayou along Allen Parkway and crossed the odd thicket of steel and glass perpendicularity that was downtown Houston as they looked toward the ship channel and the flapjack-flat coastal plain before Galveston Bay and the Gulf of Mexico.

They skirted the suburbs around NASA and the embarrassingly misnamed Clear Lake. Captain Kajerka then set a course for downtown Galveston. After making a few circles above the area, he turned to the passenger area and made an announcement: "Okay, team, this is a big day of flying, and y'all are getting to see the ship really put through her paces, but on top of that, I've got a treat in store."

He raised his mirrored Ray-Bans with a thumb and forefinger and barely winked at Svetlana. "I figured we'd all deserve a break after a morning of flying, so I accepted the invitation of an old friend on Bolivar who's invited us by for lunch."

"Lunch!" Merlin exclaimed with unfiltered exuberance.

"That's right, big fella, a real Gulf Coast throw down, complete with an old-school fisherman's platter."

Merlin's eyes grew wider, and he jumped into the swim of the conversation.

"A fisherman's platter! I love fisherman's platters! I used to eat them down the coast with my grandfather during my childhood and adolescence."

While Merlin became as glassy-eyed as a freshly caught grouper on ice in anticipation of this culinary relic of simpler times, Dirk made a hard left with the rudder, and the *Airmadillo* began to turn toward the Bolivar Peninsula. Merlin's thoughts began to shift toward Bolivar, too, as he considered how its southern end was almost completely wiped out during Hurricane Ike. *The negative vortex at its most savage*, he mused. Vexed about arrival logistics, Merlin queried the captain, "But where will we land?!"

"Got that under control, professor. There are some big concrete bulkheads with heavy rebar loops in the salt grass next to the parking lot, right across from the restaurant and marina. I think they're left over from World War II. And they've got plenty of heavy-gauge marine line to tie us down."

"Ha!" Svetlana offered tersely at the utterance of "tie us down." "In my country, fisherman's platter was maybe head of counter-revolutionary fisherman on platter during visit of Stalin to Crimea."

Dirk nosed the *Airmadillo* downward toward its noonday resting spot near the parking lot in front of Stangaroo's marina and restaurant. Helpers were already in place on the ground to secure the blimp during this unusually calm seaside day. With the *Airmadillo* moored, the trio made their way up the outdoor stairway to the restaurant's entry a good fifteen or twenty feet above ground. They turned right after passing the host's station and were met with the untempered glee of owner Constantine (Tino) Smakaporpous, a Dionysian ray of Texas Gulf Coast Greek-American sunshine.

"Dirkie!" Tino exclaimed.

"Hey, Tino! How's tricks?"

"Better all the time. Come on. I got the best table ready for us."

Dirk introduced Svetlana and Merlin to Tino, who gave Dirk a sidelong wink after meeting Svetlana. They arrived at the table overlooking the intracoastal canal where a couple of Smakaporpous's friends were already seated. More introductions followed as they sat down and a server arrived to take drink orders.

"I know you're flyin' today, but I gotta tell you we got a new local beer we found that goes perfect with seafood," Tino offered.

Dirk jumped right in. "Hey, a couple o' brews never hurt anyone." Then, with a cartoonish look around the table, "As long as we're friends here and it doesn't leave the table!"

This bit of cringe-worthy buffoonery elicited guffaws from Tino and his friends, and lunch was soon underway. Iced gulf shrimp cocktails with remoulade and horseradish-y cocktail sauce and plates of lemon halves in fine meshed netting led the way. The shrimp clung to the rims of each of the cocktail glasses, and Merlin went to work on his using the little seafood fork with clinical efficiency, stabbing each jumbo crustacean at the perfect spot in its deveined back to ensure maximum stability before its plunge into either the remoulade or cocktail sauce as his parted lips quivered in anticipation. As he relished each bite, he wished for his smock, but that thought fled as he fixated on the arrival of the next course—cups of gumbo with morsels of fresh seafood suspended in a smooth perfectly executed glistening dark roux.

Dirk was owning his role of gallivanting entertainer-in-chief as Tino and his friends encouraged him. "Tell the one about the geese following you!" Tino beckoned, and Dirk launched into another theatrical recounting. Everyone was playing into Dirk's hand—everyone except Merlin. While the group laughed more loudly a creeping concern worked its way up his spine, and as it reached the nape of his neck, he noticed the wind had picked up and the flags at the marina began to whip vigorously. He looked at East Bay beyond the marina and the intracoastal and registered that it was getting choppy, with white caps beginning to emerge here and there like dollops of meringue atop a churning, unpleasantly green dessert.

Three big oval plates constituting the fisherman's platters for six arrived and were set in the middle of the table. They were piled with mounds of fried fin fish and shellfish along with crab cakes and oysters Rockefeller on their own bed of rock salt. From the bay system there was redfish, speckled trout, and flounder. From the Gulf there was red snapper, ling (called cobia in Florida), and dorado (called mahi mahi in Hawaii and dolphin in Texas by the old-timers). In former days, the platters would perhaps have included gar, but with city folk and the massive influx of people from other parts of the country finding their way to traditional Gulf Coast restaurants (called inns) out-of-town diners began to avoid the gar when they found out what it was. Tino squeezed mesh-covered lemon halves over all of it in a kind of priestly, ritualistic fashion and opened his palms to his guests, signaling it was time for them to dig in. Svetlana seemed to be confounded at the sheer volume of fried, baked, sautéed, and grilled gifts from the sea, but Merlin was in his element and loaded his plate.

Watching Merlin, Tino offered, "Hey man, take as much as you like! The food keeps coming 'til everybody's full!" Dirk shot Tino a concerned look, but the proprietor of Stangaroo's didn't see it as he continued to hold court.

"And how 'bout you, little lady? Did they have anything like this back in the old country?"

Svetlana just shook her head in awe and said, "Never have I seen such a feast. Not at Caspian Sea, not on Gulf of Finland, not even in Crimea."

"That's right," Tino said, "and do you know why? Because everything is bigger in Texas, and Texas eats bigger than anywhere else in the world!" All the men except for Merlin broke out in hearty laughter, buoying up Tino on his sea of homespun bonhomie.

The group had been enjoying the feast for a good half hour when a waiter arrived tableside, leaned over, and whispered something in Tino's ear. When the waiter had finished the message, the wattage behind Tino's already bright presence increased, imparting an even higher degree of luminescence to his jovial visage. Tino whispered something back to the waiter, who nodded and gave him a "Yes, sir" before leaving the table. Raising his palms, Tino spread his arms out above the table, signaling that conversation should stop.

"Okay, folks," Tino announced, "have I got a treat for you!"

Svetlana perked up and paid attention. Merlin released the piece of snapper he was dredging through a white-wine lemon-butter caper sauce on one of the big platters.

Dirk said, "Okay! Whatchoo got, Teen-areen-o?"

"We just got a delivery of some beautiful local oysters. We're at the tail end of the season, but the water's still cool enough that they're sweet and prime to eat. But that's not the biggest news. One of the coast's legendary oyster bar tenders arrived a little earlier than planned. Seeing this man work is like watching a ballet of hands, knives, and shells."

Merlin forgot his concern for the weather and focused on Smakaporpous as fresh raw oysters were on his list of some of the most exquisite things in life and getting to watch them opened by a seasoned expert was a rare feast for his eyes. "So," said Tino as he turned his hands upward, "shall we go to the bar?"

The group agreed, rose from the table, and walked to the bar at the front of the restaurant. Merlin brought up the rear and cast a regretful eye toward the big spoonful of sauce-drowned snapper he left behind on the platter. His melancholy vanished when he saw that two thin rectangular slabs of what looked to be marble had been placed at the fore part of the bar, covering the lower part of the L that it made.

Behind the bar was a tall, thin black man whose air of authority was reinforced by an exquisitely pressed white apron tied securely behind his back. Next to him was a smaller, younger man ready to do his bidding. Tino sat at the corner of the bar, his two buddies to his left. This put Smakaporpous in the optimal position to greet incoming restaurant patrons while holding court with his guests.

To his right, down the short base of the L, were Dirk, Svetlana, and Merlin, in that order. Merlin was seated next to a small window through which he could see the blimp. He also noticed two large margarita machines behind the bar and various drink names etched in garish multicolors on a chalkboard behind them. The one that really caught his eye read "Stangaroo's—Home of the Juggarita!" Next to it was a cartoonish drawing of a couple of glass jugs in an oblong bucket on ice whose contents were electric lime green, the international signifying color for frozen margaritas. He then noticed behind the bar a very buxom young woman in a low-cut T-shirt bearing the same images that read "Ask me about my Juggaritas!"

Tino's bar-side speech began again, snapping Merlin's attention back toward the group's host. Tino extended his left arm in the direction of the man behind the bar and announced, "Okay, folks, I want you all to know Charles Bouchard. He's a legendary oyster bar tender, and he's here to do a little demonstration for us."

Bouchard nodded to the assembled group and made eye contact with each diner, but he did not smile as he was focused on preparation to practice his art. He motioned to his assistant, who provided small ramekins of horseradish-y cocktail sauce for each diner. He also placed bottles of Worcestershire sauce and Louisiana hot pepper sauce within each diner's reach, along with freshly cut wedges of lemon. Bouchard looked at his assistant and said in a flat commanding voice, "Mediums." The assistant began to pick medium-size oysters right from the bushel sack and place them on the marble in front of the master. Each oyster was turned so Bouchard could make the quickest possible work of them, which he did with blindingly fast precision. He perfectly opened each oyster in what seemed like no more than a couple of seconds and used his oyster knife to detach the muscle from the bottom shell before sliding the half-shell-bearing oysters, one by one, to Svetlana first and then to the men.

Now Tino was holding court in full, not only presiding over the bar at the corner of the L but also serving as a glad-hander for arrivals at Stangaroo's entry, greeting each group with his signature hail-fellow-well-met *bon vivance*. With great flourish, he announced to the group, "Y'all are experiencing something very few people get to. And watch out! Charles is as quick with a joke as he is with that oyster knife."

Bouchard shook his head quizzically in mock skepticism as he stayed focused on the oysters.

"I'm thinking about making this a reservations-only thing,"

Tino said, "and calling the experience 'A Boatload o' Bolivar Bivalves Featuring Charles Bouchard, the Oyster Slayer!'"

Bouchard gave Tino a you-can't-be-serious look and went back to work with an incredulous wince.

Dirk showed Svetlana how to eat oysters in the style of the region—no fancy thin *mignonette* sauces here—first squirting a few drops of lemon onto the oyster, then sliding it onto a saltine cracker and topping it with cocktail sauce and one drop of Louisiana hot sauce. He adjured her with a roguish mustache twitch: "You have to eat it in one bite."

"No problem," she replied with a smirk and opened wide to down the sauced, mollusk-topped cracker.

The others accepted their first oysters and each exclaimed in turn how wonderful they were. Merlin was transfixed as Bouchard slid him a slightly larger, but perfectly formed oyster with the statement "Now this man looks like an oyster eater." Indeed Merlin was, as he dispatched oyster after oyster in the time-honored fashion Dirk had demonstrated to Svetlana. Nevertheless, he continued to glance out the window across the parking lot at the blimp. Its nose began to bounce more and more as the gusts grew stronger and more frequent. Unusually for Merlin, after putting away his first dozen oysters, he became less and less interested in them and more distracted as the *Airmadillo* bobbed more wildly in the wind.

The rest of the group, however, had refocused on Dirk as he continued with story after story at Tino's urging. A group of sport fishermen, most with necks burnished red after a morning on the bay, entered the restaurant, and Tino went back into jovial greeting mode. The men were fat, squat, and wearing shorts, water shoes, hi-tech fishing shirts, and ball caps or Florida fisherman hats with ear and neck flaps and sunglasses with a strap connecting each of the temple bars to one another around their thick napes.

Svetlana was dealing with a petite oyster Bouchard had sent

her way when she saw there were no more Saltines. She nudged Dirk and said, "We don't have any more of these." Dirk forthwith looked up at Bouchard and said, "Charles, we don't have any crackers." In mock theatricism, Bouchard looked at Dirk and Tino and his friends with dubious wide-open eyes and then dramatically scanned the newly arrived fishermen behind Tino with the same theatrical eyes before locking Tino and Dirk in his view and offering, "Oh yes, we do!" This oyster-knife jab of a quip caused Dirk and Tino to double over in uncontrollable waves of laughter, and when Tino caught his breath he said to Dirk, "See! I told you so!" And then they began a new round of their laughing fit.

The blimp was now bobbing so wildly it looked like some kind of animal trying to break free from a snare, or maybe a bucking bronco about to explode out of a rodeo gate. No one paid attention to Merlin when he rose and sidestepped behind the oyster tasters to the restaurant's entry. He descended the stairs to the parking lot, never taking his eyes off the *Airmadillo*. As if in a trance, he began to shuffle across the crushed oyster-shell lot. About two-thirds of the way, he could see that most of the knots in the lines securing the blimp had become precariously loose and that the blimp was just on the verge of breaking free from its moorings. Deducing that it was a matter of mere seconds before the *Airmadillo* assumed unmanned, undirected flight, he broke into his own version of a dead sprint, heading straight for the passenger/pilot compartment.

Just as he opened the door and stepped inside, the blimp lurched upward, belly-flopping him onto its floor. Merlin grabbed the back of the pilot's seat and pulled himself to his feet as the *Airmadillo* continued to rise and head toward the colorfully painted houses of Crystal Beach and the Gulf of Mexico just beyond them. He squeezed into the pilot's seat and tried to start the engine. The first try failed, and the blimp barely missed the rooftops of a couple of beachfront houses on stilts.

As the *Airmadillo* crossed the beach and headed seaward, another buffeting sent its nose sharply downward toward the surf and the swells past the last sandbar. Merlin knew what he had to do. He spun the elevator wheel backward as fast as he could, then he glared at the ornery start switch and pressed it again.

The engine cranked, and the propeller whirred to life, and just as a spray of sea foam hit the bow of the airship, it began to nose sharply upward past the sandy brown beach water toward the opaque military green of the nearshore ocean. Merlin had failed to notice his phone buzzing in his pocket. He stabilized the blimp as best he could in the capricious wind and reached for his phone.

"Hello?"

It was the captain.

"What the hell happened? Why didn't you say anything?"

"Well . . I . . . I just saw the blimp moving and instinctively headed toward the door. I don't really know why, and by the time I reached the cabin, she had broken free of her moorings, and all I could do was jump in."

"Why didn't you say something?"

"You were all engaged in conversation, and I didn't know how to interrupt."

"From now on, interrupt when the blimp's getting away!"

"Oh, okay, I will. Even if it seems rude."

"Rude, shmood! The *Airmadillo* comes first!"

"Yes, captain."

"Now let me talk you in so Svetlana and I can board."

"Uh, okay. You mean to land?"

"Yeah, to land. What do you think I mean?"

"I've never landed the vehicle."

"Well, you've never soloed either, but you seem to be doing fine with that."

Too unsettled to recount the blimp's brush with the near-shore whitecaps, all Merlin could manage was "Uh, okay, um, thank you."

"You're welcome, cowboy. Now let's get you back to Stangaroo's."

Dirk talked Merlin in with considerably more precision than one would expect from someone who had just downed copious amounts of rich food and ale. Merlin had steeled himself for a round tongue-lashing from Dirk, but instead he watched the captain hold the cabin door open for Svetlana, Tino, and his chuckling sidekicks whose names he had forgotten after initial introductions at the table but now registered as Dirk directed Dogboy and Virgil to their seats.

A server stood beside Tino at the blimp's door and handed him a cardboard cake box, which Tino in turn handed to Svetlana to stow under the seats. Then came a tall thermos-like container and an insulated box of crushed ice. As Tino entered the *Airmadillo*, he said in Merlin's direction, "We decided to get airborne for the last course."

Merlin began to dislodge himself from the pilot's seat, but, again to his surprise, Dirk stopped him, saying, "No, stay put! You've proven yourself. I'll talk you through the standard take-off." Dirk angled himself in the passenger seat behind Merlin such that he could instruct Merlin if he turned left and cut up with the men and Svetlana if he turned right. Svetlana pulled the cabin door closed, and Dirk talked his attentive protégé through the takeoff procedure as an impromptu ground crew from the marina released the blimp from its moorings. Merlin experienced a stratospheric level of satisfaction as he piloted the oblong vehicle toward its cruising altitude.

Someone in the back shouted, "Hey, can we turn over to the right a little?"

Dirk turned to see Dogboy pointing and answered, "Sure! Whatcha got?"

"Ole Murphy got him one a them mail-order brides from across the pond, and they say she lays out on the deck outside their bedroom European-style."

Virgil chimed in, "That Murphy always was a good 'un for findin' the fillies."

Dogboy sat up and said, "Then why'd he have to git him a mail order?"

"She wadn't no mail order, Dog; he met'er on a business trip over yonder. I think it was to Row Mania."

"Business trip? Monkey business prolly more like it."

Merlin maneuvered the blimp, and the passengers looked downward through the right windows.

"Yep! Thar she blows!"

"Well, I'll be!" offered Virgil.

The passengers saw a topless woman sunbathing on the third-floor deck of a house on Crystal Beach.

Tino chimed in, "Just like the German and Swedish girls back in the old country!"

Dirk turned in Merlin's direction. "Take 'er down a couple of hundred feet and circle."

Merlin complied silently and saw what was causing the ruckus—something he had never witnessed.

"Yeah, ole Murphy got 'im a live one, that's for sure!" Dogboy said.

Virgil piped up with the arrival of a new player on the scene. "Hey! Who's that?"

A young man in swim trunks brought the woman a drink, and she accepted it moving only her right hand.

Dogboy answered, "It shore ain't Murphy."

Virgil responded with a terse "Nope."

Dogboy continued: "Naw, this feller's got a headful of hair, no beer belly, and from what I can tell, Murphy's got about twenty years on him."

Now it was Tino's turn. "Looks like a little harmless rubbernecking just turned into a dirt-gathering session! I think it's called espionage!"

Dirk winked at Tino, and his mustache twitched as he responded, "More like *air*spionage!"

Tino let out a few guffaws, and Dogboy jumped in. "Hey, I don't want no kinda trouble."

"Me neither," Virgil protested. "We'll just keep it between us. Ain't no sense in hurtin' ole Murphy."

Svetlana remained completely blasé during this interchange and after the first silent pause, offered, "It reminds me of Crimea on Riviera of Black Sea."

Dogboy responded, "Cry me a river of black tea?"

"No," Svetlana responded firmly. "Is summer place for Russian people."

Now it was Virgil's turn. "Yew never did any a that, did you, missy?"

"Eez normal. Eez cahstum on lot of beaches."

"It costs 'um a lot?" queried Dogboy.

"And I'm sure most of them are nice young ladies," said Virgil the diplomat.

"No! Eez *cah*stum! Like cowboy wearing het!"

"Easy costume?" Virgil wondered.

"I reckon it is," replied Dogboy. "Bikini bottoms and sun-glasses must be about as easy as it gits!"

Virgil tried to turn the conversation. "Dis-irregardless of all that, I still think we oughta keep quiet about the cabana boy!"

Tino squelched the inane banter. "Hey, you guys cut it out! Our Russian friend is getting upset, and I think all she wants you to know is that Murphy's wife's sun-tanning mode is not out of the ordinary across the pond."

"Yes, it's de rigueur," offered Dirk with mock sophistication.

"Dare a girl?!" questioned Dogboy. "Like dare a girl to take 'er top off?"

"Stop!" commanded the Greek-American restaurateur, and Dogboy and Virgil finally desisted.

"Time for dessert!" Tino proclaimed. He picked up the cake box and opened it to reveal triangles of baklava and tiny key lime pie tartlets, complete with house-made whipped cream and freshly grated lime zest. Everyone took a couple of pieces, and Merlin craned his neck to see the contents of the box. Tino held the box toward him with a jaunty "Here you go, Captain!" Merlin sat up reflexively on hearing himself called "captain" for the first time and swiped a couple of tartlets from the box.

Tino picked up the thermos and announced, "And now for my new specialty cocktail of the month!"

As he unscrewed the top of the container, Svetlana took a small stack of plastic cups and filled each one about halfway with crushed ice.

"What is it?" queried Dirk.

"Rhum Agricole from Martinique, crushed mint, lemon, chopped ripe mango and a little mango juice, and a capful of Metaxa to honor my heritage. Oh, and topped off with cold Topo Chico to keep it light."

Virgil chimed in, "Wow! That sounds pretty fancy!"

"Not meant to be, Virge. Just refreshing in the hot weather."

"What d'you call it?" asked Dirk.

"The Smakaporpous Smash."

"Now that's one I can remember!" enthused Dogboy.

"Yeah, not like all them drinks with foreign names!" rejoined Virgil.

"Yeah, like a 'Booleemi' or a 'Queer Royale,'" declared Dogboy.

"I *love* Bellini and Kir Royale!" protested Svetlana.

"Enough!" Tino poured some of his concoction into each of the glasses as his cocktail testers held them forward. He then topped each one with the effervescent Mexican mineral water.

"Tell me what you think of the Smakaporpous Smash!"

The group complied.

Virgil was the first to weigh in. "Dang! That'll drink!"

Dogboy followed, "It knows it's good!"

Dirk said, "Ah, reminds me of my days island-hopping in the Caribbean." Svetlana rounded out the assessment. "I love! Makes me think of amazing trip to St. Barts with Missoni bikinis and all Louis Vuitton luggage."

Dogboy responded, "I don't know who Miss Oni is or what part of Japan she's from, but this here shore is a good drink!"

Dirk lifted his Ray-Bans and said to Tino, "Looks like you've got a success on your hands."

"Great," responded Tino. "The Smakaporpous Smash goes on the menu today!"

The passengers enjoyed their libations as Merlin flew the *Airmadillo* in increasingly expanding circles over the Bolivar/Galveston area. Captain Dirk ordered the blimp back to Stangaroo's, and Merlin did an even more masterful job of landing it as the wind had diminished. When the airship was securely moored with staff to watch it, everyone disembarked for a restroom break inside the restaurant. Dirk, Svetlana, and Merlin thanked Tino and bid him, Dogboy, and Virgil goodbye. As the three returned to the *Airmadillo*, Dirk informed Merlin he could continue to man the pilot's seat. Although Merlin nodded in silent compliance, his spirits leapt at the prospect of piloting the *Airmadillo* cross-country on its homeward flight. Captain Kajerka specified a route different from the outbound course, sending the blimp southwestward alongside Galveston Island's beachfront, passing the communities of Pirate's Beach, Jamaica Beach, and Sea Isle.

Merlin looked out on a ranch pasture in the center of the island to his right and noticed a solitary bull taking the meager shade a scrubby tree offered. He looked at the content animal and wondered if his name was Ferdinand. He then chided himself for speculating this way as he recalled that nowadays livestock were alphanumerically ear-tagged and microchipped, obviating their individual identities and reducing them to little more than fungible commodities. Still, he wished the solitary bull had a name and hoped he was enjoying the springtime afternoon.

Although Merlin didn't turn around to look, Svetlana and Dirk had fallen asleep. A zen-like calm descended over the passenger pod and cockpit, and Merlin observed the sparsely peopled weekday beach scene with the satisfied serenity of a Japanese monk regarding his freshly raked rock garden. He looked down on the treacherous currents roiling the water and snaking their way around the supports of the toll bridge at San Luis Pass.

As the *Airmadillo* motored past Surfside Beach near Freeport with its huge Dow Chemical complex, Merlin looked one last time at the gulf and turned the blimp northward on a direct line for home base per the route Captain Kajerka had programmed into the GPS. A few minutes passed, and Merlin heard the curtain snap shut. He then noticed an errant empty plastic cocktail cup roll forward to the right of his seat, but this little intruder did not disturb the pro tempore blimp flyer's reverie. Ten minutes before the blimp's arrival at the base, a refreshed Dirk switched seats with Merlin. When the ground crew had secured the blimp, the three departed the passenger pod.

Instead of escorting Svetlana as usual, Dirk called to Merlin: "Hey, junior birdman!"

Merlin stopped in his tracks, wondering if he was in trouble. Dirk assuaged his concerns as he strode next to Merlin with a smile that extended the breadth of his mustache.

"You did great work today."

"Oh! Thank you."

"Meet me in my office."

"Aye aye, Captain." (Merlin sometimes liked to think of the *Airmadillo* in nautical terms.)

Dirk caught up with Svetlana, and they veered toward the little warren of offices attached to the hangar. Merlin followed suit several steps behind them. When Merlin entered the captain's office, Kajerka was sitting with his zipped-up half-booted feet propped on his desk. He pretended to look at something important on his computer screen.

"Have a seat!"

Merlin found a faux leather rolling chair and complied.

"What you did today was impressive, Merlin—not to mention heroic." Merlin received this praise in wide-eyed silence, realizing this was the first time Kajerka had addressed him directly by name.

"I made a deal with the guys back at lunch that if we could all go for a little dessert and cocktail tour in the blimp, they would promise not to say anything about the little mishap this afternoon."

"Just like the way they are not going to mention seeing Murphy's wife and her assistant?"

"Uh, yeah, I guess. Something like that, but what you accomplished today also has a lot of importance for you, personally."

"It does?"

"Yes, my friend, it does." There was a slight twinkle in Kajerka's eye and an equally constrained mustache twitch as he continued: "You soloed today. You may not have been counting on it when we left the base this morning, but you successfully solo flew a large airship—and in treacherous conditions at that."

"Oh!" Merlin responded.

"Do you know what that means?"

"Um, no sir, not really."

"It means that you joined a special club today. Even though you haven't completed the formal classroom training, which I know would be no problem for you, you did the most important thing. In the eyes of pilots, you are now a pilot, too."

At this, Merlin sat back into his chair as if buffeted by one of the gusts that took the *Airmadillo* off its moorings earlier that very same day. Dirk continued, pointing to a framed, yellowed piece of material on the wall.

"See that?"

"Yes."

"Know what it is?"

Merlin thought and responded with a bewildered no.

"That's a shirttail—mine to be exact—cut off and signed by my instructor after my first solo flight when I was sixteen years old."

"Ooohhh," Merlin said with the wonder of the sudden realization of a great mystery.

"It's a longtime tradition among pilots. They did the same thing with my dad after his first solo."

"Ooooohhh."

"So, stand up, untuck your shirt, and come over here."

Merlin obeyed immediately and rose as quickly as he could from the rolling chair to present himself to Dirk, who was now standing with military gravity.

"Turn around."

Merlin waddled in place 180 degrees.

Dirk took a pair of office scissors and made quick work of cutting the back tail from Merlin's shirt. While Merlin was still facing away from him, Dirk took the shirttail and secured its edges with paperweights on his desk. On it, he wrote with a black felt-tipped indelible marker Merlin's name and the date. He then signed his own name underneath, authenticating the solo flight.

"Okay, you can turn around."

Merlin complied and saw Dirk holding up the corners of the cut-off shirttail so the new pilot could see the inscription. Merlin stood in stony silence and took in the import of the moment as he looked at the official commemoration of his new status.

"Take it. It's yours."

Merlin reached up with both hands and took the same corners that Dirk was holding as Kajerka released the shirttail. He held it closer at his own eye level as if mesmerized by its totemic power.

"Okay, now," Dirk said.

Merlin lowered the shirttail to chest level so he could see the captain.

"Becoming a pilot carries some responsibilities and burdens."

Merlin nodded.

"Obviously, you've got to keep your passengers safe, but among themselves, pilots, from time to time, may have some information that needs to stay quiet, like in a secret society."

Merlin lowered the shirttail to his waist level, where it resembled a freemason's apron.

"What happened today is like what in the military and intelligence world they call black ops and any further talk of it is what the old spooks in the CIA used to call dead man's talk."

Merlin's eyes widened again.

"What happened today is under the umbrella of the pilot's code of silence. If anybody asks you about what went on today, your response is that all went as planned, and there was no deviation from the normal course of blimp operations."

Merlin's jaw dropped open slightly.

"What about Mr. Smakaporpous and his friends?"

"Like I told you, we've already made our deal. As freewheeling as they may seem, they are good secret keepers."

"Like the way they are not going to tell Mr. Murphy about his wife's sunbathing assistant?"

"Yes, exactly."

"What about Miss Slahtskaya?"

"I'm not worried about Svetlana. The former Soviet Union was built on secret keeping; it's part and parcel of her cultural DNA to stay mum. They look at getting to keep secrets as a badge of honor."

Dirk nodded toward the inked-up shirttail. "Just like your new certificate there."

Merlin looked down at the lowered shirttail.

"So can I rely on you?" Dirk asked.

Merlin was quiet for a few seconds as he continued to look Kajerka in the eye and gave the barest nod of accession. A complicit smile cracked the corners of Dirk's mouth.

"Good! Welcome aboard!"

Dirk reached out and Merlin offered his big right paw, and they shook. In a flash of creative manipulation, Dirk straightened and saluted the credulous blimp of a man. Merlin, astonished and honored, also straightened and slowly raised his hand to his brow, returning the gesture. It was with this salute that Merlin felt that he had crossed a line somehow, but the nature of the line was something of which he wasn't quite sure. Dirk lowered his hand, and Merlin mirrored the move. Kajerka's smile was full now as he continued the military ruse.

"That'll be all, lieutenant. At ease."

He motioned toward the office door and Merlin nodded again and started toward the door, then turned to Kajerka and said, "Thank you."

Dirk gave a silent nod of reassurance, and Merlin exited toward his office.

At his desk at the base and all the way home in the Alles car, Merlin reflected on the day. He was particularly vexed by the prospect of having to lie if asked about the day's events. He had been taught not to lie as a child and had always held this as a cardinal tenet of his code of living. But, he reasoned, no one ever asked him anything important anyway. And although his physical presence was imposing, he had a way of blending into the background, kind of like a Sasquatch, with whose kind he had always felt a particular affinity. Also, he had an inkling that most of those who were accustomed to seeing him thought of him as perhaps a bit out of the ordinary but thoroughly inconsequential as far as anything that might impact the serious world of adult business affairs was concerned.

Finally, he remembered something his youth minister who trained him to be an acolyte said. The young Episcopal priest always insisted that lying was bad but that not volunteering information when not asked about it was okay. He called it the doctrine of selective truths. Merlin hoped he would not have to invoke this doctrine regarding what had happened on what proved to be a very auspicious day for him.

· Nineteen

On his return to the observatory, Merlin was drained in a way he hadn't been since taking multihour exams for his master's degree. Nevertheless, he trudged up the stairs with anticipation of a deep sleep in the security of his own little castle of a lair. He expected the observatory to present itself as the womb of safety it so often was for him; however, he had dubbed it the observatory many years ago for a reason. Its primary function was as a watchtower and a place where data was to be gathered, sorted, and analyzed. When he opened the hatch and entered, it was this latter and primary aspect of the place that held forth. Namely, orange dots were flashing on each of his computer monitors, signaling the Agglomerator had an important message for him. He opened the program on his central screen, and in letters the same hue of orange as the alert blips, the phrase "Event Horizon Update" flashed with ominous urgency.

Merlin clicked past the warning window and the live-action map showed a gray gyre tightening over Greater Houston. He clicked on an icon called "time window" and saw an orange-shaded calendar with the orange darkening between late July and early September. "Deep summer indeed," he mused, the middle of what he had heard people in South Texas refer to as "the enchilada." The gray gyre indicated a negative energy field event. If it continued to darken toward black, the predicted event would be no cause for little concern. Merlin was impatient to know more, but he also knew he could not push the Agglomerator. It processed data thoroughly, but at its own august pace.

Now the fatigue was pulling him down like he was carrying lead-filled grocery bags, and despite the growing alarm sounded by his cherished computer program, he found himself lumbering, eyes half shut, toward his big reinforced bed, the sleep wagon on which he had come to rely to spirit him to a land of relief from the mounting concerns of his increasingly complicated circumstances. He flopped onto the bed and was out cold before he could undress and get under the covers.

————

Tite Dûche sat in a dark corner of a *bruine* café in the De Pijp neighborhood of Amsterdam looking at photos on his electronic tablet. He was choosing new pictures for the updated Dûche Ovens website. They featured his new Super Dûcherator 5000 shot from several angles using various lighting effects. He closed the file and opened another.

Also a photo file, this one featured all human subjects, none of whom appeared to be the sort of people with whom Tite would associate socially. There were both female and male, perhaps in their early adolescence, but really most of them seemed to be no more than girls and boys. Their eyes bespoke lives of deprivation and existential fear unknown to the majority of North Americans. Each of the photographs had a caption with a single name that often had the look of a nickname—Paquito instead of Francisco or Mayte instead of Maria Teresa. There were no surnames accompanying any of the images.

A tall man in a black outfit wearing dark glasses and tightly cropped gray hair walked slowly toward Tite. He was utterly expressionless. As he arrived at the table, Tite offered him an equally emotionless mien. Tite looked at his Cartier tank watch and said, "You are exactly on time."

"We Dutch pride ourselves on our punctuality, especially when it comes to business meetings."

Tite motioned toward the chair and the man seated himself. He declined the menu Tite offered him. A server arrived, and the Dutchman ordered a pint of beer in his native language.

"What else are you all proud of?" queried Tite.

"Our taciturnity in trading," responded the Amsterdammer, now removing his sunglasses.

"What about fair trading?"

"Of course! We may negotiate with vigor, but when mutually agreeable terms are struck, a deal is a deal."

"Alright. Well, I suppose we have reached that point."

"Agreed. So, then, let's have a look at the candidates."

Tite nodded and slid his electronic tablet to a neutral zone between them where they could see its screen.

———

Mickey McNaughton sat at his desk in his Dutch client's corporate headquarters. Most of the employees had already left the building, a contemporary structure in the Zuidas business district of Amsterdam. His mobile phone rang. It was a call from Houston.

"Hey, Mick?"

"Yeah! Jim?"

"Yeah, hey, I hate disturb you at the end of the business day across the pond."

"So, how's everything in the world of putting bad guys away?"

"Committing felonies continues to be a burgeoning enterprise in Harris County."

"So, what else is new, right?"

"Exactly. Hey, we found out a few things about the mad eggers outside your house."

"Outstanding."

"I don't know if it's outstanding, but I think we have ID'ed the egg hurlers."

"Okay, so what gives?"

"The vehicle is registered to N. Teitel Dûche V."

"Tite Dûche?!"

"Yep. A friend in the video lab did me a favor and analyzed the footage. He thinks our egg tossers may be Tite's sons."

"What the hell?!"

"I don't know, Mickey. But we have a pretty good visual of those two. The elder son is N. Teitel Dûche VI, aka Titey, and the younger one is Duke Wayne Dûche, aka Dukey."

"So, that's really weird, right?"

"Maybe. Maybe not. Could be just some punk kids picking on the neighborhood oddball."

"I guess the whole world has its share of punks, right?"

"Yep. Even Bayou Boughs."

"So weird. I think I saw Tite on the street here in Amsterdam a few weeks ago."

"I don't think that necessarily has anything to do with the defacement of the structure."

"No, but it's just weird is all I'm saying, right? A Dûche here doing God knows what; a couple of Dûches there causing trouble. So, what's the next move?"

"We could go after them right now, but my gut is telling me, if you'll forgive the figure of speech, to sit tight." His years in the justice system had taught him the value of circumspection. "If they do it again, maybe we can put a good scare on them."

"Yeah. Yeah, I understand. Makes sense. Thanks."

"You bet. Over and out."

Mickey tapped his smart phone to close the call. He opened his private e-mail and began to type. After a minute or so he sent the message. In Houston, Merlin was getting ready to leave the blimp base for his lunch break when his computer made a dinging sound, and he saw one of the rare e-mails from Mickey—so rare it was almost like seeing a unicorn. Merlin opened the communiqué and read.

So, my ace in the hole at the DA's office has come through. He has ID'd the license plate and is pretty certain of the identity of the actual eggers themselves. That said, he thinks we should hold off on pursuing any action against them for the time being. If the same guys strike again, a friend of his in the video lab downtown can compare the two video captures, and we can move forward from there, right?

I'm also disclosing to you who we think the vandals are with the understanding that you won't try to take any retaliatory action on your own. It looks like the culprits are Tite Dûche's sons. Stay in contact—especially if more dodgy stuff goes down. So, this is just a heads-up, right? Will keep you posted if I hear anything salient on my end.

Merlin read with concentrated focus that intensified when Mickey revealed the likely identity of the assaulters of his sacrosanct white tower and just as quickly asked him to keep it to himself. This was a tall order, even for the rule-following Merlin, but he understood by the way Mickey presented it to him that he was treating Merlin like an adult. Musing on the phrase "discretion is the better part of valor," Merlin then realized that he had been implored in the space of a mere couple of days to keep a couple of things secret. Was this how the adult world of commerce and justice really worked? Was it a place of strategic restraint and selective truths? He wondered. Perhaps keeping information under his hat might be one of his untapped talents. Equipped with the frequency listening device, his hats themselves were imparting to him privileged information all the time, the nuances of which only he was qualified to interpret.

Not speaking to others was something at which Merlin was accomplished, so adding a few items that required secretive restraint might not be so challenging. And, at the end of the day, Merlin was proud that people in authority around him had entrusted him with information and trusted him to keep it quiet.

They were indeed treating him like an adult now, he continued to muse—not like an overgrown child. He sat for a moment feeling the weight of his newfound maturity then closed the e-mail program and headed for the door, the internal debate on where to go for lunch returning to the forefront of his ever-ranging thoughts.

———

At the *bruine* café in De Pijp, the Amsterdammer and Tite Dûche concluded their meeting. The Dutchman slid the tablet with the photos of the young people back toward Tite and spoke: "So many little brown ones."

"Well, we are meeting in a brown café," responded Tite, taxing his cleverness resources.

"How appropriate."

"Is there anything else I can do to help move things along?"

"No, I don't think so. The company will come to a decision within a fortnight. You must remember that we Dutch have a considerable history managing the little dark ones from the tropics."

"Oh?"

"Of course. As you may recall, we originally colonized the archipelago now known as Indonesia; it was the Dutch East Indies for almost one hundred and fifty years."

"Oh, yes, of course."

"Some of my ancestors were there for a time."

"Really?"

"Yes, so engaging in this kind of business is, you might say, in my blood."

"And blood will tell, as the saying goes."

"But we tell no one."

"Agreed."

"And a deal is a deal."

· *Summer*

· Twenty

June arrived with a one-two punch of heat and humidity, eliminating any residuum of springtime lightheartedness. June 1st also marks the official beginning of hurricane season. As a young man, around Memorial Day weekend, Merlin kept a sharp eye out for the Sunday paper containing the annually distributed hurricane tracking charts. He penciled the familiar gyre symbols onto the chart as each system developed, scratching the little circles with the whirling semicircular arcs into the thick cross-hatched paper with its grid of latitude and longitude lines.

Unsatisfied with the consistency of his symbol-making skills, he created a stencil for the storm graphic. He left the center blank to denote a tropical storm and penciled it in if it developed into a hurricane. He also added tiny numbers with adhesive backing to the center of the design to indicate a storm's intensity. He was particularly proud of the apposite arcs in the stencil. They seemed kinetic to him somehow, intimating a storm's menacing power with their fat, stubby blades churning over the Atlantic, Caribbean, or Gulf of Mexico—the terrible sign of a twin-scythed maritime grim reaper.

Although it may seem macabre, it was actually quite common for families to keep the charts magnetically clamped to kitchen refrigerators and update them now and then. As a young person, Merlin, however, was particularly fastidious with his chart updates. His fascination with the annual ritual did not wane through the years, and, as the world became progressively digital and computerized, Merlin created his own electronic hurricane tracking charts, adding special functions for visual enhancement of the experience, like different colors representing each strength category of a storm. These first early efforts spawned projects that had ultimately led to the complex, and Merlin believed, beautiful information synthesizer of the Agglomerator. This morning, however, was blazing hot and almost cloudless, and the prospect of imminently approaching hurricanes, generally a late summer phenomenon, was neither on the horizon nor animating Merlin's thoughts.

On learning Tite Dûche's sons were the perps of the eggings, Merlin went back into online shopping mode, searching for tracking devices that could be affixed by magnet to automobiles. He found just what he was looking for—a tiny gadget with an equally tiny, but powerful, battery-powered electromagnet. The device reported its whereabouts both to his computer and through an app to his smart phone. It also had an emergency feature that disengaged the magnet, allowing it to detach from wherever it had been placed.

The tracker arrived in a nondescript little box he opened with anticipation. Getting past the bubble wrap and packing paper, he excised a smooth, thick wafer—matte black plastic on the top and sides, and the bottom consisting entirely of the magnet. It looked like a miniature hockey puck. "Not much bigger than a macaroon," he observed. He put it in the palm of one of his hands. Closing his fingers around it completely hid it from view. He went to work linking it to his computer and phone, which took just a few minutes. The manufacturers had even sent a fresh, strong battery with it, which he installed without difficulty. Then he thought, *Why not today?* He dropped the little device in a trouser pocket and set off for the club.

He saw neither father's nor sons' Dûche mobiles on entering the club, but when he left after breakfast, he saw Tite's bright yellow Porsche parked in a row reserved for board members. Although he had planned to affix it to the offending SUV, on a whim he decided to attach it to the club president's car. He saw a place where he might secrete it in a rear wheel well, but he wondered how to do it without being noticed.

He began to sidle toward the roadster and noticed an errant UPS delivery truck heading his way. He shuffled out of the way of its path and quickly scanned the lot as he approached the sports car. The truck began to pass slowly, blocking the view of the parking lot's security camera. Just to be safe he feigned dropping something, and on the way up, firmly affixed the tracker out of sight on the undercarriage of the car. It adhered with a muffled metal-on-metal clink. By the time the delivery truck rolled past, he was once again upright and on his way home.

The Saturday mail had been delivered by the time Merlin reached the main house, and sorting through it as he headed toward his observatory, he recognized the familiar shape, texture, and coloring of the Bayou Boughs Country Club monthly newsletter. As much as he found the new president's letters far from pleasant reading, they took up most of the cover of the update and were impossible to ignore, so he began to read.

> Summer has arrived and many of you will be jetting off (flying private, of course) to your fabulous homes in Aspen, Santa Barbara, or Nantucket. The more adventuresome among you will be leading lives of colonial splendor in San Miguel de Allende or perhaps Antigua, Guatemala. The French Riviera even calls some of our more Cosmopolitan Members to its glittering hillsides and shores. (I have heard the Wine Committee may convene at a Chateau in the Rhone Valley for their Summer Session if the stars line up right.) Tappi and the kids and I will be in and out of town between trips to Europe and South America.
>
> If you find yourself at the Club, there will be plenty of

Fun Activities to attract you. Even if the outdoor temperature and humidity are high—the energy level at BBCC will be even higher. There's a great day camp for the kids with loads of activities. Golf, tennis, croquet, and badminton (wear your whites!), yoga, and Pilates will keep the parents interested. And our chef has come up with some cool Summer Specials to tantalize your sophisticated taste buds.

As much as I don't like having to bring up Rules and Regulations, it is incumbent upon me in my Treasured Role as Your President, to do so as part of my Duties. Looking appropriate at the Club is crucial to ensure the mutual enjoyment of our World Class Facilities. Bayou Boughs' dress code comes from years of Thoughtful Reflection, and we all know that looking appropriate is looking good and makes for a harmonious Club Atmosphere. With that undisputable fact in mind, we must call it to the Membership's attention that the wearing of large, dyed-to-match-an-outfit hiking boot–styled shoes is not appropriate at BBCC. Perhaps during a nature trek on the bayou, it might be acceptable, but certainly not at any of the Club's dining facilities. Such coarse and unusual footwear denigrates the Club when worn within its walls. The only time I could ever imagine such footwear as appropriate would be as part of a Frankenstein costume at a Halloween party. Needless to say, most of you are benchmarks of fashion and sartorial taste, with several BBCC Ladies appearing regularly on the city's Best Dressed List. Nevertheless, Duty calls me to point this out.

Another issue vexing Your Board of late involves the ordering of outsized portions with special Club Member names or nicknames. Granted some of our lunch items have hallowed, time-honored nicknames, like the Bogie Salad Trio or the Ron Coffee, but these items have been part of Lunch Menus at Bayou Boughs for at least sixty years, if not longer. No, this is not the problem.

Specifically, certain Members (again, the Offenders are very Few in Number) have become accustomed to eating amounts in single meals that on most occasions might satisfy two or three diners with the healthiest of appetites.

Calling it by a clever name (like a Magic Meal, for instance) makes it sound like a legitimate order. But seeing such a repulsively large amount of food placed before a single diner is beyond reprehensible. In this "Day And Age," when Being Healthy and Fitness Consciousness in general is on everybody's mind, just seeing such an order arrive shocks the Collective Conscience of a Membership as with-it and good-looking as BBCC boasts. The Club is already a pinnacle of eating and drinking well, but with so many Leaders among our Membership, I know we all agree that Eating Right is equally important as we continue to set the pace as exemplary, albeit Highly Privileged, members of the Greater Houston Community. Future Offenders will be dealt with harshly and swiftly.

Wishing you cool summer breezes
and regal travels,
Tite

On finishing the letter Merlin dropped his small stack of mail to his feet on the worn-brick, moss-intersticed walkway from the main house to his abode. His eyes closed, and his chin fell like a leaden door knocker to his chest.

In a leafy neighborhood near the medical center, Dr. Mac Swearingen put down his coffee cup and finished reading the same letter. "Geez, what the hell's next? Compulsory morning calisthenics?" He tossed it aside and reached for the weekend edition of the *Wall Street Journal*.

Lindley Acheson picked up the mail from behind the front door slot of her father's house and leafed through it. She saw the Bayou Boughs Country Club newsletter and began to read. As she got to Tite's interdictions, she pursed her lips and glared at the page. She plucked a thorn from the stem of a rose in an arrangement in a vase near the entryway of the house and stuck it right in the middle of the dot of the *i* in Tite's printed signature. In the rose world, the plant's thorns are referred to as prickles. As Lindley drove the thorn into the *i* on the page, she said, "A prickle for a prick."

· Twenty-one

The *Airmadillo*'s nighttime missions continued into the summer, with Captain Dirk Kajerka giving Merlin license to fly where he liked after the key terrestrial audiences were checked off the blimp's advertising route. Merlin also took a little license of his own by bringing his hat-embedded listening device, his thumb drive with his warning messages for the populace, and his mobile phone with the app connected to the tracking device on Tite Dûche's Porsche.

When Dirk and Svetlana retired to the passenger area and Dirk drew the curtain shut, Merlin went to work. He popped his thumb drive into the onboard exterior display computer, and his messages began to run on the big screen in the sky. He then donned one of his device-modified hats and lodged the ear buds in the primeval overgrowth of the cilia forests crowding his auditory canals, turning his head this way and that trying to discern the source of the strongest energy signal. But it was the automobile tracking device that yielded the most interesting information. The app gave a history of Tite's routes that in many ways was unremarkable. Predictably, the destinations included the headquarters of Dûche Ovens, the family residence, locations that would seem reasonable as venues for charity events, board meetings, and strictly social gatherings, along with high-end restaurants. There were a couple of aberrations, however.

One was the location of a leather shop in the Montrose area

that catered largely to a specific segment of the gay community, and the other was equally surprising—an address in Northeast Houston—an area one would presume the president of Bayou Boughs Country Club had never seen or even traversed on the way somewhere else. The app's real-time functionality was particularly energizing for Merlin, and it worked while in the *Airmadillo* because the blimp flew low enough to receive signals from the cellular network.

Checking the app tonight as he piloted the blimp over the trendy area east of downtown, Merlin noticed the little blinking dot was on the move. Fascinated, he saw it shift from Allen Parkway to Interstate 45 North. "He must be picking up someone at the airport," Merlin reasoned, but he decided to depress the left rudder pedal and try to follow it anyway. Although the blimp's cruise speed was slower than a highway-darting Dûche Porsche, Merlin did not have to deal with the impediments of traffic, street signs, and streetlights and could pursue the yellow roadster as the crow flies.

To Merlin's great surprise, Dûche's vehicle moved to an exit lane not too far north of downtown. As the Porsche slowed, the *Airmadillo* caught up with it. It moved down a major thoroughfare then took a turn into a neighborhood Merlin had never visited. He had the presence of mind to turn off the outdoor advertising screen in an attempt to make the airborne vehicle as invisible as possible—a ninja blimp. He also slowed the *Airmadillo* considerably to remain at a judicious distance behind the two-seater on the ground, which slowed and pulled into a driveway. Someone opened a gate, and the Porsche pulled into a carport behind it. Merlin took note of the address and made sure the app saved it as he held the blimp in a wide circular pattern over a place that looked like a house with some sort of small compound behind it consisting of a few buildings and an open area. Merlin's attention was broken by a kick to the curtain and a gravelly shout from Dirk Kajerka.

"Hey, big guy, let's head 'er back to base!"

Merlin straightened, and in his most professional blimp pilot tone replied,

"Roger, captain. Setting a course for home."

"Good work. Carry on."

Merlin angled the blimp toward FUBAR as the carrying-on continued behind the curtain.

· *Twenty-two*

It makes perfect sense for June to be wedding season in temperate climes. A June wedding on Nantucket or in Vermont or the intramontane West can promise pleasant, still springtime weather. In the same way people in Honolulu and Miami watch holiday specials featuring snowy Christmas imagery from higher latitudes, Houston has traditionally done June weddings as if the region enjoyed the milder climates of more northerly and upland parts of the United States. Houston's humid heat has contributed to a steep rise in destination weddings in places like Aspen or San Miguel de Allende or Portofino that are not only beautiful but also promise reliable escapes from the steamy Gulf Coast. For classic June Houston weddings, however, the old school considers country clubs the ideal air-conditioned reception oases.

This Saturday night, Merlin found himself at one of the giant wedding receptions Bayou Boughs Country Club was so expert in producing. The bride's and the groom's families were both friends of the McNaughtons, and Merlin knew the couple, as he tutored them when they were in high school, so he made the guest list. He finished his second appetizer plate of roast beef on puffy rolls slathered in mayonnaise-y horseradish sauce and went to the bar at the corner of the big room. Shep Pasteur was pulling extra duty that night, working the wedding to pay for the latest improvements to his tricked-out vintage El Camino. As Merlin approached, Shep began to assemble his drink.

To prepare children for their future worlds of adult cocktailing, parents ordered Shirley Temples for their young daughters and Roy Rogers for their young sons. By the time they were preteens, they were well accustomed to the idea of a mixed drink. Merlin, however, never graduated to cocktails or the social skills of drinking them in the company of one's peers. He kept ordering Roy Rogers well into his teens, and by the time he hit twenty, Shep Pasteur decided that something needed to be done about this. Shep tweaked the ingredients; instead of Coca Cola, this concoction contained Dr Pepper, along with grenadine, lime, a dash of Peychaud's Bitters, and three maraschino cherries. Although the bitters contained alcohol, Shep put so few drops in the drink it still qualified as a mocktail. And he named the drink in Merlin's honor, eponymously after the nickname he'd given Merlin in his youth.

Merlin approached the bar, and Shep said with professional authority, "One Magic Man coming right up," never taking his eyes off the drink and each ingredient as he added it. Merlin accepted it and said, "Thank you." With a quick nod, Shep said, "Any time." Magic Man in hand, Merlin sidestepped the press of people at the bar and ambled toward the entrance hallway that gave onto the big room. He found a spot near the wall, and when he looked up after having a sip, he saw Lindley Acheson looking his way as she talked with a couple of young women. She smiled at him, and he returned the gesture. Lindley excused herself from her friends and moved toward Merlin. He noticed she was in high heels and a green dress with a slightly plunging neckline.

"Hi, Merlin!"

"Hi, Lindley! Are you enjoying the reception?"

"Yeah, you know, it's nice to see people you haven't talked to in a while."

"Yes, that's true. I talked with some kids I tutored when they were in middle school and high school. And the flowers at the church and here are beautiful! Did you have anything to do with that?"

Lindley smiled, blushed a little, and replied, "Yes, the bride's family called me in for a little consulting."

Merlin caught a glimpse of the blush continuing toward her décolletage.

"Well, they are very nice." Now it was his turn to blush. "I mean the flowers! Stunning arrangements and very striking color combinations!"

Lindley's blush deepened as she demurred, "It really wasn't that big of a deal, but thank you."

Two society dowagers approached, and the one closest to Lindley tapped her on the shoulder. "Lindley, dear, we have a botanical question for you. Could we trouble you for a moment?"

"Oh, sure! Sorry, Merlin. I'll catch up with you in a bit."

"By all means!" Merlin replied with a smile and all the graciousness that had been ingrained into him throughout his upbringing.

With Lindley's departure, he spotted what appeared to be the platonic ideal of a cold-boiled shrimp display. Its sculpted icy tiers glistened at him the way the graduated glass components of his armonica had just a few mornings earlier, but this artwork held the ne plus ultra of Texas cold seafood favorites—very large, perfectly shelled and deveined U10-U12 count wild-caught Gulf shrimp—each curling around the carefully crafted lips of several ice-sculpted bowls, with the bowls themselves containing more luscious crustaceans. As Merlin approached, he saw just how perfect they were, and in perfect complement below them, silver bowls of white remoulade, red cocktail sauce with a smaller bowl of horseradish at its side, and dozens of halved lemons covered with mesh cloth tied behind the skin of each one like a short ponytail.

Merlin picked up a pair of silver tongs and began to arrange the large shrimp on his cocktail plate. Instinctively, he chose to place them in a circular pattern with their tails pointing outward toward the edge of the plate. They created a design that looked as if it might start turning in a counterclockwise direction. On top of the center of the shrimp gyre, Merlin placed a single mesh-covered lemon half. He found a ramekin for the sauces and chose to divide the contents between remoulade and cocktail sauce, adding a little horseradish to the already piquant red cocktail sauce. He spotted a high table near a corner of the room by one of the rarely lit fireplaces. He began to enjoy his seafood inter-lude, holding each shrimp by the tail and dipping it in the sauce of his choosing on a bite-by-bite basis. The shrimp were so big, he could get two and sometimes three bites from each one. On the last bite of each he pinched the little shell by the tail and tugged with his incisors to pull away the last morsel of meat. As Merlin placed a de-shrimped tail on a plate near the ramekin, Rex Mondeaux walked by and stopped to greet him.

"Well, if it isn't the guy who whipped the blimp base into shape!"

Merlin quickly swallowed his last bite and managed a slightly muffled "Hello, Mr. Mondeaux!"

"Please, Merlin, call me Rex. We're professional colleagues now!"

With this statement, Merlin righted himself from his slump. "Mr. Rex?"

"No, just Rex, like your grandfather called me."

"Yessir, Rex."

"Good! Now, tell me how life is at the home of the *Airmadillo*."

Merlin made some noises that sounded like an attempt at lan-guage, but he couldn't get anything out. He then heard himself saying, "I like it. I find it inspiring."

"Inspiring, huh?"

Merlin was worried that he said the wrong thing, but Mondeaux assuaged his fears by jumping right back in with his good-natured banter: "Well, good! Let's hope a bunch of folks are inspired to change their electricity provider to Fandango Utilities!"

"Yes, sir, Rex!" Merlin got this line out so fluidly it seemed to him that it sounded like the banter of the fraternity boys in the room.

"That's right! Good work!"

A trio of bejeweled, designer-gowned women of a certain age beckoned Rex their way, and he excused himself. "Sorry. Gotta go!"

Rex Mondeaux winked, and Merlin nodded with a smile, again feeling like he was fitting in, even if just for a moment. As Rex angled toward the ladies, Merlin felt so confident he decided to move one table closer to the center of the room. Although it was another high four-top, which made it still seem somewhat peripheral, the stream of social interaction was flowing around him, regardless of the degree to which he remained a boulder in that waterway. A few people even said hello as they passed.

Just as he was feeling comfortable in his new forward position, he heard a group talking behind him—three male voices that sounded to be in their twenties or early thirties. They were the same three who had scoffed at him in the locker room after his chair broke.

"He probably still sleeps with a pacifier."

"Ha, yeah, like Baby Huey from those old cartoons!"

"His toilet is *prahbly* some industrial-sized setup, maybe rebar-reinforced concrete with hand grips on both sides."

"Yeah, he'd crush a regular one at one sitting."

"I hear a couple in the locker room have taken some wear and tear from him."

"Like cleaning up after a circus elephant."

"I feel sorry for whoever does his laundry."

"Don't go there, Chad."

Merlin knew they were talking about him and that they had positioned themselves so he could hear them clearly. He didn't know what to do, but he knew he felt uncomfortable, so he decided to fall back to his previous redoubt at the more remote table.

"Uh, oh, looks like he's moving."

"He oughta have one of those 'beep beep' beepers like garbage trucks when they're backing up."

Merlin took his Magic Man mocktail and pivoted to walk back toward the other table. A one-man army in retreat, he focused on his destination and tried to ignore the wiseacre voices behind him. He would not challenge them, but he would not give them the satisfaction of seeing his discomfort. He took one step and another, but on his third step his foot caught on something that, as he began to fall, he realized was a shoe—a man's dress shoe. Just as his fall started, a cocky, designer tux–clad young buck in front of him pronounced an over-acted "Oops!" and tossed all the red wine in his full glass squarely at Merlin's floor-bound pressed shirt and white dinner jacket. As Merlin tried to get his footing, his own drink went vertical, then plummeted and doused his jacket from behind. The glass didn't break, as this part of the room was carpeted, but down Merlin went with the full force of his tonnage. Later, nearby guests agreed they felt the floor shake when he hit and flattened against it.

Merlin rose. His white dinner jacket looked like Jackson Pollack had done a practice session on it. He focused exclusively on the exit door and moved toward it with single-minded resoluteness, not looking at a soul as he departed from the room and the building. He walked home in the sticky night, with the concoction covering him making it even stickier.

Shep saw the fall from the corner of his eye; he bowed his head and closed his eyes for a couple of seconds before taking the next drink order. When he looked again, Merlin was gone.

· *Twenty-three*

Tite Dûche reclined in the big leather chair in his grandiose office at Dûche Ovens and noticed a call on his silenced mobile phone. He recognized the number and answered.

The man on the other end of the line spoke with an accent. "The Indians are coming to the cowboys."

"How many?"

"Twenty-two."

"I thought there were supposed to be twenty-five."

"There were. Three fell asleep."

"Then put them in the dormitory when they get to the fort."

"At night?"

"Yes. Do it late. Feed the others and separate them."

"Consider it done."

"Good. Update me tomorrow."

"Okay, boss. Will do."

Tite touched the red disc on his phone that ended the call.

"Three out of twenty-five," Tite said aloud. A twelve percent attrition rate, he calculated on his phone. Not great, but not too bad—within the deal tolerances for the cost of doing business.

· *Twenty-four*

Merlin sat at his usual spot at the corner of the bar in the locker room at Bayou Boughs Country Club. He rested his gym-shoed feet on a support bar of the high barstool.

"Hey, Magic Man," Shep said, "you sportin' some fine kicks, *cher*!"

"I had to get them."

"Oh, yeah. The new rules. I know, but hey, I think you might be onto something good."

"Really?"

"Yeah, man, they suit you."

"They do?"

"Yes sir. Wouldn't say it if is wadn't true."

"I found them online."

Shep and Merlin looked at the giant untied white high-top basketball shoes embroidered with red Houston Rockets logos on the outside of their uppers at the ankles.

"An' you supportin' the home team at the same time."

"I found them on a fan site. They were pretty expensive."

"Hey, but they worth it. Like I said, they suit you."

Merlin's expression turned from dubious to hopeful, and he almost smiled.

The second stage of Merlin's Magic Mountain breakfast special arrived.

"Now, like I tole you, we're doin' this in courses now so nobody gets in trouble," Shep said in a low voice.

Merlin nodded. A few seconds passed, not enough time for the runner from the kitchen to completely clear Merlin's first course from the bar top beside him after placing the steaming hot plates from the tray in front of him. Tite Dûche emerged from a locker room hallway next to the bar, glaring at the plates, then at Merlin, and then at Shep.

"Hey, Chet!" Tite called to one of his cronies.

Chet Fettle looked up from his breakfast at one of the center-of-the-room tables.

"Mind coming over here?"

Fettle rose from his table and joined Tite beside the bar.

Dûche queried him: "Do you see this?"

Fettle nodded in grim silence. Tite glanced at Shep, then glared at Merlin and said, "This will be dealt with at the board level." Merlin looked back at Dûche in terrified silence as Shep lowered his head, now looking at his own shoes.

———

As a crescent moon waned above steaming Bayou Boughs, Merlin stood at his armonica, its glass discs spinning away from him. His hands hovered over the instrument for a pregnant moment, and with great deliberation and gravitas, he began to play the first part of the first movement of *Carmina Burana* by Carl Orff—*Fortuna Imperatrix Mundi: O Fortuna*. He sensed his world gyrating off its axis as he watched the graduated glass bowls turn, but this apprehension did not diminish the quality of his playing. If anything, it intensified the seriousness with which he approached the piece, its mournful strains filling the upper reaches of the observatory. The very walls, ceiling, and floor seemed to vibrate in sympathy with the foreboding tone of the iconic opera introduction.

As he was about to begin the second part of the first movement, *Fortune plango vulnera* (I lament the wounds Fortune deals), he heard a ding from the computer alerting him that an e-mail had arrived. He left his post at the armonica and went to his workstation. It may have been because it happened while he was playing O *Fortuna*, but the computer ding also seemed to have a foreboding timbre. The message was from Lyudmila Sukhova, marketing director of Fandango Utilities.

To: FUBAR Team
From: L. Sukhova, Dir., Mktg.
Subject: *Airmadillo* Repositioning

Fandango Utilities is opening new market in Midwest U.S. Also, two major golf tournaments will be in that region over remainder of summer. This is great opportunity for *Airmadillo* to highlight F U services and get extra exposure for company as aerial shot source for high-profile, nationally televised golf events.

    Airmadillo will remain in service in Greater Houston area until end of month at which time it will relocate to Ohio for rest of summer. Captain Dirk Kajerka will fly blimp to base outside of Akron where a full ground crew and maintenance unit is already in place serving other blimp, which will be relocated to New England until end of summer.

    Fandango Utilities will assign Houston ground and maintenance crew other tasks until end of summer. FUBAR offices will close for rest of summer on July 1st. Company will do its best to assign remaining office employees other tasks, but Fandango encourages them to find short-term work while blimp is gone. Management apologizes for the inconvenience, but we trust you will understand this great opportunity to open new market for increased corporate revenue must not be missed.

Sincerely,
L. Sukhova
P.S. Please direct any inquiries to HR.

Merlin's brow furrowed on reading the news and did not unfurrow thereafter. What would he do? The *Airmadillo* had become what New Agers might call his spirit vehicle, and he the spirit animal animating it. (If pressed, Dirk Kajerka might confide that he and Svetlana were really animating it, if not simply mating in it.) A young woman as attractive, worldly, and demure as Miss Slahtskaya could find compelling employment quickly, Merlin mused, but he guessed his skill set might be a bit more challenging to market. Additionally, the price of oil and gas remained low and was reflected in the still less-than-abundant monthly distributions from his trust. Perhaps Fandango Utilities could find something for him in its IT department. Still, the most important thing was the blimp. What would he do without the *Airmadillo* in his life on a regular basis? He knew that like a giant mechanical migratory waterfowl it would return in the fall, but still, he had become attached to the slow-moving, low-flying whale of an aircraft.

When this level of anxiety assaulted him out of nowhere, Merlin struck back with a tried-and-true antidote: an Axis Powers progressive dinner. Several years earlier, after a bout of anxiety over one of his cable TV channel's canceling reruns of *Xena, Warrior Princess*, he found himself on Westheimer Road, where he decided to let the 82 Metro bus spirit him where it would. The 82 runs up and down this east/west artery, and Merlin headed eastward toward the restaurant-dense zones of Montrose and Midtown. He spotted a Japanese place first, where he commanded a central position at the sushi bar, ordering the chef's omakase of the day, which consisted of a variety of nigiri featuring fish both standard and exotic. He then returned to the 82 and exited near a Neapolitan pizzeria, where he established a temporary beachhead and downed an order of gnocchi in a white truffle sage cream sauce after dispatching a medium-size pizza margherita. Not finished, he once again boarded the trusty 82, and after a few minutes disembarked for the third time, finding himself deployed at the doorway of a Bavarian restaurant, where his entrée included sauerbraten, bratwurst, sweet red cabbage, and Swiss-style rösti potatoes. A slice of Schwarzwälder kirchtorte à la mode rounded out his assault on the German position.

On this sad, humid June evening years after the first of several ensuing Axis Powers progressive dinners, Merlin's sweat-drenched march toward the nearest Westheimer Road bus stop helped take his mind off of his concerns, and his entry into the cool air-conditioned confines of the bus seemed to begin the process of focusing him on the mission at hand. As reliable as an infantryman's semiautomatic M82 anti-materiel rifle, the Houston Metro 82 bus remained the surefire answer for projecting his indomitable gustatory power toward this varied and formidable culinary triumvirate. A Japanese izakaya restaurant came into view; he steeled himself and focused as he prepared to once again vanquish the first of this unlikely trio of national cuisines.

· Twenty-five

That night Merlin slept without stirring for quite a while, but he awoke with a start in the wee hours. He looked at his phone: 3:33 a.m. His mouth was an arid cavern, so dry he couldn't swallow. He went to the refrigerator and focused on two full quart containers of hibiscus ginger tea sweetened with agave nectar. He quartered a lime and squeezed the juice into each container. He stirred and drank from one pitcher directly, completely draining it. Hydrated and wide awake, he was anxious for an update from the Agglomerator. He brought a glass and the remaining tea with him, situated himself before his three screens, and clicked the program to life.

The Agglomerator's warning panel flashed orange. He clicked on the Event Horizon window and saw a new message reading "Event Horizon—August." Merlin was intrigued and pleased his brainchild had continued to grind away—even as he slept—and was unwaveringly generating increasingly specific predictions. Additionally, the gyre moving over Houston appeared to be tightening and thickening. Merlin clicked on the Projected Gyre Track button, and a real-time animation played, showing the whorl just east of town, traversing downtown, and arriving at a stationary point west of the city's business hub.

Merlin turned to his right screen, and a button he named "Cryptid/Energy Event Nexi" caught his eye. He knew that energy events throughout recorded history were often accompanied by sightings of strange creatures. He had coded this part of the program to collect, slice, and dice data regarding this phenomenon. He was reading an account of werewolves roaming the Black Forest in late 1300s Bavaria after a freak summer snowstorm when he noticed the Sasquatch icon slowly pulsing in the corner of the right screen. He clicked on it, and a highlighted message read, "Sasquatch Nexus Possible." Seeing this alert caused a tingling sensation at the nape of his neck, where each curly hair felt as if it stood straight up.

He had always had an affinity for this allegedly mythical beast. The obvious connections were the dimensions and reported hirsuteness of the creature, but there were other, more subtle aspects that imparted a sense of kinship. Although immense, they were said to move deftly and stealthily through dense forests and over steep, craggy mountainsides. Additionally, they were reported to be telepathic, for instance, mentally communicating to humans who sighted them not to approach them too closely. Their keen attunement with their woodland worlds most attracted Merlin to these creatures, as he considered himself especially attuned to the energy of his own environment.

He had coded each cryptid with its own identifying color for the program—werewolves were silver, chupacabras were brown, and thunderbirds were black. The color he had chosen for Bigfoot was purple, doubtless alluding to what he considered the regal bearing of this legendary king of the forest. He looked back at the main central screen and noticed that the approaching gyre had a slight purple hue. "An energy event with a Sasquatch nexus. Very auspicious," he said with satisfaction. Then, just as suddenly as his neck fur had straightened, a heavy drowsiness overtook him. He rose and stumbled toward the bed.

He fell into a very deep sleep. Just before dawn, he began to dream intensely. He saw himself in the passenger pod of the *Airmadillo*, but instead of manning the pilot's seat or sitting in the passenger area, he was floating in midair inside the space in the flight position of a superhero, with his head facing the front windows and feet pointing backward. His arms were stretched perpendicular to his body. He was even larger in his midair dream position inside the blimp passenger compartment than he was in real life. When he angled his body to the right, the *Airmadillo* turned right; when he rotated his body to the left like a banking airplane, the blimp turned left. Lifting his chest and looking upward caused the airship to rise, and as he cast his gaze downward, raised his feet, and assumed a slight swan dive posture, it descended. To accelerate, Merlin swept his arms backward, and to slow down, he moved them forward, turning his palms toward the windows of the cockpit.

He saw himself as somewhat akin to a Third-Stage Guild Navigator from Frank Herbert's *Dune*, but instead of finding himself suspended in massive amounts of transformative orange spice mélange, the air surrounding Merlin seemed to be suffused with a faint mist of seasoned crawfish boil water, its madder brown tint providing him with whiffs of cayenne, garlic, onion, black pepper, and a host of other South Louisiana seasonings. He could smell the pungent spices, but they caused his eyes neither to burn nor to precipitate tears.

He then saw himself as a much larger floating mass filling the giant envelope of the blimp itself and taking up the space where its helium ballonets should have been. The same crawfish boil mist surrounded him, but it seemed slightly denser. Additionally, the fore part of the blimp's skin was transparent, providing him with a huge view of the sky and landscape. It was like the blimp had been circumcised, but a transparent skin remained at the fore of the craft.

The same body movements that directed the blimp from the passenger pod also worked for Merlin in his supersize, blimp-filling mode, but the results of his actions seemed more immediate, more dramatic, and maybe more graceful than they were in the passenger pod. The *Airmadillo* responded instantly to his movements, with no delay from the blimp pilot's promptings of rudders and elevators as in the real world. His body moved forward, and his face was near the transparent front of the blimp, just the way the Guild Navigator Oberon floated forward in his glass-encircled container to speak with the Padishah Emperor Shaddam Corrino IV in the David Lynch version of *Dune*, but, as far as Merlin could tell, his body had not morphed into a grotesque shape like the navigator of the classic science fiction tale. He was just a proportionate, blimp-size version of his already substantial earthly self.

He was enjoying swoops, climbs, and steeply banked turns in this mode when he suddenly found himself floating once again as the formerly smaller version of his larger self in the passenger and pilot pod of the *Airmadillo*. Now the madder brown of the crawfish boil mist had become so dense it was almost liquid, and as he brought his arms and hands forward, he registered with horror that they were no longer arms and hands but the giant red pincers of a gargantuan crawfish. Even greater existential terror ensued when he looked back toward his legs and feet. They, too, had been transformed and were no longer legs and feet but the large, muscular downward- and inward-curling tail of a super-size crawfish. He flicked his tail slightly and moved backward a few feet in a quick, jerking motion. He then used his right claw to feel his face. Had it changed, too? He sensed the contours of his own familiar mug and was relieved he had not been completely morphed into a mudbug.

His relief was as short lived as the bright burning fire of a shard of ignited flash paper, however, as when he looked forward into the dark opacity of the seasoned mist, he could make out a menacing figure heading directly toward him. The first things he saw were violently snapping crawfish pincers, not as big as his own, but supersize just the same. On seeing this, he swam backward reflexively, but the most horrifying aspect of this claw-flailing assailant was about to appear.

Where the head of the crawfish should have been was that of N. Teitel Dûche V. He was wearing a stylish pair of designer faux tortoiseshell eyeglasses. A sea-green cashmere pullover sweater was tied with studied casualness around Tite's neck, with the body of the sweater draping most of the top of the hard carapace of his cephalothorax. Tite's lips were pursed in rigid determination, and his eyes burned with rage as he angled both of his snapping pincers toward Merlin's vulnerable, non-exoskeletally-protected face and neck.

As Crawfish Tite moved within striking distance, Crawfish Merlin flicked his tail with all his might and shot backward several feet. He saw the pincers relentlessly approaching him and flicked his tail again, but after moving backward a couple of feet, the hard chitin of the posterior dorsal segments covering his abdomen and the powerful musculature enabling swift backward movement rammed into the much harder metal arc of the interior of a seafood boiling pot, causing a terrible clanging that woke him with a start. Eyes wide open on the bed with his heart racing, Merlin lifted his arms and held his hands in front of him. To his great relief, they were no longer giant pincers but the familiar puffy paws he knew as his own. Additionally, he was covered in sweat. After he wiped his brow and eyes with his fingers and the heels of his hands, he looked at the liquid sheen on them. It glistened with the slightest of reddish-brown tinges.

· *Twenty-six*

Svetlana, Dirk, and Merlin stood in a solemn triangle outside the passenger pod of the blimp. Dirk cleared his throat and began to speak in a tone almost as serious as the one he used the night he cut off Merlin's shirttail after the trip home from the coast. "Okay, as we all know, this is the last Houston mission for the *Airmadillo* before its scheduled return in the fall. I am already preparing for the overland repositioning flight to Akron."

Tears formed at the corners of Svetlana's eyes.

"We need to make the most of it," Dirk continued. And then, unable to contain himself, a smirk emerged; the left and the right outer whiskers of the mustache twitched in turn as he winked at Svetlana and said, "I know some of us will!"

All of her Slavic steeliness depleted, Svetlana rested her head on Dirk's shoulder and began to cry buckets as he put his arm around her. Merlin was confounded by this display and felt even more anxiety than he had just thinking this was the last flight of the summer and that he was bringing a full complement of devices in as discreet a black nylon side pack as he could find.

They boarded the *Airmadillo*, Dirk helping the distraught Svetlana into the passenger compartment, then holding the door open for Merlin.

"Hey, whatchoo got in the bag, junior birdman?" Dirk asked.

The question surprised Merlin and was particularly unsettling as he was in medias res boarding the blimp. Eyes wide and dumbfounded, he attempted an explanation, but all he could do was look at the black heavy-duty zipper on the side pack and say, "Zipper!" Immediately the idea of food came to him and he said, "Snacks!"

"Zipper snacks, huh? Well, okay, we've got some of our own zipper snacks in the back, too!" rejoined the captain.

The mustache gave a quick double twitch, and Dirk winked at Merlin with his signature fiendish grin. With a professional-sounding "All aboard!" he gestured for the big man to take a seat inside. As Dirk boarded he said with military frankness, "Alright, last mission. Remember, team, we need to make the most of it." As he settled into the pilot's seat to prepare for takeoff he said under his breath, "I know *I* will."

The *Airmadillo* was freed once again from its terrestrial bonds. In her seat in the rear of the passenger pod, Svetlana tried to fix her mascara with the aid of a small lighted mirror plucked from her Dolce and Gabbana clutch. Merlin sprawled across a seat in the fore of the passenger area and tried to savor all the wonder of blimp takeoff as he knew this was a special mission.

When they were at cruising altitude, Dirk handed off flight duties to Merlin, and as usual, he joined Svetlana in the aft of the passenger compartment where she had arranged antique tortoise-shell caviar spoons, two small silver glasses for vodka, and two champagne flutes. From a cooler Dirk had loaded before take-off, she removed a container of beluga caviar from the Caspian Sea. She had a plastic container with freshly baked blini. On ice in the cooler was a bottle of Perrier-Jouët champagne and a small bottle of Stolichnaya vodka. In a nod to local customs she had observed, there were also a few half-sized bottles of Topo Chico sparkling mineral water from northern Mexico for palate-clearing purposes. "Wow! What a spread!" Dirk enthused before snapping the curtain shut and leaving Merlin once again alone and unsupervised at the controls.

Merlin followed the preprogrammed flight plan on the GPS

map, heading east above Westheimer Road toward the Galleria. As he approached the sprawling monument to consumerism, he carefully removed the thumb drive containing the approved Fandango Utilities marketing messages and inserted his own. He had taken time to embellish his slogans with what he considered compelling complementary graphics. Preceding and following his messages, colorful spinning gyres that looked kind of like animated moving versions of the static symbols for hurricanes scrolled and tracked across the big screen in the night sky. Merlin considered a couple of his favorites as the huge words scrolled down the blimp's illuminated skin:

Solstice approaches! Steel yourselves
as the gyre tightens!
Urgent Notice to Houstonians!
Energy vortex reversal imminent!

The messages continued to scroll, and Merlin took shallow breaths, hoping no one from the Fandango Utilities marketing department would see them. The blimp traversed the airspace above Montrose Boulevard and approached Midtown.

Just like one of the 82 Metro buses turning left onto Louisiana Street toward downtown but riding smoothly aloft, with steady pressure on the left foot pedal Merlin initiated a similar turn in the direction of the great steel and glass temples to commerce in the city's central business district. Hoping he might connect with some brave souls out strolling in the spirit-wilting weather, he banked the outside screen toward the ground as more messages cascaded down its surface.

Energy dissipation must cease!
Defeat the negative energy cyclone!
Prepare to vanquish the negative gyre!

The Astros were on the road, and except for some activity around the theater district, downtown looked quiet, although he did note a few floors of skyscrapers lighted for cleaning crews, and a few offices where, even in this low-energy time of year, some hungry young capitalists were burning the midnight oil in hopes of making names, if not fortunes, for themselves. The assigned advertising route was complete, and as the *Airmadillo* crossed Buffalo Bayou at Allen's Landing, Merlin continued northward and fumbled for the tech gear in his side pack. The pack began to spill its contents toward the cockpit floor, but he caught the first device before it tumbled out and carefully placed it along with the others on the flat surface above the airship's instrument panel. He'd brought everything he considered might be germane to the mission: night vision goggles with a camera attachment; a heat sensor that attached to his smart phone and could detect variations in heat and cold at great distances; and his energy-detection device embedded in a ball cap.

As he angled toward the address to which Tite had driven his Porsche, what looked like fog came into view. As the *Airmadillo* neared the house, he realized it was not fog, but smoke. Merlin slowed the vehicle and used the GPS in his smart phone to fly directly to the address. He dived as low as he thought he could without getting in trouble and turned off the airship's headlights outside the passenger pod. On arriving at the address, he further slowed the blimp and held it in a tight circle as he donned the military-grade night vision goggles/camera apparatus.

Looking down at the small compound, he noticed immediately that the smoke was coming from something that looked industrial, like a pipe, and the metal building from which it protruded looked utilitarian, like some kind of small warehouse or storage room. When he had a good view of the smokestack, he took still images and video of it. He then noticed someone leading a group of people from one building in the compound to another. Someone walking behind the line of people had a rifle. He kept the camera rolling and captured video of the group.

He knew he needed to work fast not to arouse suspicion, so he doffed the night vision goggles and grabbed his smart phone. He attached the heat sensor to the bottom of the phone and pulled up its corresponding app. When he aimed the sensor in the direction of the compound he saw several heat signatures. Someone led another group to a waiting vehicle, and he could see the heat their bodies produced on his phone screen. But by far the most intense heat signature emanated from the chimney pipe and the end of the building directly beneath it. Merlin was astounded to see that the app indicated that the thermal detector had basically red-lined past the highest temperature it was capable of registering. He took a picture of the reading with his phone and saved it to his photo album.

The curtain separating him from the passenger section protruded briefly with the impression of an elbow or the heel of a foot, breaking Merlin out of his wonder at the intense heat reading. He pulled the blimp out of its holding pattern and turned the elevator wheel backward with his right hand to gain altitude as he pushed forward the throttle control with his left hand to increase the airship's ground speed. This maneuver may have caused the next kick or elbow to the curtain as a disheveled Dirk quickly poked his head through the side of the curtain to ask, "Everything okay up here, ace?" Quickly recovering from the shock of the unexpected inquiry, Merlin replied, "Oh! Yes! I have us on a direct course for FUBAR. Is that okay?"

"Right-o," replied Dirk as his uncharacteristically haywire mop of pilot hair disappeared behind the curtain.

Merlin straightened himself in the pilot's seat with one great inhalation and exhalation and leveled off the *Airmadillo* at its standard cruising altitude and speed. A few minutes after he turned the elevator wheel downward to begin the initial descent toward FUBAR, the curtain opened and a once again professional-looking Captain Dirk Kajerka sidled toward the front. Merlin hoisted himself from his beloved place at the helm of the *Airmadillo* and squeezed past Kajerka as they traded places. Before he flopped onto a seat at the fore of the passenger area,

Merlin noticed Svetlana on the bench seat in the aft of the craft. She was sitting on it lengthwise with her back to a window and her ankles crossed in front of her. She gave the giant interim pilot a quick look and returned to scrutinizing her fingernails as she vaped an e-cigarette.

· *Twenty-seven*

Merlin arrived home very late that evening. He had been at FUBAR since early morning and was dog tired. He asked the Alles driver to go to a Whataburger drive-through on the way home for a triple-meat, triple cheeseburger with bacon, grilled onions, and jalapeños. He bought two orders of fries—one for himself and one for the driver—and snacked on a few fries on the way home. He decided to take his meal in the kitchen of the main residence where there was a large refrigerator with a full complement of condiments. Normally, Merlin got the mail and sorted it on the way through the house to his observatory, but this evening, with his appetite in command, he picked it up from the floor beneath the mail slot and placed it on a front hall desk on the way to his feasting post atop a high barstool at the kitchen counter.

He turned on the kitchen television. There were lions in Africa attacking and tearing apart an unfortunate impala. Merlin eyed his Whataburger with an equal degree of savage focus and determination. First, however, he went to the fridge to make a concoction. He mixed mayonnaise, yellow mustard, and a little Pickapeppa sauce in a bowl. He then opened the top of the burger and lathered the underside of the bun with a generous glob of the sauce. His first bite was pure bliss. He applied a little more of the sauce to each successive bite as he held the paper-cradled Whataburger at a high angle almost perpendicular to the countertop surface to keep his prized sauce from dripping. More waves of bliss ensued as he watched a lion tear a hunk of bloody flesh from the hindquarters of its kill.

He spooned some of his concoction into a ramekin, added a bit of ketchup, and stirred. This became the dipping station for french fries on their journey over the well-worn terrain of his taste buds. Judiciously, he began to intersperse handfuls of fries between every other burger bite, ensuring they remained warm while he ate them. There was nothing as unwise as getting too enthralled with the main event of the burger itself and disregarding the fries until the end of the meal when they have grown cool and their flavor value has declined precipitously. His feast complete and feeling full beyond satiety, Merlin wadded up the burger paper, Whataburger bag, and french fry container and threw them into the kitchen garbage can. He rinsed the bowls and spoons and wiped away any telltale residue from the counter.

He waddled back to the front hall and retrieved the mail from the little entryway table where he had left it. He sorted it by recipient—the important-looking pile added to a larger pile to be sent via air express next week to Mickey in Amsterdam and the more humble pile with a couple of catalogues interspersed for himself. The first thing he noticed was an envelope addressed to him on Bayou Boughs Country Club stationery. It didn't have a cellophane window with the address showing through like a monthly bill. The stationery stock was heavier than that used for any communication he had ever seen from the club excepting the monthly newsletter, which wasn't stationery, after all. He slit the top of the envelope open with a paring knife and pulled the single sixty-pound-stock folded page from it. He opened it and read the words beneath the BBCC emblem.

Mr. McNaughton:

Because of your Continued and Flagrant Violations of Bayou Boughs Country Club Rules & Regulations, the

Board of Directors has been faced with no other choice than to suspend you from Membership in the Club for a period of not less than Six Months, beginning immediately. After this time has elapsed, the board may consider your reinstatement at its convenience.

Sincerely,
N. Teitel Dûche V
President and Chairman of the Board of Directors,
Bayou Boughs Country Club

The letter was signed with Tite Duche's official signature, not the glib and unctuously chummy "Tite" that ended his monthly updates. The *V* signifying "the fifth" at the end of the signature seemed to be etched onto the page with malicious force. It was a dagger, and it stabbed Merlin right in the heart.

He sat staring at the letter and felt a sinking feeling unlike any he had ever experienced in all his days. Nausea ensued, and he felt his Whataburger on the verge of convulsing its way up his esophagus. It did an about-face, threatened the valves of Houston at the other end of his alimentary canal, and desisted. He placed the open letter on his kitchen counter and rested his forehead, now covered with a cold sweat, on top of it. In a couple of minutes, the nausea subsided enough for him to gather his mail and himself and exit the main house for his observatory.

Looking at his feet, Merlin trudged up the stairs to the observatory. The room was dark, but as he neared the top of the stairway, he could see that the Agglomerator was once again flashing bright orange. He looked toward it on entering the room, but before he stepped closer to see the latest message, he noticed the same orange light was glinting back at him from the floor. Shards of glass were reflecting the warning color onto the walls of the observatory, and Merlin gave his signature perplexed look—the golden retriever with head cocked sideways. He took a few more steps to reach the light switch. When he flipped it on and saw the room, he took a step backward and then another.

Glass chunks and shards of varying sizes were all over the place, but they were most concentrated in the space dedicated to his beloved glass armonica, which was now smashed to smithereens. The intruder did a very thorough job, not just obliterating all the instrument's spinning cylinders but also dismembering the structure of the apparatus that held them. As for the armonica's motor, it looked like someone had taken a sledgehammer to it. The window behind it was shattered.

Still clutching his mail, Merlin took another step backward and wilted onto the floor. He sat with his back against one of his galley kitchen's cabinets in one of the few glass shard–free spots of his cherished home. He couldn't think. He could barely breathe. He just stared at the devastation. After several minutes had elapsed, the only thing he could think to do was to call Bayou Boughs Patrol, which he did with a kind of mindless, zombie-like deliberateness. When an officer answered, it took everything Merlin had to try to get some words out. Finally, in a stunned monotone, he managed to utter, "Hello? Yes. I would like to report an incident." When he finished the call, his valves of Houston once again began to falter. He looked like a defeated sumo wrestler as he got to his feet and bolted for the bathroom.

· *Twenty-eight*

Late the following morning, Merlin awakened groggy and disoriented. The officers' questions and inspection of the scene had taken quite some time. Bayou Boughs Patrol arrived first; they called the Houston Police Department to take fingerprints and lodge an official burglary and vandalism report. By the time it was all over, it was almost 3 a.m. Other than the destruction of the armonica and the broken window, everything else seemed to be in place. Merlin's antique astrolabes and sextants still dangled from the ceiling undisturbed.

This was a case of quick-strike break-in and destruction of property. The neighborhood patrolmen and the officers from HPD admitted that this case was unlike anything they had seen or even heard about as far as burglaries in Bayou Boughs went. Usually in this neighborhood, the wife's jewelry was gone and maybe some free-standing electronic devices. The husband's hunting rifles and shotguns were also typical stolen items. Additionally, the officers had never seen a residence quite like Merlin's observatory. They marveled as much at the strange living space as they did at the unusual crime after Merlin explained to them what a glass armonica was, that Benjamin Franklin had invented it, et cetera.

"Whoever did this knew what he was doing," said one of the officers.

The cop with the fingerprinting kit said, "Yep, not a print in sight."

At that point Merlin remembered his outdoor mounted camera and said, "Oh, officers, I think I may have the perpetrator on video!"

Merlin, the patrolmen, and the HPD officers watched the video and saw a man completely covered from head to toe in black, including black gloves. He had a small backpack he opened to produce a heavy-headed hammer to smash the casement window glass and enter the observatory.

"Doesn't do much for us," the officer with the fingerprinting kit said.

"Nope," the other officer agreed. "Wearing a ninja suit during a Houston summer! This guy was hard-core. Operated like a pro."

The officers had Merlin sign the incident report, and all offered their condolences to him on the loss of his beloved armonica.

With the summer sun glinting through the observatory's blinds as he lay on the bed, Merlin reflected on his exchanges with the officers. The room took on a strange, soulless orderliness as the police and patrolmen had helped him clean up the broken stuff. They took the bigger chunks as evidence. They had even helped him tape a plastic bag to the casement window frame, and now the observatory was back to its icy-cool, air-conditioned state—cool enough to chill a big man, a very hairy big man.

He looked at the place where the glass armonica had been intact just a few hours earlier. How could this be? He thought that if he had only been at home, it would not have happened, but the final *Airmadillo* night flight of the summer was a long one, especially with the added time for surveillance above the strange compound that Tite Dûche's Porsche frequented. On a morning he would have normally worked up an appetite shuffling to the club for breakfast, thanks to President Dûche, he couldn't. And he couldn't lament that situation with a baleful dirge on his armonica, either. He was truly hamstrung, manacled by the callous dictates of bad fortune.

After performing his morning ablutions, which became simultaneous ablutions of mourning, Merlin sensed that he needed to get out of the house as soon as possible. He didn't even call for an Alles car or finish tying his bootlaces. He just marched toward the street. He had to leave behind the scene of the crime, at least for a while.

Looking downward as he emerged onto the sidewalk in front of the house, he noticed a new crack was forming. "Probably buckling from the heat," he mumbled aloud to no one. "Merlin!" someone called from up the street. He looked up and saw Lindley approaching on a retro Schwinn bicycle with a wire basket attached to its handlebars. Two bunches of just-picked roses lay crosswise inside the basket. The bottoms of each bunch were swaddled in damp kitchen towels.

The instant she saw Merlin's face, she knew something was wrong. He didn't say her name and smile like he usually did when they met. He just gave her a sad, silent look, like he was asking for something. As she coasted to a stop next to him on the street and put out her right foot to balance on the curb, she asked, "What's wrong?" Merlin's brow furrowed, and as he tried to get words out, he pointed at the plastic-covered broken window.

"You were burglarized?" Lindley asked.

Merlin looked back at her and nodded. Then he managed to produce speech, but only haltingly. "They smashed it," he said.

"What? The window?" Lindley queried.

"Yes, but, also the armonica," Merlin replied.

"The instrument you play to make that beautiful music?"

"Yes."

"They damaged it?"

"Smashed."

"They broke it?"

"Destroyed. Smashed into pieces."

"Oh, Merlin! I loved listening when the sound carried to my back garden!"

Merlin received and mirrored her gaze in mute despair.

"And especially when I passed by your place while you were playing."

"You did?" Merlin asked with a bit of the surprised golden retriever look. He noticed a glimmer in her green eyes, and it sparked a flicker of hope in his own.

"Who would do such a thing?" Lindley continued.

"Someone who doesn't like my playing, I guess."

"I can't imagine. I think your playing is inspired."

"You do?"

"Yes, I do."

Lindley looked at her watch. "Oh, I'm late."

"You are?"

"Yes, Chloris Godley, a friend of my parents, is recovering from surgery, and I'm taking her some roses."

"Oh," Merlin said.

"But here."

Lindley chose two of the fullest blooms in the bunches and offered the long-stem roses to Merlin. "But," she began, and before she could say "be careful," Merlin had reached for and taken the thorny stems. He closed his meaty mitt around them and immediately winced and said, "Ow!" Blood was oozing from a thorn prick to the palm of his right hand. He carefully shifted the stems to his left hand as he looked at the fresh puncture.

"Oh, shoot!" Lindley exclaimed. "I was going to tell you to be careful! Wait! I have something."

Lindley took a pair of gardening shears from the courier bag at her side and cut a strip from a bandanna tied to the bicycle basket. She used the remaining large piece of bandanna cloth to wipe Merlin's palm. She wet her fingers with saliva and wiped away the blood. Then she very swiftly and deftly tied the cloth strip around his hand, covering the wound. Merlin watched the whole operation with amazement that turned into gratitude.

She looked him in the eye and said, "Put pressure on your palm with your other hand."

"Okay," Merlin offered with the empty, guileless eyes of the bereft.

As Lindley got back on her bike, she said, "I'm so sorry, Merlin."

He said, "Thank you, Lindley. And thank you for the roses."

Something he couldn't articulate moderated his despair as he noticed how the sunlight fell on the nape of her neck and her right shoulder.

Lindley smiled and rode away. Merlin stood with his left thumb pressing down on his right palm and kept a delicate hold on the roses between his left fingers and the back of his right hand. He looked down the street and saw Lindley rounding a curve and pedaling out of sight. He then looked back at the vibrant deep crimson of the two roses, forgetting for a moment the sting in his palm.

· *Twenty-nine*

Merlin looked up again to the place where Lindley had disappeared around the bend of the street and saw a dark-colored vehicle rounding it in the opposite direction and moving toward him. Before he could make out what kind of car it was, he heard the low rumble of its engine and then its horn sounding several short blasts. Could the honking be for him? He stood wondering with his signature quizzical look, then recognized the vehicle was a black El Camino. The only person Merlin knew with an El Camino was his friend, erstwhile defender, and recent coconspirator in the breaking of a new Bayou Boughs Country Club rule—Shep Pasteur.

The El Camino slowed, and the driver's side window lowered. Shep called to him. "Hey, Merlin!" Shep pulled over to the curb, and Merlin crossed the street to talk with him. Merlin's expression telegraphed a clear signal to the long-suffering Cajun.

"What the problem is, *cher*?"

"They smashed it."

"Smashed what?"

"My armonica."

"A harmonica?"

"No, the instrument I play. The glass armonica."

"Oh, you mean dat fancy spinning glass contraption that make such pretty music?"

"Yes. They are rare and difficult to procure. Benjamin Franklin invented it."

"I know. I remember you telling me about it and then playing me a recording of you playing it. So, it's broken?"

"It's utterly demolished, Shep. Someone broke into the observatory last night before I got home and destroyed it."

"Oh, man, that's terrible! I'm so sorry, *cher*. Who would do such a thing?"

"Someone who hates me, I guess. All I saw on my security camera was a guy completely covered in a ninja suit and gloves."

"A ninja suit?"

"I guess that's what it was."

"It was even worse because it came right after I got some bad news."

"And what was that?"

"I got a formal letter from the board suspending my membership."

"That ain't right. You never hurt no one or called nobody names or nothin'. Magic Man always mind his own business and polite to everyone. I'm sorry, and I'm sorry times two, *cher*, but if it's any consolation to you, that makes two of us."

"Two? It does?"

"You and me. That's why I'm riding this way on your street this time of day. They told me not to show up for ten days and not to count on any pay for that time either. Now how long they get you for?"

"Six months."

"Six months! That's not a suspension! That's a sentence! Hell, suspendin' Merlin McNaughton 'cause he eat a big hearty breakfast oughta be a crime. The suspenders are the ones who oughta be suspended!"

Merlin hung his head. Whenever Shep saw Merlin in this state, he usually tried to think fast to buoy him up, at least a little.

"An' the blimp done flown to Iowa?"

"Ohio."

"Whatever. I mix 'em up. They sound like the same kinda cold place to me. Either way, it's a long way from Houston."

"Yes," Merlin said.

"An' the company still han't found you any other work?"

"Not so far."

"Then I got a plan."

"A plan?"

"Yes, sir, a plan."

"What's the plan, Shep?"

"The plan is Lumbeaux Jump."

"Your hometown?"

"Callin' it a town is a little bit of a stretch, but yeah. It's gonna be our base of operations."

"Operations?"

"With hook and line."

"Fishing from Lumbeaux Jump?!" Merlin's droopy face brightened.

"Dat's right, *cher*. Seeing as you and me got no work to go to an' the moon's new an' I jus' got a report from ma sweet cousine that the fish are active, I don't see a whole lotta other options for us."

"Oh! Okay! What do I need to do?"

"All you gotta do is bring whatever tackle you want and any rods. I got everything down there anyway—extra rods and reels, lures, shad heads and tauts, topwaters, swivels, leaders, *tout ça.*"

"Oh, okay, I have some stuff. Should I bring snacks?"

"Hey, Magic Man, we goin' to the *land* of snacks. On top of that, you know the Black Ghost flies down the highway. Before you can say *loup-garou,* we'll be crossed that Sabine River and pickin' us up a big sack full o' boudin links that'll do us all the way to da Jump."

"Ooooh!" Merlin became bemused imagining a bag full of

authentic, spicy boudin links. He asked, "Can we have sauce with them, too?"

"Hell, yeah," Shep countered, "hot sauce, pickles, onions, whatever."

"Oh, wow, Shep. Wow. Thank you."

"Hey, what friends do? Dey look out for each one another, hey what?"

"I always wanted to go over and fish in that part of Louisiana."

"Well, even though the sky looks a little dark here, you got a silver lining shining just to the east. Now I can't guarantee anything. We all know that's why it's called fishing and not catching, but we gone give it the best shot we got."

"When should I be ready?"

"How 'bout day afta tomorrow?"

"Okay!"

"An' I spec we stay for five or four days so we can hit a few different spots."

"Okay."

"Ma sweet cousine say they got some big trout bitin', and the bull reds ain't shy neither."

"Ooooohhhh!" Merlin responded with a faraway look toward the sky.

"Now all you gotta do is get yourself together an' we go."

"Okay. I'll get ready."

"An' I see you half pass eight in the morning here day afta tomorrow."

Shep gave a little half-salute of a wave from his left brow and put the same hand on top of the steering wheel as he eased away down the street. He raised the window and adjusted his reflective wraparound fisherman's sunglasses. Turning the corner at the end of the street, he stepped on the gas and let the 454-horsepower engine roar within earshot of Tite Dûche's faux Tudor manse.

· *Thirty*

In his office at Dûche Ovens, Tite Dûche wadded a one-piece black bodysuit into a ball and tossed it into a trash can in a corner of the room. His mobile phone buzzed. He touched the answer button and said, "Yes." As he walked to his desk, he said, "I'll check that right now." And then, "They'll make a delivery tomorrow night. Russian-flagged vessel."

Tite listened for a moment and said, "Yes. I'll call after the drop." He thumbed the red end call button without saying goodbye.

· *Thirty-one*

Shep had filled a big ice chest in the truck bed on the driver's side of the El Camino in an attempt to offset his passenger's weight, but this tactic was to little avail as Merlin caused the vehicle, even with all of its state-of-the-art springs and shock absorbers, to list toward the right lanes of the interstate. Shep couldn't put a larger ice chest in the rear of the vehicle because its bed, at seventy-five by forty-eight inches, was just big enough to place a few seven-and-a-half-foot fishing rods on the diagonal across it with less than an inch to spare. (The diagonal of the El Camino bed was almost ninety-one inches and the rods and attached reels spanned ninety inches.) The use of space was actually pretty elegant, and it sectioned the El Camino's truck bed into discrete compartments for various fishing-related supplies and gear.

From the rear, the look of the vehicle on the highway was a bit cartoonish—a souped-up but not flashy vintage El Camino with the dual exhausts and covered bed looking muscular while leaning to the passenger side like an unevenly loaded barge. Everything else was the soul of bayou cool. There were no garish flame decals or brightly colored effects on the vehicle. The only appliqué was at the center of the rear window, a fleur-de-lis composed of redfish and trout. It said Cajun fisherman, and that's who Shep was.

They motored eastward past petrochemical plants and refineries, crossed the Trinity and the Old & Lost Rivers, then moved into a blank lowland prairie as they approached Beaumont. A truck slowed in front of him, and Shep signaled with his left blinker. He gripped the classic eight-ball knob atop the Hurst shifter, jammed the Nixon-era muscle car down a gear, and mashed on the gas. The big 454 roared, sending Merlin backward in his seat like an astronaut in one of the 20-G centrifuge training machines down at NASA. The El Camino rocketed into the left lane, leaving the eighteen-wheeler and slower traffic behind them in a cloud of exhaust.

During the powerful acceleration Merlin flattened to his bucket seat and overhung it like one of those droopy pocket watches in Salvador Dalí's *The Persistence of Memory*. When the Black Ghost leveled off at a considerably higher speed in the left lane of the interstate and Merlin reassumed his usual shape, he said, "Wow, Shep, this vehicle has considerable power."

"You can say that again, Magic Man."

"How much horsepower?" Merlin queried.

"She got a LS6 turbo jet 454 under the hood."

"And was that flap that popped open on the hood for the carburetor?"

"You got that right, too. Dat little flap is what you call a cowl induction hood. It forces the air right into the Holley 4150 four barrel. Got a vacuum secondary that kicks in the second two of the four barrels when I ask the ghost to fly. Got a Erson 120320 flat tappet camshaft with a dual valve spring, a Mallory dual point distributor wit' a Accel super coil and yellow solid-core ignition wires, a Muncie M21 transmission. What else you wanna know?"

"What about the differential?"

"Ain't no sissy factory ten-bolt. Da Black Ghost got a big, fat twelve-bolt differential. Big ring and pinion inside make it some kinda strong."

"What's the ratio on the differential?"

Shep turned to Merlin with a quick, slightly miffed glance and just as quickly resumed his even-tempered concentration on the fast lane.

"Twenty year ago I had a 4.11 cause I liked it to pop off the line, but I changed it out to a 3.55 cause I wanted the Ghost to move real smooth-like on this here Hi-10."

"And how much does the Black Ghost weigh?"

"Well, when it's just me and a full tank and no cargo in the back, she run about 4100 pound."

"How big is the gas tank?"

"Twenty gallon."

"And the horsepower is 454?"

"You got it."

Merlin stared forward intently through his thick round eyeglass lenses. "So, it would probably do a quarter mile in between 11.80 and 11.95 seconds."

Shep whipped his head around to Merlin and looked at him in shock.

"Not just probably, but exactly! Last time I checked, she clock in a quarter at exactly 11.87 seconds. How'd you do that?!"

"I just made the calculations and compensated for the weight of the fuel and an average driver."

Shep put his attention on the fast lane again, and his shocked countenance now hosted a wry, satisfied smile.

"Dat's why they call you the Magic Man."

Merlin just sat expressionless, looking forward down the interstate.

"I think all dat calculation work calls for a little music. We on vacation anyway, *cher*. You like Clifton Chenier?"

"Zydeco?"

"Yeah, you right!"

"Sure!"

Shep cued up "Hot Rod" by the legendary Zydeco king and turned up the volume as the punchy, driving, freight train beat hustled them toward the Louisiana border.

· *Thirty-two*

Mickey McNaughton sat at the bar at Mossel & Gin in the converted Westergasfabriek complex in Amsterdam. He was enjoying his second artisanal gin and tonic and looking around the web on his laptop. He checked his e-mail and scrolled backward to an unopened message from Merlin. He shrugged and decided to click on it. He was Merlin's trustee, after all, and even though Merlin's messages were often tedious, it was only right that he at least read them. Besides, the egging affair captured his attention, especially now that he knew Titey Dûche was the culprit.

Mickey opened the e-mail and read.

Dear Mickey:

I don't mean to bother you, and I thank you for taking time to read this.

The observatory was broken into through a window. The intruder destroyed my armonica, but it does not appear that he committed robbery. Also, just before I ascended to my abode and refuge, I opened a letter the purport of which was suspending me from the club for six months.

I implore you for your confidentiality in what I am about to tell you, as it involves some actions on my part that might be considered well beyond the pale of the good citizenship our forebears instilled in us.

Mickey read about the tracking device and Merlin's flights to the property in Northeast Houston. When he read the details of the last night flight, his mood changed from slightly annoyed to intrigued. He responded to Merlin with a terse, but civil reply.

Merlin: so sorry to hear about the break-in and the suspension.

So, just want to confirm with you that you have my complete confidentiality regarding the details of the flights.

Best and wishing you well, right?
Mickey

He looked at his watch. It was still morning in Houston. After paying the tab, he walked to his apartment a few blocks away and placed a call to his friend Jim Atlas in the office of the Harris County District Attorney.

· Thirty-three

The Black Ghost crossed the Texas–Louisiana line on the bridge over the Sabine River. A few minutes later, Shep decided to switch from his recorded playlist and search for a radio station.

"This is for old times' sake."

He went to the AM dial, and the plaintive, high nasal whine of sung Cajun French crackled through the speakers as the singer wailed the time-honored classic "Jolie Blonde."

"Dat sound like da Hackberry Ramblers," Shep mused. "An' why not start our time in Cajun country with a little 'Jolie Blonde'." Shep sang along for a few bars of the melancholy refrain. *"Jolie blonde, jolie fille, tu m'a quitté pour t'en aller."*

Merlin looked at Shep with mild amazement as he heard him sing in Cajun French for the first time in his life. He nodded in silent assent, taking in the experience now that he was not in his home country. The next song was a contemporary rendition of the plaintive murder ballad "Les Oiseaux Vont Chanter" by the Red Stick Ramblers, and Shep and Merlin listened to it like it was a requiem.

Within an hour's time, they were off the interstate and motoring through the flat, water-sliced terrain of deep Southwest Louisiana—cayenne pepper country. As they approached the flashing lights of a country crossroads, Shep announced, "Okay, now we gonta make a stop." Merlin looked at the little gas station and saw a faded hand-painted sign that read: "P'tit Pirogue's Pump n' Run."

Merlin said, "But this looks like a gas station."

Shep said, "It is."

"But I thought you said we were gonna get boudin and cracklins."

"We are."

"But it's a gas station."

"One thing you got to know, Magic Man, is that things in South Louisiana are not always as they appear. A lot a times, if it's a gas station, it's kind of a restaurant, too, or at least it has a kitchen and a coupla tables."

"Oh!" Merlin said, now regarding the ramshackle petrol dispensary with wonder.

Shep pulled up to the gas pump and a scrawny, sun-burnished man with a pronounced limp on his right side emerged from the doorway shouting salutations as soon as he saw Shep emerge from the driver's side of the Black Ghost.

"*Eh la bas! Pasteur! Il y a très longtemps, cher!*" the small overall-clad strip of human beef jerky enthused.

"Eh, Boudreaux!" Shep responded with equal vigor, and they greeted one another with a kind of simultaneous hand-shake and hug.

"Whatchoo doin' down in the home country?"

"Ma sweet cousine tole me the fishin' switched on."

"So you up and leff work?"

"Yeah, hell yeah. Got my priorities, *cher*."

"Hanh! You right on that one! Hey, who's your fishin' buddy?"

"Merlin, I got someone I want you to meet," Shep yelled in the direction of the open driver's side window as he prepared to refuel the El Camino.

Merlin dislodged himself from the passenger side bucket seat, opened the wide muscle car door, and stood to present himself to Shep's friend. On seeing Merlin, Shep's friend exclaimed, "*Oooo, cher, tu a porté avec toi un vrai* bigfeet *paramafait*!!"

"*Mais non*, Zimou, he ain't no Bigfoot. This ma fren Merlin McNaughton. They call him the Magic Man."

Merlin dutifully presented his right paw to shake hands, and the diminutive Cajun beheld it with wonder as he extended his own leathery hand in greeting.

To Merlin, Shep said, "Dis here my ole fren—but still not dat ole—Onézime Boudreaux."

Boudreaux raised his gaze to Merlin's bespectacled eyes and said, "Magic Man. *Bienvenue*. My friends call me Zimou. Since you wit' Shep, you can call me Zimou, also too."

"Okay, thank you," responded Merlin with his signature mannerliness.

"Now afta da tank is full up and you boys done waterin' the yard, come inside. You got perfect timing for rolling up on the P'tit Pirogue."

"Whatchoo got, Zee?"

"All ahm sayin' is you gotta come see."

"Okay, you gotta deal."

The bathroom was out of order, so Shep and Merlin relieved themselves near an elevated propane tank out of the sight of passersby. They used a faucet, industrial soap, and some rags hanging on a nail to wash and dry their hands before heading for the station's office.

On entering, they were overpowered with a host of savory aromas announcing that one was in deep Cajun country. The air was thick with cayenne pepper, garlic, and roasted meat smells. Standing atop a little wooden box behind the counter, the now elevated Onézime Boudreaux commanded the room with the authority of a Michelin-starred chef or maybe even some kind of Cajun culinary evangelist.

"Step raht up," Zimou adjured the two unlikely wayfarers.

Shep led the way and Merlin followed. The counter was faded white linoleum, chipped at the edges and worn through at its center. From a small steam table behind him, Zimou removed the lid from a metal container and used tongs to retrieve a couple of hot boudin links. He put them on butcher paper, stood back, and crossed his arms.

"Fresh made today," Zimou said.

"Ooo, yeah! That's what I'm talkin' about!" Shep replied.

"You ain't seen nothin', yet!"

Zimou produced a grease-stained paper grocery bag folded at the top.

"Diss from a big *cochon de lait soirée* just last night."

He dried the tongs with a clean rag and pulled out a couple of big pieces of spiced and roasted-to-a-crisp pork cracklins.

"Now, this don't come around every day!" Zimou announced.

"Hoo! Thassa rare delicacy indeed!" Shep picked up the banter.

"Try some," commanded the high priest of the P'tit Pirogue.

Zimou broke off a couple of morsels from one of the big pieces. "*Seulement des petits morçeaux,*" he added.

"Come on up, Magic Man! Let's check this out!"

Merlin moved to the counter at Shep's side, and they each tried a piece. Merlin's eyes grew to fill almost the entire aperture of his glasses. Shep just closed his eyes in a delirium of rendered porcine skin and fat ecstasy and said, "Now dat taste like home."

"These are the best pork rinds I've ever had."

"Bite you tongue!" said Boudreaux. "These are real Louisiana *crack*lins! Pork rinds is them little *crottins* you buy in a plastic bag at the truck stop."

"Then they're the most triumphantly excellent cracklins I've ever tasted!" Merlin averred with an equally triumphant smile.

"Now you got dat right. Triumphally excellent. I'm gonna file that one away for when I need it," Shep offered.

"Okay, *mon frére*," Shep said to Zimou, "sold."

"You fellas want what I got right here on the counter?" asked Zimou.

"Double it," Shep said and looked at Merlin, who had his quizzical look working.

"Ah, triple it."

"Triple?!"

"Hey, tree's a lucky number. You got enough?"

"Yeah, man!"

Zimou sacked up the order. He sliced part of a white onion and put it in a small Styrofoam bowl, covered it, and added it to the contents of the bag. He walked around from behind the counter, selected a jar of spicy thin-sliced pickles, and put it on the counter with a resolute, percussive thunk. Punctuating the gesture, Zimou added, "Pickles on da house."

Shep paid, and Merlin thanked Zimou and headed for the car. Shep lingered at the door and thanked his fellow countryman Onézime Boudreaux. Zimou replied, "*Il n'y a pas de quoi* any time," and continued to watch him for a couple of seconds as he headed toward the car.

Zimou looked toward Merlin in the car and back at Shep with his palms upturned and a questioning look. "Who's Baby Huey?" he asked.

"I known him since he was a boy. A little different but got a good heart. He don't really seem to know it, but he don't have almost nobody to look out for him, and he just kinda got his rug jerked out from under him on top of that."

"Looks like he still eatin' pretty well."

"Yeah, not eatin' is not a problem for Merlin McNaughton."

"Well, you make one helluva camp counselor, ma fren'. Y'all go get on 'em out on the water."

"We gon' try. Hey, I got a line on some brand-new linoleum for that counter if you want to re-lay it."

"Hey, man, ain't nothin' or nobody roun' here gettin' laid, not even the linoleum!"

Shep burst out in unrestrained laughter as he waved goodbye to Zimou and stepped through the doorway into the steaming midday heat.

· *Thirty-four*

During the drive between P'tit Pirogue's Pump n' Run and Lumbeaux Jump, Shep cued up one of his favorite playlists on the Black Ghost's sound system. They listened to Michael Doucet & BeauSoleil, then to a hit parade of Zydeco artists, including Terrance Simien, Wayne Toups, Rosie Ledet and the Zydeco Playboys, the whimsical Boozoo Chevis, and the cowboy hat–wearing Southwest Louisiana showman, Geno Delafose. When they were just a few miles away from the Jump, Shep put on the screaming slide guitar–playing Sonny Landreth to further amp up the energy. Merlin was astounded at Landreth's playing. He looked at Shep and said, "Wow!" as loudly as he could over the music. At the end of a song, Shep turned down the volume a little and said, "That's Sonny Landreth."

Merlin asked, "How does he get that sound?"

Shep responded, "I'm not sure how he does it exactly, but he uses a slide and some kinda special way of playing that's all his own. That's why they call Sonny 'the king of slydeco.'"

Merlin asked, "Is the slide made of glass?"

"Well," Shep replied, "come to think of it, I think it is. I seen him play, and I recall that slide was see-through."

"Doesn't surprise me," offered Merlin.

"Oh yeah? Why's zat?"

"It's the glass. Besides glass itself as the instrument, glass on strings produces some of the most compelling music in the world. I knew there was a reason I liked it so much."

"Hey world, the Magic Man is on it! He can even tell Sonny Landreth uses a glass slide! Hooooo!"

Shep mixed up the playlist a little and the unusual fishing duo was jamming out to "Alligator_Aviator_Autopilot_Antimatter" by R.E.M. as they passed a painted sign that read "Welcome to Lumbeaux Jump—Louisiana's premier jump-off spot for the outdoor sportsman and sportswoman" and underneath it in French, *"Bienvenue au Saut des Lumbeaux. Faites votre saut içi."* On the left side of the sign were leaping trout and redfish and on the right were several migratory ducks flaring for landing into a decoy spread in front of a blind on a bay. Merlin read the sign and noted that nothing appeared to be jumping in this quiet little outpost of French Louisiana. The sun was still high in the afternoon sky, and it looked as if the locals had left the out-of-doors to the mad dogs and Englishmen of musical yore.

Shep turned down a street whose asphalt pavement soon became crushed oystershells. He made another turn into an oystershell driveway that became a neatly paved motor court surrounded by a group of dwellings. The main house was freshly painted and on tall stilts. There was what looked to be a cosmetically improved double-wide mobile home across the driveway from it, and next to it a single-wide. Both of these were on stilts also and just as high as the main house. Beyond the motor court was a driveway that led to a small boat ramp. Merlin could see there was also a covered boat slip with a hoist behind the main house. The hoist held a shallow-draft bay and marsh fishing boat. Underneath the houses were parking spots and utility rooms.

As Shep angled the Black Ghost toward a parking spot under the shade of the main house, Merlin saw the first resident Lumbeaux Jump presented him. The house obscured the view initially, and all he could see were thin, deeply tanned legs taking delicate steps down a stairway in flat white shoes that looked like ballet slippers. Then a white cotton dress and a petite woman who looked to be not too much older than Merlin himself came into view.

"Now you get to meet ma sweet cousine," Shep said.

Shep opened the driver's side door and stepped out onto the concrete of the covered carport. The diminutive woman was beaming from ear to ear as she and Shep embraced in greeting.

"Cousine Marie Mado, you just get prettier every time I see you!" Shep proclaimed. Merlin registered that she was indeed very pretty in a very natural, unaffected way with long black hair, glowing olive skin, and fiery hazel eyes. Shep beckoned Merlin to exit the El Camino with a wave and as Merlin unfolded from the bucket seat, Marie Mado exclaimed, "Hoo, Shep, I heard they grow 'em big in Texas, but I never 'spected to see one like this!"

"Hey, this my fren Merlin I was telling you about!"

Merlin extended his right paw and uttered a perfunctory "Pleased to meet you" as Marie Mado bypassed the handshake and gave Merlin a hug, which he slowly returned in a gentle one-armed embrace.

"If you with Shep, you family, too, *cher.*"

She was still smiling as Shep announced, "Now this ma sweet cousine, Marie Mado. She and her kids live here and take care of the camp for the whole family."

"Enchanté!" Marie Mado said to Merlin with a slight theatrical curtsy.

And then to Shep, "Where y'all been?"

"We had to make a stop up the road to see ole Boudreaux at the P'tit Pirogue."

"Oh yeah, ole Zimou. How he's getting along?"

"He still cookin'!"

"That's good, and guess what, I am too. Got a big bowl of cold-boiled shrimp right off the boat this morning for y'all. And I already mixed up cocktail sauce for them also too."

"Aiiieeeee!" Shep let out a Cajun party whoop and waved Merlin toward the truck bed of the Black Ghost to get their gear.

Before Merlin crossed the threshold of his temporary home he saw a carved and brightly painted wooden alligator above the door. Shep showed him to a small bedroom with a big king-size bed. Out a side window, Merlin could see a canal that passed by the fishing camp. On a wall near the galley kitchen, there was a barometer, and on seeing it, Merlin's eyes lit up. "A barometer!"

"Yeah, you know us Cajuns got a pretty good sense of the weather, but every once in a while it don't hurt to consult a meteorological instrument just to confirm our gut."

"This place feels like home," Merlin said.

Shep didn't miss a beat. "Wait 'til you taste ma cousine's cookin'!"

· *Thirty-five*

At 4 a.m. a group of people followed a tall man in single file, walking from the Amsterdam cruise ship terminal toward the Red Light District. After moving a few blocks into the infamous part of the old city, the group stopped in front of a nondescript house, the only identifying marker of which was a dark plaque with the image of a circular band with a smaller circular band hanging from a metal loop at its base. It looked kind of like something used to lead livestock, with the larger band capable of encircling a neck and the smaller one serving as a place to attach a lead. A door opened, and the tall man stood aside for the group to enter. He then entered and shut the door tight.

· *Thirty-six*

Over the next few days, Shep and Merlin fished all the habitats of the area—broad, open bays Shep called lakes; narrow, labyrinthine sloughs whose twists and turns Shep navigated with expert precision; and even the surf on a beach on the northern Gulf Coast south of the Jump. They waded some of the shallow water littoral areas and drifted in the middle of the open bays. It was hot, but there was enough breeze to make the day tolerable without being so windy as to shut off the fishing. When they got in the boat after wading, the air hitting them when they were up on plane and cruising cooled them a little and dried their clothes.

On the first day, they caught fish here and there—a few trout, but mostly redfish, the majority of which they released unless Shep deemed them the perfect eating size. Merlin brought two bait-casting rods and reels and an 8-weight fly rod and saltwater reel. He had a plastic box full of tackle and a box affixed to a Styrofoam donut for wading with netting material at its center for keepers.

Uncharacteristically, Merlin showed no concern for determining latitude and longitude as he trusted in Shep's guidance through his home country. The twenty-two-foot center console Hanko was constructed of heavy-gauge aluminum painted dark green and did winter duty getting hunters to and from duck blinds. There was a flat area on the foredeck where an angler could stand and cast. There was a padded leaning post for Shep as he ran the boat. In front of the captain's console, a big marine cooler with a cushioned top was Merlin's seat when they were moving across the water. Behind the leaning post was a big heavy-duty cooler, which doubled as a lookout stand for Shep when they weren't running. The weight distribution onboard worked pretty well with Merlin sitting forward of the center console as they ran and fishing from the foredeck and Shep at the console working the 200-horsepower Mercury outboard and fishing from the aft.

On the second day, the fishing wasn't very productive at first, and as they drifted in a bay called Spirit Lake, spirits were low. They pulled in small gaff-top catfish that slimed their lines and whose needlelike dorsal gaffs they were careful to avoid as they used hookout pliers to release them. Shep stood on top of the box behind the leaning post and scanned the horizon with a monocular. He paused, looking in one direction for a moment, and then said to Merlin, "Okay, let's go." Merlin reeled in his lure and sat as Shep started the engine. They were up on plane in seconds, and there wasn't a lot of chop in the water, so the running was smooth. Merlin began to see some commotion on and above the water, and as they approached their next fishing spot he looked back at Shep and flapped his arms with a questioning look. Shep nodded.

They neared the place where the seagulls were feeding, and Merlin could see the big trout slick. Shep guided the boat around one edge of the slick to position it to drift into the trout-feeding frenzy. He queried Merlin, "Smell dat?" Merlin smiled and replied with even greater enthusiasm, "Watermelon!" confirming the distinctive smell of a school of feeding speckled trout. Shep cut the motor behind the slick and deployed into the water what fishermen call a parachute, basically a small facsimile of the airworthy variety that slows a boat as it drifts. As they floated into the slick, the much stronger smell of an entire field of ripe, split-open watermelons enveloped them.

On their first cast beneath the swooping and screeching birds, they both hooked small trout, which they released. Their next casts brought keepers—beautiful fish that would yield perfect pan-size filets. After they drifted the slick, Shep pulled in the parachute, started the engine, and repositioned the boat to drift it again, putting out the underwater parachute a second time. The following casts proved just as productive as those of the first drift, and after a few minutes, having drifted the breadth of the big slick, which was beginning to break up, they had each nearly limited out on keeper-size trout.

A few fish stowed in the iced fish box were still flopping around as they washed their hands in the bay water and dried them on their clothes. Merlin produced a small container of hand sanitizer and offered some to Shep before taking some for himself. They dried their hands a second time on a clean towel Shep pulled from a dry box, and Shep looked at Merlin matter-of-factly and said, "Lunch?"

With unguarded enthusiasm, Merlin brightened and responded, "Yes!"

Lunch was dressed roast beef po'boys with a spicy chopped pickle and mayonnaise spread, some cracklins (a few chips of which Merlin deftly placed inside his po'boy for added flavor and crunch), and apples for dessert. Shep drank water, and Merlin opted for his favorite: Dr Pepper.

"You know, Magic Man, some folks who maybe fish five or four times a year can go a lot of years without getting into a hungry school like that."

"It was almost surreal," Merlin replied. "Like magic."

"You said it! Hey! I got the Magic Man in the boat!"

"Well, you saw the birds and put us on an ideal perpendicular drift right across the middle of the slick."

"But we're in Louisiana, and we never discount luck over here."

They ate in silence for a minute, and as they drifted toward shore, Merlin spotted two strange-looking animals and pointed.

"What are those?"

"Nutria rats."

"Rats?"

"Yeah, they're like big water rats, but they got nice pelts that they used to make fur coats out of. On top of that, some people say they're good eatin' but they still look like rats to me."

"They're big."

"Yep. Biggest rodent you'll see around here."

"Looks like they see us."

"Yeah, momma and poppa nutria out for a walk, having a look at what's going on in the neighborhood."

"You think they are a male and a female?"

"It wouldn't be two males or two females together. You lookin' at Mr. and Mrs. Nutria there."

Merlin continued to watch them, and Shep saw his opportunity.

"You know, Magic Man, that's kinda the way it's spose to be—momma and poppa out for a walk together."

Merlin nodded and continued to look at the nutria.

"And that's the same for us, too. Out there somewhere, there's someone for each of us. Even no matter how different we think we may be from most folks. There's somebody just as different, or different in a compatible way, for every single one of us."

This time, unlike when Dr. Swearingen tried to engage him on this subject, Merlin didn't protest. Maybe it was the setting and the soul satisfaction of just having caught a mess of trout. Whatever it was, Merlin just sat and nodded and listened as he watched the nutria peering out from above the salt grass on shore.

"What about you, Shep?"

"I'm still trying to get up on plane after ma sweet Clothilde."

"How long has it been?"

"She passed away five years ago. Five years next week."

"So, you are still feeling loss."

"I'll always feel it, Magic Man, but there's a time and place for everything."

Merlin nodded.

"See, Clothilde changed me. No, really, I changed by being with her. She made me a better human, and I realized, after a long time with her, that that's what she was angling for the whole time in her own gracious way."

"Really?"

"Yes. For sure. And you know what? It stayed with me."

"It did?"

"Yes, it did. Even after she's been gone these last years. Maybe even got stronger."

Merlin looked at Shep with wonder.

"Yes, sir. Not just someone for everyone, but the right someone. I guess the right someone can kinda bring you into yourself or a better self you didn't have no idea you could be."

They sat in silence for a moment and finished their lunches. Shep took a big drink of water and wiped his mouth.

"What you say we go for a ride and look for some reds back in the marsh?"

It took Merlin a second to snap out of his reverie, but snap he did. "Oh! Yes! That sounds great!"

Shep started the motor, and Merlin hunkered down in front of the console for the run. In a flash, they were skittering across the water at speed.

They neared the marsh and headed toward a narrow, winding slough. Shep slowed the boat, and Merlin pointed at a small structure on the shore covered with dried sticks, salt grass, and weeds. He queried Shep, "Duck blind?"

Shep answered, "Yeah, you right, Magic Man. That's where you come back in winter and bring wit' you what ole Justin Wilson used to call a double automatic twice-barreled over-and-under twin carabine shootgun!"

Merlin wasn't exactly sure how to process Shep's recounting of the famous Cajun humorist's quote, but it made him smile just the same as they passed the blind and entered the twisting slough.

After a quarter mile or so, Shep cut the motor, and they anchored in the middle of the waterway. They switched lures from shad heads and rubber tauts to weedless silver spoons and started casting to within a foot or so of the shoreline grass, working the spoons carefully to attract feeding redfish. They fished for a while, then Shep used the electric trolling motor to move farther into the slough and anchored again. This time, during the course of forty-five minutes or so, they caught some nice keeper reds within the slot limit of sixteen to twenty-seven inches. Louisiana law allowed them to keep one bull red over twenty-seven inches, but the bulls were running elsewhere. They moved again and didn't catch any keepers over the course of twenty minutes or so.

Shep asked Merlin, "Want to try one more spot?"

"Sure!" Merlin replied with the enthusiasm of a kid asked if he'd like to ride the roller coaster again.

Merlin pulled the anchor and washed the silty mud from it in the opaque marsh water. Shep started the outboard, and they cruised farther into the marsh. After rounding a sharp bend, Shep cut the motor abruptly. He saw something. The boat drifted, and he continued to cast an eagle eye on something at the water's surface. Without looking at Merlin, he said, "See that dark spot over there next to the right bank where I'm looking?"

Merlin looked and after a moment said, "Yes. It's kind of round."

"Yep," returned Shep, "looks kinda like a hole. Go ahead and drop anchor."

Merlin deployed the little anchor, and it caught bottom and spun the boat around slowly until it stopped.

"Okay, Magic Man."

An idea came to Merlin. Instead of grabbing his bait caster with the weedless silver spoon for redfish, he selected his salt-water fly rod. It was an even stranger move because the line was rigged with a special shrimp-pattern fly he usually threw for speckled trout, not redfish. Shep looked at Merlin dubiously, but something kept him from quizzing the big fisherman on his choice of tackle. They were a judicious distance from the hole; a strong cast with a bait caster could reach it, but Shep thought it might be too far for a fly line.

Merlin had not seen Shep's befuddled expression. He was completely focused on the task at hand. He stepped onto the platform that was the foredeck, unhitched the fly from the hook keeper just above the rod's grip, and with a grace that belied his substantial mass, began to build his loop for the cast. He double hauled the line the way bone fishermen do, building a beautiful looping length of line moving forward and backward over the water in perfect rhythm, like a thin littoral metronome. He made the cast, and the lure alit atop the calm water at the far end of the hole. He let it sink a little, then began to strip line and work the shrimp pattern through the water with quick double pops of the rod between line strips. For a few seconds, the only thing disturbing the calm of the green hole was the lure dancing through it.

Then it happened. Something major blew up on the fly, gobbling it in one resolute bite, and Merlin's 8-weight rod doubled over as it strained against its adversary. Shep's mouth dropped open when he saw the bite and stayed open as he realized what kind of fish it was. Merlin fought the fish resolutely but carefully as he knew something special was happening. Instinctively, Shep put the handheld net within Merlin's reach on the fore deck.

Shep found himself in continued mute awe for several seconds and with enthusiasm increased by the delay in his response, he yelled, "It's a trout! A huge spec! What he's doin' back here?"

Shep's thrilled outburst somehow served to focus Merlin even more intensely on the fish. The writhing spec breached the water's surface a couple of times. Shep counseled, "Careful, steady, let him run just a little, *mais, ne lache pas la patate!*" Merlin complied as the fish stripped line and started reeling when it finished its run. The trout made several runs, but Merlin held it.

Shep had the presence of mind to grab his smart phone, pull

up the camera, and put it on video mode. The camera recorded as Merlin worked the trout closer and closer to the boat. Then Shep said, "Okay, Magic Man, I got a feeling about this one. The net is right next to you, so you can boat him all yourself." Merlin looked at Shep and down at the net near his feet. He held the rod and reel as high as he could in his left hand as he squatted to grab the net with his right hand. He passed the twine loop at the end of the net through his hand and let it dangle from his wrist as he worked the massive trout closer to the boat.

The water at the boat's side boiled with intense thrashing as the big man stepped down from the foredeck next to the mid-boat gunwale. He slipped the net under the fish with authority, like he was sliding a sheet of paper under a door. As Merlin raised his catch out of the water, Shep took a step backward but kept the video on his friend and the fish. It was the biggest speckled trout he had ever seen. Shep was at a loss for words for a couple of seconds, then began to shout in utter glee while instructing Merlin on what to do.

"Okay, Magic Man, I got this all on video. Now hold that fish up for the camera—real carefully."

Merlin embraced the fish, doing his best to throttle its thrashing so Shep could continue his video documentation. Shep opened the fish box, and Merlin dropped it inside. Shep slammed down the box door, and Merlin fell backward onto the fishing platform, his posterior hitting first and the inertia of the fall splaying him out with arms wide, supine on the foredeck. The trout percussed the box's interior like there was giant popcorn popping inside it.

"Ho! Merlin! You okay?"

Merlin raised only his head and nodded in silent assent that all was well.

"We gotta weigh him and measure him, but I think you got some kinda trophy on your hands, ma fren."

Merlin looked up at Shep again and lay his head back down, staring at the immense cumulus clouds of the coast. Shep walked forward in the boat and put out a hand to help Merlin to his feet. Merlin accepted the help, and they celebrated with double high fives and double fist bumps that they both blew up like fireworks with wiggling fingers. The celebration was short lived.

The upright rods in holders on both sides of the center console began to buzz and whir. Shep hadn't paid attention to what was going on in the heavens during the drama of the surprise lunker trout, and on hearing the rods begin to sing he looked up to see threatening cumulonimbus clouds moving toward the boat. He shouted to Merlin, "The anchor! Get low and pull it in as fast as you can!"

Merlin bounded to the front of the boat and knelt; he hauled in the rope line, then the silted chain, and the anchor. He stowed it all in a forward hatch on the foredeck. Shep pulled all the rods and reels from their holders and placed them on the lower deck's walking space at the bottom of the boat between the gunwales on both sides of the console. Merlin heard the outboard start as he stowed the anchor.

Shep yelled to him: "Get back here and get as low as you can! Lie down next to the gear!"

Merlin's eyes were at full aperture as he obeyed orders and lay prone on the boat deck while Shep turned the boat.

Shep yelled over the motor, "Hang on!" He jammed the throttle forward as he crouched low behind the center console. Thunder was rolling and the lightning was almost on them. Shep negotiated the twists of the slough at precariously high speed. He spotted a straight trenasse to port that provided a short cut to the open water in the direction of Lumbeaux Jump and away from the storm. He veered into the trenasse and pushed the outboard to its limit.

Big drops of rain began to pepper the two fishermen. When they reached Spirit Lake, bright lightning flashed and almost simultaneous thunder clapped and jolted them in the boat, but Shep was not deterred in his mission. He glanced backward and saw that the duck blind they had passed when they entered the slough was on fire. He figured there must have been something metallic protruding upward from the blind and that, if it wasn't for that trenasse, they might have been passing the blind about when the bolt struck.

They continued to run fast for several minutes with Merlin acting as forward ballast and Shep hunched behind the console and peering out over its control panel. The rain slackened, then stopped, and Shep stood and took in the view. The storm had moved on, and they had dodged potential disaster. Shep yelled over the whining motor, "Dey's a lesson in dat, Magic Man." Merlin looked up the way he had a few minutes earlier when he was supine on the foredeck fishing platform after landing the trout.

"Never let your guard down," Shep said.

Wide eyed, Merlin nodded in assent, then got to his feet and returned to his seat on the cushioned cooler in front of the console.

Their quick getaway had them running on fumes as they approached the little Cajun outpost. Next to the Lumbeaux Jump public boat ramp and docks, a crude, hand-painted sign outside Jupiter's Bait, Tackle, Fuel & Supplies read "The best little bait shack on the planet." They needed to officially weigh, measure, and document Merlin's catch.

The portly Jupiter Robichaux sat at his post on a high swivel chair behind a circular counter in the middle of the store. Jupiter barked orders at his diminutive assistant, Callisto, who ran wide circles around the store getting things as Robichaux pivoted this way and that calling for them. A couple of officers from the Louisiana Department of Wildlife and Fisheries happened to cruise by, tie off at the dock, and enter the shop to add an even more official air to the proceedings. Jupiter's orders to Callisto began anew.

The scale and yardstick did not lie, and Jupiter pronounced that the trout was likely a state record for the year thus far. A quick internet search indicated that Merlin's catch might even be the biggest spec taken in Louisiana waters over the preceding five years. Jupiter asked Callisto to take a photo of Merlin and Shep, the game wardens, and him with the fish.

They all laughed about a seriously dangerous situation when Shep made light of it, saying that thenceforward he was going to call Merlin's 8-weight "the lightning rod." There was a moment of quiet, and Shep broke it with a decisive "I think this occasion calls for a beer." Jupiter Robichaux agreed, but the officers deferred that they were on duty. Shep cajoled them a bit, and they capitulated, agreeing that it was indeed a very special occasion and their shift was almost over. Merlin opted for a big Barq's root beer as the other men told fishing stories from decades past and sipped ice-cold Abita Andygators. Jupiter and the wardens reiterated that this was indeed a very special afternoon, and they would be glad to be able to tell folks they were there for the weigh-in.

The men finished their libations and Shep, Merlin, and Jupiter said goodbye to the Fish and Wildlife officers. Shep went outside and filled the boat's gas tank as Merlin placed the rods back in their holders. Merlin stepped inside and paid for the gas over Shep's protests. They unmoored the boat from the dock and putted at a no-wake pace over to the little covered boat slip at Shep's family's fishing camp. As they unloaded the boat and began to hose it down, fatigue hit them like a sledgehammer.

· *Thirty-seven*

Eating lunch at his desk, Junior Trust Officer Curtis Bumpers moused around a regional hunting and fishing enthusiasts' website on his desktop computer. Under the Latest Reports tab he saw the heading "NEWSFLASH!" followed by a few lines: "Reports of a potential season-record speckled trout (spotted sea trout) caught near Lumbeaux Jump, Louisiana. Details to follow on official confirmation."

"Probably a pro guide on his day off," Bumpers mumbled aloud to himself.

· *Thirty-eight*

That evening on the deck above the canal in front of the house where Marie Mado and her daughters lived, the oil was boiling at a roll in a deep metal pan. Around the pan's edges, spread newspapers fanned to catch errant spatter. Although the flame from the propane burner and the heat of the oil increased the already high ambient temperature on the deck, Shep commented to his supersize sous chef that the cooking setup didn't seem to disperse the mosquitos a bit.

They took a break and went inside. Merlin closed the sliding glass door to the family room as he and Shep entered the cool of the air conditioning to confer with Marie Mado about timing for supper. Her twin daughters, Pélagie and Thétis, were chasing each other around the room and nearly collided with the men when they were a couple of steps inside the doorway.

"Lagie! Tay Tay!" Marie Mado adjured her girls. *"Tranquillez! Vous aller faire un grand mess avant de que tout les gens arrivent!"*

They stopped and bowed their heads slightly.

"Now come help your maman. These tables aren't gonna set themselves."

Lagie and Tay Tay washed their hands and went to work; Marie Mado wiped her hands on a kitchen towel and looked at Shep and Merlin in mock exasperation.

"They maniacs is what they are. Only why they have to get they maniac out right when a buncha people come over, hanh? Splain me dat!"

Shep laughed, and Merlin smiled because he had begun to understand the way Marie Mado talked, and he was able to tell by now that she was not really being completely serious.

All three went to work patting each trout filet dry, passing it through the Zatarain's spicy batter mix and then through an egg wash and then back through the mixture of Zatarain's fish-fry spice and white flour mixed with cornmeal before placing each one in a big bowl ready for the fryer. They also had spicy boudin balls ready for a swim in the hot, popping oil. The guests were bringing the rest of the fare, including vegetable maque choux, spicy cole slaw, and a special tartar sauce for the fried trout. For dessert, there was chicory coffee–flavored ice cream.

In a few minutes, the men were outdoors again by the fryer. Shep was the fry chef, and Merlin kept everything in order on the little card table they had set up for pre- and post-fried trout. Merlin watched with anticipation as the golden-brown pieces of trout surfaced and bobbed before Shep used a long-handled Asian-looking wire mesh skimmer/strainer to remove each filet and set it atop layers of paper towels and newspaper into which excess oil drained. Merlin decided it was a good time to query Shep. "What was that you said to me in French when I was fighting the trout today?"

"Hey, man, I don't remember with all the excitement."

"It was something about *la patate*."

"Oooooh, yeah! *Ne lache pas la patate*! Ha!"

"Yes. That's it."

"It means 'don't let go of the potato.'"

Merlin gave Shep his cocked-head golden retriever look.

"Okay, I'll splain it to you. Real basically, it means 'hang on,' but in a deeper way. The potato stands for life itself, and it means 'don't let go of life' or maybe something like 'hold on for dear life,' but I think it sounds more powerful than that in Cajun. The guys on the floor of the drilling rigs used to say that to whoever had the chain and was moving pipe into place over the spinning drilling table because if something went wrong, a man could lose a finger or two, if not his life all together. So *ne lache pas la patate* maybe means something like 'hang on like your life depends on it,' and you did dat for sure today, Magic Man."

Merlin's eyes widened a bit with the enlightenment of learning something new about this culture that seemed so different yet was so geographically close to Houston.

"Only don't say nothing about the oilfield or drilling platforms or any o' that around ma sweet cousine," Shep said. "She lost her husband in that big offshore explosion a few years ago."

Merlin's brow furrowed as he responded, "Oh, okay, I won't say anything about it."

Guests bearing side dishes and sauces arrived. Shep and Merlin had filled a tray with fresh-fried speckled trout filets. Shep picked up the tray with care and said, "Okay, Magic Man, this is just like your days on the front line. You block for me so I can get the main event inside to the buffet." Merlin complied and walked in front of Shep to open the sliding glass door and deflect any potential forward-progress inhibitors. With the spread set up in a little buffet line and high-decibel Cajun banter for a kind of musical accompaniment, the guests lined up, and the feast was underway.

After supper, everyone was still in high spirits, especially with all the talk of Merlin's record trout and the near miss of a lightning strike, so they decided to pile into cars and trucks and head to a place up the road called Hebert's Haut Mercure, which featured cold beer, live music, and a well-worn dance floor. All the generations were on the dance floor at one time or another that evening—from toddlers all the way up to great-grandparents. Lagie and Tay Tay danced holding hands with a couple of their cousins in ring-around-the-rosie style.

The band played a Cajun waltz, and Merlin watched Shep and Marie Mado glide like pros around the room in perfect rhythm to the music. Merlin was amazed. It almost seemed like a rehearsed performance to him, but he knew that Shep and his younger cousin were simply reveling in the music, the moment, the culture, and what must have been the joy of the dance. Shep and Marie Mado sat with Merlin after their waltz, and Merlin said, "That was amazing!"

Shep replied, "Hey, it's just what we learn to do as kids around here."

Then Marie Mado, "Yeah, and it's really not that hard once you get it. Specially the waltzes."

The band began another waltz. Marie Mado looked at Merlin and said, "Hey, Merlin, I'm gonna teach you to waltz!" Merlin offered his signature wide-eyed-deer-in-the-headlights look and hesitated, but Marie Mado persisted. "Naw, come on!" she said. "There's no time like the present!" Tentatively, Merlin rose from the table and took the hand that Marie Mado offered him. As they walked onto the dance floor, the size difference between the two of them was comical—tiny, waif-like Mary Mado and huge, lumbering Merlin.

Merlin told Marie Mado, "I haven't tried to waltz since eighth-grade dance class." And she came right back with an encouraging "Well, then, it's time to try it again! It'll come back to you in snap."

Marie Mado did her best to guide Merlin through the ONE, two, three; ONE, two, three steps of the dance, but Merlin was slow to catch on. And the size difference made it look like Merlin was dancing with a child's doll. After a minute or so, though, Merlin did seem to get a rudimentary sense of the dance. He was not the smoothest waltzer on the dance floor, but certainly the most appreciative of his partner's pedagogical ability and patience. As the song drew near a close, he was concentrating intensely on the step count, and he and Marie Mado moved around the dance floor, not as fluidly as she and Shep did, but at least in time with the music like the other dancers at Hebert's Haut Mercure that muggy July night in South Louisiana.

· *Thirty-nine*

The next day on the drive back to Houston, Merlin and Shep saw thick black smoke rising ahead of them in the distance. Merlin spoke first: "Maybe someone's car is on fire. Should we stop to help?"

Shep responded, "Well, Magic Man, maybe it's best we wait and see as we get closer."

"But it could be bad!"

"I know, but we don't know yet, so no reason to get worked up."

Merlin sat with concerned eyes fixed on the thick dark cloud rising ahead of them. As they approached, Shep said, "I think I might know what that is." And then, after a couple of minutes he said, "Yep."

When they neared the source of the smoke, they saw that it was a pile of old tires that had been set alight on property just off the roadside. As they passed, the flames were so intense they looked as if they were powered by gas jets and the thick black smoke blew across the road, forcing Shep to slow the Black Ghost like it was passing through a heavy thunderstorm. They both looked with wonder at the angry flames.

"I think that's illegal," Shep said. "The environmental pollution agency gonna get after them for sure if the state don't get to 'em first."

"I've never seen anything like that!"

"Yeah, Magic Man, sometimes things aren't what they seem like they are from a distance—whether the distance is on the road, or on the water, or in life."

Merlin's brow furrow relaxed and flattened, and he slumped back into his bucket seat in the El Camino.

"And sometimes we don't find out what's really going on until we are a lot closer," Shep said. "And even sometimes we don't figure it out until we way, way past whatever it was we were wondering about."

Merlin turned and looked at the wise Cajun.

"And putting the wheels in motion to try to help based on what we think we see where we are at the time," Shep opined, "well, all that does is it can put us in danger where if we were more patient, not disinterested, but more patient, and stayed on the road—stayed on our course—things might work out better for everybody and a whole lot less frettin' and energy would get spent up."

Merlin looked at Shep with awe as, somehow, he had a sense that he was listening to something important. He took it in and nodded silently as Shep rested his left palm atop the steering wheel, accelerated, and resumed his usual unperturbable countenance, bespeaking his internal cruise control, as he gazed down the highway.

· *Forty*

Merlin was still enjoying the satisfaction of catching the record trout and the tranquility induced by listening to Shep's life lessons when he reentered his home. Moments after he opened the hatch to his observatory, his calm mood leapt out the window like a glass armonica–smashing phony in a black ninja suit. The Agglomerator was going berserk, blinking and buzzing with a vigor it had never registered. He chided himself for not checking the program remotely while he was in Louisiana.

He dropped his duffel and went to his workstation. The orange warning flashes were now tinged with red, indicating an energy event was considerably closer. The cloud indicating its location had moved just west of downtown Houston, but the program suggested that it had not yet stopped over the final event point. The hue indicating a Bigfoot nexus had also remained and intensified. This development puzzled Merlin, as he was accustomed to understand the creatures avoided the limelight whenever possible, but he reminded himself that such momentous events like large hurricanes are sui generis and can obey their own logic as they express their unique storm dynamics.

It was clear to Merlin that the whirling cloud on the screen would soon come to a nearby resting place where the event would occur. It was also clear that the time for action was at hand. He had to steel himself.

· *Forty-one*

Sitting alone at a Danish modern dining table in his third-level corporate apartment on Fannius Scholtenstraat in the Westerpark neighborhood of Amsterdam, Mickey McNaughton looked at his laptop screen and took a couple of sips from a wide glass goblet containing La Trappe Quadrupel ale. He reread Merlin's e-mail for the third or maybe fourth time. Merlin may be a little out there, he reasoned, but his nighttime airborne description of the goings-on at the out-of-the-way address Tite Dûche's Porsche had frequented continued to bother him. He looked at his wristwatch and subtracted seven hours, determining that it was still before noon in Houston. He picked up his mobile phone and called the Harris County District Attorney's office, and when the phone system prompted him, he keyed in the extension for Jim Atlas's office.

· *Forty-two*

Merlin was caught up in rapt attention at the colorful whirling and flashing images the Agglomerator was producing on his monitors. Although he understood what the program was predicting was serious business, he had to admit that the visual effect was quite compelling—even beautiful—like tongues of fire or the moving satellite image of a well-defined high-category hurricane. A ding broke his reverie, and a small rectangular frame appeared on his central screen. Normally, he would ignore this kind of intrusion, but he noticed the message was from Rex Mondeaux's personal assistant. He opened the e-mail and straightened in his chair when he read the subject line: "VIP Tour of NASA Johnson Space Center." Merlin read:

Dear Mr. McNaughton,

Mr. Mondeaux has arranged a special VIP tour of Space Center Houston for some of his most valued clients and associates. In appreciation of your work for Fandango, he would like to include you on the guest list for the tour tomorrow. I apologize for the late notice. Please RSVP to me ASAP. If you can attend, I will send you details of the specific start time and location of the tour.

Sincerely,
Sherry McQuerry,
personal assistant to Rex Mondeaux

Merlin's eyes were at full aperture. A VIP tour of NASA! He had heard of these special tours and rumors that the guests on them were privileged to see the veritable sanctum sanctorum of the legendary aerospace compound down by the bay. With loud and resolute keystrokes, Merlin replied immediately and enthusiastically. The event horizon deserved his attention, but the opportunity to *be* one of the VIPs on a VIP tour of NASA was not to be missed.

· *Forty-three*

Mickey McNaughton and Jim Atlas were finishing their phone conversation when Atlas said, "Yeah, I'll have to admit these are some pretty strange facts. I can't put anybody official on it at this point, but I agree with you that something seems fishy."

"So, we're dead in the water?"

"Not quite."

"What does 'not quite' mean?"

"It means there's another way for us to proceed. And by us, I mean just you and me."

"And that would be?"

"A private investigator."

"Alright, go on."

"I know a very good PI here in town. A lot of folks think he's the best. If there's anything there, he'll find it."

"What about his expenses?"

"I propose that we split his expenses for a month."

"Deal. If there's something there, we'll be lauded for doing our civic duty, right?"

"Maybe, but all this is weird enough that it's worth it to me to try to turn over a few rocks."

"Alright, I'm in, and I appreciate this, Jim."

"No problem."

"Roger. Over and out."

· *Forty-four*

Uncharacteristically for such an important day, Merlin overslept by half an hour, so he was in a rush to shower, dress, and be on his way to Space Center Houston. He was so busy getting ready he didn't have time to check the latest from the Agglomerator. An idea out of left field popped into his mind and without ruminating on it, he grabbed a thumb drive and inserted it into his computer. He dragged an Agglomerator file titled "morning update" into the thumb drive. Before leaving for the JSC, Merlin snatched the thumb drive from his workstation computer and dropped it into his pocket. He then shouldered the strap of a messenger bag containing a small laptop, a legal pad, pencils, and erasers and was out the door.

He arrived at the prearranged meeting point at the visitor's center out of breath and in the nick of time but relieved and excited to participate in the special tour. And the tour lived up to his expectations. The group saw areas where astronauts and NASA personnel were working. They saw up close the newest space robots that could be sent ahead of a human mission to do construction on Mars. They also got to walk on the huge air-bearing table. It was like a giant, industrial-strength air hockey table that simulated weightlessness and could lift up to twenty thousand pounds. Merlin thought about how it could lift him and an armonica simultaneously. He wondered if there would be enough stability for him to play the instrument as they hovered.

When she was talking about the Apollo lunar mission, the VIP guide reminded the group that the very first and very last words spoken on the moon were "Houston": "Houston, the Eagle has landed" and "We're on our way, Houston."

They even had the opportunity to walk through the newly refurbished Apollo Mission Control room. Everything was true to the era, from the onscreen graphics to the four rows of consoles for the twenty-two controllers. After that astounding stroll back through time the guide announced, "I have a very special destination for this very special group."

With the entire group's attention on her, the guide said, "For quite some time, the Johnson Space Center has had five mission control rooms, but we are now adding two more to provide state-of-the-art support for future missions. NASA has cleared this group to see one of these new rooms this morning." Everyone oohed and ahhed, and Merlin brightened and pursed his lips into a small O of anticipation.

The group went up a flight of stairs, and the guide opened the door onto a gleaming newly outfitted floor of the building. As the group walked into the corridor, the guide went ahead of them to open another door, which led onto the floor of one of the new mission control rooms.

The look of the space was night and day from the Apollo room, as different as an early Buck Rogers movie from a contemporary high-tech intergalactic sci-fi thriller with all the latest CGI special effects. There were arced rows of sleek modular workstations descending on a slight incline, and the screens on the room's front wall were more impressive than any displays Merlin had seen. As with the Apollo room, there was a central rectangular screen with screens flanking it, but all of them were considerably larger.

The tour guide said, "We are particularly fortunate today that the testing of the screens is underway. It might be quite a show."

A couple of technicians were in the room working from one of the workstations, and the side screens suddenly lit up with graph-ics. Then the central screen displayed a high-resolution video of a slowly rotating earth. This image was so stunning that the tour group took it in with silent, mesmerized stares. Next, an image of the Martian surface appeared, and then a dazzling real-time video of a supernova from the Hubble Space Telescope.

"When they are fully operational," the tour guide said, "these screens will constitute the highest-resolution, most state-of-the-art video and image display of their kind in the world, as far as we know." Merlin listened, but his eyes stayed on the screens. He heard the tour guide ask, "Does anyone have any questions?"

Like a bolt from the blue, Merlin felt an alien surge of confi-dence rise in his spinal column. "I do," he said. "Yes?" the tour guide responded.

"I captured a video update on a thumb drive this morning from a program I wrote. Would it be possible to see it on the display?"

Some of the group chuckled, and a couple of men who knew of Merlin from the country club rolled their eyes and looked at one another with dubious grimaces.

"Gosh, I don't know. Let me find out," the tour guide responded. She then walked to the two technicians and con-ferred with them quietly for a few seconds. Merlin saw one of their heads nodding and then the other. He took quick, shallow breaths. The tour guide stepped away from the technicians and motioned to Merlin, smiling.

"They say to bring them the thumb drive—as long as it doesn't have any viruses on it!"

The group chuckled again, but Merlin was already on his way toward the technicians, twirling the drive between his thumb, forefinger, and middle finger in his left front pocket. He handed the drive to a NASA employee, who plugged it into a slot on the official NASA laptop from which he was working. Merlin asked, "May I drive?" and the technician made a faux gallant "be my guest" gesture with the sweep of an arm. Merlin sat at the computer and clicked away. All the screens went black for a moment.

Razor-like flashes of red arcs describing ley lines raced across the screen and pulsated in the background as multicolored eddies of light whorled on a section of the globe that included Europe, northern Africa, North America, Central America, and northern South America. Every few seconds, whooshes of lavender and violet blew across parts of the map. Merlin looked up and took in the view with amazement, but he quickly realized that he needed to make the most of his time. He clicked on a tab that read "Houston Center Morning Update" and the next screen was a map of the Greater Houston/Upper Texas Gulf Coast area. There were similar red hash marks, whorls, and eddies on this map, but the most intense action seemed to be right over the city itself. He zoomed in tightly and enlarged the map to include downtown Houston. It comprised an area as far east as the ship channel and as far west as West Loop 610.

Now the intensely colored, counterclockwise rotating whorl was flashing, indicating it had stopped over the exact location of the energy event. It looked to Merlin like it was in his neighborhood or maybe over Memorial Park, so he made one final close-up zoom. He was so astounded that he stood, left the computer, and approached the giant central high-resolution screen. He stood directly in front of it, and the sinister gyre whirled in place near Buffalo Bayou, but not on the north bank in Memorial Park. The eye of the storm had targeted a spot just behind the sixteenth green of the golf course at Bayou Boughs Country Club. Merlin took in the whirling image as if in a trance, and then, just below it on the screen, in numinous white letters and numerals, the message appeared. It read: "Event Time Coordinates: Friday, August 13, 23:33."

The other members of Merlin's tour group continued to laugh uncomfortably and make comments under their breath, but Merlin did not pay attention to them. Here, in the newest, most awe-inspiring chapel of the cathedral of manned space-flight, he stood enraptured at the beauty and majesty of the Agglomerator's work, and at the ominous event it so definitively and precisely foretold.

· *Forty-five*

Eating lunch at his desk, Junior Trust Officer Curtis Bumpers scrolled down a screen of his favorite fishing website. A boldface headline read "Record Spec Confirmed!" He scrolled until he saw a photo of an oversize human holding an enormous speckled trout. Picking up a pencil with his left hand, he drummed it nervously on the surface of his desk. He lifted his right hand from the mouse and held the pencil in both hands as he read the caption: "Angler Merlin McNaughton of Houston, Texas, Catches Record Trout in Waters Near Spirit Lake, Louisiana."

Bumpers looked at the name in disbelief, then his eyes went to the face of the large man in the photo. He was wearing round-lensed wire-frame glasses and a mop of unruly hair bushed out beneath a long-brimmed fisherman's cap. Bumpers' face flushed bright red as his lips drew into a tight thin line of pure ire. As he broke the pencil he was holding in half, he inadvertently jammed the sharpened lead into his palm. He threw the pencil pieces across the room and then looked at his punctured hand. He could see a piece of lead under his skin, but there was no blood.

· *Forty-six*

Of any of the days it was fortunate for both Merlin and his fellow humankind that he did not drive, this one was right up there at the top of the list. His stunned reverie stayed with him through the rest of the tour and the remainder of the day. He was not so engrossed with it as to not think of lunch, however, prior to his departure from Space Center Houston. Crowding in on his visions of the energy event were visions of multipattied hamburgers and enormous piles of battered, thick-cut onion rings. He had heard that Spookie's had an impressive new location near the channel from Clear Lake out to the bay, and he asked his Alles driver to spirit him there *tout de suite*. Spookie's, in fact, had bifurcated into two restaurants after the last big hurricane—a seafood café north of the bridge and a hamburger place south of it near the Kemah boardwalk. Merlin had put the correct address into the Alles program for the driver, but he made certain to clarify that it was the burger joint that was the object of his lunchtime desire.

As they crossed the bridge, Merlin took in his first good view of the opaque greenish-brown waters of the strangely named Clear Lake to his right and then a longer, sweeping view of Galveston Bay out to his left. He considered what a different perspective of the bay it was from what he experienced on that auspicious day when the *Airmadillo* crew flew to lunch at Stangaroo's on Bolivar Peninsula. The car exited the bridge on its southern side and made a quick left to arrive at Spookie's Burgers. Merlin entered the green-and-yellow-painted building and took a seat at the bar, which was directly in front of him.

He ordered a spicy Double Trouble Spookie Burger with cheese ("It's scary good!"), Aunt Bertha's oversized "dungeon ring" onion rings, and a large Dr Pepper. He took the laptop computer from his messenger bag, opened it, and inserted the thumb drive. The same graphic that had filled the giant screens of Mission Control now appeared on a thirteen-inch screen, but it still enraptured him. He looked at various metrics surrounding the event while trying not terribly successfully not to drip burger juice and sauce onto the keyboard as he ate and considered the imminent event.

Just like tropical cyclones in the northern hemisphere the whorl signifying the negative energy event rotated in a counterclockwise fashion. Was the incoming energy cyclone also somehow subject to the Coriolis effect? He wondered for a moment but didn't have time to ponder the possibility even though the energy gyre had bands and an eye like a hurricane. He noted that the place where the Agglomerator predicted it would stop and intensify behind the sixteenth green of the Bayou Boughs Country Club golf course was a relatively small patch of earth.

As he took another bite of the massive burger and sauce oozed and dripped onto the computer's edges, it was clear to Merlin what he must do. Concentrated counterclockwise energy required concentrated clockwise energy to neutralize it. He would design and construct a compact but powerful clockwise particle accelerator. Come hell or high water, he was determined to have it functional and in place on the quickly approaching August night.

· *Forty-seven*

Over the following days Merlin focused almost all of his attention on his energy reversal project. He also became increasingly agitated and absentminded. His first challenge was constructing his portable particle accelerator. After an angst-laden day or two, his brain fog burned off, and the answer appeared. He would call Angus McQuirkidale, the owner of Hephaestus Tool and Machining on North Shepherd Drive a few miles beyond the North Loop.

Merlin had met Angus at a gathering of the Houston Medieval Swordsmen's Association. They had also participated in demonstrations at the annual Renaissance Festival northwest of Houston between Magnolia and Plantersville. Merlin had asked him about his work and Angus had been very forthcoming with him regarding the company's clients and the capabilities of Hephaestus. Angus told Merlin of the over-hundred-year-old behemoth drill presses and metal-bending machines that were a part of the company's arsenal, along with metal lathes and brushing and finishing equipment. Merlin admired the old-school way McQuirkidale approached his vocation as he spoke with a kind of reverence toward his brawny old machines dating from an era when America was a heavy industry manufacturing powerhouse.

Merlin also sensed that McQuirkidale might actually comprehend the work of the Agglomerator and the exigency for constructing something that might counteract the concentrated negative energy of the event it predicted. What this really meant, although Merlin wasn't fully aware of it, was that Angus McQuirkidale might listen to him, and, most importantly, not make fun of his ideas the way most everyone else did.

Merlin e-mailed Angus, who got right back to him with unvarnished enthusiasm, suggesting they meet at Hephaestus the following day. Merlin went to work researching and sketching a rudimentary design for the contraption, which he dubbed the Vortexan Cyclonic Reverser. He was so enraptured with his planning that he didn't even leave the observatory to feast, instead opting for home delivery from a nearby Thai restaurant. He opened and arranged large white Styrofoam containers on the desk at his workstation. The cold dishes like Nam Saad glistened in their clear sweet and tart sauces, while the hot dishes like Pud Prik Thai and Tom Kha Gai in its own special soup Styro disgorged themselves of massive amounts of steam, like an incense offering to the Buddha.

The desk at Merlin's workstation featured angled sides that corresponded to the two angled screens flanking his main computer monitor and the way he had his lunch set up. It kind of resembled an edible drum set, except, instead of drum sticks, he wielded chopsticks and swiveled in his chair to take a bite of something on his right and then reach across his keyboard to snag a morsel on his left side from a dish a couple of boxes deep atop a thick catalog, like he was hitting a hi-hat cymbal to punctuate the hook of a top-ten pop song. Except, instead of a percussive pop, the chopsticks were nearly silent pincers grabbing food and sending it with a muffled kerplop into his greedy mouth. During this noontime exercise, he was actually wearing earphones and listening to music, which made his performance all the more reminiscent of famous drummers like Gene Krupa, Keith Moon, Ginger Baker, and perhaps even one of his idols—Neil Peart.

As he consumed his Asian delights, he ingested a massive amount of information from the Agglomerator and myriad websites regarding cyclones, anticyclones, vortices, and particle accelerators. He was beginning to visualize the Vortexan Cyclonic Reverser, but his boots needed to be on the ground at Hephaestus to determine the fearful symmetry of his device and proceed apace with its fabrication.

· Forty-eight

This time it was Assistant District Attorney Jim Atlas who checked the clock before placing a transatlantic call. It was midmorning in Houston, so he reasoned he might catch Mickey McNaughton at the end of his workday or perhaps at the onset of the brief but reliably daily Dutch workweek happy hour.

His conjecture paid off as Mickey was seated at the bar at Arendsnest Proeflokaal, the Amsterdam temple of on-tap artisanal Dutch beer. Although there was no denying the place was in a pretty touristed part of the city, it was equally irrefutable that the breadth and quality of its brews was without equal. The bartender had just scraped foam from the top of a glass of a highly recommended farmhouse saison. He placed it on a paper coaster in front of Mickey, whose phone rang as he was taking his first blissful sip. He drank with his left hand as he pulled the phone from his pocket with his right.

"Hello?"

"Mickey?"

"Yes! Jim?"

"Right you are. How's the afternoon?"

"Bright like midday. It's still summer in northern Europe, right?"

"Well, lucky you."

"How's H-town?"

"Like a kitchen full of steamers in a Cantonese restaurant."

"Sorry, man."

"Well, something else looks to be getting warmer."

"Our PI is turning over some rocks?"

"Yes, and he appears to be finding lizards and bugs under them."

"Do tell. I'm all ears, right?"

"Okay. He saw a lot of comings and goings over several nights. He saw a couple of fair-size trucks—kind of like small moving vehicles—drive past the gate of the place and leave a few minutes later."

"Okay."

"After this happened a couple of times, he decided to follow one of them at a discreet distance. It ended up at the port of Houston at three in the morning and drove past an electronically controlled fence gate toward the docks."

"So that's a little odd, right?"

"Yes, I think that's a little odd."

"Okay, carry on."

"He followed another vehicle a few nights later, and it went all the way to Galveston, to the cruise ship terminal. Same program—entered past a security gate in the middle of the night."

"Wow! So what do you make of it?"

"I'm not sure yet, but I do think it surpasses the strangeness barrier sufficiently to tell my boss and see if we can get the official authorities on it."

"Great work, counselor."

"Hey, it's our PI. And there's another tidbit that might be of interest to you. The ship in port at Galveston was from a Dutch-American cruise line—headquartered in . . ."

"Amsterdam."

"You got it, Sherlock."

"Damn!"

"Is that a joke?

"No. Just processing, right?"

"I'll blow up your cellie when I know more."

"Right! Thank you, brother."

"You got it."

Mickey closed the call, shook his head in disbelief, sighed, and quietly uttered a single word: "Merlin."

· Forty-nine

At Tellicherry on a steamy deep-summer morning, Lindley Acheson was drinking an equally steamy cup of masala chai as she answered e-mails, browsed a few gardening websites, and waited for a prospective client to arrive. She heard something and looked up as the restaurant's large and weighty glass and steel door opened. A small, sharp-featured woman with a leashed Chihuahua at her heels was on the way out with a to-go cup of masala chai. From Lindley's vantage point she couldn't tell who was on the inbound side of the doorway, but she did hear the little dog yapping. She leaned out just in time to see the incoming customer was Merlin and the officious, sunglassed woman's pet was nipping at his ankles from all sides like a relentless canine mosquito.

The dog's rapid-fire attempts to bite were enough to knock Merlin off balance, and as he tumbled earthward like a mouse-besieged elephant, the paper-stuffed clipboard he was carrying sailed upward and descended to a loud, clacking crash on the polished concrete floor. A few sheets detached in midair, and when the clipboard hit the floor, everything it was holding popped loose and scattered across the entryway. Immediately after slamming into the concrete, Merlin scrambled to retrieve the sheets of varying sizes, colors, and thicknesses, some bearing pencil scribbles, some with writing in firm dark pen strokes, and a few with what looked like multicolored pencil drawings and diagrams.

The woman with the Chihuahua sniffed and jutted her chin skyward in disgust. Her stiletto heels clicked their disapproval as she gathered up her snarling pet and made an imperious exit toward her red Mercedes convertible. Merlin gathered the sheets and held them against the clipboard with one of his paws while he made his way to the counter to order. Lindley's initial concern that Merlin might have broken a bone or twisted an ankle was assuaged when she saw him rise unscathed and approach the register, but she was still worried.

Merlin started to pass her table with his eyes trained on the banquette at the far end of the restaurant where he could hide behind a tall gauzy curtain, await his breakfast, and attempt to gather himself like he had gathered his papers. Lindley arrested his progress by calling to him, and he almost did a repeat performance of the confetti parade of a paper storm that the aggressive houndlet had precipitated at the entryway.

"Oh, hi, Lindley!"

"Hey, Merlin! Is everything okay?"

"Oh, yes, just a mishap on entry."

Lindley's prospective client had entered and approached the table. Lindley stood to greet her, and Merlin shuffled off with an "Okay, good to see you." During her meeting with the new client, Lindley glanced Merlin's way from time to time. She could see that things were not okay. He seemed very disturbed as he studied his notes while he cradled the top of his head in his hands. As Lindley left with her client, she noticed a paper scrap Merlin hadn't retrieved, picked it up, and put it in her satchel. Final goodbyes with the client ensued, and she forgot to take the piece of paper to Merlin. When she arrived at home, she saw it as she pulled her laptop from her commuter bag. It was folded closed, but she opened it and read: "Event Horizon 8-13 @ 23:33 hrs CDT." Beneath this line was what looked like latitude and longitude coordinates. Something inside told her she needed to keep this scrap.

· *Fifty*

At Hephaestus Tool and Machining, Inc., the following day, Angus McQuirkidale scrutinized Merlin's drawings and notes in his office in front of the big warehouse of a shop. He asked a few questions but didn't raise any red flags about the project's feasibility.

"So, four two-foot-by-two-foot sections?"

"Yes," replied Merlin.

"Each with a quarter-circle conductive metal arc?"

"Yes."

"And one electromagnetic accelerator per section?"

"Yes," responded Merlin again, barely able to contain his excitement.

"And they fit together like this?" asked Angus, motioning with his fingers.

"Yes," responded Merlin eagerly, "like Hot Wheels tracks, except the connectors are a conductive metal."

"Okay, but what keeps them connected?"

"Oh! I haven't really thought about that."

"Okay, how about some clamps like you would see on an old-school suitcase or steamer trunk?

"Uh, okay."

"I think if we put two clamps on the edge of each section you will have a more stable platform when you set it up."

"Ah, I see! Okay, sounds good!" said Merlin with renewed optimism.

McQuirkidale called his CAD expert to refine and digitize the design.

He then pulled up the McMaster-Carr website on his desktop computer, and the two began to look at parts.

In the flash of an eye, Angus began to search through the materials necessary for the successful construction of the Vortexan Cyclonic Reverser, which they were both now referring to as the VCR. He showed Merlin electromagnets, rubberized pads to which the tracks of the VCR could be attached, and even metal connectors that could work like the plastic Hot Wheels track connectors. Angus then said, "We might be able to use these, but we can certainly fabricate our own back in the shop, if the need arises." Merlin nodded in rapt agreement to everything McQuirkidale said.

"How did you learn how to do this?" Merlin queried in amazement.

"Trial and error, I guess. I studied engineering in college, but there's no teacher like the university of adversity," offered Angus.

"Wow," said a still amazed Merlin.

McQuirkidale nodded at what looked like an over-one-hundred-year-old photo of a youngish military officer on horseback. Merlin looked where Angus was nodding, and Angus continued: "That's my great-grandfather, Colonel Angus McQuirkidale. He was a battlefield engineer in World War I. He went on to have a productive engineering career in the UK and later in this country."

"Oh wow! I kind of see a resemblance," offered Merlin in awe of the proficient lineage from which he was so grateful to benefit.

"Well," said Angus with a smile and barely squelched pride, "I like to think so."

· *Fifty-one*

Near midnight one night in late July an unmarked Houston Police Department vehicle sat in a dark patch of street a half block from the compound on Snuffmeister Road in Northeast Houston. The officer inside took note of a yellow Porsche slowing in front of the address and entering the driveway. He captured the vehicle's license plate on his exterior camera and scribbled its letters and numbers on a small notepad. The officer pulled his vehicle up to a spot to try to get a look at the goings-on behind the fence. He saw a man exit the Porsche and confer with someone. The two men directed a group of people into a cargo area at the rear of a panel truck parked in the lot behind the fence and facing the driveway as if poised for departure. The officer reversed his blacked-out vehicle to its former, less visible location. In a few minutes, the truck carrying its human cargo departed; the HPD officer followed it at a discreet distance.

· Fifty-two

Riding her bike through the neighborhood on a stultifying late July morning, Lindley approached the McNaughton residence. She looked toward Merlin's observatory and noticed something new. On its surface, near the ground-floor doorway, was a freshly painted design. It looked more like a schematic of something than the depiction of a scene. She stopped and walked her bike back to the gate of the residence. In black paint there was a narrow, vertical ruler-like image with strange markings and what looked like letters at regular intervals. She took out her smart phone, zoomed in, and snapped a picture of the odd painted design.

When she arrived at her destination, she looked at the photo again. It seemed the markings might have something to do with an ancient writing system. She texted Polly Andry, her friend in the anthropology department at Rice University. Since it was summer, Polly was researching, writing, and enjoying the more pleasant climate of Tuscany. Polly responded immediately, and Lindley sent her the photo and texted, "I have no idea what this is, or what it means, if anything, but I thought if anyone might have a hook for it, it would be you." Polly responded, "It's no problem at all. I love puzzles. Will get back to you ASAP."

Late that same afternoon, Lindley's phone rang. It was Polly.

"Hello?"

"Lindley?"

"Yes. Polly? How is Florence?"

"Work is inspiring, for sure, but I'm finding *gli uomini Italiani* seem to be vying for a greater share of my attention."

"Oh, fun! I guess?!"

"I think I can handle them—not my first rodeo, so to speak. But on to business. I got a pretty quick answer for you, once I narrowed down the culture."

"Oh, great! But what culture?"

"I thought the markings resembled ancient Norse runes."

"Wow! Okay."

"So I contacted a colleague with expertise in that field, and he got right back to me."

"That's great! What was it?"

"The diagram is a depiction of what's called a runic staff calendar. Usually they were narrow, vertically oriented wooden pieces carved with runes and other etchings to mark seasons and dates."

"Okay."

"Now, here's the interesting part. The one in the photo you sent me keys in on a date in the future—the very near future."

"Uh, okay. Any ideas?"

"My colleague said he tried to make an accurate translation from the runic to the Julian calendar date, and it looks like a day roughly late in the second week of August—maybe the twelfth, thirteenth, or fourteenth of the month."

"Oh, god. Merlin."

"Merlin? Who's Merlin?"

"That's who painted it."

"Well, if you'll notice in the photo, Merlin even used red paint for the date. Must be important to him."

"Oh, wow. Wow!"

"Was this helpful?"

"Yes! Very! Lunch is on me when you're back in town."

"That's not necessary. I'm glad to help, but it'll be good to catch up!"

They said their goodbyes, and Lindley closed the call. She sat looking at her phone like it was a Sith oracle stone from the *Star Wars* series. She pulled the scrap of paper she had found at Tellicherry from her purse. She opened it and read the date and time again. As she looked at the latitude and longitude coordinates, her phone buzzed. It was a text from the person she was going to meet telling her she would be five minutes late. Lindley searched the coordinates on her phone and was puzzled when she saw that they corresponded to a place just behind the sixteenth green near the bayou on the Bayou Boughs Country Club golf course.

· *Fifty-three*

At Hephaestus Tool and Machining on North Shepherd Drive, Merlin and Angus McQuirkidale watched as two machinists drilled small notches into four quarter-circle arced segments of steel. The notches interlocked the arcs to form a circular whole. When they were done, at Angus's request, the technicians assembled the pieces into a complete circle, and for the first time, Merlin saw the perfect steel circle of his Vortexan Cyclonic Reverser. He took a step backward when the final piece was in place, so awesome was the sight to him. Angus spoke: "Now we need to add the electromagnets and clamps to keep the circuit together."

"Yes," said Merlin in a near trancelike tone. "The circle must remain unbroken."

"And we have another problem to solve," McQuirkidale continued. "What is it going to sit on?"

"I have thought about that! I had a train set when I was young, and its rails were affixed to heavy-gauge plywood painted a dark green."

"Well, that sounds good. And you can paint the plywood whatever color you like, but there's another issue."

"Oh?" Merlin queried.

"We probably ought to raise and cushion the steel arcs an inch or so above the platform sections with some rubberized pieces between the wooden platform and the VCR."

"Ooh," replied Merlin.

"That way, you'll be able to ensure nothing on the platform is touching the track. And the pieces I am thinking about are completely nonconductive, so there won't be anything interfering with the current running through the circuit."

"Wow, that sounds right!" enthused Merlin.

"Plus, it will look really cool," said Angus with his signature eye twinkle.

"And, of course, in addition to the clamps for the tracks, you will have a couple of closures on each piece of plywood so the platform stays secure and intact, especially if it needs to sit on uneven ground."

"Yes! Of course!" agreed Merlin, amazed at the thoroughness of Angus's planning.

"As soon as the electromagnets arrive and we attach them, we can proceed apace with the rest of the plan."

"Excellent! Thank you, Angus!"

"It's my pleasure," responded the idiosyncratic engineer.

They exchanged more pleasantries, and Merlin departed Hephaestus when his Alles car arrived, starry-eyed over the prospect of seeing his idea birthed into the realm of functional, three-dimensional reality. On return to the observatory, he checked the Agglomerator. The data had remained constant, but the colors attached to the energy event had intensified considerably. The approaching cloud had darkened, and the vortex appeared to spin all the more tightly.

· *Fifty-four*

Lindley Acheson was driving a load of potted plants to a client's garden in the cargo area of her vintage hunter's green and cream-colored International Harvester Scout. As she passed the McNaughton house, she saw Merlin exiting what looked like an Alles car. He seemed more distracted than usual—even more than he did after the unfortunate collision with the Chihuahua and its owner at the threshold of Tellicherry. She didn't stop because she needed to get to her client's house, but she did take note of Merlin stumbling on the baking deep-summer sidewalk while holding a large pizza box. She exhaled in relief when she saw he recovered from the trip-up and shambled on toward his place, the odd satellite of the rarely occupied McNaughton house.

· *Fifty-five*

In a windowless room outfitted with apparatuses including black leather harnesses, chrome chains, and handcuffs suspended from steel beams spanning the breadth of the room's ceiling, Tite Dûche stood at the center of a group of men wearing black. Two of them were wearing rubber butchers' aprons and black elbow-length rubber work gloves.

The tallest man in the group spoke: "We intend to provide you with the premier experience of its kind in the world. What your mind may interpret as pain will certainly be a component of it. If the experience becomes too intense for you, we have a safe phrase for you to say, and we will stop. We encourage you, however, not to use this phrase unless you deem the sensation intolerable. Is that understood?"

Tite replied with an emotionless yes and a quick nod.

The tall man continued: "Very well. Our group is quite fond of this place, The Umber Tulip. Our pet name for the hotel is UT.

"UT?" Tite asked.

"Yes," the tall man continued, "UT. And your safe phrase for this session will be 'I love UT.' Say it now so you will remember it if you need it."

"I love UT?" queried Tite.

"Yes, but without the intonation of a question. Just 'I love UT.'"

Dûche complied: "I love UT."

Twenty minutes later the proud former University of Texas fraternity man was suspended spread-eagled with chains attached to hand and ankle cuffs and a wide leather strap around his waist holding him parallel to the floor and ceiling. Covering his head and most of his face was a skintight patent leather piece that looked like a Mexican *lucha libre* mask without the colorful embellishments. Electric current-bearing clips with wire trailing behind them were attached to his chest and nether regions. Behind him, a man worked him over with various devices, each of an increasing size, the latter ones also electrified while other members of the group pricked his back with hot needles.

The man performing the extreme mechanical violation from the rear had now donned a set of horns connected by a curved piece of metal that he could wear as a hat. The horns themselves were much larger, longer, and thicker than those on Wagnerian Viking helmets. They seemed to be very much like those of Texas Longhorn cattle but were actually from animals bred to resemble the ancient aurochs that roamed the fields of prehistoric Europe. These horns had even been sanded and stained to match the dark reddish-brownish orange that was the Umber Tulip's signature color.

Wearing this menacing headgear seemed to invigorate and empower the man as he administered increasingly larger implements of torture. He seemed to take on the persona of an ancient mating-season bull in its prime as he ratcheted up the intensity of the session. At one point, he was so carried away that he used his right hand to manipulate the instrument at Tite's posterior while he yelled and raised his left arm and hand in a skyward pointing gesture, holding the middle fingers of his left hand with his thumb in a gesture that everywhere but Texas was considered a celebratory satanic salute or a sign indicating cuckoldry.

Tite Dûche's heart rate was already racing, and increasingly frequent drops of sweat were puddling on the floor. Now the rate skyrocketed, and the sweat was profuse—so intense that it became difficult for him to see through his mask's eyeholes. As he felt he might be on the verge of passing out in agony, and in a tone with which he had never said the phrase, Tite gave two desperate squeals: "I love UT! I love UT!"

The man wearing the horns started to relent, but Tite continued, moaning and tearfully wailing, "I love UT! I love UT!" The tall leader of the group nodded at the man wearing the aurochs horns, and he desisted. For a good minute and a half after he ended the session with the safe phrase, but before his tormenters unchained him from harness and cuffs, Tite whimpered the safe phrase repeatedly, its volume finally decreasing to a whisper.

· *Fifty-six*

Mickey McNaughton decided to take a stroll as the evening was still quite bright that time of year in Amsterdam. He traversed the Jordaan and the Centrum, and once again found himself walking alongside the Geldersekade canal just above the Red Light District. He was on the same side of the canal he was on the day he saw the man who looked exactly like Tite Dûche emerge from the Umber Tulip in such unusual garb. He was thinking about that strange moment when, as he passed directly across the canal from the infamous hotel, he saw its door open and, once again, and this time he was sure, it was Tite Dûche stepping onto the hotel's landing in what seemed to be some kind of biker outfit.

Mickey was so astonished he just watched the diminutive man leave the hotel and begin to walk away. He couldn't even muster the ability to speak this time, but he did manage to pull his smart phone from his pocket. By the time his camera app was on the screen, Dûche was gone, but the door to the Umber Tulip opened again, and a group of men emerged dressed in black leather trousers and wearing black turtlenecks. A tall man who seemed to be their leader and looked like Dieter on "Sprockets" from the old days of *Saturday Night Live* directed the group down the street.

Mickey kept his camera on the screen and took photos of the dour, severely dressed group, even zooming in on the tall guy and a few of his colleagues. Somehow, he had a sense they might not be strangers to N. Teitel Dûche V.

· *Fifty-seven*

Sitting at the dining table of his apartment on Fannius Scholtenstraat, Mickey McNaughton responded to a brief e-mail from Jim Atlas, who used a private, non-official e-mail account.

> Mickey, I think your nephew's log of the Porsche's trips around town could be useful. I can't have this come through official channels right now, so if you would please use this e-mail address to send the data, I would appreciate it.
>
> Best,
> Jim

Mickey sent Merlin an equally brief e-mail requesting the data in a zip file and although Merlin was absorbed in the Agglomerator's prognostications when he received it, he sent the log of the Porsche's peregrinations to Mickey immediately. He was so absorbed in thoughts of the imminent energy event he didn't pause to wonder why Mickey wanted the data.

Mickey sent the file to Jim Atlas. He decided it was beer-thirty and was soon down his building's narrow staircase and out the door to a neighborhood bar. He led off with his usual bartender banter, and since the bartender was a good-looking young Dutch woman with the unlikely American-sounding name of Linda, the conversation flowed as smoothly as the local ale from the tap at the center of the counter. Mickey allowed that work was going fine but that he had found himself assisting in what seemed to be some kind of criminal investigation in his home city back in the U.S.

"Is that so?" said Linda in the impeccably accented English all the Dutch seemed to speak with such flawless fluency.

"Yes!" replied Mickey after taking a quick sip from his glass.

"Well, you might be interested to know that the gentleman at the other end of the bar is a detective with the Amsterdam Police!"

She said it loud enough for the man to hear and immediately reassured him. "I don't think you'll mind your cover being blown, Piet. This guy doesn't seem to be one of the characters you're looking for."

The man at the other end of the bar looked up from his newspaper, pushed his eyeglasses up to the bridge of his nose, and shrugged. Mickey was demonstrably surprised to learn this, and seeing the man's world-weary indifference to Linda's disclosure of his vocation, he ventured a question. "Hey, I know you're off work right now, so I really don't want to bother you, right? Shut me down whenever you feel like it, but would you mind if I asked you a potentially law enforcement–related question that has been nagging at me?"

"Sure, shoot," responded the Amsterdam official flatly in pitch-perfect colloquial American English.

Mickey went on to recount his sightings of whom he believed to be Tite Dûche exiting the Umber Tulip on the Geldersekade. He then described his unease at seeing the strange group of black-clad men exit the storied BDSM hotel. On hearing this part of Mickey's story, the Dutch official straightened a bit and cast Mickey an icy glance.

"What, as best as you can remember, did these men look like?" queried the detective in professional tones.

"They were all dressed pretty severely in black. Some of them wore glasses." Mickey then lifted his smart phone from the bar counter and said, "Here, I took some pictures of them. Do you mind?"

"No, go ahead," responded the detective, his attitude shifting a bit. Mickey walked a few steps down the bar and placed the phone in front of the officer.

The Dutch detective froze on seeing the image then quickly asked if he could see some other photos of the group. Mickey complied by swiping through the photos for him.

"Stop right there! Wait, go back one frame."

Now Mickey was the one who was intrigued.

"And you say you think that the man who left before them might have something to do with this group?"

"It's a hunch. Yes."

Now the detective looked at Mickey with steely eyes and said in very measured tones, "I don't know you, nor do I have any reason to trust you, but part of my work, despite all of the science and official procedural protocols, hinges on hunches."

"Okay. I mean, you can research me, right? I don't have a criminal record of any kind, have never been arrested, or in any kind of trouble with any government, et cetera, right?"

The man nodded, sat in silence for a moment, and then said, "The group you saw is one of the most notorious bondage and sadism groups in Europe. They are considered the very cream of the crop for their area of expertise. And the crop is one that a rider might use, not the kind that grows in a field. I say notorious because they have been connected to criminals and criminal activities over the years. We just haven't been able to get them on any of the specific charges because they are so secretive, so good at covering their tracks."

"Shit!" Mickey barked.

"The tall guy, as you guessed, is their leader," the Dutchman said. "He is known as Willem, a pretty common Dutch name, but some of their worldlier, shall we say, sophisticated clientele call them by a rather chillingly appropriate name considering Amsterdam is their base of operations."

"So, what's the name?"

"The Syndics of the Rapers' Guild."

"Whoa!" Mickey said in amazement as he visualized one of his favorite Rembrandts in the Rijksmuseum.

"Again, however, we haven't been able to adequately connect these guys to some of the crimes with which they are implicated. They've been pretty slippery, if you will." The Amsterdammer cracked a wry smile. "Until recently."

Mickey leaned forward.

The officer took a long pull from his beer. "As of this week, we have a bona fide mole in the group."

"A rat?"

"Yes, a kind of double agent. He provides information when we ask for it. Lately, we have instructed him to photograph anything that looks like it might be of use in the Syndics' clients' wallets, man-purses, or clothing. He uses a small spy cam, and he's getting pretty good at taking the photos discreetly."

"Okay?" said Mickey quizzically.

"Now I have a question for you," said the officer without blinking and looking Mickey in the eye.

"Sure, shoot."

"What is the name of the guy you thought you saw walk out before they did?"

"Are you ready for this?"

"Yes."

"This guy's name is Tite Dûche. He pronounces it 'duke,' but people who aren't exactly fond of him generally use another pronunciation because it is spelled d-u-c-h-e with a circumflex accent over the *u*."

"Ha!" the Dutchman allowed a second of levity before resuming his professional attitude.

"Right?" Mickey laughed. "So, his name is N. Teitel Dûche the Fifth. Here, I'll write it for you."

Mickey wrote Tite's name on a bar napkin for the detective, who looked at it for a moment, folded it, and placed it inside a coat pocket.

"So, here's another weird thing," Mickey continued. "I'm

finding myself kind of entwined in what may be a criminal investigation in my home city in the U.S. regarding this guy because of some things my nephew uncovered incidentally."

"Your nephew?" queried the detective.

"Yes. My brother was many years older than I. So, he's not even a whole generation younger in age than I am, right?"

"I don't know," said the Dutchman.

"You don't know what?" queried Mickey.

"I don't know how old your nephew is."

"Well, he's in his early thirties, okay?"

"Okay. And you said your brother 'was'?"

"Yes, he and his wife died quite a long time ago in a plane crash. Anyway, all of this started because of an egging."

"An egging?"

"That's what we call it when someone throws eggs at your house."

"Oh, I see. How American."

"So it starts with this egging, and then when this guy Tite Dûche's sons are implicated as the eggers, my nephew—don't ask me why—attaches a tracking device to the guy's car."

"I see," responded the Amsterdammer.

"And then—now get this—my cousin works for a company that has a promotional blimp."

"A blimp?"

"Yeah. A blimp, a dirigible, an airship. A big, slow-moving cigar-shaped balloon in the sky. They run ads on a giant screen on its exterior skin at night. It flies over football games and state fairs in the daytime."

"Very American."

"Yes, I'll give you that. Everyone seems to love the *Airmadillo*."

"The what?"

"The *Airmadillo*. It's a play on words. An armadillo is a kind of prehistoric-looking armored little field beast in Texas. It's iconic, kind of like the kiwi is for New Zealand."

"I see."

"Anyway, I'm getting off track."

"Okay."

"So, my nephew, who seems to have been learning to fly the blimp as a benefit of his job, tracks Dûche's car to an address in a part of Houston I'm not familiar with and notes some pretty strange activities."

"What kind of activities?"

"People being loaded into vans and delivered to the Port of Houston. Also, a very intense heat signature."

"Heat signature?"

"Yes, my nephew is not a bad guy, but he is a bit of an odd bird, to say the least—fancies himself a gadget expert. So he brought along a heat sensor attachment for his phone on the last night he flew in the blimp before it relocated to another part of the country for the remainder of the summer."

"Fascinating."

"And this whole time I'm in conversation with a friend of mine at the county district attorney's office. So I tell him about all of this and long story short, the Houston Police Department thinks there's enough questionable activity that they are now sur-veilling the property and following vehicles arriving and leaving there. And my nephew has a digitized log of all the times this guy Tite Dûche's piss-yellow Porsche has been there. It's quite a few, by the way."

"Hmmm. Egg-hurling vandals, a dirigible named after a beloved prehistoric-looking animal, and a Porsche the color of urine. Texas must be a colorful place."

"And a ninja suit–wearing vandal who smashed my nephew's beloved armonica."

"Harmonica?"

"No. It's called an armonica. It is composed of different sizes of spinning glass discs played with the fingertips. It's similar to getting sound from a wine goblet. It was invented by Benjamin Franklin."

"How very American, indeed!" responded the Dutch detective, now confused and bemused by this headstrong half-drunk American's story.

"And the intruder wore a ninja suit?"

"Yeah, a pitch-black one—in the middle of summer in Houston. He must have really wanted to do this."

"Do you think this ninja has anything to do with the other events?"

"I don't know. I guess. I thought I would mention it when you got on the theme of colorful stuff. Anyway, I'm not trying to entertain you. I'm just a bit perplexed with all of this."

"It's not a problem. This is the kind of conversation that makes my life interesting. Do you have a card?" queried the officer.

Mickey opened a silver business card case and handed the detective one of his cards. In turn, the detective opened a thin wallet containing his official credentials, including his name—Piet Penders. He then gulped down the rest of his beer and stood abruptly. Mickey also stood and noted that the man shook hands very firmly for a European as he looked at him one last time with the steely, unblinking eyes, and said, "It's been a pleasure meeting you. I will contact you if I learn anything of interest." With that, Detective Penders departed the bar, leaving Mickey even more confounded as he ordered another beer and said, "The Syndics of the Rapers' Guild" in a low, astonished voice.

· *Fifty-eight*

In the tastefully appointed café at the Embassy of the Liberated Mind in the high-ceilinged House with the Eyes on the Keizersgracht on Central Amsterdam's west side, the Dutch man who had met with Tite Dûche a few months earlier at the café in De Pijp waited for Tite on the banquette side of a two-top table at the far end of the room near a tall, opaque streetside window. His name was Nico van Rompaey, and he looked up as Tite approached his table with a slight limp. Van Rompaey motioned to the chair across from him, inviting Tite to take a seat. Dûche seated himself carefully and winced a little when he scooted his chair toward the table.

A server appeared at his side, asking if she could get him anything.

"Something soothing," Dûche replied.

"We have a very good Dutch apple pie today."

"Okay, I'll take that and a cup of tea. Decaf."

"We have chamomile. It is very gentle, particularly good for the digestive system."

"Yes. I want that one. Thank you."

"Of course."

The server left the table, and Nico fixed Tite in his gaze.

"Are you well?" van Rompaey asked.

"I think so. I seem to have strained or pulled a muscle or something—probably taking too many steps at a time up these narrow Amsterdam stairways."

"It's important not to take too much at a time . . . of any-thing," responded van Rompaey. After a pause the Dutchman said, "Are we ready to expand operations?"

"I'm ready to increase on my side. Additionally, I may be able to deliver some business out of New Orleans. Some pretty-established players handle this sort of thing over there, but I think I have a good understanding with a syndicate that can set up operations based on the Houston–Galveston model."

"Good. Instead of overconcerning yourself with how the pie is split, you are growing the pie."

The server placed a thick slab of Dutch apple pie topped with a massive dollop of freshly whipped cream in front of Tite.

"I'm quite satisfied with how well you have kept the pipe full," van Rompaey said.

"Thank you. I'm all about deal flow. Kind of goes with the pie analogy."

"Yes. Indeed, it does." Van Rompaey eased back into the cushioned banquette. "How do you feel about our enterprise in general?"

"What do you mean?"

"Are you at all concerned? Do you have any qualms?"

"I don't think so. The machinery is well oiled and under the radar screen back in Texas."

"And the same here in Amsterdam."

"So?"

"I was thinking in broader, perhaps more philosophical terms."

"Philosophical?"

"Maybe that's not the most appropriate word. Some people might have what they call a moral problem with this kind of venture."

"Moral problem?"

"Yes, but I don't."

"Me neither. Like you said before, business is business."

"I think that the simple people who have been conditioned to think in these terms are trapped behind the prison bars of Western dualistic thinking."

"Dualistic thinking?"

"Right and wrong. Good and evil. These sorts of quaint, simplistic notions."

"Oh, okay."

"It is important to remember that all is one. As humans, we are all flowing together."

"Uh, okay."

"Yes, and all is circular and inevitable. These people, who some would say we are exploiting, we are most likely simply ushering on their way to their next incarnation. Given their backgrounds, nothing good would have come their way. And if we weren't doing this someone else would have been, because Fortuna is in command."

"Fortuna?"

"Fate. Inevitable, unavoidable, inexorable fate."

"So, you're saying we're off the hook as far as the authorities are concerned?"

"Yes. And more than that, I am saying that there is no hook, or perhaps that the hook of their idea of criminality is a ruse, a chimera—a contrived fabrication."

"But it could still get us in trouble."

"Perhaps, but I believe because of our concurrence in this enterprise, we are under a kind of shield."

"How?"

"Because of my frame of mind that transcends this infantile Manichean dualism, this silly strain of the silly game most think they are playing. I have great internal tranquility. And because of that, I am happy to reap the financial rewards that flow my way. I think you may not understand it yet, but this kind of outlook provides shelter."

"Okay?"

"There is great freedom in eschewing this framework contrived from what many call Christianity or the Judeo-Christian tradition."

"There is?"

"But that doesn't mean that there still isn't the element of a game to all of our interactions."

"I agree with that."

"Good, then you'll understand why I'm showing you these."

Nico van Rompaey placed a large heavy envelope secured with a string around a central button on the table. He slowly opened it and pulled from it an 8x10 photo that showed the Syndics of the Rapers' Guild leaving the Umber Tulip, and Tite several yards away, walking away from them. Tite's eyes widened, but he kept his cool. "So what?" he said. "I was walking down the street."

Van Rompaey responded coolly, "As you say in America, nice try."

He pulled the next photo; it showed the Syndics working Tite over moments before he screamed the safe phrase. The blood drained from Tite's face. He sat bolt upright and glared at the Dutchman, who returned Tite's look with a kind of smug avuncular superiority.

"But how?"

Van Rompaey interrupted Tite with a shushing finger at his lips in the sign for keeping a secret, then dropped his hand and said, "I own the Umber Tulip."

"You? I thought—"

Van Rompaey interrupted again: "The purported ownership is a false front. You will have a very hard time finding my name associated with UT."

"Don't call it UT!"

"Why not?"

"I just don't like it!"

"My, my. Getting found out certainly makes you testy."

Tite's face flashed crimson as he sat in irate silence.

"Now, you are in my game," van Rompaey said. "Exiting it means forfeiting all you hold dear; staying in it will bring you great prosperity. There's nothing right or wrong with that. It just is. Just like there's nothing right or wrong with the private proclivity that led you to Willem's group. It just is. You have nothing to fear as long as you stay in the game. I saw when I met you that you had the mark of one of my chessboard pieces, and I knew Fortuna had dictated it."

Mouth agape, Tite stared at van Rompaey as he relaxed farther into the plush banquette and stretched his arms out wide. He looked around and said, "Isn't this a lovely room?" Tite gave him a questioning look.

"Why are you perplexed?" van Rompaey asked. "You knew I was a wealthy man when we began this."

"Yes."

"And what is the entertainment of people who can buy anything they want?"

"Being able to buy more?"

"No, of course not!"

"What is it?"

"You don't know?"

"I guess not."

Van Rompaey chuckled and said, "The chief entertainment of people who can buy anything they want is what you Americans might call messing with people. Perhaps you are accustomed to hearing the phrase with a more colorful verb that better conveys the dark pleasure of the sport. This ultimate rich man's game has provided endless entertainment for the wealthy for centuries. Yes, you and I have been making money, but now I find our association truly gratifying, and I want you to know I certainly appreciate it."

"So, I'm the goat."

"The goat—what a wonderful Americanism. Yes, you are. But you are also a good income-generating business partner. And there are others to whom I look forward to introducing you." Van Rompaey looked around the room, then back at Dûche. "Perhaps I was a puppeteer in another life." He smiled and opened his hands in a gesture of conjecture. He eased out of the banquette and stood to go.

"The strings between you and me are now very difficult to cut," the Dutchman said. And in a lower voice, "Let no independent step entangle you. Besides inconveniencing me, straying would bring you sure devastation."

He looked down at Dûche, who looked up at him with the eyes of a caged animal.

"Stay and enjoy the café. It's such a pleasant day for contemplating the ancient wisdom that resonates from these old walls." Van Rompaey pulled a deck of cards from a pocket of his sport coat and placed them on the table.

"This is an antique deck of the Tarot. Cut them."

With deer-in-the-headlights eyes, Tite cut the big deck of cards into two stacks. Nico van Rompaey finished the cut, putting the bottom stack of cards on top of the other stack, and departed with a chipper "Good day!" He smiled and exchanged pleasantries with the server as he walked toward the doorway of the famous old Amsterdam *huis*.

Tite flipped over the first card on top of the deck. It read "Wheel of Fortune." He turned over the second card. It bore the image of a skeleton in knight's armor wielding a large scythe. The numerical value of the card was thirteen and the name under the image read "Death." He hesitated, then decided to take a third and final card from the stack. He turned it over. It was The Fool, and its value was zero. He realized he was having a difficult time breathing. He glanced around the room and felt a sudden urge to get out of the building immediately.

· *Fifty-nine*

On the shop floor of Hephaestus Tool and Machining, Merlin, Angus McQuirkidale, and shop foreman Victor Martinez put the finishing touches on the Vortexan Cyclonic Reverser. Angus had decided the VCR needed only two electromagnets to operate efficiently, so they joined each quarter arc of the apparatus together such that the two arcs opposite one another had electromagnets attached to ensure the current would flow clockwise. The arcs were fabricated to overlap and touch one another, so the circuit would not be broken, but Merlin added metal clips to the places where they overlapped to ensure contact. They connected the four quarters of the plywood base using latches on the top and bottom of each piece. A single power cord and inlet connected each of the magnets, and Victor Martinez plugged a long, heavy three-pronged extension cord into it and then plugged the other end into a power source at the shop wall. He returned to the group and said, "Well, who wants to do the honors?"

Angus looked at Merlin and motioned with his hand toward the on/off switch. Merlin returned the gesture with a solemn nod and moved toward the switch. He took a couple of breaths with his broad thumb against the switch and gave it a resolute flip. The thing whirred to life, emanating a low hum. A blue light on the VCR indicated the circuit was complete. Angus touched a voltmeter to one of the metal arcs; he read it and gave a thumbs-up. Merlin felt a kind of electricity start at the base of his spine and run all the way up to his giant coconut of a head. He stood in awe as he beheld his brainchild at work. Angus smiled at Merlin's delight in the fruition of the project. The only one who wasn't in on the euphoria was Victor Martinez who, after a silent interlude, stepped back and addressed Angus: "Well, boss?" Angus refocused and looked at him. "Anything else?" Martinez asked.

Angus returned to his usual businesslike mode and responded, "No, I think we're good." He then asked Merlin, who was still entranced by the device, "Shall we box it up?"

"Oh!" Merlin said, returning to the moment. "Yes, of course! And thank you, Mr. Martinez!"

Martinez was relieved to have a pressing task as he found the whole enterprise kind of embarrassing, and he didn't have a clue what this perplexing device was for and what the big goofball was going to do with it or why his boss was so pleased.

After the Vortexan Cyclonic Reverser was placed in four heavy-gauge cardboard boxes and Merlin departed Hephaestus, Victor Martinez said, "Boss, I hope you don't mind me asking, but why'd you decide to help him make that thing?"

With a twinkle in his eye, Angus said, "How many art cars have we helped design and fabricate back here?"

"Well, plenty, over the years, I guess."

"And the people who have the ideas for them, you wouldn't exactly call mainstream, would you?"

"No! For sure not!"

"They are on the periphery, so most of the world isn't set up for people who think like they do to get along smoothly, and more than that, to feel like what they are doing matters."

"Okay."

"Then they see their art car come together and get cheered by thousands of people in the parade every spring—and I've seen this—it's like their eyes come to life."

"Yeah, but boss, this thing wasn't a car. It didn't move. It didn't even have any moving parts!"

"I know, but when he flipped that switch, and I confirmed that it was working, I saw the same look in his eyes that I see in those art car artists during the parade, and that makes the whole enterprise worthwhile."

Angus's phone rang, and he excused himself. Victor stood in motionless silence until someone from the back of the shop called to him for help.

———

Lindley rode her bike down a cross street that intersected with Merlin's street. As she crossed, she saw an SUV on the street in front of Merlin's house and Merlin and the driver at its rear hatch. She wheeled her bike in a loop and headed toward the McNaughton house to see what was up. When she arrived, Merlin and the driver were unloading what looked to be heavy two-and-a-half-foot-square cardboard boxes from the vehicle's cargo area. She glided to a stop a few feet away from them and asked, "Do you need any help with that?"

Merlin jumped, surprised that someone was observing his activities at close range, but when he saw that it was Lindley, he relaxed a little.

"Oh! Lindley! What are you doing here?"

"I saw you guys unloading, and I wanted to see if I could help."

"Oh, no. Thank you! We are just stacking them here inside the gate right now. I'll use a hand truck to deal with them in a few minutes."

Lindley noticed Merlin seemed even more flustered and out of sorts than he had been when he tussled with the teacup Chihuahua at Tellicherry. His glasses were on kind of sideways, and he had ripped his shirt in the box-unloading process.

The driver stood next to Merlin and said, "Well, that's it."

Merlin fumbled for his wallet and a few bills fluttered onto the street as he found a suitable tip amount. The driver thanked him, and Merlin and Lindley picked up the errant bank notes.

Seeing him so rattled, there was only one errant note on Lindley's mind, and it was the one that fluttered away from him at Tellicherry, which she had kept on a hunch. Merlin seemed in a hurry to move the boxes toward the garage at the base of the observatory, but he stopped and looked Lindley in the eye and said, "If you can arrange it, try not to be here—here in town—during the weekend of the thirteenth."

"The thirteenth?" Lindley queried.

"Yes, it would be advisable to be a good hundred and fifty miles away from here by sunset."

"On Friday the thirteenth?" She visualized Merlin's scrawl on the scrap of paper he dropped at the Indian restaurant.

"Yes."

"That's next Friday!"

"I know. I'm sorry. I should have told you earlier, but I think there may be some kind of disturbance."

"There's a hurricane the weather forecasters say is heading straight for the Gulf right now."

"Another good reason to depart for a while. It would be a good weekend for an Austin or Hill Country trip."

"What is it, Merlin?"

"I can't really talk about it in detail. Please just take my word for it."

"Okay."

Merlin picked up a black backpack that seemed to be rather heavy and said, "Bye, Lindley." She stood still and said, "Bye, Merlin," and watched him as the curb tripped him on his way to the front gate of the McNaughton residence. He righted himself before he hit the ground, then turned and waved goodbye to Lindley as he closed the gate and shuffled toward the base of his watchtower. Lindley was befuddled, but concern for Merlin took precedence over her confusion regarding his warning, and she watched him until he began to open the garage door at the base of the observatory. Before he could turn to wave goodbye, she hopped on her bike and stood as she pedaled to gain speed.

· *Sixty*

Over the days leading up to the negative energy event, Merlin rehearsed and re-rehearsed his moves for the critical night. He knew that, just the way the astronauts had only one opportunity to land the unpowered space shuttle orbiter, there would be but one opportunity for the Vortexan Cyclonic Reverser to be in place and operative at the moment of the event's energy discharge. With the gravity of a NASA commander of that most leaden of interatmospheric gliders, Merlin went through his checklist.

The VCR was obviously functional, but he made a special note to remember to bring the heavy-duty document clips to ensure an unbroken electrical circuit. He appraised the dimensions of the two-and-a-half-foot-square boxes and considered the VCR's transport to the spot on the far side of the Bayou Boughs Country Club golf course. He rummaged through the garage beneath the observatory and found an old, somewhat rusty red Radio Flyer wagon. It was just wide enough for each of the four boxes containing the components of the VCR to fit when stood on their sides. There was even a little room left for extension cords in the wagon's bed.

Next, his thoughts turned to logistics. The Betancourts' house was on the BBCC golf course. He had a key to the house's side gate because he sometimes fed the Betancourts' dogs when their owners were out of town. The wagon would be ideal for getting the gear there as that part of the trip would be over pavement and sidewalks, but from the home's back fence, he would need to traverse a considerable amount of grass as he crossed fairways and rough to arrive at the spot behind the sixteenth green. He could try to arrange the route as much as possible on cart paths, but that wasn't feasible as the most direct way to ground zero was over the course itself. Any way he looked at it, crossing grass was in the cards. He went back to the garage and continued to pick through its dust-coated contents. In the area with hunting gear, he found goose decoys and a couple of plastic decoy sleds. One was cracked down the middle, but the other seemed to be intact. The Radio Flyer would suffice for the first part of the trip, and he could drag a decoy sled containing his equipment the way he and his grandfather had when they prepared to shoot the honking avian behemoths in nearby coastal prairie rice fields when he was growing up.

Merlin was so focused on his mission he didn't go out to forage during the last few days leading up to the event, opting instead for home delivery from his favorite nearby restaurants and cafés. By the time the day of the event had arrived, the accreted pile of takeout boxes and containers rose precariously above the rim of his recycling bin like a new island forming from active lava flow.

———

No breezes caressed the observatory on the morning of Friday, August 13th, and thick humidity gripped it the way Merlin had handled himself during one of his many vivid waking dreams featuring Celtic goddesses and buxom mythical warrior queens. Bone-roasting heat headlined the afternoon and held on into the sunlit early summer evening. During the day, he checked the Agglomerator. Nothing had changed. It continued to register the same precise time for the event. The purple haze indicating a possible Sasquatch/Bigfoot nexus also remained, and, if anything, the color had become more saturated on his monitor screens during the final days prior to the predicted moment.

He also checked the weather. There were a couple of tropical depressions—one traversing the Florida Straits and one headed for the Yucatan Channel. Even if they made it into the Gulf of Mexico, they could end up anywhere along the coast, or dissipate completely. Besides, Merlin reasoned, the height of storm season was at least a couple of weeks away in late August and early September.

Finally twilight arrived, and night fell on the city. Although the evening was almost moonless, the familiar orange glow of urban light reflected from the undersides of low-passing cumulus clouds. And finally, after all the preparation that was almost more than Merlin could think about, the moment of his departure was at hand. He dressed for the weather—a blue fishing shirt and beige cargo shorts made from strong but lightweight material. For footwear, he considered the dampness of the golf course after the sprinklers had done their work and chose the same water shoes he had worn on the fishing trip with Shep in Louisiana.

He descended into the garage. His setup was waiting for him in the little red Radio Flyer wagon. The sled itself presented a bit of a problem, but Merlin solved it by looping marine twine through rings at the left and right sides of the fore and aft of the sled so he could wear it like a large backpack over the smaller black nylon military-grade tactical backpack he was already shouldering. As he pulled the wagon away from the garage—with the sled on his back like a giant inverted rectilinear tortoise shell—he thought of the image of the man bent forward under the burden of a huge bundle of sticks lashed to his back on the album cover of Led Zeppelin IV. But for Merlin, the sled was more unwieldy than heavy, and he leaned forward only slightly as he balanced it to walk with the Radio Flyer in tow.

On his way to the Betancourts' house, Merlin was worried that he would be noticed and questioned. What he didn't consider was that the neighborhood was so accustomed to his eccentric walkabouts with gadgets adjuring him to sometimes angle his person one way or another, like a jet crabbing in a crosswind, that seeing him pulling a child's Radio Flyer wagon while hiking with what looked like a small boat on his back would raise nary an eyebrow. Even though he tensed as he saw a Bayou Boughs Patrol car approach during the walk, his concern was unfounded. He recognized the officer at the wheel, who slowed and gave him an amiable hand wave of greeting as he passed. His relief after this interaction invigorated him and caused him to quicken his pace; the Radio Flyer clacked resolutely over the uneven tree root and heat-buckled sidewalk.

His entry into the Betancourts' property was equally uneventful. They were at their home in Jackson Hole for the summer, and their two Weimaraners had flown up with them on the family's plane. A couple of motion-activated security lights switched on, but other than that, no alarm sounded. Merlin maintained his quick pace past the home's motor court to the rear of the property. He opened a little gate in the midst of a tall hedgerow that gave onto a fairway of the Bayou Boughs Country Club golf course.

He needed to stash the Radio Flyer, but he didn't want to leave it at the Betancourts' house. He unbuttoned one of the big front pockets of his cargo shorts and pulled out his night vision goggles. He secured its elastic straps to his head and peered through the lenses. There was a thicket of bushes and trees on the far side of the fairway, and he thought he might hide it there. Then an idea flickered to full flame. He could load the sled with the VCR and tie the wagon to his back with some extra twine he had stashed in his backpack. He quickly rearranged his gear. He unharnessed himself from the decoy sled and placed it on the ground.

He placed the four boxes containing the VCR inside the sled and looked back at the wagon where he saw the extension cords, and an image flashed in his mind's eye. It was of an antique photograph of Pancho Villa, jaunty with twin ammunition-filled bandoliers slung across his body from both shoulders, making an X on the Mexican revolutionary's torso. He grabbed a long, coiled orange cord and unwound and rewound it to fit him; he donned it on his left shoulder, forming a sash to his right hip. He did the same with a yellow cord of equal length, forming a sash from his right shoulder to left hip, creating a Day-Glo X across his massive torso. He felt like a warrior primed for battle.

Merlin pulled more twine from his backpack. He held the free end in his teeth and cut a length of it to secure the wagon to the upper part of his back using his tactical backpack's shoulder loops to help hold it in place. He untied a loop on the decoy sled and ran the line through a loop at the top of his backpack before retying it to the sled.

In a couple of minutes, he was ready, the VCR on the sled behind him, and the wagon secured to his back with its front wheels by his ears. It was uncomfortable, but comfort was the last thing on Merlin's mind. The mission was underway. He gripped the twin extension cord bandoliers and gave them a tug to ensure they were secure. He flipped his night vision goggles down in front of his eyes and set off across the sprinkler-wet turf for the far side of the back nine.

· Sixty-one

Dawn of August 14th broke mild and clear in Amsterdam, and Tite Dûche was already having coffee in his hotel suite. He looked through a glossy folder detailing the particulars of a Ferrari rally in which he had been invited to participate starting on Monday on the Amalfi Coast. The cars would then be moved to other scenic drives in Italy during the week for the event to continue.

There was a welcome reception scheduled for Sunday near the rally's starting point. For Tite, the rally shimmered with glamor and prestige. All drivers received their very own custom-made leather racing outfits emblazoned with the logo and colors of the fabled Italian performance car maker. He found the jackets with their diagonal zippers and high, notched collars particularly appealing. He was almost as excited about wearing his tailored-to-fit leather race car driver outfit as he was about the rally itself.

Half an hour after finishing his coffee, he settled in the spacious back seat of a large black Mercedes sedan heading to Schiphol Airport. He checked his phone for updated information regarding the trip. His midmorning flight to Naples was on time.

· Sixty-two

Merlin was watching the clock. Everything was in place and a mere five minutes remained until the energy showdown behind the sixteenth green. He had stumbled a couple of times during his walk, but he made it to ground zero unharmed, his night vision goggles performing their wartime best to help him navigate through the darkness. He set up the Vortexan Cyclonic Reverser, locking each of its quadrants and fixing metal document clips at the places where the now complete steel rings' arcs overlapped and joined together. The exact spot for the event was in a relatively flat area, so there was no worry about the VCR sliding toward the bayou. Additionally, as Merlin had calculated, the end-on-end joined-together extension cords reached a power outlet at a shelter covering a bathroom, outdoor water fountain, and ice dispenser near the fifteenth hole's tee box with a few feet to spare.

A fine mist had been falling intermittently as Merlin arranged everything, but it ceased. He placed a small Bluetooth-enabled speaker in the grass a couple of feet away from the energy-reversal device. The decoy sled and wagon were stashed by the shelter. One minute prior to the event, Merlin flipped the switch of the VCR, and it whirred to life. Fifteen seconds before 11:33, Merlin stepped inside the ring of the particle accelerator. He hit "play" on a song he had cued up on his smart phone and the first ominous strains of *Fortuna, Imperatrix Mundi* from *Carmina Burana* began to play from the nearby speaker in the grass. With six seconds left, Merlin slipped the phone into his pocket and counted down in a whisper, "Five, four, three, two, one."

The volume of the instruments and accompanying choir soared as he stretched his arms out on either side of him. He turned his hands skyward, and as the encircling electricity pulsed clockwise, he closed his eyes and began to rotate his massive person in counterpart, a slow clockwise gesture of commitment to the well-being of his hometown and a simultaneous devoir and sacrament honoring the city of his birth. His eyes remaining closed in a kind of ecstatic prayer, this unlikely tortoise-speed dervish raised his chin from his chest toward the heavens at the music's crescendo. The fine mist began once again, filming the thick round lenses of his eyeglasses.

Merlin hadn't noticed the coating of the extension cord attached to the VCR was worn all the way through to the wire. An electrical arc had formed between the bare worn wire and the metal ring of the Vortexan Cyclonic Reverser. The music was loud and Merlin had kept his eyes shut. He was completely unaware when the arc ignited one and then another and another of the rubber supports between the metal ring and its plywood base. Several of these pieces were now burning and Merlin was oblivious that his outstretched-arm spinning was happening inside a ring of fire. The priest of the par-three hole continued to spin and the opera played on.

Then, a voice. He heard a voice! And it was calling his name! Merlin closed his eyes even harder now as he discerned that it was the insistent voice of a woman.

"Merlin!"

The voice was closer now.

"Merlin!"

He ventured an answer to what he presumed was an auspicious visitation from a goddess.

"Yes! Is that you, Britomartis? Or do you prefer Britomart?"

"No!" the ever-closer voice responded.

"Are you Queen Boudica or Athena herself?"

"No! No! Merlin! It's me!"

Merlin continued his query, racking his brain to remember the various female deities from ancient pantheons.

"Are you Hecate or perhaps Isis?"

"No! Merlin! It's me! Lindley!"

"Lindley?"

"Yes! Your friend! Lindley!"

Merlin stopped spinning and faced the direction from which the voice emanated. The opera played but now the voice was all he heard.

"Lindley?"

"Yes! Merlin, open your eyes!"

He lowered his chin from its skyward angle and opened his eyes. He used his shirt to wipe his glasses and could barely make out the silhouette of Lindley Acheson trudging toward him from the thicket at the south bank of Buffalo Bayou. He stared downward at the flames licking toward his calves and gave Lindley a desperate look.

Then, a feeling descended upon him he had not expected. It was a cavernous emptiness borne of despair, a hollowness and terrible sense of futility with the sudden certain knowledge that, other than the rubber supports for the Vortexan Cyclonic Reverser catching fire, exactly nothing had happened or changed during what he was sure would have been a propitious and clearly discernible energy shift.

This terrible apprehension was a bolt as arresting as the one that had ignited the duck blind near Lumbeaux Jump but not remotely as exhilarating. Instead of an energy depositor, it was an energy thief. He knew the plug had been pulled on all his aspirations for reversing the negative gyre and resetting his city's course. Merlin was defeated—a big overweight lumbering sweaty mass of post-delusional emptiness. And all he could do was stand motionless and hear Lindley calling to him as she emerged from the shadows, her Wellington boots trudging toward him with the same resolution that minutes earlier had animated Merlin's own march across the links.

"Merlin!" Lindley continued. "This is bad!"

"It is?"

"Yes! This is bad! We have to go!"

"We do?"

"Yes! All this commotion and smoke is going to attract attention."

"Oh!"

"I have a raft!"

"A raft?"

"Yes! A raft, down on the bayou! We have to go! Now!"

"Oh! Okay?" Merlin said with shocked uncertainty.

He looked at the flames encircling him and hopped over the fire to the damp grass surrounding the VCR.

Pointing to the VCR, Merlin asked, "What about this?" He now saw it as devalued scrap—an embarrassment and liability. Lindley saw it, whatever it was, as evidence that needed to disappear.

"We'll drag it down the bank to the bayou," Lindley offered.

Merlin then looked at the outline of the wagon and decoy sled leaning against the shelter.

"What about the sled? And the wagon? And the extension cords?"

"We'll take them down there, too."

"We will?"

"Yes! Merlin, we have to go!"

Merlin snapped to attention and went to work. He flipped over the VCR and stomped on it upside down, putting out the fire. Lindley unplugged the extension cord at the shelter, then pulled the wagon and dragged the sled toward the thicket at the top of the bank. Merlin pulled in the two extension cords and held them in the crook of his right arm as he dragged the VCR by one of its plywood edges toward the bayou. At the top of the bank Lindley put the wagon handle and the sled lead rope in his hand and said, "Take these down by the raft. I'll take the thing that was just on fire and the extension cords."

Merlin followed her instructions dutifully, almost numbly, and they scrambled down the steep bank with the gear. The black self-inflated raft was pulled all the way onto the dry part of the bank.

"What are we going to do with all this stuff?" Merlin asked.

"I don't know. Throw it in the bayou?"

"We can't litter!"

Sirens wailed in the distance.

"Merlin, we have to go!"

"I can put everything in the decoy sled. It'll float. I can tie it to the back of the raft."

Lindley was quite flustered now. "Okay, whatever, but we have to go! Now!"

Merlin put the Vortexan Cyclonic Reverser and extension cords on the sled and the Radio Flyer wagon upside down on top of everything. He cut the rope lead on the sled in half and retied it through a ring at the aft of the raft. Lindley had moved the raft halfway into the shallow water and was already aboard. Merlin flopped into the raft, loosening it from shore, and Lindley used a single oar to push off the rest of the way from the bank. She and Merlin lay prone, side by side at the fore of the craft, and Lindley covered them with a dark camouflage tarp that, at its front, she suspended from three short lengths of PVC pipe. The central length of PVC was a little longer, so the tarp made a short half tent at the front of the raft, providing them with a downstream view. There had been heavy thunderstorms west of town and the current was running at a fairly quick clip for a bayou.

Every once in a while, Merlin looked back to see if the decoy sled was still in tow. He asked Lindley where they were going, but she just told him not to worry about it. After a while they heard a police helicopter behind them, and they huddled more tightly under the tarp. Lindley hoped that from the air, the craft might just look like a piece of junk floating in the brown water along with the alligator gars.

They approached a kayak and canoe ramp near a restaurant overlooking the bayou alongside Allen Parkway, and Lindley used the oar to angle them toward the concrete incline. A man wearing black was waiting for them at the water's edge, and Lindley threw him a line. He began to pull the raft toward the ramp, and Lindley and Merlin stepped out onto the ramp's cement surface. The man in black pulled the raft all the way out of the water onto the incline. Merlin looked back and saw that the decoy sled containing all of his gear had come untied and was floating down the bayou in the direction of downtown, the ship channel, Galveston Bay, and the Gulf of Mexico.

"Lindley! It's loose!" he shouted. "It's floating away!"

Lindley responded emphatically: "Merlin, you're just going to have to let all of that stuff go! We have to go!"

Merlin watched his ill-conceived Vortexan Cyclonic Reverser and the red Radio Flyer wagon, a relic of his childhood, disappear around a bend in the bayou.

Lindley called him, and he heard an engine start and then another. Soaked with sweat and bayou water, he jogged up the ramp toward the waiting vehicles.

· Sixty-three

Detective Piet Penders had been awake all night at his place in Westerpark. He looked at the photos of Tite getting his treatment at the hands of the Syndics of the Rapers' Guild. He then looked at a photo of Nico van Rompaey and at a shot of the scrap of paper with van Rompaey's name and mobile telephone number written on it, which his mole in the Syndics had found in Tite Dûche's wallet. They seemed like the spoils of war to him.

The wheels this information had put in motion over the course of a couple of weeks or so continued to astound him as the higher-ups on both sides of the Atlantic closed in on the chief perpetrators of the ring. Being a part of the team that cracked this case would be a career maker. He finally fell asleep but awakened after a few hours and decided he needed to pull himself together for a trip to his favorite watering hole. Then, he hoped, a long afternoon nap would ensue.

· Sixty-four

At the top of the ramp, two vehicles were running and pointed toward a driveway that led to the street. Two men put the raft in the bed of a pickup truck and opened its air valve to begin the deflation process. The other vehicle was a black Suburban. After the man who had met Lindley and Merlin on the ramp opened the passenger doors, the muddy and disheveled rafters entered the vehicle. The black-clad man then drove them to a private aviation facility at Pastime Airport. On the drive to the airport, Merlin asked Lindley, "Is it going to be okay?" and Lindley nodded yes before dozing off into a brief nap.

When they arrived at Billion-Aire aviation, Lindley directed Merlin to the bathroom.

"They have a shower in there, and there are some fresh clothes for you. Leave what you have on in the bathroom. The driver will take care of it. Take your time. It's okay now."

Merlin nodded and trudged toward the restroom to the right while Lindley turned left and went to the women's restroom to shower and change.

Although he was in a daze, Merlin was surprised by how much he enjoyed his shower. He even took time to shave the parts of his face and neck where he kept his beard at bay. He changed into new underwear, sweatpants, and a sweatshirt; he unboxed and stepped into a brand-new pair of water shoes. In the lobby, he met Lindley, also showered and in fresh clothes.

A man in a pilot's uniform walked through the doorway from the tarmac. "We're ready when you are, Miss Acheson," he said.

Without looking at Merlin, she quickly responded. "Are the bags aboard?"

"Yes, ma'am!"

"We're ready."

Merlin, Lindley, and the pilot walked outside and boarded an electric golf cart–like vehicle driven by an employee of Billion-Aire. The cart took them to a small business jet with engines and lights on and ready for flight. The pilot helped Lindley and Merlin board, and they waved to his copilot, who was already seated in the cockpit and beginning the preflight check. The pilot who had escorted Lindley and Merlin to the plane turned left toward the cockpit after his passengers had settled into their seats. The plane roared skyward in the dark, quiet earliest hours of Saturday, August 14th, and after banking in a sharp right turn at takeoff, followed a direct flight vector just a couple of degrees west of due north. Lindley fell asleep again in her seat, and Merlin sprawled on a couch alongside the fuselage.

In a few hours, the jet landed on a runway beside a length of water that also looked like a runway. On landing and disembarking in the brisk morning air, Merlin and Lindley were met by another golf cart that took them and the bags that Lindley had delivered to Billion-Aire the previous afternoon toward the strip of water on which a seaplane floated by a short pier, its interior lights glowing. They waved goodbye to the jet pilot, and as they left in the cart, Merlin spotted a flag at the top of a pole near a hangar—a red maple leaf on a central white field flanked on either side by thick red bars. After Lindley and Merlin stepped up into the seaplane's cabin and exchanged greetings with the pilot, the plane's prop whirred to life.

With the sun cresting over the eastern horizon, Lindley and Merlin began the second leg of their trip. After half an hour or so, the plane made a flawless landing on the glassy surface of a pristine northern Saskatchewan lake. Its shore was forested and rock outcroppings jutted toward the water. The seaplane took them to a dock at the end of a pier that led to a small cabin up an incline near the edge of a forest. Merlin and Lindley thanked the pilot and headed toward the cabin.

The cabin was modest but very well appointed, with a fireplace, a full kitchen, and a cozy living room. It had only one bedroom, and in it a single king-size bed with an overstuffed mattress and high-thread-count sheets. The pillows were filled with pure Canadian goose down. A colorful Hudson Bay blanket was folded at its end. Dog tired, they stood at its foot, and Lindley shrugged at Merlin. They got under the covers and fell fast asleep, tucked into the northern forest blanketing the western reaches of the vast Canadian Shield.

· *Sixty-five*

Mickey McNaughton negotiated the steep, narrow stairway from his apartment down to the building's entry vestibule and emerged onto the street. He took a hard left and headed to a neighborhood place he knew would be open and serving cocktails. People were already there, arranged at tables on the restaurant's terrace in the bright summer light.

Newspaper in hand, the sunglassed Mickey strolled right past them and took a seat at the bar inside. He ordered and folded the newspaper to reveal the crossword puzzle and set the paper on the bar counter. His pencil began to scratch a few letters into the newsprint grid when he heard someone call from down the bar.

"Hey, Houston!"

Mickey looked up from his puzzle and heard another call.

"Hey, McNaughton!"

He turned in the direction of the voice, and to his surprise, Piet Penders, the Dutch detective he had met at the restaurant bar, was once again seated down the way from him. Mickey put on his most jaunty prep school mode and said, "Hey, Detective! You're not stalking me, are you?!"

This comment elicited the hint of a smile from the haggard official, who said, "I have an update for you." He then motioned him his way as he pulled an iPad from his briefcase. As Mickey approached, Penders said, "Your friend in the Harris County District Attorney's office has been very helpful. And I think some of our department's research has been of use to him."

Mickey sat at the barstool next to the detective, who was well into his cocktails. The waitress delivered Mickey his first drink of the day. Before Piet Penders opened a photo file on his iPad, he said, "Just to be clear, you never saw these images, and we never had this conversation, right?" Mickey's mirth disappeared as he looked the detective in the eye and said, "Right."

· Sixty-six

Late in the morning, Lindley and Merlin stirred from their sleep. Lindley put her hand on Merlin's shoulder, and they turned to one another and he found her. At first, he wondered if this was another of his waking dreams about Wonder Woman or Athena, but no, this was real and that was the wonder of it. He embraced his rescuer, and she was more wonderful than he could have imagined. Maybe for the first time in his life, Merlin felt as if he belonged, and then the more specific sense that he and Lindley somehow belonged to one another. He received Lindley, and she reciprocated. Their connecting was suffused with a warmth Merlin had never known until that moment. It was like some kind of case around his heart had opened and for the first time he knew its object was not an idea but a person. And that person was Lindley and she was fully with him. Somehow, he knew she was now his greatest advocate, and that together, they constituted a kind of bulwark of positive energy to counteract anything with which any sort of negative gyre might try to thwart them.

Lindley also felt a kind of belonging she had never known, and she and Merlin would talk about it during the ensuing days on their hikes in the forest and especially on their trips in the rowboat on the lake. They would look back on these conversations as pure magic—unguarded and exploratory and unlike anything either of them had ever experienced.

But Lindley felt even more than this. It was like an annoying little pebble at a corner of a chamber of her heart had melted away, or really, instantly dematerialized. She knew her mom had loved her during her lifetime and that her dad's love for her was as solid and unwavering as he was, but for the first time, she felt beloved. There was no tinge of doubt, no bitter-edged second-guessing to this sense. It was like a thick beam of warm light, and in that moment, she knew that Merlin loved her and her love for him was confirmed.

· Sixty-seven

That afternoon Merlin rowed as Lindley faced him in the boat. He pulled the oar blades out of the water to drift, and they began to talk in the way neither of them had ever talked with another person. They talked together. Lindley related to Merlin that the name of the lake was Nemihaha and that her parents had often come to the same cabin when her mother was living and that her dad loved the fishing. On hearing this, Merlin's eyes widened, and he asked, "Can we fish?!" Lindley smiled and began to laugh and replied, "Yes, all the fishing stuff is in that little shed behind the cabin." He was ecstatic on hearing this news. Before Merlin began to row toward the shore, Lindley leaned toward him and Merlin held the oars to steady himself as he leaned in her direction. The sun glinted between their foreheads as they kissed in the fading light of the long northern summer evening.

On Sunday, August 15th, they were out on Lake Nemihaha again. As the sun began to set, Lindley lit two torches she had brought aboard. She had tied colorful ribbons to each of the fire-bearing sticks, and she placed them in round metal slots angled outward at the row boat's port and starboard gunwales. When they returned to shore, Lindley placed the torches on similar holders that protruded from a couple of trees near the dock. Their flames glinted on the water and danced above the ornate ribbons beneath them as Lindley explained that the torches were a family tradition her mom and dad loved. For Merlin, the torchlight made Lake Nemihaha all the more magical.

That night they watched a television weather report courtesy of the cabin's exterior satellite dish. The news for the Upper Texas Gulf Coast—specifically the Houston-Galveston area—was not good. The depression traversing the Straits of Florida had become a tropical storm then a hurricane in the southeastern Gulf of Mexico and had merged with the system that had moved north through the Yucatan Channel west of Cuba. In just a few days, Hurricane Franklina had spun up all the way to a Category 5 as its predicted landfall cone continued to point toward the coast just below Houston. Lindley's father called and said that they would need to extend their trip.

Merlin thought of his smashed instrument and felt a kind of momentary vindication that the storm bore a feminine version of the surname of the Founding Father who had invented the glass armonica. He checked this impulse toward taking revenge on Tite Dûche and traded it for concern for the people of his homeland.

After Galveston Island and Houston took a direct hit, the storm meandered around Southeast Texas and returned to dump record amounts of rain on the area. There were huge swaths of power outages and downed trees, and flooded roadways brought travel to a near standstill.

Lindley's dad called again and said that they should stay until after Labor Day. He said the power was out all over Bayou Boughs, and it could take two weeks to restore service. He also reported there wasn't any flooding in the Acheson or McNaughton residences and that Lindley's garden had made it through the inundation with minimal damage. Lindley and Merlin were concerned for everyone at home but thrilled their vacation on the lake was becoming a sabbatical away from the hottest part of Houston's tenacious summer.

· Sixty-eight

At six a.m. on the morning of Tuesday, August 17th, the FBI raided the offices of Dûche Ovens, Incorporated, and confiscated all computer hard drives on the premises. Additionally, they boxed and sealed all of the paper files from Tite Dûche's executive office. Later that day, as the outer bands of Hurricane Franklina began to buffet the Upper Texas Gulf Coast, a plane took off from Houston for Dulles Airport containing all the hard drives and files now bound for bureau headquarters at Langley. It was one of the last jets out before the storm. Within an hour of its departure, all the area airports closed.

In Campania, the second leg of the five-day Ferrari rally was about to begin. Ferrari had arranged to clear the fabled Amalfi Coast highway for ninety minutes to accommodate its forty or so drivers who were scheduled to leave the starting point in Sorrento at thirty-second intervals. Tite was at the wheel of his bundle of Italian fire and cueing to pull up to the departure line. He noticed a voice mail on his phone and decided to listen to it in speaker mode. It was brief but arresting. The speaker sounded drunk.

"Hey, Tite, this is Mickey McNaughton. So, I just wanted to let you know that I didn't realize you were so photogenic! Kudos and have a nice day!"

He knew Mickey was a Bayou Boughs member, but how could he have known about Nico van Rompaey's photos? All of Tite Dûche's sphincters tightened as he inched toward the starting line.

With just a few minutes remaining before his departure flag wove with a gallant flourish, Tite's phone rang. It was his attorney. Tite answered and listened as his lawyer spoke in the gravest tone he had ever heard from this unwaveringly serious man.

"Interpol has just issued a Red Notice on you," his lawyer said.

"What's that?"

"It's their highest-level arrest warrant."

There was a second or two of silence as Tite continued to creep toward the starting line.

"And, ah, it's rumored there are some photographs," his lawyer said.

"Photographs?"

"Of you in, shall we say, rather compromising circumstances."

Tite was next in line to take the flag and pilot the bright yellow Pinin Farina past Positano, Amalfi, Praiano, and Maiori toward Salerno. His face was ashen, but a new determination focused his forward gaze.

"Sorry, Hedley, it's my time on the line," he said. "Gotta go."

As a golfer, Tite Dûche considered himself—without a moment of reflection on the irony of it—a master of the short game. A component of his short game of which he was particularly proud— again with nary a thought for the irony of it—was the approach shot from what is known as a tight lie. A golfer contends with a tight lie when his ball ends up stopping where there is very little or no grass underneath it or on a very closely mown lip of a green. The term "tight lie" signifies the ground under the ball is either compact or even hard. Although he wasn't on the links, he found himself in the tightest lie of his life, surrounded by the infamously steep rocky terrain of the Amalfi Coast.

He turned his phone off and rolled to the starting line. He and the flagman made eye contact, confirming the driver was ready. Tite released the clutch carefully to ensure a smooth, in no way embarrassing start and began to run through the gears as he negotiated the picture postcard beautiful but dangerously precipitous coastal drive. After several minutes, he entered a curve considerably faster than even the most cavalier or experienced of the other rally participants would have.

As he braked hard and skidded around it, he saw a huge ram jump from the almost sheer wall of rock to his left and stand in front of him. The ram's eyes burned red in challenge as they stared directly at Dûche. Tite tried to avoid it, but the animal seemed to anticipate his next maneuver. It hopped to the left in front of the car's evasive course and lowered its horns toward the Ferrari, never taking its eyes off the driver. Tite overcorrected to the right and his foot slipped from the brake to the accelerator.

The Ferrari hit the curb with such force that the vehicle's rear rose in an arc and began a dramatic tail-first forward flip over the low wall delimiting the roadway. It turned again in another impressive rear over front midair flip that seemed to Tite like a very long moment as he saw the Mediterranean sky and sea come into view through the car's windshield for the last time.

The Ferrari hit the rocks by the sea top-first and exploded into flames that complemented the color scheme of the legendary Italian sports car—a bouquet of yellows and reds. Behind the flames, the car's twisted metal and rock that held it were charred coal black. At the center of the conflagration was a roiling and constantly changing kaleidoscope of orange feeding black smoke that snaked toward the blue firmament of the southern Italian summer.

· *Sixty-nine*

On Saturday, August 21st, the float plane arrived to resupply Lindley and Merlin at the cabin. In addition to groceries and household goods, there was a large crate marked "EXTREMELY FRAGILE" and "HANDLE WITH CARE." Merlin was surprised and intrigued. To his even greater surprise, neither the pilot nor Lindley would offer a word about its contents. When they placed the crate by the window in the bedroom, Lindley asked Merlin to go fishing or take a walk through the woods for twenty or thirty minutes. Under no circumstances was he to look in through the window.

He complied, and Lindley and the pilot went to work unboxing the contents of the crate. When the job was done, Lindley draped a dark woolen blanket over the uncrated object by the window. She thanked the pilot for his help, tipped him, and bid him goodbye. The plane was gone when Merlin returned to the house, and as he was about to ask Lindley about the crate's contents, she said simply, decisively, and maybe a little winsomely, "It's a surprise."

That night, Lindley and Merlin rowed out onto the lake a couple of hundred yards from the cabin and looked up into the sky. Unlike Houston's sky, this sky was black with zillions of stars. Merlin pointed out constellations and shared with Lindley their significance in ancient mythology. He was surprised she already knew most of this information and then astonished as she pointed out even more star groupings and the significance of their Latin names. "Do you see that broad, cloudy sweep of distant light?" she asked.

"Yes, I do. What do you think it is?"

"I think it's the arm of the Milky Way that our solar system is spinning on."

Taking in this astounding revelation, Merlin looked in silence and uttered a single protracted "Wowwwwwwwww!"

Before sunrise on Sunday, while Merlin was still asleep, Lindley tiptoed from the bed and removed the blanket from what it was covering by the cabin window. She plugged a cord at its base into a wall socket and returned to bed. Merlin stirred a little after sunrise and awakened.

He looked to his left, toward the cabin window, and saw his gift, the fresh sunlight glinting from its perfectly dustless crystalline disks. It was a brand-new glass armonica, and it was even more exquisite than the one the ninja of Bayou Boughs had destroyed. If a musical instrument could be pristine, like a glassy northern lake, that was how this new armonica looked to Merlin. For a second, he thought about waking Lindley to show her, the way a child wakes parents to alert them to what Santa Claus left behind, but just as quickly, he remembered it was Lindley who had arranged its purchase and special delivery. After a necessary stop to the facilities, he approached the instrument—now even more glimmering as the sun surmounted the eastern horizon. He turned on the switch and the discs spun. He dipped his fingertips in a saucer of water and began to play.

Lindley awakened to "Ode to Joy" by Ludwig van Beethoven. Before she opened her eyes to see Merlin playing, a broad smile of satisfaction dawned on her face as she listened to the unmistakable strains of the iconic classical piece. To her delight, Merlin played the armonica throughout the morning and even began a new composition, which when complete a couple of days later, he named in honor of their time at the Canadian lake: "The Idyll of the Loon."

Hurricane Franklina devastated the Houston–Galveston area, with power outages lasting well over two weeks in many areas and floodwaters leaving tens of thousands of people without homes. Following her father's suggestion, Lindley and Merlin remained at the lake until after Labor Day. Before their departure, they spoke often of how they could contribute to the relief effort on their return.

The reservoirs on the west side of town were like giant water-holding valves of Houston. As with the valves of Houston in Merlin's formerly jammed and enervated lower gastrointestinal tract, they gave way under massive pressure and inundated more neighborhoods while sending a huge volume of water down Buffalo Bayou. The force of the water was sufficient to dislodge the sled containing the rapidly rusting Vortexan Cyclonic Reverser, Radio Flyer wagon, and extension cords from a downstream, mostly submerged tree and send it all flushing into the bay. The current created by the volume of water was so powerful these relics of a former life rode it all the way into the open Gulf of Mexico.

On Wednesday, September 8th, Merlin looked through a passenger seat window toward the lakeside cabin as the float plane sped across the water for takeoff. He saw two hairy bipedal creatures emerge from the woods near the fishing tackle shack. They were enormous, and he could tell that one was male and the other female. As a small version of the creatures scrambled around the female's feet, the male looked right at Merlin's face in the airplane window, smiled, and gave Merlin an unmistakable two thumbs up. The float plane bounced a bit as it broke free from the surface of the lake, causing Merlin to look away for an instant. When he looked back to get another glimpse of the big furry bipeds and their little one, they had vanished.

· *After*

· Seventy

On the morning of Tite Dûche's fatal crash in Italy, a caddie at Bayou Boughs Country Club had brought around his presidential golf cart to have at the ready for Tite's sons, Titey and Dukey, who wanted to get in an early round before the sun was too high in the sky. Before the boys arrived at the club, there was an electrical short in the cart's wiring, and it burst into flames, burning to a black heap with four melted tires at its periphery. Later it was determined the golf cart self-immolated at the hour of Tite's afternoon crash in Italy. After the incident, the club never again designated a special golf cart for the serving president's use.

There was upheaval on the club's board as well, and in a case of shame by association, Dûche's cronies resigned from their service en masse, and new interim board members were voted into office. Although he hadn't served on the board in many years, Dr. Mac Swearingen was called into duty as Bayou Boughs Country Club's interim president. It was reported that his in-camera declaration of disgust at Tite Dûche's activities spawned a stream of choice epithets that was unequaled in the good doctor's long history of well-placed off-color phrasings and aphorisms, but when he got that out of his system, he got down to business and went to work. His first official communication was his letter as interim president on the cover of the monthly newsletter. For his part, Merlin read it with delight, as Dr. Swearingen called Merlin himself before its publication to inform him that his membership had been fully reinstated. The letter read:

School is back in session, and it seems like everyone is ready to return to a normal state of affairs in Houston. I am happy to report that the state of affairs at Bayou Boughs Country Club also appears poised to return to equilibrium. The board is in the process of rescinding or modifying some interdictions that have been instated over the past several months. The board believes that, true to the club's history as a welcoming place for generations of families, we need to open our arms to embrace and accommodate all of our members and their loved ones. This doesn't mean, by any means, that the club should be a free-for-all atmosphere. It is the board's intention for the club to return to the baseline civility that has characterized it for generations, and that means some rules will need to be adhered to and respected to maintain the comfortable club environment so many of us have come to cherish.

In addition to being a stellar retreat for golf, tennis, swimming, and dining in the heart of the city, Bayou Boughs Country Club is a place that has fostered and nurtured lasting friendships and family ties since its founding a hundred years ago. The range of personalities among our membership is another aspect of what makes this club such a special place. We may not all be exactly straight-down-the-fairway conventional types—for my part, I damn sure have my quirks—but I think we can all agree that we are angling for a warm, genial, and welcoming atmosphere here at the club. I'm looking forward to keeping you updated on happenings over the coming months, and I look forward to seeing you around the club.

Yours very truly,
McLean Swearingen, M.D.

(The letter was signed "Mac.")

In a fall ceremony on the front steps of City Hall in downtown Houston, Merlin and Mickey McNaughton were honored by the mayor, who cited the duo's service to the community and the world for doing their part to help dismantle a major human smuggling and trafficking ring. Although Mickey and Merlin looked different in many ways, they both sported round-lensed glasses, and when excited, the eyes behind the lenses seemed similarly round and almost as large as the lenses through which they looked. During the photo op with the mayor, as Mickey and Merlin were holding the plaque commemorating the day, the nephew and uncle team were both wide-eyed, and their lips were in the signature McNaughton pursed O shape. Before ending his talk, the mayor said that the two were models of "if you see something, say something" civic vigilance.

Also in the fall, Dr. Mac Swearingen presided over the annual Coastal Sportsmen's Association dinner during which the organization highlighted its strides toward better wildlife conservation and gave awards to individuals who had made significant contributions to the organization's mission during the year and to anglers who made record catches on the Texas and Louisiana Gulf Coasts.

Junior Trust Officer Curtis Bumpers was in attendance, and when a slide showing Merlin McNaughton with his record trout appeared on the screen behind the podium, the bank employee's face flushed bright red, and he clamped his jaw shut to contain the rage boiling inside his chest. He couldn't take it, and as Dr. Swearingen began to talk about Merlin's fish, Bumpers excused himself from the table and strode toward the venue's exit, his unabated ire fueling his departure. Dr. Swearingen called Merlin to the podium and presented him with the annual golden trout award and the two were all smiles as the photographers' flashes popped like little innocuous facsimiles of the menacing lightning bolts that followed Merlin's momentous catch that July day in Acadiana.

The address of the compound Merlin discovered on Snuffmeister Road corresponded with that provided as a home address by a former kitchen employee at the club. It was later learned that this employee was Tite's main henchman in the Houston smuggling and trafficking operation. He was taken into custody to await trial and there was some conjecture as to whether he and Tite had more than just a business relationship. Additionally, authorities apprehended complicit employees at the ports of Houston, Galveston, and New Orleans.

The remaining members of the Dûche family left Houston altogether. It was rumored they had relocated to South America— maybe Argentina or Brazil. Some said they had heard they were on a ranch in Paraguay. It also became clear that Tite had thoroughly fabricated his family's patrilineal heritage, spreading the notion they came from a lineage of wealth and aristocratic prestige. After the press got on the story, it was revealed that Tite's family name was actually Dücher and that they were in no way either Alsatian or remotely aristocratic. The Düchers had been butchers in a hamlet near the Upper Austrian town of Braunau am Inn on the Bavarian border. When Tite's grandfather moved to the U.S.—to Dallas, Texas—he changed the spelling of his name and concocted the rudiments of the phony story upon which his grandson would later elaborate with lavish embellishment. He wore an ascot and a smoking jacket, and the Dallasites ate it up.

When Dutch authorities set out to take Nico van Rompaey into custody, they were confounded. He had vanished without the merest smoke trail of a lead.

· Seventy-one

Since Lindley and Merlin had become a couple, Lindley took on the gargantuan effort of setting the battleship of Merlin's prodigious and catholic culinary appetites on a more salubrious course. He was now eating more green vegetables and beginning to eschew gluten and fried things from his daily intake. Additionally, Lindley had begun to encourage him to exercise, and he now rode alongside her on some of her many bicycle outings. Merlin's bike was by no means one of those racing cycles so many enthusiasts ride. A fat-tired street bike with a wide, comfortable seat was his new mode of getting around the neighborhood and nearby environs.

On a mild day during a late autumn trip to New Orleans, Lindley and Merlin found themselves uptown on Magazine Street. Lindley spotted a bike rental place called Chez Schwinn. They were thrilled when they learned the place had a wide-tired tandem bike for rent. With Lindley at the front handlebars, the two set forth to explore. They turned down Constantinople Street, and Lindley slowed and pointed to a house on the left.

"Look how cute that one is!" she enthused as she looked toward the covered front porch of the home. Merlin saw a youngish, mustachioed man of perhaps his own age lounging on a swing behind the balustrade. Like Merlin, he was rather large. He was wearing a hunter's cap with its earflaps up no doubt because of the pleasant weather and was playing a stringed musical instrument. An older woman swept the opposite side of the porch with a straw broom.

Lindley asked Merlin, "What is he playing?" Merlin did not hesitate, as his knowledge of musical instruments both ancient and modern was encyclopedic. "It's a lute," he said with a certain winsomeness that bespoke his glee at seeing someone practicing such a noble stringed instrument that doubtless accompanied many a Renaissance feast.

"Wow! A lute! I knew you would know," Lindley said as she straightened the tandem's front wheel and stood on the pedals to gain speed. They glided past an array of New Orleans home designs—shotguns, camelbacks, creole cottages, and some stately double-gallery houses.

When they returned to Chez Schwinn later that day, they decided to drink chicory lattes in a little place adjacent to the bike rental shop called Café du Côté. As they sat across from one another at a two-top table by a window, Merlin produced a tiny jewel box.

Lindley was speechless as she took it in her hands.

"Open it," Merlin said.

She opened the little red velvet–covered jewel box that seemed like an antique. Inside was a marquis-cut diamond ring, perfectly sized to Lindley's ring finger.

"Is it okay?" queried Merlin.

Lindley sighed and sat back a little in her chair and said, "Yes! It's more than okay; it's beautiful."

"Like you, Lindley!"

Lindley started to tear up.

"Put it on!" Merlin said.

"Do you think it will fit?" asked Lindley.

Merlin said, "Put it on!" again without a bit of wavering in his voice.

Lindley slipped the engagement ring onto her left ring finger. It fit perfectly. Now she was even more thrilled.

"How did you know my ring size?"

"When we were in Canada, I traced the radius of a ring you wore on your right ring finger that you had left on a table. Then, taking into account that you are right-handed, I subtracted the standard amount of size variation of the ring finger from the dominant hand to the nondominant hand. I guess you could call it a fortuitous estimation."

"A fortuitous estimation," Lindley repeated as her smile broadened. "That's my Magic Man!"

She leaned forward and so did Merlin, and their lips met in an engagement kiss as the beguiling earthy aroma of chicory coffee rose to caress them in this magic moment. Lindley's hand touched Merlin's cheek, and the sunlight through the window glinted off the diamond and sent brilliant star-like sparkles dancing on the café's ceiling, creating a daytime visual echo of the summertime Canadian night sky they would cherish always.

· Seventy-two

Lindley Love Acheson and Merlin Mistlethorpe McNaughton were married in early May of the following year when the magnolias were at the peak of their bloom. After the ceremony in the chapel at St. James' Episcopal Church, the reception was at the club. Both of them had made this short trip many times on the Sundays of their youth—heading down the boulevard for the big buffet spread with their families after church—but this particular ride down the boulevard on this bright Saturday would become the one they would remember most. A vintage Rolls Royce with passenger doors that opened outward from the left side instead of the right spirited them to the party in regal quiet.

Halfway up the boulevard Merlin noticed in the median neat boxwood hedges circumscribing thick clusters of blooming roses. "Look!" he said.

Lindley didn't miss a beat and replied with a satisfied smile, "Double Knock Out Roses. Cherry red. I consulted on the project."

"You're my double knockout!" Merlin enthused. He squeezed Lindley's hand and her smile shone like the spring sunlight.

On their arrival at the top of the circular driveway, a raucous mariachi band greeted them with a fanfare and followed them into the reception, where the assembled guests met them with an extended ovation.

The day was neither too warm nor unpleasantly humid and,

mirroring the couple's radiant mood, the sun shone brightly above the golf course beyond the floor-to-ceiling picture windows of the big room. The weather was so nice, in fact, that Lindley's father and the wedding planner decided to move the band and dance floor outside to a raised terrace directly behind the room that overlooked the golf course, including a small lake with a fountain. While the guests greeted Lindley and Merlin, music was provided in the indoor space where the buffets and bars were set up by the Bayou Boughs Chamber Orchestra. There were two musicians, one playing a cello and the other coaxing ethereal tones from a glass armonica. Guests mingled and settled at tables as Lindley and Merlin accepted greetings and well-wishes in the receiving line.

Rex Mondeaux and Lindley's father, Gray Acheson, were enjoying cocktails and looking out on the golf course after Acheson had greeted several people. Rex toasted Gray and said, "Well, if I had a hat on, I'd tip it to you. You sure picked the right time to call in that favor you've been sitting on."

"Lindley made the call," Acheson responded. "I just passed along your gracious gesture. To say I'm grateful would be an understatement."

"Hey, I'm happy to have done it. I'm grateful that you saw a problem I didn't and saved my ass in that deal ten years ago!" Gray Acheson smiled and nodded and then suggested, "Shall we have another?" The two Houston fixtures headed for the bar. After getting their libations in highball glasses with etched BBCC crests and matching cocktail napkins, the two continued to talk until a guest pulled Acheson into another conversation.

Mickey McNaughton, who was quaffing his own cocktail of very dark liquor on the rocks, saw Rex Mondeaux had a free moment and angled in his direction like a heat-seeking missile. He shook hands with Mondeaux enthusiastically.

"Greetings, Rex. Great to see you again. How's everything in the world of Mondoco?"

"Oh, you know, just sixes and sevens."

"I guess that's better than deuces and threes, right?"

"Right you are," Mondeaux said. "Hey, I got a question for you."

"Okay, shoot."

"I heard you called Tite Dûche the day he crashed and said you'd seen some compromising pictures of him. How'd you know about the photos?"

"So I didn't say that they were compromising, but my tone might have insinuated that they were."

"Okay, but how did you know about the photos?"

"I didn't. The detective on the case showed me photos of the S&M team that Tite paid to work him over, but they were just photos of the Syndics of the Rapers' Guild in action with their clients blacked out."

"You bluffed?"

"Yeah, it's an intimidation technique they teach all the newbies in the executive track programs at the big Manhattan investment banks. Like when someone on the client or investor side challenges you during a presentation, you walk toward them as you answer their question without breaking eye contact. It's a sure-fire intimidation and domination tactic. So, we learned, is the well-reasoned bluff. There's a risk in it, but if the preponderance of factors points toward the possibility your bluff might be true, it can be worth venturing."

"Damn! I've seen plenty of New York IB and private equity guys in action, and now that I think about it, that walking toward the challenger thing is something I've seen them do. Where'd you learn that?"

"Right out of Yale when I went to work for Schitti Banca. It's an Italian–American concern like Lazard Frères is a French–American investment bank, but in this respect, they're all the same; they all teach basically the same techniques."

"So that's how the Ivy Leaguers do it?"

"I guess it's part of it. So it's probably just a culture thing, right?"

"Right you are, Mickster!"

Rex grinned as a glamorous, sophisticated-looking woman tapped him on the shoulder. He excused himself from the conversation. Mickey had drained his drink and decided to switch to gin and tonics as they seemed to befit the sparkling spring day. He got in the bar line with the same efficiency of movement that he had exhibited when he swooped in on Rex Mondeaux a few minutes earlier.

The party moved outside onto the terrace and the band, which included an impressive brass complement, took their places along the balustrade above a lawn that gave onto the golf course. They played a few songs to pick up the tempo of the party, and then, to all the guests' genuine surprise, Lindley and Merlin positioned themselves at a corner of the dance floor in the confident posture of seasoned dancers—Merlin's palm at Lindley's back and hers at his hip. Merlin's left hand held Lindley's right hand, and he was ready to lead. They had each shed a significant amount of weight leading up to their special day, but they remained large, impressive figures on the dance floor.

Merlin looked the band leader in the eye and gave him a nod, and the band began a new number. It was "The Lonely Bull" by Herb Alpert and the Tijuana Brass, and Lindley and Merlin swept and dipped and spun across and around the dance floor to a choreographed routine like competitive ballroom dancers. The crowd was astounded.

Mac Swearingen stood agog and commented on the dancers to his nephew, Luke Swearingen, who had just graduated from medical school. "Well, I'll be dipped! Who'da thunk it? The last time I saw anything remotely like this was when I was on the sidelines before a Texans' game last season. I watched the linebackers do their pregame tire drill. It was an uncanny combination of size and cat-like precision."

Luke grinned and answered in his best doctor's tone, "I concur, Uncle Mac." Some of the guests whooped loudly as the dancers executed a series of spins and dips.

The song transitioned seamlessly into "A Taste of Honey"— also by Herb Alpert and his legendary group—and the dance became even more lively. Lindley and Merlin seemed to glide across the floor almost weightlessly, but it was the spectacle of their combined mass and agility that continued to amaze the guests. A Bayou Boughs dowager standing next to Rex Mondeaux commented that they looked like animate versions of the dancers from the painting "Bailarines" by the Colombian artist Fernando Botero. "Stunning," she said. "I hope they have this on video." They did.

"A Taste of Honey" came to an end with Merlin dipping Lindley over his right thigh. The crowd roared with applause and the kind of celebratory whoops that one hears only in Texas—even at the country club. A few beads of perspiration collected at the dancers' temples, but they appeared no worse for the wear as, with flushed cheeks, they took a bow before the guests encircling the outdoor dance floor. The musicians settled into a more sedate tune, and Lindley danced with her father. Then everyone crowded the dance floor, and Lindley and Merlin danced together as the band offered an inspired rendition of "Merlin" by Tex Allen and the tempo of the music once again picked up.

Shep Pasteur was at the reception as an honored guest. (Right after the Lumbeaux Jump fishing trip during Shep's work suspension, Rex Mondeaux had strategically offered Shep a better-paying job as house manager for his Houston home and all of his vacation properties.) Shep brought his cousin Marie Mado and they cut a rug in that inimitable way that only real Cajuns can. Merlin cut in for a dance with her, and now, although the comic size difference between the two of them remained, Merlin's steps were unfalteringly smooth. Marie Mado commented with a coy smile as they danced, "You have learned a lot, *cher*!" Merlin beamed as he accepted the compliment, and they spun counter-clockwise like a tropical cyclone.

Lindley danced with Shep, and they spoke as they moved around the floor in time with the music.

"I've known you and Merlin all your lives, and I've never seen either of you smile like y'all are today."

Lindley beamed and said, "Well, Shep, you were a part of the plan. I mean in a big way and in a really granular way. You believed in my hunch and gave me Merlin's clothing and shoe sizes without questioning me."

"And I never said nothin' about it to nobody."

"I so appreciate that," Lindley said as they turned and smiled even more brightly.

Shep returned the smile, winked, and said, "An' I never will."

At this, Lindley threw her head back in laughter at the inside joke she and Shep would get to share for years to come.

At a corner of the terrace, Dirk Kajerka was chatting with one of Lindley's friends from college, a sandy blonde with classic East Coast style he found very attractive.

"My ancestors came to Texas from what's now the Czech Republic back in the 1800s," he said. "The original name was spelled K-j-r-k-a but my great-great-grandfather figured that was too many consonants in a row for English speakers so he added an *a* and an *e*, and that's how it ended up being Kajerka."

"That's fascinating!" the young lady replied. "In Connecticut, we think Texas is just kind of homogeneous. I had no idea."

Dirk winked at her and said, "Sometimes I think there's more to this place than the world gives it credit for."

Then, uncharacteristically while chatting up such a compel-ling prospect, he looked at his watch and said, "Oh!"

"What?" the young New Englander asked.

Dirk responded with all the graciousness he could imagine a Southern gentleman might muster: "I'm sorry, Isabel. I must excuse myself. Now is the time for all good men to come to the aid of the party!"

"Of course!"

"It's been a pleasure talking with you!" Dirk excused himself and headed down the terrace steps.

The revelry continued at a fever pitch and those who enjoyed their cocktails took this as a perfect opportunity to indulge in their bibulous proclivities, displaying a few more flamboyant-than-usual moves on the dance floor. A couple of guests even sang with the band. A vociferous cluster of merrymakers shouted "Encore!" to Lindley and Merlin, and the couple obliged as the center of the dance floor cleared. The band launched into a rollicking rendition of "El Toro Valiente" in the style of John Coltrane backed by Art Blakey's Big Band and Lindley and Merlin once again dazzled the crowd, sailing diagonally across the dance floor like twin caravels under full sail on a beam reach for home port.

Teetering at the rail on one of the terrace's edges with his back to the music, Mickey McNaughton missed Lindley and Merlin's finale. He had cornered Isabel from Connecticut and, although slurring his words more than a little, he was doing his dead-level best to display his prep school, Ivy League, and Wall Street bona fides by playing "who do you know" in glib, rapid-fire verbal pulses, blurting the clipped syllables of jaunty Yankee-style banter. It wasn't on his calendar the afternoon of the reception, but in a few short weeks, he would check in for an extended stay at Trembling Hills Ranch Recovery and Wellness Center on the Central Coast of California.

The band took a much-needed break, and its roadies turned PAs, monitors, amps, mics, and instruments around to face the golf course. A few minutes later, the whir of an airplane prop approached, and then, astoundingly, the huge blimp—the *Airmadillo* itself—emerged from above the trees over the back nine and headed just a couple of hundred feet above the ground directly toward the thick, verdant, meticulously manicured lawn below and in front of the outdoor second-floor terrace where the revelers chatted and toasted one another and the new couple. As the blimp landed and some of the grounds crew at the club held the lines dangling from it, the band returned to their places.

The guests were given little bags of rice, and they formed a long line leading from the terrace, down the stairs, and onto the lawn all the way up to a place near the blimp's passenger pod, where another send-off team was in place. Eight of the club's groundskeepers formed an archway the way the military does with sabers, but instead of sabers they held aloft gas-powered, shoulder-harnessed leaf blowers, with the long blower tubes held high and crossing the ends of the blowers of their counterparts standing across from them. Chloris Godley mounted a tall ladder on the left side of the passageway. She had changed into flats to ascend the rungs and held a basket of rose petals.

Merlin and Lindley emerged from the clubhouse onto the terrace in their traveling outfits and ducked their heads as they dodged the rice grains being tossed their way. On the giant screen covering the blimp's skin the words "Congratulations, Lindley and Merlin" scrolled and flashed with the image of a red rose on one side of the phrase and a counterclockwise whorl on the other. As the couple approached the leaf-blower archway, the groundskeepers blew high-powered jets of air skyward, and Chloris Godley tossed mounds and mounds of fresh rose petals onto the upwelling drafts. Even with the blimp looming behind, this created quite a spectacle, and everyone clapped at the novel gesture. Chloris was relieved and thrilled it went according to plan and was even more impressive than she thought it would be. Lindley and Merlin looked up in awe as handfuls of petals flew up on jets of air and descended around them.

When they were a few steps away from the passenger pod, the door opened and Tino Smakaporpous greeted the newlyweds with his signature bonhomie. Gold chains swung from his neck as he offered the bride a gallant hand to step aboard, and Merlin followed. Dirk Kajerka was at the controls of the *Airmadillo* wearing all of his captain's regalia, including a jacket with epaulets, captain's hat, and Ray-Ban aviator sunglasses. He turned to Lindley and Merlin as they entered and gave them a big smile and a tip of his hat. The couple settled into their seats.

"Nobody ever eats at their own wedding reception," Tino said, "so I brought along some snacks for y'all's first flight of the day."

Tino lifted a big white cardboard box and opened it to show them an array of appetizers. He put it down and said, "I got dessert, too!"

"Baklava?" Merlin asked.

"That and the little key lime tarts you liked so much!"

Merlin and Lindley beamed, and Dirk said, "Okay, everybody hold on, we're taking off!"

The groundskeepers released the blimp's rope lines and as the *Airmadillo* nosed skyward, the band broke into "Up, Up and Away" by the 5th Dimension. The vocalists sounded astoundingly like Marilyn McCoo and Billy Davis Jr., et al., in the original version of the song, and the guests marveled at the newlyweds' duly idiosyncratic yet spectacular departure from the reception. As the *Airmadillo* rose and banked northward for the trip to George Bush Intercontinental Airport, everyone waved and shouted, and the newlyweds responded with equally enthusiastic waves. Captain Kajerka got Lindley and Merlin to the big airport with time to spare for their evening flight to Europe.

· Seventy-three

Lindley and Merlin spent a few days in Paris and then flew on to Malta, where Lindley's father had chartered a private cruise for them. They motored around the island nation for several days on the *MY Ruby*, a thoroughly comfortable, but by no means ostentatious yacht. Its helmsman, who asked the couple to call him Captain Omar, was Iranian by birth. Before dinner every evening, he recited ancient Persian love poetry to the couple in Farsi followed by the English translation.

Like Merlin, Omar was a fan of antique navigational instruments, and even brought a few old astrolabes and sextants on board. Merlin and Captain Omar took readings with various instruments a couple of times a day, and Lindley chuckled as the two men indulged their nerdy navigational and meteorological obsessions. She asked Captain Omar after he and Merlin had worked with one of the old sextants, "Do you know those levels that carpenters use?"

"Yes, of course. I use one myself on projects at home!"

"Well, we've taken up golf, and Merlin brings one onto the green and puts it on the grass to determine which way the putt will break!"

"Ha! That's wonderful! I must do the same the next time I play!"

Lindley liked watching Merlin have a buddy to talk to. It made her almost as happy as she was about being with Merlin on the deep blue sea and swimming with him in coves where no one could see them.

To indulge her own interests, Lindley brought along a nice digital single lens reflex camera with a macro lens and a field notebook to record the local flora they encountered during their onshore hikes. One day, with the aroma of wild oregano in the air, they found a rock outcropping that served as a natural diving platform and they jumped and swam and jumped and swam in the clear cool water to their hearts' content.

As the *Ruby* cruised the opalescent turquoise and indigo seas, they talked of the new developments in their lives—including their new home, an Arts and Crafts–era one-story bungalow not too far from Bayou Boughs—and of their careers. Merlin had accepted a job to teach at St. James' School and coach the offensive line of the varsity football team in the fall, and Lindley had recently been named the executive director of the Bayou Boughs Garden Club, a position that would include frequent appearances as the gardening expert on Houston television and radio shows. She was also being courted to write a regular column about rose gardening for the *Houston Chronicle*.

At twilight one evening, Captain Omar anchored the *Ruby* in a protected cove. After night fell, Lindley and Merlin decided to take a swim. The dark water felt cold, but they adjusted to it and floated on their backs, looking up at the stars the way they had in Canada. They held hands as they floated and identified constellations.

"Look, you can even see that kind of snowy sweep of background stars," Merlin said.

"Yes, this part of our arc of the galaxy—just like we saw at the lake."

They released each other's hands, then, like recombinant strands of DNA bridging the twin helixes, they extended their arms and joined both hands behind their heads—Lindley's left hand in Merlin's right and Merlin's right hand in Lindley's left. Merlin began to kick sideways a little, ankle over foot, and Lindley did the same until they were rotating in the water like a slowly moving twin-bladed propeller with the axis of the turning between each of their heads.

They spun like that and continued to talk. Then they spun in silence beneath the starlit vault of heaven—twin mimics of the Milky Way's turning—consecrating the revolution in each of their lives that had created their lives together. They pulled one another close until the tops of their heads touched. They released hands, turned to face one another, and treaded water. They embraced for a kiss under the cool fire of the night sky in the bracing May waters of the ancient sea.

· *Acknowledgments*

Thank you to Greenleaf Book Group for believing in the story of Merlin; to Jay Hodges for the scrupulous copy edit and to Neil Gonzalez for the inspired cover design and illustration of Tite's spontaneously combusting, flame-engulfed golf cart; also, to Jeremy Wells for the central cover illustration of Merlin at the helm of the Airmadillo, including pocket shrimp. Special thanks to my lead editor Amanda Hughes for her patient attentiveness and for indulging me as I rattled on about Merlin, Houston and tenuously related tangents. Our conversations have been a balm for me. Thank you, Sally Garland, for your crucial help with the last-minute edits.

Thank you to rose expert Mike Stroup at the Texas Rose Emporium (no beauty without thorns) and to former Harris County chief prosecutor Ann Johnson for providing me an overview of the tragedy of human trafficking and human smuggling. And thank you Lindsey and Judge Larry, respectively, for making these connections for me. Thank you, Mike Barone, for the thorough and thoughtful muscle car tutorial regarding the potential specs of an updated, souped-up, and tricked out 1971 El Camino.

Thanks to Kathy O'Brien Adjemian and Ellie Maas Davis for the timely encouragement. Thank you to my friend Sara Essex Bradley for the author photo and for being unwaveringly pro-Merlin.

Thank you to my friend and book doctor Ann McCutchan for the enthusiastic support for the project, yet requiring an outline to pass muster with her before allowing me to proceed beyond the book's initial pages.

Major thanks to my friends and colleagues in the Indiana Street Group for their crucial help in shepherding this project toward the pasture of its culmination. Christa, my friend, special thanks for the good word you spoke over it.

I reserve most heartfelt thanks for my dear friend and mentor Emily Fox Gordon who brought me into what would become the Indiana Street Group at its inception; her wise, steady and insightful counsel as the story of Merlin developed and matured was indispensable. Thank you for raising flags when necessary and for affirming me when needless doubt arose. Our conversations kept me on course and left me with a sense of relief and renewed motivation. Most of all, thank you for reveling with me in all things Merlin.

Thank you, Lucy Herring Chambers for hipping me to Greenleaf and encore thanks to the gate keepers at Greenleaf for the green light.

Finally, I thank God for revealing Merlin Mistlethorpe McNaughton and his world to me and for giving me the inspiration, grace and determination to follow this project to fruition. I am so grateful.

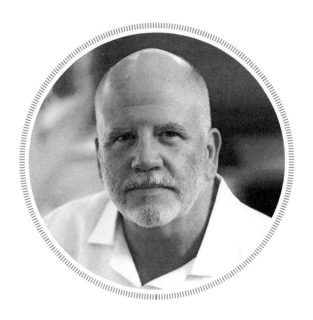

LOUIS GARDNER LANDRY

graduated from the College of Arts and
Science at Vanderbilt University in 1985
with a Bachelor of Arts in English, magna
cum laude. He is a native Houstonian.